I0676141

WAIT

Until The

Dark Of Night

WAIT Until The Dark Of Night

A Joseph Cross Adventure

Arthur A. Lee

LEEWARD PUBLISHERS, LLC
Orlando, Florida

WAIT Until The

Dark Of Night

By

Arthur A. Lee

This is a work of fiction. Names, characters, places and incidents are either the product of the author's imagination or are used fictionally, and resemblance to actual persons living or dead, business establishments, events or locales is entirely coincidental.

Copyright © 2015 by Arthur A. Lee &

LEEWARD PUBLISHERS, LLC

All rights reserved. This book, in whole and in part, is the property of the author. No part of this book may be reproduced or transmitted in any form or by any means, graphic, electronic, or mechanical, including but not limited to photocopying, recording, taping, or by any information storage retrieval system, without the permission in writing from the author.

ISBN: 978-0-692-53802-9

In accordance with the U.S. Copyright Act of 1976, the scanning, uploading, and electronic sharing of any part of the book without the permission of the publisher constitute unlawful piracy and theft of the author's intellectual property. If you would like to use material from the book (other than for review purposes), prior written permission must be obtained by contacting the publisher at

editor@leewardpublishers.com.

Silver Cat Press
An imprint of Leeward Publishers, LLC

This Book Is Dedicated To
Captain Edmund E'Stran
A Professional Soldier,
A Leader Of Men

Other Books by the Author

The Morgan Crew Mystery Series

A Storm In From The Sea
The Las Vegas Murders
A Deadly London Fog
The Four Seasons Murders
The Hawaiian Sunset Murders
The Spy Who Would Not Speak
The West Texas Murders
The Hawaiian Island Murders

The Mystery and Adventure Series

Three Families

WAIT Until The Dark Of Night

A Joseph Cross Adventure

CONTENTS

PROLOG

BLOOD DIAMONDS

Blood Diamonds – also referred to as Conflict Diamonds or War Diamonds – are terms used for diamonds mined generally in Africa, in a war zone, and sold on the black market to finance a rebellion, a civil war, or a Warlord's bloody activity.

Throughout Central and Southern Africa in the 1980s and 1990s diamonds were mined in very remote areas and sold to finance, at first, Warlords and small bands of thieves and brigands. As the market for these cheap diamonds grew, they became the chief financial source for terribly destructive wars throughout Central Africa.

In Angola, between 1992 and 1998, Angola's UNITA rebel group mined and sold an estimated $3.72 billion (that's right, **BILLION**) in blood diamonds in order to finance its war against the Government of Angola. Tens of thousands of people died horrible deaths during this six year conflict.

In 1998 the United Nations passed a resolution banning the purchase of blood diamonds from Angola. This slowed the sale but did not completely stop the black market of the diamonds. During this terrible period, UNITA commonly used captives as slaves to mine their Blood Diamonds.

The Democratic Republic of the Congo, The Republic of the Congo (these are two separate nations), Liberia,

Zimbabwe, and Uganda have all produced and traded in Blood Diamonds. Today, most of these diamonds are mined by individuals in remote tribal areas and are a source of income to those marginally surviving in these very remote areas rather than to finance wars. But still, in the most inaccessible areas, far from government controlled regions, small Warlords have used and still use captives as slaves to mine the diamonds.

"Mining" of diamonds should not be confused with what one might think of as mining, as most of us know. There are no tunnels in the sides of mountains or mines dug deep into the ground with elevators taking miners down. African Blood Diamonds are dug out of the African soil, most often in muddy or swampy areas. Holes may be dug into the ground, but few are deeper than would require more than a ladder to climb in and out.

The 'Kimberly Process Certification Scheme' was adopted on July 19, 2000 by the World Diamond Congress. It seeks to register legally produced diamonds from Africa and to monitor diamond production from member States. The Governments of most of the Central African States are now members, although Blood Diamond production does still continue in these states in the most isolated areas.

Legally produced diamonds today are given a laser produced registration number, internally within each diamond, in order to tell a legally produced diamond from a Blood Diamond. These internal numbers can be seen with a jeweler's loupe (eyepiece).

In spite of all the laws, the monitoring of production, the fines and penalties, Blood Diamonds continue to be dug and sold in a few areas of Africa to finance vicious Warlords' private armies, Communist and Muslim insurgencies, and even larger wars throughout the Middle East. Several Muslim areas of Central Africa produce Blood Diamonds and send the profits to the Middle Eastern Muslim armies, such as ISIS.

When any civilized person with a conscience shops for a diamond, the buyer should always use a loupe to see if the diamond has a serial number cut inside by laser. Buying a good diamond at a cheap price without an internal serial number may save the buyer some money, but remember that the diamond was probably produced by a tortured slave.

SLAVERY

It is commonly believed that slavery ended in April 1865 when the American Civil War – The War Between the States – ended. The truth is, slavery has existed as long as man has walked the earth and fought other men for dominance, and it still exists today.

Today, slavery exists in almost every Country on Earth. Slavery exists in many forms, from laborers in chains, to household labor held in bondage, to children and young adults held as sex slaves. Many Nations, such as North Korea, hold prisoners-for-life who are worked as slaves doing heavy labor until their short lives end from starvation and the labors they are forced into.

Men and women held in prisons in many Asian Countries are forced to make goods, often under contracts with American companies, which will be exported to Europe and The United States. Their labors bring cash into the countries that work the prisoners to death.

Men, women and children from Central and South America, and from many areas of Mexico, are worked as unpaid, forced farm workers, and yes, some of these unpaid farm laborers are working right here in the United States.

Young women, boys and girls from Asian Countries and from Mexico and Central America are sold to criminal organizations to be used as sex slaves around the world. Suicide amongst this group of slaves is common as the only perceived way out of their terrible lives.

In Eastern Europe and Russia young women are kept as sex slaves and are often exported to Western Europe and the Americas. Their lives are short and terrible.

Throughout the Middle East, slavery and slave markets, where human beings are sold like cattle, exist today and are overlooked by the 'civilized' world, perhaps in exchange for the flow of oil or perhaps for political influence. In India and Pakistan, the very wealthy hold men and women from the 'lower castes' in bondage as household workers and gardeners.

And today, in the most remote areas of Africa, men, women and children are held in slavery mining diamonds for rebels and petty Warlords. Hence, we present our story of one man's fight against a brutal warlord.

BOY SOLDIERS

Wherever in this world of ours a war of terrorism and cruelty exists, children – for the most part boys – are kidnapped, or their families are murdered, and they are educated in murder. Children in the Middle East and in Africa, barely old enough to hold an AK-47 rifle, are sent out to fight in battles and often are told to kill prisoners.

In the Middle East, ISIS (or ISIL) operates schools where boys are brainwashed into believing that murder will assure their pathway into heaven. They kill without thought and put pistols to the heads of prisoners, Christians, and Jews.

In Africa, when groups of boy soldiers are finally freed, they face many years of psychological and psychiatric care to mend the damage done to them. Their memories of family and anything other than cruelty and murder had been wiped from them. Many never return to normality and spend their lives in protected environments.

Young girls in the Middle East, pre-teens, are recruited as sex-soldiers to provide sex to Islamic terrorist soldiers, often old men, and the boy soldiers in these groups. They are all too often sold to old men as wives in order to bring money into groups like ISIS or to gain political influence in the tribes of that area of the world.

The fact that this happens in this 21st Century world is probably, in this writer's opinion, the cruelest thing African and Islamic terrorists can do. The fact that boy soldiers and girl sex-soldiers exist needs nothing more to be said. Remember this when any thought of compassion comes to mind for Islamic or African terrorists.

MERCENARY ARMIES

The idea of a group of soldiers who fight wars and kill for money is, at first, abhorrent and repugnant. Imagine, hired killers! How bad can that be?

But the reality of the history of professional mercenary or civilian armies is long and oftentimes good. Going back to the ancient Roman Empire, Rome had hired foreign, non-Roman armies from the Germanic and Franco tribes of the North. In the 'Middle Ages' even the Pope of the Catholic Church hired professional soldiers from Switzerland (that was a fierce fighting Country of the time) to protect the Church in Rome. These 'Swiss Guards' remain today as security for The Vatican.

For more than 2000 years, governments of all nations have hired professional, civilian, or as they are derogatorily referred to, 'mercenary' armies. During the American Revolution, Britain hired Hessian (German) soldiers to fight against the American Colonies in rebellion. Prior to the American Revolution, France and Britain waged war against one another over the lands of Canada and the western Appalachian regions. Both sides hired Native American tribes to fight for them.

In the 1960s private, civilian armies became famous in world news when the continent of Africa fell into terrible civil wars as the result of the European nations relinquishing their control of their "Colonies."

Tens of thousands of people were murdered during those years. Tribes that held centuries old anger against other tribes were suddenly free to wreak bloody vengeance. Petty Warlords rose from the chaos. Newly formed governments of the new and free African Nations did not have the power to stop the near anarchy.

During the 1960s, The Congo was a most violent and dreadful place. Any semblance of humanity and civilization had disappeared. In 1964 Congolese Prime Minister Moise Tshombe hired Mike Hoare, the most famous mercenary leader of the time, to fight and bring to an end the Simba Revolution. Major Hoare had an 'army' of 300 men – professional soldiers from several European Countries and South Africa – and the Simba Revolution was brought to a quick end.

I had dealings with one small mercenary group under Captain Edmund E'Stran. I am proud of that association, and it gave me first hand insight into what professional soldiers can do.

Many other civilian armies were hired during that time period to put down the most vicious of rebellions and criminals in Africa. Most recently, in 1995, the company, Executive Actions, was hired to end a violent revolution in Sierra Leone. With 119 professional civilian soldiers, the revolution was ended. That's right, 119 professional soldiers brought a rapid end to the killing and brought peace to a Country that had not seen peace for many years.

Unfortunately, the United Nations thought it was unconscionable that paid, civilian, private armies were being used anywhere in the world. By U.N. decision, Executive Action was pulled from Sierra Leone and 35,000 U.N. 'peace keepers' were sent to replace them. The revolution, once ended by 119 mercenaries, arose once again, and 35,000 U.N. troops could not end it.

Today, in the wars in the Middle East, the United States and several European Countries hire civilian 'contractors' to do primarily security work. The U.S. Military has budgeted tens of millions of dollars to hire these contractors. But often these mercenaries are caught up in hot battles. Due to politics and short sighted thinking on the parts of Governments, even the U.S. Government, these professional soldiers are not supported in hot battles and are left to die at the hands of overwhelming odds against them.

The story that follows is, of course, fictional. But a large part of it concerns a civilian group of professional mercenaries, a group that is based entirely on real groups that exist today, often very quietly in actions that do not reach the news media. They fight short, quick wars that bring an end to violence and peace to ravaged people.

Without these very professional soldiers the world today would be a very different place. Consider, if you were caught in a hot battle with people who wanted to kill you, would you rather have at your side a 19 year old boy fresh out of basic training, or a professional soldier with many years of warfare behind him? The answer seems simple enough.

WAIT Until The
Dark Of Night

CHAPTER ONE – Into The Storm

Michael Finnegan paced across the open deck, cupping his cigarette in both hands to protect it from the rain. The cabin of the North Star was nearby and dry inside, sheltered from the biting wind. But Michael stayed outside on the deck in the heavy weather, wishing he could see the stars above, remembering the clear, cold nights at home in Ireland, but knowing the black clouds of the dark of night, covering the sky were what he needed to do his job. The bumpers at the side of the long craft bounced against the wooden dock, preventing the boat from crashing against it in the wind. The thumping sound was almost rhythmic.

He wore a black slicker that fell to his ankles. It would have been short for anyone else, but Michael was short, barely 5 feet 6 inches tall. On his head was an old, wide brim hat, covered in black rubber that sagged in back, letting the rain pour down his shirt collar and across his back. His old brogan boots were soaked through, the wool socks as wet as a sponge. But he didn't notice. He paced, smoked his cigarette, and paused long enough to drink straight from the bottle of Bushmills Irish Whiskey he kept close by at all times.

After his long drink he started to pace in the rain again. He slipped on the wet deck, swore a Gaelic profanity, kicked at a coil of rain soaked rope lying nearby, and continued his pacing, his back at first to the blowing gale rain, then turning to face into it.

Michael was a short, heavily built, red haired, freckle faced Irishman who had a history of taking dangerous jobs and staying drunk most of the time. It would be easy to think he was a leprechaun from Irish folklore.

He had been a petty thief as a teenager, stealing fruit and cigarettes from local street vendors and neighborhood shops in the Belfast he grew up in. He was a burglar as a young man, seeking out the homes of wealthy Protestants during the conflicts. He moved into being an assassin for the IRA until he was forty-five years old. It wasn't the one-on-one killings, the gun fights, or the murders done in the dark of night that bothered Michael. He objected to the random bombings that killed everyone nearby, Catholic and Protestant alike, innocent children, and civilians only trying to live as normal a life as is possible in the middle of a warzone.

He had argued with the IRA leaders that they should be careful in their targeting, seeking out the British and Protestants and not children. Michael had a choice given to him by the IRA Captains: Use the bombs or be executed as a traitor.

He decided to leave Ireland in the dark of one moonless night and debated where he could go to not be found by his former comrades. He came across a job that he thought he might be well suited for, and an employer who could offer him protection from the IRA. He took a job as a boat Captain, making the smuggling run between Calais, France and Yarmouth, England for Joseph Cross.

For years Joseph Cross had been running a smuggling operation throughout Europe, and part of that operation was running guns into Ireland for the IRA. That work gave him a semblance of authority within the ranks of the IRA. When Michael Finnegan was hired by Joseph Cross, the IRA commanders were told that Michael Finnegan was working for him now and he was to be left alone. Michael was in fact left alone.

The runs Michael made between France and the U.K. were done in the dark of night, in the heaviest of storms that rage ever so frequently down the English Channel, out of the North Sea. Michael was captain and crew of the North Star, an aged and ragged fifty-eight foot trawler, making the run in the face of death, alone, over and over again.

The old North Star had been reinforced with steel beams in order to keep it from falling apart as it crashed through the heavy seas of the worst storms possible. She was painted black to blend into the dark night. She was powered by the two 1250 horsepower Rolls Royce airplane engines that had been squeezed into her hull. Those engines shook the ship almost to the point of breaking apart.

Michael waited patiently for the peak of the storm to fill the English Channel that night because the North Star was packed tightly with contraband: wines and liquors, cigarettes and cigars, and anything else that would be of value on the Black Market in and around London. But the most important cargo carried by the North Star was a leather sack the size of a cricket ball, full of diamonds, some legal and some illegal. That sack was in Michael's Pea Coat pocket, under the wet slicker. If he went down, the diamonds would go with him.

In the thickness of the storm, other ships, especially Her Majesty's Maritime Customs Patrol, would be safely tied up in port, assuming that no one would be insane enough to take on the storm. The North Star, with its powerful engines, would be able to cut through tall waves and whatever else may lie in its way. It would run through the dark of night without any lights onboard, and, if Michael's Irish luck held out, it would deliver its cargo to Michael's employer, Joseph Cross, the owner of the ship and its cargo.

The maritime weather radio and the ship's weather radar indicated that the peak of the storm would be over the course Michael would take in a few minutes. He tossed his cigarette over the side of the ship, took one more drink from the bottle, stepped under the corrugated steel cover of the flying bridge, ignoring the closed cabin, and started the engines. They kicked in immediately, and the North Star rattled into life. Michael walked through the rain to the rear and then to the bow of the ship, letting the lines go. The wind and the waves inside the little harbor along France's Pas-de-Calais coast slapped the North Star against the dock, the big heavy rubber bumpers struggling to protect the hull of the ship.

At the ship's wheel, Michael pushed the two control sticks forward slightly, enough to move the ship away from the dock and out of the small, private harbor. The North Star rocked on the harbor's waves and moved past the few, seldom used yachts of the very rich, tied amongst the derelict fishing vessels that were bouncing up and down with the rough water, and into the blackness of the storm-filled channel. He stepped out onto the deck once more to pull the bumpers into the boat.

If he made it to Yarmouth, which he never gave more than a 50 – 50 chance of doing on these runs, there would be money and another bottle of whiskey. If he didn't, 'What the bloody hell,' he told himself. "Life's short and never certain, ain't it," he said out loud to himself, not realizing he had said it. It was the same thing he said at the start of every run.

The North Star slipped into the heavy sea, past the break water and into the ten foot waves. Ahead was dark nothingness. Michael pushed the double engines to full throttle, casting the ship into the storm. Waves that would crash against the concrete breakwater lifted the North Star and then threw it down into a valley of black water, only to have the next wave cover the ship, as the two powerful engines that turned the two oversized props pushed the ship through one wave and into the next.

The two Rolls Royce engines were shaking The North Star bow to stern. Half the time, as the ship rammed into wave after wave, the ship, and Michael at the wheel, were under water. But the two powerful engines in their sealed, water proof compartment pushed the ship forward, with Michael hoping the next wave would not capsize the ship or break it in two. He would have said a prayer, but with his life behind him and all that he had done, he doubted God would listen.

Hours later he saw the faintest of lights through the grey rain. He checked the GPS monitor and corrected his course three degrees to the south. Yarmouth was ahead, and the worst was behind him. He had done the impossible once again. That, he reasoned, deserved another drink from the bottle at his side.

Waiting behind the steering wheel of a black Jaguar XKR-S, in the parking lot of the Millbanks Yacht Club at Yarmouth, was the owner of the North Star. Joseph Cross sat patiently, listening to some good jazz from Miles Davis on the CD in the dashboard. The rain was hitting the windshield like sharp knives; the sky was black; the wind was blowing out of the north. Inside the car was as cold as outside, but Joseph Cross didn't care. Michael Finnegan would be on his way, making another impossible but successful run. And there would be profit as a result.

****

Michael had met Joseph Cross four years earlier. Cross, having acquired a reputation for running guns into Ireland for the IRA, was running guns into Southern Ireland for what he was told was an offshoot group of the IRA. It was a small group of young men and women who called themselves "The Army of Free Ireland." Their 'army' consisted of six men all in their twenties and four women, all again in their twenties. They were college students, and none of them were religious. In fact one of the women and two of the men were Protestant, while all of the others were from Catholic families. It was merely great fun to them, acting out what they had seen in movies so many times.

They were well funded by wealthy parents who didn't know they were more than students of Irish history. And they were excited enough about what they had planned that they bragged about it to 'friends' in the Harp Pub while laughing over pint after pint of Guinness.

'The Army of Free Ireland' had paid Joseph Cross four times the black market value of 50 used SA80 rifles. It was easy for Cross to obtain the rifles. They were to be discarded and destroyed by the British Army. He merely paid an underpaid Sergeant who was nearing retirement ten Pounds for each rifle. Cross would receive forty Pounds for each from the young people who had no idea what a good rifle was.

Michael Finnegan had heard the young people bragging about the 'dark of night' delivery of the rifles as had a dozen other people. He knew what would happen. Either the bloody Provos or the bloody British would have heard also; someone would tell one authority or another for a small price paid to traitors. Whoever was told would, of course, meet the delivery and kill everyone involved. Michael decided that he could not let happen what would happen.

Michael knew the name Joseph Cross as did anyone deeply into one sort of crime or another. He had an idea, and he would work on that idea. The night that the guns were to be delivered, Michael was waiting behind some boulders along the beach where Joseph's small boat would land and offload the guns.

It was a quarter to one in the morning. It was the dark of night, and the sky was blanketed with a thick cover of black clouds, but there was no rain, and the sea was calm. Michael watched as Cross slowed the outboard motor on the small open boat as he neared the rocky beach. In the boat with Cross were five wooden boxes of rifles. He stopped the motor and let the boat coast quietly onto shore. He stepped out into the ankle deep sea and pulled the boat up onto the shore.

There was a light breeze, a cold breath of air, coming in from the ocean. The night was deadly silent. The only sound was the lapping of small waves onto the rocky beach. The black sky would have been full of a million stars on such a night had they not been hidden by clouds. And the young people who were to buy the rifles weren't there. He looked into the blackness of the trees and bushes. Nothing.

He walked along the beach to the right, stopped, turned and walked back. 'Oh well,' he thought. 'Maybe next time.' And then a slight crack, almost too quiet to hear in the still night air, came from the trees twenty yards inland. A shrieking whistle blew, and five well-armed Irish Garda Police ran from the shadows. They carried Lee Enfield rifles, not new by any means, but Cross knew they could still kill.

He raised his arms and waited calmly. No sense, he thought, trying to shoot it out with five of them. A good lawyer and some well-placed bribes would have him free in a matter of days. The financial loss would be minimal. He would do nothing that would result in the Police shooting him.

The five policemen approached slowly, carefully, but Cross was alone and unarmed, his arms raised tall over his head. They started to walk a little quicker towards him. They had nothing to fear, they thought . . . Until Michael Finnegan stepped from behind the boulders at their rear and opened fire. He killed the five of them with five head shots from his Russian Makarov pistol.

Cross watched as the five quickly fell to the wet, rocky ground. It all happened so quickly that none of the five had a chance to react before they were killed.

Keeping his arms raised, he turned and saw the little man run toward him. Cross had the same thought so many others had when first seeing Finnegan. He could have been a Leprechaun; his diminutive height, his bright red hair, pale skin and chubby freckled face stood out even in the dark of night.

The little man stopped at the five bodies, kicked each to be sure each was dead, pocketed his pistol, and turned to look at Cross. He smiled broadly. He looked up from his 5' 6" height and said in a deep Irish accent, "I need to get out of bloody Ireland, now don't I, Mr. Cross. I thought you might oblige me with a nice little boat ride across the pretty water?"

"To where?" Cross asked, unsure of what else to say.

"To anywhere, Mr. Cross."

"How do you know me?" he asked.

"Ah, then.   And don't everybody in the bloody

business know you, Mr. Cross? The little boys and girls you were to be doin' business with . . . Don't you know they was talkin' in the Pub about you and all the damn big guns you was bringin' them. It was not only me who heard them. These here fellas' . . ." Michael said waving his hand at the five dead policemen . . . "These boys also heard, much to their bad luck. Now, do I get a pleasant boat ride out of me own lovely homeland, and probably never will I ever again set me own eyes on the lovely green of Ireland?"

Cross lowered his arms and looked down at the little man. "Who the hell are you?" he asked.

"Aye, and me name is Finnegan . . . Although me sainted mother would be ashamed of that fact."

"And why do you want to leave Ireland?"

"Ahh, and ain't it me own home where I was born and raised. But I've got boys from both the north and south after me now, don't I? The IRA and the Prods from Belfast . . . And leave us not forget the damn Brits . . . They all want me dead. Even in the warmth and comfort of me own home an' bed, don't ya' know, I ain't safe from the bloody bullet that'll kill me."

Cross grinned, laughed and nodded, understanding fully what the little man was saying. He knew how easy it was to offend any of the various groups who were at war with one another. A mix of politics and religion – a combination that spells trouble anywhere in the world – filled Ireland, and death was the easy way out.

He got in the boat and started the outboard, waving to Michael to join him. Finnegan pushed the little boat back into the water and jumped in, sitting on the boxes of rifles. Michael was smiling broadly and began to sing a lilting Irish tune in the ancient language of Ireland, a language that was fast disappearing.

Before they reached the British coast, Cross had hired Michael Finnegan to work with him smuggling anything of value back and forth between the U.K., the Continent, and the west coast of Africa.   Cross had, as part of the agreement, guaranteed Michael's freedom from the threat of the IRA and the British governing Northern Ireland.   "The Ulster Protestants may still be a problem, Michael," Cross said. "They want to kill me almost as much as they want to kill you."

"Aye, and ain't that the bloody shame of it all. People fighting because they pray in different ways to the same God. Will they ever bloody learn how foolish it all is?"

****

The night Michael had finished his run across the Channel, Joseph Cross was waiting for him in a lot at the small harbor near Yarmouth. He stepped from his Jaguar and looked down the wet, wooden docks to where Michael was securing the North Star. He smiled once again, as he did every time Michael Finnegan had not been killed crossing the English Channel in a storm. It would be difficult . . . Impossible . . . To replace Michael.

Joseph was tall, six foot two, with the build of a man ten years younger, and in good physical shape. His hair was dark with a little grey showing at the temple, revealing his real age of forty-eight. That night he had brought an ankle length, black leather overcoat to protect his suit from the weather. He stepped carefully over and around puddles of rain water so as to not damage his custom made, Italian leather shoes.

It was half past three in the morning, and it was cold and brisk. An icy wind was blowing onshore from the remains of the Channel storm. Cross took his long, black, leather jacket from the rear seat of the car and put it on, pulling the collar up around his neck.

The North Star rocked in the swells of the harbor, as Michael secured the lines and bumpers that would hold the ship until the dark of some night, when he would return it to France for another stormy run across the channel.

At the tattered ship, Cross stood with his hands in his jacket's pockets. He looked up onto the deck at Michael Finnegan who was, as usual, drinking deeply from his bottle of Bushmills. Cross called up, "Michael! I see you made it!"

"Aye . . . And ain't it the bloody truth that I'd be crazy to do that again!"

"It was bad?" Cross asked.

"Bad ain't the word Joseph, me old mate. But I'm here ain't I? And you've got all the bloody booze and wine and other things you wanted."

"And the diamonds?"

"Aye, and the bloody diamonds. Wouldn't I have jumped into the bloody storm tossed ocean itself had they gone overboard?"

Finnegan tossed the leather sack over the ship's side. Cross caught it and hefted its weight. He smiled, satisfied at the bag of cut and uncut diamonds. He turned and walked away towards his Jaguar as three men approached and passed him. They would unload the North Star's illegal cargo, move it to the canvas covered bed of the truck that would carry the wine, cigars, cigarettes and everything else Michael had managed to bring safely across the Channel back to the South London warehouse where it would wait to be sold.

Michael watched the unloading as he drained the last few drops of the whiskey from the bottle. When the ship was empty, he would lock and secure it and walk through the cold, wet morning to the small room he kept in Yarmouth, where he would sleep the daylight away until night fell once again.

CHAPTER TWO - The Rochester Club

London's Soho District is an area of the West End that for two hundred years has been the District where the people of London go for entertainment. In the late seventeen hundreds and through the eighteen hundreds, visitors, rich and poor, from the European Continent and a few from the Americas sought out what Soho had to offer, which was at that time sex oriented entertainment in the taverns and pubs, and on the dark, bleak streets.

Soho's streets in those years were filled with prostitutes, and its cellars housed Chinese opium dens. There were cheap Public Houses where cheap beer and cheap gin flowed. There were dark and dirty rooms where gamblers were sure to lose their money. And from these dank parlors, Captains of sailing ships kidnapped men for their crews. Thieves roamed the area at night, stealing from anyone not in rags, often killing their victims. The dark of night was not a time to be roaming the dirty streets.

In the late Twentieth Century, X-rated movie theaters took over as the major form of entertainment, and the drug trade came out into the night from the cellars. Street roaming prostitutes were replaced with call-girls. Sex clubs, offering every form of deranged sex, took to the back alleys and cellars. But all that began to change when, in 1996, a very private gambling club opened in the middle of Soho.

The Rochester Club is a very exclusive, very expensive, very high-stakes, and very private, members only gambling club. It is located in a four-story building in the midst of the bright neon lights of the Soho nightlife district. Without warning to the inhabitants of the surrounding streets, one early morning, day crews showed up and began demolishing buildings in a square block area of central Soho. Eighteen months later the Rochester Club was born.

The front of The Rochester Club is reminiscent of a palace. White, carved granite walls rise tall above the street. A curved drive off the main street enables cars and taxis to stop and unload passengers, and an adjacent porte cochere protects guests from London's rain.

Black Italian marble stairs rise from the sidewalk to eight-foot tall double doors of polished brass. The doors had been imported from Florence, Italy where they had once hung at a 16th Century church.

Two tall columns with Corinthian finials, imported from Greece, stand at the top of the wide stairs at each corner and hold a tiled roof above The Club's entrance. A white, green, and red striped awning extends from the porte cochere to the tiled roof to keep the visitors dry. Two doormen, dressed every evening in white tie, tails, and tall black silk top hats stand at the doors, waiting to open them for guests with fat wallets. A liveried footman stands at the curb, waiting to open the doors of the limousines and taxis that deliver members and guests to The Club.

Inside, The Rochester Club's Grand Hallway is magnificent in Victorian grandeur and splendor. Red flocked wallpaper stands out amidst fine, white Italian marble, Iconic columns and gold light fixtures on the walls. The gray marble hallway floor is graced by fine Turkish carpets.

Five huge crystal and gold leafed chandeliers hang in

line along the extended first floor ceiling of the Grand Hallway, light dancing off them much like thousands of the diamonds that the club's owner, Joseph Cross, is enamored with.

Ornate tall-backed chairs, upholstered in Asian gold and green line the walls. Big, centuries-old, Asian pots hold tall fan palms that sway gently against the cool air of the fans high above. On the walls hang the works of the old masters of France, Holland and Italy.

To the left is the splendid and dimly lit Venice Bar. Inside the Venice Bar the walls are carved mahogany and polished brass with secluded and very private booths, their benches covered in the finest leathers Asia has to offer. Tones of softly flowing jazz fill the air.

Next to The Venice Bar is a small Public Casino. Its walls are lined with slot machines and video poker machines, and a few table games with small gambling limits fill the center of the room. The room is crowded with the cacophony of the gambling machines, coins dropping into tuned metal baskets, and old ladies yelling joyfully at winning a few Pounds, and the air is filled with cigarette smoke. All this is carefully shielded from the hallway of The Rochester Club by thick glass doors that are kept closed to keep the cigarette smoke and noise from the Grand Hallway. The glass allows small time gamblers, non-member visitors, to see into the brightly lit casino.

Non-members, tourists mainly, fill the Public Casino, dropping coins into machines as they hope to walk away wealthy. They go home bragging that they actually gambled in the world famous Rochester Club, not realizing that the real gambling club is on the floors above them and open to members only and the very wealthy of the world.

Along the Grand Hallway to the right as one walks

through the ground floor of the club is The Hunter's Room, a restaurant that is famous for its cuisine and list of rare wines. The Hunter's Room is booked a solid three months in advance. Non-members of The Rochester Club are allowed into the Venice Bar, the public casino, and with one of the very hard to get reservations, into The Hunter's Room – if they are dressed properly – but never onto the floors above.

At the far end of the polished gray marble floor of the hallway is a grand, white marble staircase, with elaborately carved handrails gilded in 18 karat gold. It is carpeted in Chinese royal red. The staircase curves upward both to the left and right from a landing halfway up. And on the landing is a ten foot tall painting of Black Beard the Pirate, its meaning known only to a very few who know of Cross' criminal and smuggling operations. Non-members and tourists attempt to ascend the stairs to take a photograph of the pirate, but they are stopped from doing so.

At the base of the staircase, two very large men in crisp tuxedos stand guard in front of a red velvet rope draped across the first step of the staircase. Non-members, tourists for the most part, with cameras slung around their necks, dressed in casual clothes or blue jeans and shorts and sandals in the heat of summer, are politely pointed toward the Venice Bar or the small public casino nearby. They are offered a complimentary glass of champagne – ordinary champagne rather than the rare and expensive wines served in the private casino – but they are never allowed to ascend the staircase to the upper floors and that exclusive and private casino.

On the stair's right hand side, stands a very large, extravagantly carved, cream and gold Louis XIV desk, at which sits a man in splendid white tie and tails. Members stop at this desk before venturing up the stairs. The man stands, politely bows with a nod of his head, and checks the

IDs – passports, driver's licenses, etc. – presented to him by everyone: commoner or nobleman, kings and queens. He then compares the IDs he has been given to the membership records that flash onto the big computer screen on his desk before allowing members up the stairs to the private casinos. He nods to the two men at the foot of the stairs telling them who can ascend. The velvet rope is opened, and the lucky few ascend.

Stored on his computer is a list of the world's wealthiest people. These people, although they are not members, are allowed up the grand staircase to the private casino.

The walk up the magnificent staircase is done slowly, royally. Female members and ladies escorted by members want to be seen in their finest designer gowns and jewelry. Tourists are stopped from taking photos of those climbing the stairs. A record of members and the ladies they escort is kept very private from the public.

The hallway is seldom crowded, as most people head directly for the gambling tables in the public casino. Occasionally small groups of non-members will stand in the hallway talking, drinking the complimentary champagne, marveling at the luxury all around them, and taking photos of the hallway to brag about when they go home.

They take those photos with flash cameras that bother others. When this happens, white gloved waiters in full dress will appear with silver trays of canapés and remind the visitors, while smiling graciously, that flash photography is not permitted. And as soon as these people realize that they have seen all they will be allowed to see, they leave, envious of and curious about those lucky few who are allowed upstairs.

The second floor is the private casino, a grand and

very formal room of marble, gold, thick carpets, and walls carrying original works of art. Members can lose their money there, and some few will walk away winners. The casino is absolutely honest, and as is in any casino, the odds are always with the house, guaranteeing Joseph Cross millions every year. Members are never without the best champagne, rare champagne that was smuggled in on one of Cross' boats. Caviar, and anything else they ask for, flows freely so long as they stay at the gambling tables.

The air is cool and clean in the upstairs casino. Gentlemen and a few ladies are offered the very best cigars. There is an air filtration system that cleans the air efficiently and very quietly. A string quartet plays soft music by Mozart and Brahms. There are no slot machines in the upstairs private casino, but every form of table game, Western and Asian, is available for the members.

One quarter of the third floor is a cigar bar for the members. It stocks the best of Cuban and Dominican cigars, also smuggled in by Joseph Cross to avoid the heavy taxes on tobacco products. It is walled in the rarest of Brazilian rosewood and dimly lit for an atmosphere of quiet calm, while the members, men and women, enjoy their cigars and cocktails. The bar serves the best brandies and cognacs, smuggled into Great Britain of course. It is a men's bar, but women will occasionally be seen inside enjoying a cigar.

The remaining third floor is a private, member's only restaurant. It is unrated by Michelin because no public, non-member is ever allowed in it, even Michelin reps. The food would be five star if it were rated by anyone. The wines are exquisite and rare, and smuggled of course. The menus have no prices listed. The old adage applies: If you can't afford it, you shouldn't be there.

The fourth floor of The Rochester Club is the private

residence of Joseph Cross. It is an expansive apartment, furnished simply but suited for a man's taste in the very best contemporary styles. There is an elevator at the far end of a hallway that is the only access to Cross' home. The grand staircase below ends at the third floor.

The elevator rises from the underground parking garage and stops at each floor of The Rochester. A guard stands at each level to ensure the elevator is used only by their employer and his guests. All others use the staircase.

Inside the apartment, at the elevator door, in an oversized chair, constructed especially for him, is Billy Volgar. Billy is a giant of a man, powerful and frightening to look at or be near. His hands are like a bear's, his face scared by years of fighting and killing. He has dedicated his life to the protection of Joseph Cross. Billy is a killer. More than once he has put his own life at risk to save Cross. He has taken bullets, and he has been cut by knives, all willingly and without fear or after-pride.

That evening, the evening Michael Finnegan crossed the Channel, Billy sat in his chair near the elevator doors, reading his ever present sports magazines. He waited for Cross to return from meeting Michael Finnegan and collecting the diamonds Michael brought from the Continent. Next to Billy's chair is the only other piece of furniture in the hallway, a small table with a lamp lit so that Billy can read about Manchester United, his favorite football team. Next to the lamp is a black phone. It rang once, only once, meaning someone downstairs wanted to come upstairs.

Billy carefully closed his magazine, laid it on the floor at his feet, and lifted the phone off its cradle. He said nothing. George, the man at the desk at the bottom of the stairs, on the ground floor of the Rochester Club, knew it would be Billy Volgar.

"There is a lady here who asks to see Mr. Cross," George said, his voice trained to be refined and soft. Both the lady and Billy could hear the smile as George spoke. He was standing in deference to the lady who sat on a white and gold Louis XIV chair in front of his desk, and the polite smile never left his face.

"Mr. Cross don't see no women," Billy said. Billy's voice was deep and full of gravel. "You know that. He ain't interested in no tourists."

"The lady is The Most Honorable Mrs. Margaret Fullsome," George said. He smiled at the woman and bowed slightly as he said her name.

The name was familiar. Billy seldom read newspapers, except for the sports pages, of course. But he was at Cross' side when Cross watched the news on television. He asked, "Who is she? I heard her name somewhere, ain't I?"

"Yes, sir," George said, a smile still in his voice as the woman sat patiently in front of him at the desk. She was not smiling. Her foot, tapping on the marble floor, told George she was impatient. "Mrs. Fullsome is a Member of Parliament."

'A fuckin' M.P.' Billy thought. 'Bloody hell. What the hell does she want?'

He spoke into the phone, "Mr. Cross, he ain't here. He'll be back soon. Tell her to wait in the bar. She don't pay for nothin'. Unner'stand?"

****

While Margaret Fullsome, MP waited patiently at a

secluded corner booth in the Venice Bar enjoying a few glasses of fine Spanish sherry and excellent caviar and hors' devours, and while Billy Volgar paced nervously back and forth in front of the elevator doors, Joseph Cross drove his Jaguar from Yarmouth back to London. The rain had stopped, and the clouds had drifted further south. The night became clear and cold. The sky began to be filled with stars. The roads were clear of heavy traffic as he drove. He glanced to the seat next to him on the left. On it was the small leather pouch that was filled with diamonds. He patted the little bag as if it were his favorite child.

Cross checked the time on his watch. He was late because Michael Finnegan was late. But he couldn't blame Michael; he had made it through the storm after all. So Cross put more weight on the gas pedal and watched the speedometer rise.

Jacob Rosen would be at his shop, waiting for Cross to arrive with the diamonds he would cut. He would wait patiently, of course, and not be upset at Cross' delay. There were too many years of good profits between Joseph Cross and Jacob Rosen. Too many diamonds had been cut and resold over the many years he and Joseph Cross had done business.

It was fourteen minutes past four in the morning as Cross pulled his car to a stop in front of Jacob Rosen's little shop in London's East End District of Bermondsey. Above the shop was Jacob's home. It was a small flat, old but comfortable. Jacob was waiting at the front window of his home, every few minutes pulling the thin curtain aside to look down to the street for Joseph Cross. When he saw the Jaguar pull to the curb, he ran downstairs for the door as Cross jumped from the car and ran up the steps. Joseph smiled broadly as he handed Jacob the little bag that contained the uncut diamonds Michael Finnegan had smuggled in.

Jacob hefted the weight of the bag, and he also smiled broadly. He nodded his satisfaction and shook hands with Cross. No words needed to be spoken. Cross smiled and returned to his car. He knew Jacob would cut the diamonds to perfection, and he would laser-print a counterfeit number in each finished piece that would fool buyers into believing the diamonds were legal.

Jacob is the son of a well renowned Dutch diamond cutter. Jacob learned the trade at a young age, before he met and married the Protestant daughter of a wealthy businessman. Jacob's father would have none of it, insisting Jacob marry the plump and short Jewish girl who lived next door to them. It would be a good business arrangement, the joining together of two prominent families. After Jacob married his Protestant lover and fled to London, he found a job re-cutting diamonds and cutting raw diamonds for Joseph Cross, turning them into valuable gems. It was a good life. Jacob, his wife and their three children were happy.

****

Cross stopped at the steel gates to the underground parking garage of the Rochester Club, waiting for them to rise. Inside, he parked his jaguar, nodded to the guard at the elevator who saluted as Cross walked past, and took the elevator up four stories to his home. Billy Volgar was waiting impatiently at the elevator doors as they opened. Cross saw the expression on the big man's face. Something had happened that worried the big man. He seldom worried about anything, so whatever it was had to be important.

"Good morning, Billy," he said as he walked past the giant. "You look like you drank some bad beer. Did somebody break the house downstairs? Are we broke again?"

"No boss," Billy said as he opened the doors at the end of the hallway and followed Cross into the living room. He waited while Cross took off his leather jacket and tossed it onto a chair.

"Can I pour you a drink, Billy?" Cross asked as he poured cognac into a large snifter. "How about some food? Are you hungry?"

"No boss. You got somebody waitin' to see you, ain't you?"

"And who might that be?" Cross asked as he tasted the strong liquor. He looked at his wrist watch and wondered who would be downstairs at five in the morning.

"That woman, boss. Margaret Fullsome. Ain't she the one been after shuttin' you down?"

"You mean the MP? *That* Margaret Fullsome?"

"Yes, boss. She's down in the bar. Been waitin' a long time, ain't she?"

Cross drained the snifter and smiled at his friend. "Why are you so worried, Billy? That woman has been a pain in my ass for years. I think we should let her wait a while longer, don't you? Phone downstairs. Tell them to let her wait, and when she gives up and starts to leave, tell them to stop her and bring her up here. I think we should let her sweat a little. Maybe she'll know what it feels like to be treated like nothing."

Billy walked back down the hallway and went to the phone on the table next to his chair by the elevator. George picked up his phone and said merely, "Yes, sir." He listened and hung the phone onto its cradle. He looked across the hallway, into the Venice Bar and saw the MP still sitting in the dark corner. He looked at his watch; it was approaching six AM. The Venice Bar had closed, the grand hallway was empty, and all the tourists had left. The MP and a single bartender were the only people in the bar. She sat alone, a full glass of Sherry in front of her. The one remaining bartender was wiping down the granite bar that had been wiped clean a dozen times already. He would not leave until the MP left. In the meantime he would keep her supplied with Sherry, and he would wipe down the granite bar.

At twenty past six, Margaret Fullsome rose and walked with an angry stride toward George, her heels clicking loudly in the empty hallway. He stood and smiled as she approached. Except for a few members still gambling upstairs, George, the bartender and the MP were alone in The Rochester Club. She stopped at his desk and said angrily, "I assume I will not be speaking with Mr. Cross this morning. Tell me when I should come back and speak with the man."

George walked from behind his desk and with a gracious and very formal wave of his arm he said, "This way, Mrs. Fullsome."

George led the way to the elevator that was hidden behind the staircase. He pressed a button, and the bright brass doors slid open silently. The MP stepped inside. George slid a small keycard into a slot above the five buttons that allowed the elevator to go to the fourth floor of the Club. He pressed the topmost of the five buttons and stepped out of the elevator car before the doors closed. He stood outside, facing Mrs. Fullsome and continued to smile until the doors had closed, leaving the woman alone in the elevator. "Finally!" he said out loud as he turned to go home.

When the doors opened again, at Joseph Cross'

apartment, Billy Volgar was standing in front of the elevator, waiting. His hands were folded at his waist, his black suit jacket with the dandruff dusted collar, was unbuttoned, so that he could quickly reach for the big gun he carried under his left shoulder. Margaret Fullsome, startled at the size of the giant, froze, looking up at the ugly man.

Billy spoke in his bearlike, growling, deep voice, "This way please. Mr. Cross, he said you should wait in the living room."

He led her to the big double doors at the end of the hallway that would open into Joe Cross' private apartment. As the doors were opened, the woman looked at an exquisitely decorated apartment, larger than she could have imagined. The furnishings were all contemporary, well placed and well chosen. The walls were muted grey with bright white crown molding and trim. Original works of art of old masters hung on the walls, lighted from above. The floors were carpeted in thick pile, a pale beige in color. And in the center of the main room, the living room, was a sunken seating area. 'What kind of man,' she thought, 'What kind of criminal can live like this?'

She was wearing tan slacks that were obviously expensive, and a high collared white shirt, buttoned down the front. She carried a brown tweed jacket she had removed hours ago while waiting in the bar for Joseph Cross to make an appearance. And she carried a large brown leather purse with shiny brass fittings slung over her shoulder. Her hair was colored blond but not overly blond, and done perfectly by London's best hairdressers to reflect a conservative, motherly appearance. She was the perfect example of casual wealth one might see in the countryside of Southeast Britain. She herself modelled her appearance after Margaret Thatcher, a Prime Minister she had detested but whose appearance she had admired.

Billy led Mrs. Fullsome into the living room and down the three steps to the circular, sunken area centered by a stone fireplace, hooded in copper. A couch, upholstered in dark red very soft leather, ran the circumference of the sunken living room. The three sections of the couch were separated by carpeted stairs, leading down into the sunken area. Billy said, "You should sit and wait here. Mr. Cross, he'll be here soon."

Mrs. Fullsome sat, uncomfortable and angry, but afraid to say anything that might bring on the wrath of the giant. She leaned back and crossed her legs and tried to put on the appearance of being relaxed. She continually looked at her wrist watch every few seconds as the minutes passed by. She realized she was tapping her foot on the floor and wishing she had another glass of Sherry.

Twenty minutes later Joseph Cross walked through a hidden doorway in the wall to the MP's left. He was dressed in light blue silk pajamas with a navy blue terry cloth robe tied at his waist. His feet were bare, and he was smoking a long cigar.

The MP stood, her face red with pent up rage. "How dare you . . ." she started.

Cross interrupted and said, "Gosh, I'm so sorry you had to wait. I wish someone had told me you were here."

"Mr. Cross . . . Do you know who I am?"

He slowly stepped down into the circular sitting area, smiling broadly as he locked his eyes on the MP's. Billy Volgar stood at the top of the three steps. Cross looked behind her at Billy. He laughed a little and said, "Well, I was told you are Margaret Fullsome. Was I misinformed?"

"I have waited for hours, Mr. Cross. I was shuttled off and ignored."

"I'm so sorry, Mrs. Fullsome," Cross said. "I hope you enjoyed the Sherry. It's very expensive you know." He looked back again at Billy and said to him, "I think some cognac, Billy. The Martell Creation Grand Extra."

Billy walked to the bar against the wall of the living room and filled two large, cut crystal snifters with the dark cognac. He stepped down carefully into the sunken seating area and handed one to Cross first, intentionally walking past Mrs. Fullsome. He then turned and walked the other to the lady. She was still standing. At first she stared at the glass and then up at Billy looming over her. She finally took the glass from him, afraid to anger him by refusing it.

"Please sit, Mrs. Fullsome. What can I do for you?" Cross asked as he took a seat across the room from her, not waiting for her to sit first. The fireplace hood was between them, but if Mrs. Fullsome bent, she could see him. He leaned back casually and crossed his legs. He held the long cigar in one hand and the crystal snifter in the other, smiling at her.

She moved to her left a few steps and sat away from the fireplace hood. She looked around for a place to lay the snifter. Not finding any place nearby, and unwilling to get up and go to the stone fireplace, she carefully laid the snifter on the floor without tasting it. "I need your help, Mr. Cross," she said, her voice shaking and soft, and her eyes looking down.

Cross sat unmoving on the couch, his legs still crossed casually. He drew deeply on the cigar and blew the smoke out slowly, towards the ceiling. He sipped the cognac and stared at Mrs. Fullsome. Her face was blushed red, and her hands were shaking. Cross wanted her to be as uncomfortable as possible, to be as nervous as possible. Whatever she wanted, he was preparing himself to say, 'NO!'

He didn't like Margaret Fulsome. She had spent her five years in Parliament speaking against Joseph Cross, sending Scotland Yard and the Inland Revenue after him, time after time. She often referred to him as "that American" with an inflection to the words that made it sound as if she were spitting out something fowl or swearing in the most vulgar fashion.

She was never successful in having him arrested and deported, but she kept trying. She was public with the fact that she did not like this American ex-patriot, making himself rich by skirting and often breaking the law and flouting the Queen's society. She knew, but she could never prove, that Joseph Cross' business was the black market, smuggling and selling, ignoring the tax laws of Britain. Cross was too smart for her and for Government in general. He employed a small army of accountants and solicitors to make his business appear perfectly legal.

Mrs. Fullsome's husband was a wealthy industrialist, owning businesses across Europe. For years there had been rumors of how he bent the laws of many Countries, evading taxes legally via his own personal army of accountants. He hid money in banks that protected him from the too curious eyes of the tax men of many Countries, including his own. Mr. Fullsome had moved several of his manufacturing companies to Asian Countries where labor was cheap, while putting thousands of English men and women, and Europeans of many other Countries, out of work. But no one ever heard Mrs. Fullsome, Member of Parliament, speak against her husband's businesses.

Joe Cross waited, while he slowly sipped on his cognac. Mrs. Fullsome said nothing and couldn't bring herself to look at the man she had hunted and haunted for so many years and was now pleading with for help.

Finally, Cross said, "You need *my* help? I thought

you hated me and you wanted to have me deported back to the States? Haven't you made a career out of political campaigns centered on me? You've been trying to turn the population against me for years. Now you need my help? Why should I care about whatever trouble you're in?"

The MP wiped a tear from the corner of her eye. That almost shook Cross. He wondered just what the hell kind of trouble she had found herself in. The only thing he could think of, to make a powerful MP cry and shake fretfully was blackmail. So, what had she done, he wondered. Sex? Money? Bribery? Maybe a little of everything. It had been his experience that politicians who were publicly too good were all too often not very good at all in their private lives.

She slowly looked up, and with clouded eyes stared unblinking at Joseph Cross. She quickly wiped the tears from her eyes with the back of her hand, first her right hand and then her left, childlike in the gesture. Billy Volgar went to her with a box of tissues, which she took gratefully, managing to smile up at the giant in thanks. She wiped her eyes and nose and tightly twisted a handful of tissue in her fingers. Her eyes filled with tears once again as she tried to speak, her voice weak and fretful. "Mr. Cross . . . I have no place else to go. My son . . . My son, Robert . . ." she sobbed.

"What about your son?"

She let the tissue drop to the floor and reached into her purse. Billy Volgar took a step closer to her, and his hand went inside his jacket to the Colt .45 he carried. If the woman pulled out a gun, she would die quickly. She quickly pulled out a small linen hanky, and Billy stepped back, his hand coming out of his jacket. As she did so, her foot tipped over the snifter of cognac she had laid on the floor. It spilled onto the carpet. Billy Volgar went to it, picked up the snifter and blotted at the spilled cognac with his handkerchief. She wiped her eyes once again and said in a quavering voice, "I'm sorry. I'm not asking for me . . . It's my son . . . He's been kidnapped . . . They want ransom."

"I'm very sorry, Mrs. Fullsome. But are you asking me for money? Are you really asking me to pay the ransom?"

"No, of course not," she said. "He's going to be killed, Mr. Cross. The people who have him are animals. I'm sure they will kill my son."

Cross paused, laid the glass of cognac on the stone rim of the fireplace, folded his hands in his lap, leaned forward and stared deeply into the woman's tear filled eyes. He was silent as he studied the woman. Finally he sat back and said, "Mrs. Fullsome. You're an MP with some influence. Why not just call in Scotland Yard . . . Or your military . . . Use your political power. Go have your people rescue him. Why come to me?"

"I've tried all that, Mr. Cross. Robert isn't in this Country."

"So use your Foreign Service . . . Send out your SAS, your Special Air Service Commandoes. Again, why come to me?"

"Mr. Cross," the woman started. She was now crying openly, wiping the tears first with her small handkerchief, and then with one or two tissues she pulled from the box on the seat next to her. But the tears would not stop flowing freely from her eyes. "I've tried all that," she sobbed. "The Government will do nothing. There is a lot of foreign policy involved. They can't just invade a foreign Country on my behalf."

"But you have a Foreign Service," Cross argued. "Get your diplomats on it. Surely there is something in the way of diplomatic arrangements that can be done. Offer whoever it is who has your son money . . . Or military assistance . . . Give them what they want. That's how it's done, isn't it? Diplomacy is merely commerce . . . Buying and selling, so to speak."

"They can do nothing when there aren't any diplomatic relationships existing. These people are criminals. They are not a government we can deal with," she said. She was not able to fight back the emotion and tears, but Joe Cross, after years of having to deal with people of lesser conscience and humanity, could hear fear and a sense of pleading in her voice. He would always listen carefully to the voices of people he dealt with; he would watch their faces and their body movements.

Listening to her, watching her as she spoke, Cross was starting to feel sorry for the woman. He was fighting that feeling; he didn't want to feel sorry for her, he wanted to hate her, but seeing her sitting there crying uncontrollably made him feel some pity for her. He thought, 'Here's a woman who hates me, and I feel sorry for her! What the hell's the matter with me? I should have Billy Volgar throw her out onto the street.'

At first he had wanted to embarrass her, insult her, and then hand her over to Billy Volgar. Now, he was beginning to feel some sympathy for her.

She was not young, she was not pretty, and she was crying freely. She was pale, and she was shaking, her shoulders bent and her head down. She seemed to be trying to be contrite but could not bring herself fully to it. She had money and power, both of which she had used effectively to rise in her party and gain a high position of influence in Parliament. Yet there she was, crying and asking for help from someone she had very publicly hated for years.

Without moving from the couch, Cross said, "Mrs. Fullsome, I think you need to tell me what the hell is going on. But first you need to calm down and regain your composure. Would a cup of tea help . . . Perhaps a glass of water?"

"Yes," she said, wiping her eyes and nose with the small hanky. She tried to sit up straight and struggled to fight back more tears. "Water please," she whispered.

Billy Volgar turned and went through a door that swung on silent hinges, returning almost immediately with a tall glass of water. He stepped down the set of steps into the sitting area. He handed it to the MP, and she sipped at it. Billy stayed, standing next to her awkwardly, not really knowing what to do, but knowing he had to be there to help if his boss needed help. He took the glass from her when she had finished half of the water and walked back up the steps to wait, holding the glass in case she wanted it.

Cross waited while she wiped the last of the tears away. It seemed she was beginning to calm herself, struggling to regain some composure. He waited a minute or two. She breathed deeply and wiped her eyes. When he thought she was a bit more in control of herself he said, "Start at the beginning, Mrs. Fullsome."

She took a deep breath and began, holding back further tears as best she could, "My son, Robert . . . I don't think you know of him . . . I try to keep my family out of the public eye . . . Robert had taken a year off from his schooling at Eton. He went to work as a volunteer with St. Anthony's Purse. Have you heard of them?"

"No, please go on."

"It is a private, charitable organization. They send food and medicines to the poorer parts of the world, generally Africa and Asia, and some parts of South America.

They also send doctors and nurses who volunteer their time and expertise to treat the sick. Robert joined the group, he said for only one year. My husband and I tried our best to dissuade him. They sent him with a team of doctors and nurses to some remote area of Southern Congo, near the border with Zambia I think, I'm not really sure. Although the Foreign Service says it is more likely near the southern most border of Uganda."

"You don't know exactly where your son went?" Cross asked. "Doesn't the organization know where they sent him?"

"The people at St. Anthony's Purse will not speak with me in any detail for fear other of their people will be hurt. They seem to be afraid of bad publicity.   I find it unconscionable that they place the organization above the wellbeing of one of their people. But they did tell me it is a very remote area of swamps, rivers, and grasslands. They said there was an outbreak of yellow fever in one of the villages, at least that's what they say, but they won't tell me exactly which village or where it is. Many villages and tribes were affected. He could be anywhere in that area."

"OK," Cross said. "So your son is down there with a group of charity folks. You said he was kidnapped."

"I received a letter three weeks ago.   It was postmarked Geneva, Switzerland.   There was no return address on it."

She pulled a wrinkled and worn beige envelope of good quality paper from her purse and held it out to Cross. Billy walked down the steps and took it from her. He walked across the room, unsure and hesitating. He wanted to throw the note into the unlit fireplace and set a match to it. But he wouldn't do that unless his boss, Joseph Cross, told him to.

He held it out to his boss. Cross paused at first,

staring at the piece of paper Billy held out to him. He was fighting back the desire to do anything to help this woman who hated him so much. His first instinct was not unlike Billy Volgar's. He wanted to refuse to take the envelope and read what it held. But in spite of his dislike of her, in spite of what he thought of the woman, in spite of his hatred of the MP, he could not help feeling somehow sorry for her. He knew he shouldn't, but he couldn't shake that feeling of sympathy for a woman who had lost her only son. He stood and took the envelope from Billy. Inside was a one page, hand written demand on similar paper to the envelope. It read:

"I have Robert. You may have him back for five million United States dollars in cash. All one hundred dollar bills, please. You will be contacted in one month's time.

Gen. Simba Azubuike"

The handwriting was good, by a well-educated person. The ink was blue, common to the wealthier of Europe, and not black. That fact, added to the words used and the sentence structure told Joe that the person writing it was European and of a good standing in that society. Cross knew General Simba Azubuike, and he knew that the man certainly did not write the note himself. He was an uneducated man who could speak little English and was certainly not able to write in such a good, clear hand. It had to be someone in the blood diamond business, Simba Azubuike's business, someone doing business with Azubuike.

Cross read the note twice more and then held it out

for Billy, who took it into his bearlike hands. He read it and handed it back to Cross. He said, "That's bad, ain't it?"

"Yes, Billy," Cross said. He tossed his cigar into the unlit fireplace and quickly drank down his cognac, draining the crystal snifter. "It's worse than bad."

CHAPTER THREE – General Simba Azubuike

Mrs. Fullsome looked from man to man and then back again. She saw the expressions on the faces of the two men change suddenly. There was surprise there certainly, but there was also worry and maybe a little fear. Joe Cross' face flushed red. Billy's face was the ruddy, rock hard, and scarred face of a fighter that never changed. The name on the note obviously frightened them. It must be a name they knew, a man they knew who alarmed them. Yet these were two men who had risen to become the most powerful criminals in the entire United Kingdom.

"Do you know this General Simba Azubuike?" she asked.

Cross looked at Billy who could not control his outward emotions as well as Cross could. Billy wanted to shout out, 'NO!' and tell the woman to leave, to go away. He wanted no part of anything Simba Azubuike was involved in. But he held himself back. His boss would make the decisions, and whatever his boss said, would be done.

It took only a look from Cross to Billy Volgar to ask the unspoken question, should they escort Mrs. Fullsome out of the Club or answer her question? Billy shook his head at first, indicating that Cross should go no further with this woman. Seeing that his boss might not do that, he shrugged his shoulders. "I don't know, do I?" he said, answering the look on Joe Cross' face. "That bloody bastard ain't no good, is he?"

Cross turned to the woman and said, "If this man has your son . . . It's bad."

"Can it be worse than a kidnapping?" she asked.

"You don't know who this man is, do you?" Cross asked.

"No. Who is he?"

"Didn't your Foreign Service tell you anything about him?"

"No. I had my office make enquiries, but they said nothing in return. They said they had no information on the man. I asked personally, and they said they knew nothing once again. I got the feeling they weren't telling me the truth."

"Mrs. Fullsome," Cross started. "You are a highly respected and powerful Member of Parliament. And you mean to tell me that your Government's entire Secret Intelligence Service . . . MI-6 and everybody else . . . Couldn't tell you about this man?"

She didn't answer immediately. Her face blushed and she lowered her eyes as she admitted, "I did ask . . . But they told me nothing. I guess I just assumed they didn't know of him."

'And maybe this MP isn't as powerful as she thinks she is,' Cross thought without speaking the words. Maybe the people in her Government didn't fear her as much as she wanted them to; maybe they just didn't like her and wouldn't cooperate with her on something not Government related? Maybe they just didn't care what happened to her or her son?

Cross looked up at Billy, and Billy said in his bearlike growl of a voice, "Maybe they just don't want t'scare her." He knew the real reason, of course. Billy Volgar was a giant of a man and an ugly killer. But he wasn't stupid. He knew that Margaret Fullsome made enemies everywhere she went, as she propelled herself up the ladder of British Government. She was a strong woman who demanded rather than reasoned or even manipulated, as so many politicians did. People were scared of her more than they respected her. Billy was trying to be nice, as nice as the violent man he was could be.

Cross nodded and said to Mrs. Fullsome, "Simba Azubuike is a criminal, a self-appointed revolutionary, although he isn't in it to take over Governments. He has his own little empire, and he's satisfied with that. He is the head of his own army of boys and drugged out men, a dealer in slaves, and a cannibal . . ."

The MP's face paled at the word; she sat back on the couch, obviously in shock, and her jaw dropped.

"That's right," Cross said. "I said a cannibal . . . Who finances his little kingdom through the blood diamond trade. He keeps slaves, working chained to each other, digging diamonds in the African sun until they die of hunger and beatings. His nighttime entertainment is watching people be tortured to death or burned alive. He eats captives' hearts and livers. He thinks it will give him strength. Mrs. Fullsome . . . The man is certainly insane and possibly the incarnation of Satan himself on earth. I've never met or known anyone as cruel and vicious as he is. He took the name Simba . . . Which means "lion" . . . And Azubuike . . . Which means "he has much strength" . . . And he calls himself a General. If he has your son . . . I suggest you pay the ransom and anything else he demands. Then just hope that he will eventually release your son. Doing anything else will certainly mean you will never see your son again."

"You say I should '*hope*' that he releases Robert. You mean he may not?"

Cross hesitated to answer her. He looked once again at the giant, Billy Volgar, who could only shrug his wide shoulders again. Billy knew his boss was right, and he knew his boss should walk away, throw the MP out of The Rochester Club, and get on with his own life. But he watched Cross closely, and he could see the man edging toward helping this woman.

She needed to know the truth, Cross knew that. He was about to say something, but before he could answer, the room was lit by a flash of lightening across the black early morning sky outside, followed quickly by a loud crash of thunder that shook the room. Cross thought it was perhaps a warning from whatever gods there may be who protect people like him, to not get involved in this.

Cross would tell her, he decided, and then he would have Billy escort her out and downstairs to the front door and into the rain on the street. He owed this woman nothing. He had wasted enough of his time with her. All she had ever done was to make life more difficult for him. Without her constant insistence and prodding of the police and Customs Service, they might go after other smugglers and criminals, dealers in the drug trade, instead of wasting more time on Cross then they would normally do. But she never gave up on her public outrage at the American Joseph Cross, using that to advance her career.

There are criminals in the United Kingdom who are worse than Cross, violent men and women who kill and live on the drug and prostitute trade. He felt he was sure in saying too many police were assigned to hunt down Joseph Cross, urged on by Mrs. Fullsome for her own personal political advantage, who could be out stopping these violent criminals. The streets were often dangerous places, but not by the fault of Joseph Cross.

But she was also a woman, a mother, and he felt some pangs of compassion despite all she had done to him. He needed to shake off that feeling of sympathy and worry about his own life and businesses. Whatever was happening to her was what she probably deserved anyway. He liked to believe that 'bad things happen to bad people,' and he certainly felt this MP, this Margaret Fullsome was a bad person whose only goal in life was to rise in the political world at the expense of everyone she encountered.

He took a deep breath and explained, hoping his words could be harsh enough to hurt the woman and maybe drive some sense of the real world into her.

"I mean, the odds are better than even that you will never see your son again, regardless of what you do. Simba takes great joy in watching people suffer. He will probably kill your son no matter what you do. Don't count on him releasing your son. I suggest that all you can do is pay the ransom and pray. Or accept the fact that your son is probably already dead and save your money."

His words seemed to have little effect on her. Her eyes seemed to be looking at Cross and yet seeing something far, far away. "May I ask you something, Mr. Cross?" she said in a bare whisper.

He nodded, and she asked, "You deal in diamonds. Please don't deny it . . . I know, and it makes no difference right now. Have you ever bought diamonds from this man?"

"Once, many years ago. Before he became what he is today. I would not buy anything from him today. In spite of what you may think of me, I do have some moral standards left. I don't deal in drugs, slaves, prostitutes or murder. And I don't do business with Simba Azubuike."

"So you know the man personally. And I believe you have some experience with mercenaries? Men who fight wars for money?"

Cross didn't answer, and his face remained expressionless. Mrs. Fullsome, he considered, could be here on a mission to get him to incriminate himself in a crime. Was she wired? Was their conversation being recorded? That would not surprise him; the damn woman would stop at nothing to see him in jail.

"Mrs. Fullsome," he asked. "Are you wearing a wire?"

"A what?" she asked and frowned questioningly.

"Are you here to record what I say and then use it to have me arrested?"

"Mr. Cross, please believe me, I am sincere. My son is in danger. If you want, I shall submit to a search. Your man here has my permission to do a thorough search of my person. To save my son I will strip naked in front of you, if you wish."

"Alright, Mrs. Fullsome. Stand up please."

The woman stood immediately and started to undue the buttons on her blouse. Cross stopped her and waived Billy Volgar to her. He picked up her big leather purse and upended it, dumping everything onto the floor at his feet. He quickly rummaged through the pile and found nothing that could be a recording device.

He stood behind the woman and held her arms out to her sides. Billy started to move his hands to the woman to pat her down but stopped when Cross held up his hand and said, "OK. I believe you."

Billy stepped back, and Mrs. Fullsome buttoned her

blouse and sat down. She bent and pulled her things from the floor into her bag. She asked, "Please may I have some more water?"

Billy took the half full glass from a nearby end table and disappeared for a moment, returning with a full glass of cold water. The MP drank most of it and handed the glass back to Billy. She smiled up at the man in thanks.

Cross waited until she had settled back on the couch, and then he asked, "You wanted to know about mercenaries? Why?"

She paused a moment, took a deep breath, and then said, "I assume my own Government will not send our military to rescue my son because they don't want a diplomatic incident with the Republic of the Congo . . . or wherever my son is. I've sent letters and done all the normal Government to Government diplomatic routine, but the Congolese will do nothing. No one will do anything to help Robert . . . and me. How do I contact these mercenaries and hire them to rescue my son?"

"Where is your husband, Mrs. Fullsome?" Cross asked. "Why isn't he here? Why isn't he doing something? He has businesses all over Europe, Asia, and the Americas. Certainly he has contacts who can arrange such a thing."

"Taylor, my husband, was extremely angry when Robert left school. He thinks doing charitable work of any kind is a waste of time and energy. He believes tax revenues should provide needed assistance and will do nothing to help anyone himself. He wants Robert to come into his businesses. Robert has told him many times that he wants his own life. He's told us, Taylor and myself, that he doesn't want to be like his father. Taylor thinks this whole thing will teach Robert a good lesson. He brushes aside the idea that Robert may not survive this. He says that things like that happen only in the movies. If the ransom is not paid, he insists, then this Azubuike will just let Robert go."

"But he will pay the ransom?" Cross asked.

"He says he will . . . I insisted on that. I hope he will. He controls the money we have. I have little money of my own."

Cross stood and walked up the three steps of the sitting area. He went to the bar and poured another small cognac. Billy Volgar walked with him. They whispered back and forth for a minute or two. Billy argued against helping the woman. "You don't owe this bloody bitch nothin'," he said. "That Simba bloke, he's too damn dangerous to fool with, ain't he?"

Cross was beginning to bend and thought he might be able to profit if he did offer some assistance. He drank his cognac and returned to Mrs. Fullsome.

He said, standing in front of her, "I'll make a deal with you. You lay off me . . . Stop trying to destroy me . . . Find some other cause to keep your career going . . . And I'll make some enquiries. Go home. Talk to no one. Especially not the press and the police. I'll contact you in a day or two. If you tell anyone what we've talked about, you'll be on your own, I won't help you. If I help you, and then you come after me again . . . I'll send Billy there after you. He will kill you, he will kill your husband . . . And if your son survives Azubuike, he will kill him, too. If you have other children, if you have sisters or brothers, he will kill them, too. And your nieces and nephews. Do you understand me perfectly?"

She stood, standing uneasily, shaking, her knees ready to collapse under her. The threat was something she had never heard before, but she knew that Joseph Cross . . . And Billy Volgar . . . Were capable of carrying out that threat. Her face was red from her tears and now from the threat of death; her eye makeup had run down her cheeks. Her eyes had dark rings around them, both from the makeup and her not having slept for three days before coming to Joseph Cross. She said in a weak, quavering voice, "Thank you, Mr. Cross. I do promise. Thank you."

****

Neither Joseph Cross nor Billy Volgar slept that day. As the winter's sun rose, Cross looked for the twelfth time at the letter Fullsome had received. It was in a very good handwriting, and the English was perfect. But who had written it?

Cross knew General Azubuike before he was a General and before he took the name he used as a General. His name had been Stephen Okeke a few years before, and he had been a petty thief. He plied his trade in Kampala, the Capital of Uganda. The day Cross met him, Stephen was thin, dirty, bare footed, hungry and desperate. He had a small leather bag of raw diamonds, his only thing of any value in the whole world, but he was having a difficult time selling them. People who would buy diamonds assumed by looking at them that they were illegal, either stolen or blood diamonds. Honest jewelers wanted nothing to do with them. But Stephen had dug them himself, out of the mud, out of desperation. He was unable to convince anyone that they were his and not illegal.

De Beers Diamonds was well known for its near monopoly of the diamond industry throughout the 20th century. That monopoly began to shrink in the 1980s when Russia, Canada, and Australia began to produce and distribute their own diamonds, ignoring the De Beers' decades old control of the market. The price of diamonds began to shrink until De Beers started to withhold many of its own diamonds from the world market.

And, in the mid-Twentieth Century, in secret and remote areas of Central Africa, tribes and individuals began digging in mud and river banks for diamonds to sell for pennies to whomever would buy them. These diamonds began to be produced to finance violent revolutions and tribal warfare in Africa. These cheap diamonds bought guns and bullets and whatever other instruments of death could be had. These cheap diamonds flooded the markets. The profits from the sales were used to wreak death among the African tribes.

Raw diamonds from Africa, without provenance, not coming from a known diamond producer, without the laser carved number inside the cut diamond which is recognized around the world, are considered contraband and are shied away from in most parts of the world. Hundreds of thousands of deaths, perhaps uncounted more, are the result of the world wide trade in these diamonds. Hence their name: 'Blood Diamonds.'

But the value and profit from these diamonds can only be recognized if they can be moved out of the African Continent. And Stephen Okeke had no way to do that. It was easy for everyone to assume that the raw diamonds in the little bag were illegal and therefore trouble for anyone buying them.

So he walked the streets of Kampala, stealing food when he could, eating out of garbage cans when he couldn't. He slept in muddy, dirty alleys and searched out someone, anyone, hoping to find a buyer for his leather bag of red-mud covered raw diamonds. The police would find him asleep somewhere and beat him with clubs until he would run away. Desperation enveloped Stephen Okeke, and thoughts of suicide filled his head. Only hatred for the civilized world, that cared nothing for him, kept him alive.

In 2008 he came across an old man, Ruben Decker, a white man with thick, uncombed grey hair that hung in unkempt knots to his shoulders. His aged, wrinkled face was hidden behind a gray beard that was as thick as the hair on his head. It covered his mouth so that his lips disappeared under it. Flakes of food stuck to the beard. His clothes, ill-fitting and mismatched, were old, wrinkled, and stained.

Ruben carried a great weight of age and troubles on his shoulders. He was bent over from a past that haunted him throughout his life. Ruben had been born in the Auschwitz concentration camp just days before it was liberated by the Russian Army. His mother, weak from starvation, had died giving birth to Ruben. He was handed around by the Russians from a number of ramshackle military hospitals to the remnants of civilian hospitals until the Swiss Red Cross stepped in, took him from the Russians and found homes for Ruben and thousands of other nameless children from the camps.

Ruben was adopted by a farming family in Holland. The family needed male children to work the farm, and Ruben grew up doing that. His adoptive parents were strict believers in the teachings of the Protestant Bible, especially that one phrase Ruben came to know very well: '*Spare the rod, spoil the child.*'

At thirteen years of age, while working in the fields one hot afternoon, Ruben dropped his hoe and walked away. He spent the next four years walking aimlessly around Europe, working when he could find work, stealing when he had to. At seventeen years of age he was caught stealing a car in France and sentenced to five long, hard years in prison.

Over the next 35 years Ruben was in and out of prison, learning to accept the beatings and gang rapes. Then, upon his release from a prison in Germany, he left Europe and found his way south, into Africa. He fled one African revolution and tribal war after another until he settled in Kampala, Uganda, after the major wars had ended and Idi Amin was deposed in 2003. He opened a small shop in a decrepit area of the city selling whatever people would buy: cigarettes, cheap whiskey, straw hats, and anything else that people asked for.

It was into that shop that a ragged and hungry Stephen Okeke walked. His thin body was dressed in dirty, torn shorts and the remnants of what was once a T-shirt but was now merely rags of cloth hanging across his shoulders. The acrid smells of the filthy back streets enveloped the young man.

He had pulled one dirty stone from his little bag and placed it on the crowded counter next to the old cash register. He wanted to trade it for a few cans of food. Ruben recognized what the dirty little stone was, and he knew there was an American in Kampala who was buying uncut diamonds. He fed Stephen Okeke a meal in the back room of the shop while he sent a ragged, skinny boy from the streets to find Joseph Cross and bring him to the shop.

Ruben filled Stephen's stomach for the first time in days. After eating he sat on an old couch in the rear of the room, and then he lay down on it and quickly fell asleep. Ruben covered him with a frayed, knitted, red shawl and waited for Cross to arrive. The boy he had sent to find Cross came back an hour later with Joseph Cross.

"Hello, Ruben," Cross said and shook the old man's boney hand. "You have business for me, I understand."

"Hallo mijn vriend," Ruben said in his childhood

Dutch. He smiled through his thick beard and bowed his head slightly as he held Cross' hand in both of his own. "Business, ja, natuurlijk. But first, please give the boy a few coins."

Cross laughed and took a handful of Ugandan coins mixed with a few British pennies from his pocket. The boy nearly jumped as he ran from the little shop to buy whatever food and cigarettes he could with the handful of coins.

Ruben explained that a young man had come to him with a bag of uncut diamonds. "I do not know the quality of them," he explained. "But I thought you might be interested. So I sent the boy to find you. Did I do right?"

"You did right, Ruben. You always do. Where are they?" Cross asked. He was always interested in raw diamonds that could be smuggled into England and cut and sold.

"He is asleep," Ruben said. "In the back room. He was very hungry, and he may sell the diamonds cheaply. He looks in a bad way."

Ruben led Cross into the back room where Stephen lay curled under the red shawl. He was snoring softly. Ruben asked, "Shall we wake him or let him sleep more?"

"Wake him," Cross said. "I have other things to do today."

Ruben gently touched Stephen's shoulder. "Young man," he said. "Young man. Here there is a man who wants to see your diamonds."

Stephen groaned and rolled onto his back. At first he didn't know where he was. He was used to local police hitting him with their clubs to wake him and move him off the streets. When his eyes were able to focus, he recognized Ruben. He smiled slightly and said, "Thank you, sir."

His English was heavily accented, but Ruben and Cross understood. Stephen sat up, rubbed his eyes and looked at Cross. "You will buy my diamonds?" he asked.

"Maybe," Cross answered. "Let me see them."

Stephen reached into the pocket of his torn shorts and pulled the small bag out. He hesitated at first and then held it out. He asked in a quaking voice, "You will not steal them from me, will you?" Cross smiled and took the bag, pulled the cords to open it, and spilled the mud covered stones into his palm.

He had experience with diamonds; he could recognize the real thing from cheap crystals. These were good diamonds, but not great diamonds. A few of the bigger stones could be cleaned and cut into something of medium value. The smaller ones might be sold as industrial diamonds. In any case, Cross could see value in what Stephen had.

He put the stones back into their little sack and handed it back to Stephen. "Where did you get these?" he asked. If they were stolen or worse yet, smuggled out of a De Beers mine, he would not buy them.

Stephen explained to Cross that he had dug the diamonds himself in a swampy area along the southern border of Congo and Uganda.

"You found these yourself?" Cross asked.

"Yes," Stephen answered simply. He nodded quickly, nervously and held the small bag tightly in his thin fingers.

"And how did you get to Kampala after finding these? Where you say you found them is a couple hundred miles south."

"I walked," Stephen answered.

"You walked hundreds of miles to Kampala?" Cross questioned, finding it hard to believe what Stephen had said. He looked at the boy's bare feet. They were leather-like and carried the scars of years of walking without shoes.

"Yes," Stephen said once again. He remained seated and looked quickly from Ruben, to Cross and back to Ruben. The old man was smiling with a great deal of compassion for the ragged boy. He had seen too many of this kind of person over his years. People, men and women, whom society had passed by. People whose lives were filled with hungry days and pain-filled nights. So many of them lived short lives, while others walked by them as if they were invisible.

Ruben's life had been like that, and in his aged years, when he could manage it, he had helped as many of these people as he could. He often fed the hungry who came to him; he clothed those who needed clothing; he comforted those in need of some kindness. Life had taught him to do these things, things he wished had been done for him.

"How long did it take you to get here?"

Stephen's forehead wrinkled as he thought. He said, "I don't know. Many days, I think."

"You would have had to come across villages . . . Maybe thieves," Cross said.

"Yes," Stephen answered. "Many beatings . . . But some people gave me food and water. Not all people are bad," he said trying to smile. "I am here now."

Cross bought the diamonds for a fair but meager price and paid in U. S. Dollars. Okeke was happy, and for the first time in as long as he could remember, he smiled broadly, showing all of his uneven teeth. Stephen used the money to buy good clothes and a backpack full of food. He walked back to the isolated swamp and forest area along the southern border of Uganda. He dug more diamonds.

That was the start of Stephen Okeke's career. It took some time and some work, but soon the dirty and ragged Stephen Okeke was General Simba Azubuike, well dressed, with money, and fat.

****

A little more than two years later Cross had returned to Kampala in search of more diamonds. He knew even then that not all raw diamonds taken from the ground were a means of survival for men who wanted to feed their families or for tribes to survive. More and more, over the years, too many of the diamonds coming out of central Africa were being sold to finance wars and petty dictators and bands of thieves. He avoided these, knowing where to go to buy the diamonds he wanted and where to avoid the ones he would not buy.

He was in his hotel room, resting after a mediocre dinner of tough beef or something closely related to beef, and over cooked vegetables. The room was basic at best, fairly clean but old. The bed's springs squeaked loudly, and the mattress was lumpy. It was a place far from the eyes of police. But he would be there for only a few days, three or four, just long enough to buy some diamonds that he could have smuggled into Britain.

He was listening to a radio broadcast of some station that played years old music of all sorts, and whose DJ spoke in very deep, broken English that the locals could understand, but Joe Cross could only get a word or two out of it. He busied himself by reading a four day old British newspaper, when a knock at the door startled him. He opened the door and was faced with an African, smiling broadly, and sweating profusely.

"Good this morning, Mr. Cross," the man said.

"It's evening . . . Not morning."

"I am truly so sorry, Mr. Cross. Good this evening to you."

"Who are you? What do you want?" Cross stood in the doorway, holding the door open a bare eight inches with his left hand, his right hand on the revolver tucked under his belt at his back. The man was dressed in khaki fatigues, wrinkled and dirty. He was short and thin. His hair was matted and thick with dirt.

"I am the pleasure of a message carrier for General Simba Azubuike."

"And who is that?" Cross asked.

"My General, he asks that you should remember him when he was Stephen Okeke."

Cross did remember the man. But now the ragged, skin and bones Stephen Okeke was a General. Cross thought, 'He's come up in the world.'

"What army is he a General in?" Cross asked.

"Why, my General he is Supreme General of The Army of the Heart of God," the man said with a wondering expression on his sweat drenched face and in a tone suggesting he should not have to tell anyone this, that it should be known throughout the entire world.

"OK, so what do you want?" Cross asked.

The smiling man relaxed a little and said, "My General he asks that you to his ultimate headquarters come with me.

He has diamonds for you to sell to you."

"So have your General bring them here, and I'll look at them," Cross replied and started to shut the door.

The thin man pushed back on the door and said, "I am the much pleasure to drive to you my General, Mr. Cross. My General commands."

"He may command you, but he doesn't tell me to do anything."

"I am who is sorry, Mr. Cross. My General to me commands to drive you to him. Do I say the words right? Do I make myself to you to understand?"

Cross said nothing, wondering what the hell was going on. Some skinny kid is now a General of his own damn army, and Cross was supposed to go to him?

The man had both hands on the door as he smiled even more, showing off big, yellow and black teeth. He said with a deep bow, "My General he has good whiskey and pretty women. He has for you diamonds. My General commands I say the please to you."

"OK, come back in the morning," Cross said. "I'll sleep on it and tell you at nine o'clock if I'm going with you or not."

The broad, toothy smile fell suddenly from the man's face. He said, "But . . . But my General, he has told me . . . He has the command to me . . . He will be angry . . ."

Cross pushed hard closing the door in the man's face. He locked it and laughed. "That little guy must be something else," he said out loud.

He slept with the revolver on the nightstand, and in the morning, as he ate a breakfast of over cooked eggs and burnt toast in the hotel's small restaurant, the man in the wrinkled fatigues walked in and stood in the restaurant's entrance. Cross saw him and intentionally finished his coffee very slowly. He lit a cigarette and smoked it as slowly as he drank the coffee, while looking directly at the man. When he was done, he stood and walked to him. It was half past ten in the morning. Cross had intentionally taken his time bathing and shaving, hoping the skinny man would give up and go away.

"OK, I'm ready now. Where are we going?" he asked.

"It is a drive very long, Mr. Cross. I have the truck, water and food. We should go now, yes. The General has the command he said."

And it was a very long drive. It didn't take very long in the battered and dirty old Toyota pick-up truck to leave the paved roads of Kampala and start to bounce along semi-paved rutted roads and then dirt tracks that ran through grasslands and forests.

Big, black storm clouds raced in, bringing with them crashes of thunder and flashes of lightening. In the distant horizon Cross saw herds of antelope running from the storm. Elephants grazed near the side of the road, apparently not caring about the noise of the thunder or the flashes of lightening. Like most things in life, Joe Cross knew that if you were big enough in size or reputation, very little would scare you.

They drove very slowly along the rutted dirt road. The driver stopped once and pulled a thermos from the bed of the truck. He handed it to Cross and smiled. Cross found it held water that must have come right from a muddy river somewhere. He refused the water that the man drank deeply. The driver stepped to the side of the road and relieved himself into the tall weeds.

As they drove on, Cross could see an occasional

village in the distance. Small thatched huts rose from the brown grass all around them. Plumes of smoke rose from the villages, curling into the darkening sky. People were gathering together for dinner and perhaps protection from what the approaching dark of night might hide.

Evening was fast approaching. Soon it was too dark for Cross to see the time on his wristwatch. The driver slowed the pick-up as he approached a small, thrown together hut. He pulled to a stop, and Cross looked out the window. Two thin and ragged men sat in the dirt, asleep, with old rifles lying on the ground in the dirt next to them.

Cross asked, "What's this?" The driver said nothing and put his foot down on the gas pedal.

A short drive later they pulled into what might be called a village of thatch roofed huts. Small fires burned on the ground in front of a few of them, but no residents could be seen. The entire village was surrounded with a fence of cut acacia thorn bushes, making a formidable wall of protection from anything . . . or anyone . . . who might want to enter.

Cross looked around. It was dark, but he could see that this little, decrepit village had been cut out of swampy forest. The bare ground was muddy and dark reddish-brown. He could smell the stagnant swamp all around.

The driver pulled the pick-up to a stop. In the middle of the village, a tall, rusted iron I-beam stood askew in the middle of a pile of ash and rock. Chains had been bolted to the beam, and handcuffs hung from the ends of the chain. He saw piles of burnt bones in the ash. He hoped they weren't human bones, but he had a feeling they were.

An old woman appeared from inside one of the small huts and bent to stir a pot of something over one of the fires as she looked cautiously at Joe Cross in the truck. Little children, most of them naked or nearly so, ducked outside from the cover of the huts and ran away to hide in the shadows as two men, ragged and skinny, opened the doors of the truck.

Cross climbed out of the truck and stood on the wet dirt, looking around. There was a smell of damp rot and old death in the air. A nightmarish scream suddenly rang out, a woman's scream, a scream filled with pain and suffering. It was so fearful a scream that it seemed to shake the entire little village. The old woman who had been stirring the pot over the fire dropped her wooden spoon onto the dirt and crawled quickly through the low doorway into the hut behind her. Cross looked around, and no one was there but the skinny driver and himself. The two men who had opened the truck's doors had disappeared. And the driver was shaking in terror. His yellow eyes were about to pop from their sockets. His face was covered with sweat. He was quivering with fear.

"What the hell was that?" Cross asked the man.

"That is nothing," the man said, frightened obviously, speaking in a whisper. His eyes were bulging, foamy saliva ran from the corners of his mouth, sweat ran freely across his black face, soaking his dirty shirt. "You are to please come with me to my General."

Cross followed the man to the biggest of the huts, a round building, roofed in tin sheets, raised up off the muddy ground on wooden stilts three foot tall. There was a porch of sorts covered with a roof of brown, dried palm fronds and tree branches along the front of it. Two planks of rough wood on piled stones served as steps up to the porch. A double door of polished wood stood open. Cross, standing on the ground near the stairs, looked inside. The big room was lit brightly inside, casting light out into the dark night.

The truck driver stood in the doorway, holding the doors open for Cross. He stepped aside as Cross walked into the room. The driver walked away, almost running as fast as his skinny legs would carry him when Cross had passed him. He had closed the door behind Cross before he ran away, leaving Cross standing by himself in the eerie quiet.

The room was big and round; Cross thought it might be forty-five or fifty feet across. Polished wooden planks lined the walls, and African shields and spears hung here and there. The floor was also polished wood and darker than the walls. The floor was spotted with the brown tell-tale remnants of dried blood, but otherwise very clean.

The ceiling above was thatched under the tin roof and held above by thick timbers that rose from the walls to a high peak in the center of the room. Hanging from the peak of the ceiling was a large, primitive looking chandelier holding a dozen very bright light bulbs, the only light fixture in the room. Cross wondered how a building this far out in the wilderness could have electricity.

The air inside was still and humid. There was a foul odor hanging heavily all around him. Even the worst lockers in the worst gymnasiums didn't smell as bad as the big room did.

A tall chair sat lonely on a bright red, raised platform, across the room, the only furniture in the hut. The chair was highly polished black wood, ebony Cross thought. It was carved elaborately with small lions' heads sculpted at the shoulders. It was upholstered with a zebra skin that was well worn at the back and seat of the chair. He wondered just what the hell he had walked into.

Behind the chair he saw a wall that extended from one side of the platform to the other. On it hung spears and tall shields, and several stretched skins of animals.

His footsteps echoed across the bare, wood floor as he walked slowly into the center of the room. The floor's loose and warped floorboards squeaked as he circled the room. He stopped when the door behind him opened once again and two men, tall and thin, wearing filthy tan shorts, shirtless and shoeless, stepped inside. They moved aside slowly and stood on either side of the open door.

They had with them old, dirty, scratched, and pitted AK-47 rifles. They each carried them loosely in one hand, almost too casually, by the ends of the rusted barrels, letting the battered wooden stocks drag across the floor. And hanging from hemp robes that served as belts at their waists, were long bolo machetes, perhaps rusted and dirty, but still dangerous in any case.

Both men seemed to be only half awake; their eyelids hung thick and long over their eyes. Their dark, black skin was shiny with sweat over ribs that appeared to have little flesh on them. Their hair was a jumbled mass, matted and dirty with embedded shards of grass. Cross could see, in the light from the chandelier, small insects crawling through their hair. They stood to either side of the open door as General Simba Azubuike strode in proudly, smiling a big, toothy smile and throwing his big stomach out in an arrogant advertisement of his appetite.

Cross recognized the face of the man, although it was a much fatter face than he remembered. It was Stephen Okeke, but this Stephen was close to two hundred pounds heavier than the last time Cross had seen him.

He stopped in the doorway, threw his fat arms out and shouted, "My old friend, Joseph Cross! And I thought you weren't coming to see me after all this time!"

"Stephen," Cross said, using the name Cross had

known him as, the man's real name. "It's very good to see you again. And I see you've been eating well. The last time I saw you, you looked like you needed a good meal."

The General laughed a thunderous laugh that shook the very walls of the big room as he walked in a rambling step to Cross. He took Cross up in his thick arms and lifted him off the ground. The General may have been dressed in good, clean camouflaged fatigues with rows of medals and ribbons stuck all over the shirt, but he smelled like animal dung. It was apparent that he hadn't bathed in weeks in the tropical African heat.

He let Cross go and strode to the platform where the big chair that seemed to be his throne waited for him. He struggled to climb up the three steps and flopped down into the chair. He laughed again, shaking the timbers of the hut. "Why are you so late, my friend? I expected you for breakfast this morning."

"I told your driver to pick me up this morning. I wanted to get some sleep."

A volley of gunshots rang out from somewhere in the compound. Cross turned, flinching at the shots.

"Ahhh, well," Azubuike said, shrugging his fat shoulders and staring deeply at Cross to see his reaction. "That was your driver. If that man he had done what I told him he should do, he would be alive right now." He broke out suddenly in another hut shaking laugh.

"You killed that man because I wanted to sleep?"

"Discipline my old friend, Joseph. Discipline. An army runs on discipline. But now, it is late, and you must be hungry. I have a bed ready for you and some food. We will talk of business in the morning."

He stood and waived his fat arm. The two men

standing at the doorway stood aside and waived for Cross to follow them. Cross waited for Azubuike to leave his thrown, but the fat man remained seated, staring down at Joseph Cross. So he turned and started for the double doors.

Outside, he saw a bloody body being dragged by its feet across the muddy ground. It was the driver, he assumed, although the body had been torn apart by the volley of bullets. He again wondered just what the hell he had gotten himself into.

He followed the two men, soldiers to use the term loosely, who had led him out of the big hut, to a small grass and stick shack with a low opening in it. They motioned for him to go inside. He bent and managed to enter.

Inside it was barely tall enough for him to stand up straight. It was perhaps eight feet in diameter with a mud dirt floor. An oil lamp on the floor lit the inside faintly, the smell of the burning oil filling the small hut. Smoke filled the ceiling and slowly made its way through the thin thatch. A stench of filth and unwashed bodies permeated.

A blanket had been laid out on the dirt floor. It was roughly weaved of crude, uncolored hemp. Dark stains dotted the cloth; Cross hoped they weren't blood stains, but they could have been. There was a small, yellow pillow at one end that was dark from overuse by unwashed heads. A covered, clay pot sat on the mud near the bed. Cross took the lid off and smelled what was inside. Corn, he imagined; some kind of corn meal mash, with maybe some kind of meat and possibly some peppers. The smell was strong, too strong for Cross to want to eat any of it.

He sat on the blanket, determined that the morning would find him on his way back to the hotel in Kampala, even if he had to walk. Then two women, one after the other, bent down low to enter the little hut. They were completely naked, bone skinny, with sunken eyes that were looking at something far, far away, and with breasts that hung flat against their ribs. 'Drugged,' Cross thought.

They each laid themselves down on the dirt, on their backs, and spread their legs. Cross stood and stepped away from them. He waived his arms back and forth and repeated, "No . . . No . . . No . . ." He was not sure they could understand what he was trying to tell them. Their eyes were glassy, and they seemed to ignore him, or possibly not hear him because of the drugs they had been fed.

His first thought was to push them out of the hut. He had no intention of screwing a couple of sickly, drugged out women. Then he remembered the fate of the man who had driven him to see Azubuike. He stood and helped each woman to her feet. They were much shorter than Cross, and as he lifted them to their feet, he guessed each could not possibly weigh more than a hundred pounds.

He took each by a skin covered boney hand and led them to the pot of food. He lifted the top from the pot and said, "Eat . . . Eat." He made motions of putting food in his mouth, and the two women finally understood. They fell to their knees and took the food, whatever it was, by handfuls. They stuffed the food into their mouths, moaning and even crying a little. Cross had no idea how long it had been since they had seen food of any kind. The clay pot was empty in a few minutes.

Still on their knees, they turned to Cross and smiled. He folded his hands together and put them to the side of his head. He pointed to the blanket on the floor, trying to tell them to sleep. They finally understood and lay down on the dirt floor, avoiding the blanket, perhaps in deference or maybe fear of Cross. They huddled together, holding each other tightly, and fell into a deep sleep almost immediately.

CHAPTER FOUR - The Heart Of My God

The morning was greeted by a lot of shouting outside the little hut where Cross had spent the cold night. Sunlight filtered in through the grass and thatch matting of the hut's thin walls and roof. Cross had managed a few hours of sleep, curled against the wall of the little hut, as far from the two women as he could manage. He had pulled the dirty blanket from the middle of the hut and lay on it to keep from sleeping in stinking mud. When he awoke, the two women were gone. He rubbed the sleep from his eyes, stood and bent to leave the hut.

Outside, in the grey cold of early morning, he watched as a line of men and women, covered in red mud and filth, filed through the middle of the village. They were chained together. Steel cuffs were fastened around their ankles and locked with padlocks. Lengths of heavy chain hung from each, from one to the next. They were all very thin, like the two women the night before, mainly skin and bones covered with red mud.

There were both men and women in the line; all were naked, and scars and bruises left by whips and beatings were easily recognizable. They were being herded by four men in ragged shorts and shirts, like the two guards the night before. But these held big, nasty looking clubs.

When the chained slaves had passed out of sight,

Cross looked around him. Groups of skinny men and a few very young boys stood in the red dirt watching Cross. Each held a weapon of some kind, mainly old AK-47s, some of them with old British Enfield rifles, one or two with long spears and machetes. A few of the young boys, children really, held old rifles as big as they were. Cross was very familiar with weapons, having run many into Ireland and Africa over the years. What he saw in the hands of these pitiful people would probably blow up in their faces if they were fired.

Cross walked as fast as he could back to the big hut where he had spoken with Azubuike the day before. There were two guards at the doorway, standing beside the closed double doors, at the top of the wooden stairs. They wore filthy and tattered shorts with lengths of rope tied as belts. One had a dirty and torn yellow T-shirt on; the other wore nothing above his shorts. They were covered with sweat and red dirt. Flies circled above their heads, ignored by the two of them. Both were barefooted.

They stood leaning against the wall of the hut; their AK-47 rifles had been propped up against the wall next to them. One of them smoked a hand rolled, very fat cigarette, the smell of which was easy to recognize. Marijuana. The other was chewing on a wad of something. Probably, Cross thought, some kind of drug.

Their eyes were glazed over and filled with drugged near-sleep. They stood motionless and stared off into deep nothingness as Cross opened the doors and walked past them. They did not stop Cross from entering Azubuike's chamber.

The General was sitting on his tall-backed chair, his throne, while two women knelt on either side of him, holding wooden trays out towards him that were filled with food. There were fruits, bananas and a couple of melons. There was a dish of some kind of meat, a bowl of corn meal mash, and a plate of dark bread.

Azubuike was dressed in bright orange silk pajamas. The buttons of the top were left open exposing his huge belly, matted black hair, and scars telling the story of his violent life.

The women were dressed in brightly colored cloths wrapped around them. They wore necklaces of red beads, and their heads were crowned with colorful flowers. They had good makeup on their attractive faces. They were not skinny and dirty as were the others Cross had seen.

"Ahhh! My old friend Joseph has awakened!" Azubuike roared and let loose with another of his booming laughs that shook the building. His fat mouth had been filled with food which sprayed out, down his pajamas, and onto the floor in front of him as he laughed. The two women, still on their knees, turned to look at Cross and laughed gently along with Azubuike.

"Please come in, my old friend! Have some breakfast!" he yelled, spitting food out with the words. "Did you enjoy the women last night?" It seemed that Azubuike could not speak without shouting as loud as he could.

Cross thought the best thing to do was to try to defend the two women. He didn't want them murdered as the driver had been the day before, so he said, "They were very good. Thank you for them and the food. But I need to go home now. May I get a ride back to Kampala?"

"Breakfast first . . . Then business . . . Then we shall see about a ride back to Kampala," he laughed and shouted, spitting more food.

Azubuike motioned to the trays held by the two women. "Please come up onto my throne platform and join me, my old friend. Not everyone may walk upon my throne platform. You are my good friend Joseph, so you may do so. These are two of my wives. They cook for me. The food is good, and you need to keep your strength up, my old friend."

Cross walked softly, uneasily, across the wooden floor and stepped cautiously up the three stairs to them. He took a slice of dark bread from one of the trays. There were a few bananas; he took one. He figured that if Azubuike was eating it, it wouldn't have been poisoned. Biting off little pieces, he finished the bread and peeled the banana. Then he asked, "Are you selling diamonds or not, Stephen?"

The broad, yellow tooth smile suddenly left Azubuike's fat face and was replaced by a maniac's glare of anger. He leaned forward, his elbows on his fat knees, letting food fall from his mouth. He said in a threatening, low whisper, "I am no longer the man Stephen. I am General Simba Azubuike. I speak with my god, and he has given me that name. My army is The Army of the Heart of God, and I have been given the heart of my god . . . It is inside of me. I am not Stephen any longer. Be careful, my friend Joseph. Be very careful how you address me."

"I am sorry, General," Cross said. He bowed his head slightly. There was no sense at all in arguing with the man. He was obviously insane and dangerous. The best Cross could do was agree with the man, humor him, give him what he wanted, and try to get the hell out of there somehow. He bowed his head slightly once again as he said, "I didn't know you have been so blessed. I am honored to be able to speak with you again. And I am honored to be in your presence. Business with you will put me in a privileged place in the world. People will hold me in honor having spoken with you and eaten food with you. What business can we do?"

The smile returned to Azubuike's broad face. He sat back on his throne and clapped his hands like a child at a circus. "That is so good!" he laughed and roared. "Business is so good! There is no one in the world I would rather do business with than my old friend, Joseph Cross. You were the man who helped me, and without that help I would not be so close to my god. My god has told me this is good. You will certainly hold an honored place in this world and in my god's heaven."

Cross bowed, grandly this time, from his waist, and said, "I am truly honored, General." He was having a difficult time keeping the smile off his face. If Azubuike knew how funny Joe Cross found all this, it would be dangerous for Cross.

Azubuike clapped his fat hands, and a woman, dressed as the two who remained kneeling at his side, walked into the hut through a hidden door at the back of Azubuike's throne room. What had appeared to be a zebra skin hanging on the wall was in reality a door. This woman, rather than being attractive as the two holding the trays, was beautiful.

She stepped down off the platform to the center of the room. She carried a short stool and placed it carefully in the middle of the room, in front of Azubuike. Quickly, almost running, she stepped up onto the red platform and left through the door she had come through. The General motioned toward the stool with his hand, and Cross went to it, down from the throne platform, as quickly as he thought would keep him out of trouble. He bent and sat on it, so low to the ground that his knees were up to his chest.

The General waived his hands, and the two women holding the trays rose to their feet and walked out, backing away from Azubuike, bowing over and over as they left the platform, leaving Cross alone with Azubuike in the big hut.

The General reached down beside himself and pulled up a small cloth bag which he had been sitting on. He tossed it to Cross who caught it with one hand. Cross opened the bag and spilled the small, dirt covered stones into his hand. He knew what raw diamonds looked like, and he knew that these were of only medium value. Most would be cut to sell as industrial diamonds; a few might be cut into smaller gem stones. But he couldn't tell Azubuike that for fear of offending the man.

"So what do you think, my old friend?" Azubuike asked, smiling and leaning forward.

"Very nice . . . Very nice," Cross said, smiling and nodding as if very satisfied with what he was looking at, while fingering the stones as if he were interested in them. "You mine these here, General?"

"Yes, of course. I discovered the places where these are dug years ago. The diamonds I sold to you back then I dug myself. Now I don't dig anymore." He laughed, and the rafters shook once again.

"The people I saw marching out this morning . . . They dig your diamonds?"

"Yes . . . They are my prisoners of war. They have been tried and found guilty of offending my god. They work off their guilt."

"You are at war, General? I didn't know that."

"Ahhh, yes, my old friend. I was once of the Bellawaa tribe. I am, of course, no longer of such a lowly state since the heart of my god entered me. The Lucentee tribe has been the enemies of the Bellawaa for many generations. The Ng'uluu tribe has been fighting with the Lucentee. The Bellawaa and the Ng'uluu have taken to that loathsome religion of Christianity. The Lucentee they are Muslim for many generations. All these non-believers are offensive to my god. I am at war with everyone who offends my god. All these loathsome people have offended my god."

"Well, I can understand that, General. Do these non-believers ever attack you here in your village?"

"This land is my kingdom. It is not a welcome place to nonbelievers. It is swamps full of mosquitoes, snakes, and mamba . . . What you call crocodiles. It is no good this land for anything but for my diamonds. My army is strong and when these . . . Christian and Muslim pigs . . . When they come, my army destroys them. My army cuts them to pieces, and they are too frightened to return."

"What about the Government up in Kampala? Do they ever come here?"

"One day my god will make me strong enough to kill that Government, as they, too, are non-believers of my god. Until that time I buy things from them. I buy guns and bullets. I buy food . . . And other things," he laughed. Cross assumed Azubuike meant the drugs he fed to his 'army'. "As long as I do . . . I give that Government money, you see. They leave me here to fight my war. They are stupid and do not understand that my god will one day rule everywhere, even in Kampala."

"Well, General," Cross said. "I'm very glad you have god on your side. In the end, I am sure you will win your war." He tried to sound sincere; anything else, the truth for instance, that this man was absolutely insane, would certainly mean his death.

"Thank you my good friend, Joseph. I am certain I will, also." Another booming laugh filled the throne room as he clapped his fat hands together. "Now how much will you pay for my diamonds?"

"We can come to a very fair price, General. How much do want for them?"

"I think fifteen thousand American dollars would be fair," he said in greed and anticipation. He leaned forward again, his elbows on his fat knees. "After all, they are very raw. I would not ask for more even if their value would increase once cut."

Cross knew the stones he held in his hand weren't worth half that, but he couldn't offend the maniac, so he said, "Please forgive me, General, but you underestimate their true value. You are being too kind to me. I appreciate that. Believe me. You and I are longtime friends and you are being kind to me. I could not think of cheating you in any business we do now or in the future. Please don't be offended, but they are worth twenty thousand dollars."

Azubuike broke into another of his booming laughs that shook the thatch covered hut. "Oh my old friend, Joseph!" he shouted. "I knew I could do good business with you! Twenty thousand it is!"

"Fine," Cross said. "Shall I write a check?"

"Oh, my old friend, Joseph," Azubuike said, feigning a childlike disappointment. "I have no way to cash a check. I need cash."

Cross forced a frown and lowered his head, as if he were in deep thought. Then he said, "OK, have your most trusted soldier, one who would give his life for you, drive me back to Kampala . . . He will hold the diamonds, of course . . . I will get the cash from my bank there and give it to him in exchange for the diamonds."

"That is very good, my old friend. I trust you very well. Of course, if you don't keep your word I will kill you," he laughed and slapped his hands on his fat knees.

The General stood, pushing on the arms of this throne, struggling to get his huge bulk onto his feet. Cross stood also. He bent his head, looking at the floor, trying to look humble in the crazy man's presence.

"No, please sit, my old friend," Azubuike said as he stepped carefully down the three stairs and walked past Cross to the hut's door and outside, leaving Cross alone. Cross sat on the low stool and waited, not knowing if he was successful enough to keep himself alive, and hoping the fat man wasn't going outside to get a firing squad.

He looked at his wristwatch every few seconds, nervously waiting for something to happen. All he could think about was regretting not having brought a gun. Twenty minutes after Azubuike walked from the throne room, he returned, followed by the tall woman who had brought the stool Cross was sitting on. She was dressed in clean and well pressed, brown and tan camo fatigues. Her tall combat boots were polished to a mirror finish, her camo pants bloused into the tall boots. And she wore a webbed combat belt from which hung a brightly polished leather holster, a big semi-auto pistol strapped in it. Cross recognized her as the beautiful woman who had brought the small stool to him. She looked beautiful when she had brought the stool, but she was exotic as she stood behind Azubuike.

She was an exceptionally beautiful, dark skinned African woman, as gracious as European royalty in her facial expression and the way she walked and held herself. Her hair was cut very short, and she wore elegant makeup, bright red lipstick and a pale green eye shadow. She and the two women holding the trays of food were the first Cross had seen who were clean and with makeup in Azubuike's slum compound.

Azubuike spoke, introducing the woman, "This is my number one wife. She is Mary Ssanyu. She will drive you to

Kampala and receive the money you will pay."

The General smiled, turned to his wife and said, "Tell my old friend what will happen if he does not pay."

"I will kill him," she answered simply, in a voice as soft and flowing as silk, without looking away from Azubuike and without expression on her face.

****

Cross stood and bowed once again to Azubuike and then once again to the woman. The three walked out onto the thatch covered porch, standing in the shade of the hot African morning. After a few minutes of small talk between Azubuike and Cross about the weather and their future business dealings, Azubuike patted Joe Cross on his shoulder. He kissed Mary Ssanyu hard on the lips, bending her backwards enough that Cross was certain he would hurt her. He turned and walked inside his throne room, the guards at the door closing the doors behind him.

There was an almost new and very clean Toyota pickup truck waiting on the red, muddy dirt for them outside the throne room hut. In the bed of the truck was a large cooler that Cross later found was full of food: cooked chicken and fruits of a better quality than he had seen since arriving there. Inside the cab there were two big thermos jugs of water. When he had opened one, he found clear, clean water, not the muddy stuff that was in the truck that brought him to Azubuike.

Cross followed the woman to the truck. He at first opened the passenger side door for her. She ignored his gesture and stepped slowly, elegantly, like a queen, around the truck to the driver's side. Cross ran to get to that door before she could open it. She waited for him, a regal expression of royal prerogative on her sculptured face.

He opened the door for her, holding it as she got in, and he even bowed slightly. Azubuike had stepped outside, now smoking a fat cigar. He was watching from the porch of his hut as Cross closed the door and bowed. Azubuike laughed once again, clapping his hands in delight. He shouted, "Oh, my old friend, Joseph! You are such the fine gentleman!" He turned and walked back into his throne room, laughing uproariously.

As they drove from the compound, bouncing along very slowly through the mud, people in rags came from mud huts and stood like statues, all forcing cheers and clapping without expressions on their sad, gaunt faces. Mary drove slowly at first, trying to avoid most of the ruts and holes and rocks in the dirt path that headed north from Azubuike's little kingdom. She said nothing as she drove.

Cross took one of the thermos jugs and drank deeply from it. It had been nearly twenty-four hours since he had tasted water, and his stomach growled in hunger.

They sat in silence for the first hour and a half as they bounced along, gradually gaining in speed as the dirt road would allow. Cross again picked up one of the thermos jugs of water and drank. He held it out, offering it to the woman who seemed not to know he was in the truck with her. And then Cross thought he might risk some conversation. He said, "So you're the General's wife. That must be quite an honor."

She didn't answer him.

"This is a nice truck," he said.

She said nothing.

"The weather should be nice. Hot but nice."

She said nothing.

"Look, we have a long drive ahead of us," Cross said. "It would make the time go by faster if we could talk about something."

Mary turned and looked at him. She said in what turned out to be a very soft, educated, and refined voice with a British accent, "Mr. Cross. We are doing what General Azubuike wants us to do. We have no options. Please just sit quietly, and we will be done with this as soon as possible."

Cross thought for a moment or two and decided to press his luck. Mary Ssanyu was wearing a pistol at her waist. She was probably dangerous, but he had to risk a chance.

"Do you always do what he wants you to do?" he asked.

"Of course," she answered, her forehead frowned as if it were a stupid question.

"Why, if you don't mind my asking, is that?"

"I am married to the General. I would dishonor the memory of my father and mother if I would not obey my husband."

"Are your parents dead?" Cross asked.

"Yes, they were murdered by the Lucentee tribe. I am Ng'uluu."

"You're Christian then? Isn't the Ng'uluu tribe a Christian people?"

"I was Christian, Mr. Cross. Now I worship the true god and the General who carries god's own heart within him."

"I'm sorry if I sound too inquisitive," Cross started. "But you sound educated."

"I am . . . as you say so quaintly . . . educated. I went to school in our parish mission. There were British missionaries there. They are not there now . . . They are dead. And for two years I was in school in France."

"And your goal was to marry the General after you finished school?"

"Don't be rude, Mr. Cross."

"I'm sorry," he said sincerely, and he was honestly interested in this woman who began to seem out of place living with Azubuike.

She drove on without speaking for a mile or two. She slowed the truck and pulled to the side of the dirt road. She opened her door and got out; Cross followed on the other side of the truck. They were in an area of tall, brown-grass savannah. A light breeze moved the grass as if it were a sea somewhere. In the distance, Cross saw tall giraffes rambling slowly, and some birds took to the air ahead of them.

Mary went to the bed of the truck and opened a cooler. She took some bananas from it and tossed one to Cross across the bed of the truck. "Eat, Mr. Cross. You look as if you need some food. Please help yourself."

She sat on the ground, leaning against the side of the pick-up, taking advantage of the little shade it provided. Cross sat next to her, a respectful foot or two away, and ate some fruit and two pieces of chicken. She ate some fruit, delicately and slowly. They ate in silence.

Mary ate the few pieces of fruit but nothing else. She finally turned to look at the man sitting near her and then said, "My life is what it is, Mr. Cross. There is little choice for a woman from the remote tribes. I make the best of what I have."

"But you've been away from here. You've been to France. You must know there is a better life out there . . . Away from here."

"There is no 'away from here,' Mr. Cross. I am the property of the General."

And that gave Cross an idea. It might just work. He would wait. Mary stood and got in the truck. Cross wiped his hands first in the dirt of the road and then on his cotton pants. He returned to the passenger seat and rolled down the window, hoping to catch a breath of a breeze as they drove on.

A mile or two later he slouched down in the seat of the truck, closed his eyes and slept. It was dusk as he awoke, and they were on a paved road with the lights of Kampala on the far horizon. Mary glanced to the side and saw Cross awake finally. She pulled the truck to the side of the road and turned the engine off. She looked at him and said, "We have several hours before we reach Kampala. You should eat something and drink some more water. It will do no one any good if you fall ill."

Cross nodded, and both got out of the truck. He pulled the cooler from the truck bed, and they sat at the side of the road, in the shade of a Jackal berry tree, eating the fruit and chicken that had been prepared for them. Cross drank two full cups of the cool water. Mary ate a little, this time nibbling on a small piece of chicken, and drank a little water, but she said nothing in the hour they spent resting in the early evening shade. Cross was leaning against the tree trunk, feeling full and almost free of any danger. He glanced to his side and saw that Mary had stretched out on the grass, her back turned to him, and was sleeping, breathing deeply. He closed his eyes and was soon also asleep.

****

It was half past one in the morning when they arrived at Cross' hotel. She pulled the pickup to a stop across the street from the hotel, turned off the engine, turned and looked at Cross and said, "Tomorrow morning, at precisely nine AM, I will be here. We will go to your bank, and you will get the money you have promised the General."

"Where will you sleep tonight?" Cross asked.

"I will be fine right here. I will be safe."

"I can't let you do that," he said. "The streets are dangerous after dark. Look, unhook the gun. Lock it inside the truck. Take the diamonds. You can sleep in my room. There's a couch, and in the morning we can get some breakfast."

Mary looked at him, trying to understand if he was being honest, trying to seduce her, or just trying to steal the diamonds. "Why leave the pistol here, Mr. Cross?"

"Do you trust me not to take it while you are sleeping and perhaps kill you or just run off with the General's lousy diamonds?"

"I do not trust you, Mr. Cross," she said. "But you say 'lousy diamonds.' Are they of no value?"

"Don't worry," Cross said and smiled. "You'll get your money. Now sleep in my room, OK?"

Finally, she said, "Alright." She unbuckled the web belt that held the holster and pushed the pistol under the seat. They both got out of the truck, and she locked the doors.

The lobby of the hotel was empty at that time of the morning. The night clerk was asleep in a chair behind the front desk, snoring loudly. The elevator had been shut down for the night. Cross and Mary took the stairs to the third floor and into his room. Inside, he switched on the lights, and Mary looked around the big hotel room.

A king size bed was against the far wall, sagging in the middle of the mattress. A couch and two matching chairs, well-worn but clean, were against the windows overlooking a small garden area below. A scratched and battered desk on the opposite wall made a work station with a telephone and small lamp.

The room was carpeted in thick wool carpet that was also clean, although it was old and well worn. There were framed pictures on the walls, old prints of good paintings, faded with age and sun, but still attractive. Nothing in the room was new. In the UK it would be merely a cheap, two star hotel, but the room was cool when the two windows were open to let in night air, and a fan spun slowly on the ceiling above. Mary had not seen such luxury in many, many years. Cross went from window to window opening them, and a breeze flowed into the room.

"This room is yours?" Mary asked.

"Yes," Cross answered. "Is it OK? I can sleep on the couch, and you can have the bed. The sheets are clean I think."

"Is there a bathroom nearby?" she asked.

"Through that door," Cross said, pointing to a door to the right of the bed.

"Is there a shower?"

"Of course. And a tub. Please use it if you want.

There are clean towels in there I think."

"I have not seen a shower or a tub for a very long time. The General's village doesn't have running water. I would like to use the shower, please. And then perhaps soak in the tub for a while."

"Sure, help yourself. I'll go downstairs and see if I can get some food."

Mary walked quickly to the bathroom. She found a fresh bar of soap and stripped off her clothing as she ran the hot water for a seemingly endless shower. She stood naked under the shower letting the stinging beads of water bring life back into her body. She used a rough wash cloth to cover herself with soap, rubbing harsh memories away as she washed her breasts and stomach and legs. She stood under the water, turning the faucet to make the water even hotter and then washed herself again.

She at first didn't want to leave the shower, but a glance at the white tub across the room made her turn the water off. She stepped from the shower, water flowing from her as she walked across the tiled floor. She filled the tub with hot water and slowly sank into it, sighing at first and then crying, wiping the tears of joy away with a soapy hand.

Cross took the stairs down to the lobby, and then walked lightly past the still sleeping night clerk and into the kitchen. No one was there. He searched around and found some bread and some left over roast beef in a small refrigerator. He sliced off big chunks of the beef and layered them on the bread with some very sharp cheese he found in a big refrigerator on the other side of the kitchen. Also in the fridge he found bottles of beer, African, but he recognized the labels and knew they were good beer. He took four of them, and with the sandwiches he walked back upstairs to his room.

The sound of the shower had stopped before Cross returned to the room. He thought that Mary had moved to the tub and was soaking as she said she wanted to do. He called out through the closed door, "I have some food and a couple of beers."

"I'll be a few minutes, Mr. Cross, if I may. The water is hot, and it feels so good."

Cross peeled off his dirty clothes and pulled a thin cotton robe he had brought with him from London around him. He would shower when Mary was done enjoying herself, and then he would eat and try to get some sleep. He had an idea, but it had to wait for the morning.

He knew how Azubuike came by his diamonds. The people he had seen chained together were slaves, digging in the mud and dirt under a blazing African sun and horrendous physical conditions. Cross knew he could not take part in that. He could not do business with Azubuike. Diamonds were one thing, one thing he loved and liked to buy, smuggle, and sell. But he had a conscience, and he would not do business on the backs of slaves. Diamonds dug by a poor villager trying to feed his family were one thing, but diamonds dug by slaves was not something Cross would buy at any price.

He could easily kill Mary Ssanyu if he had to; while she slept would be the easiest. Or he could rush into the bathroom and drown her in the tub. And Azubuike would have a hard time killing him if he never went back to Azubuike's hell hole of a petty kingdom. Or, he could just say 'no' and have Mary go back empty handed. But then she would probably be killed, as the man who had taken Cross to Azubuike had been killed. No, he couldn't do that. But he had an idea that might work.

The sound of the tub emptying ended, and a minute

later Mary walked out of the bathroom. She was wrapped in one of the hotel's big terry cloth towels. It wasn't new, and some of it was threadbare, but she enjoyed it anyway.

"My," she said, smiling happily, "But that was good. Mr. Cross, I would like to speak with you." She sat on the edge of the bed, pulled the towel tightly around her, crossed her legs, and looked down at the floor. She began, "Mr. Cross. Can you imagine how truly terrible life is under the General?"

He sat on the couch across from her, leaned back and crossed his legs, and waited. The sandwiches and bottles of beer were on a low table between them, unnoticed for the time being. She was going to tell him something, perhaps a deal, he thought, which would save him. Perhaps, he hoped, she might have the same idea he had.

She told him, "The General is insane . . . But you probably know that. The problem is, you do not know just how insane he is. He has seven wives, besides myself. In the evenings, after his meal, we all sit on benches behind the big hut in which you spoke with him. We watch . . . as an evening's entertainment . . . people . . . men, women and children . . . being tortured to death. It is quite horrible. Many times the General will consume the heart and often the liver of the dead . . . He makes a religious sacrifice out of it. He believes his so called god takes the offering of the heart into the heart his god gave him.

"The people who dig his diamonds will die as the only way to end their suffering. They work under the lash and club, and they are fed only corn meal and only if they find a diamond. The General raids isolated villages when he needs more slaves. I was sold to him as a way to keep him from raiding my village. But he lied, and the raids continued. He murdered my parents after they sold me to him.

"You saw the steel post in the center of the village? People are chained to it and burnt alive for his amusement. He keeps his army well drugged so they will do whatever he wants. When they don't . . . Even for the slightest infraction . . . He has them killed. Recruits are from captives he takes on his raids. He forcibly drugs them and keeps them drugged so they do not know what they are doing."

She paused and wiped tears that were filling her eyes. Cross waited a moment and then asked, "Why are you telling me this?"

"Because I do not want to go back there."

"You don't have to," he said. "I'll help you. I was about to make that same offer to you."

With those words Mary Ssanyu's hands went to her face. She lowered her head, and she started to sob openly, the first time she had let herself cry since being sold to General Simba Azubuike. She covered her face with her hands and bent forward. She rocked back and forth and cried in uncontrolled joy. She was wailing loudly, calling to her God, thanking Him for the chance to get away finally.

She would be free. She had dreamed of that for all the years she had suffered. She had dreamed of ways to escape, but fear was her chains. Azubuike would find her if she ran back to her village. She had no money; she had nothing but fear in her life.

The compound was too isolated, surrounded by swamps and forests that were filled with animals that would hunt her. It was too far from any protection she could run to, and Azubuike would be another animal who would hunt her. And if she ran and he caught her, he would bring her back. Her death, she knew, would be terrible. Now her dream had come true. Now there was someone who would help her, who would see her safely away and allow her to start a new life. She would be safe, she would escape.

Mary's tears would not stop as Cross went to her and gently helped her down onto the bed. She turned onto her side, away from him, and she cried into the pillow. He pulled the thin cover up to her shoulders. He looked down at her, watched her cry, but he knew the tears that flooded from her were tears of joy, not pain. They were tears she had to let loose, tears that had been inside her for years.

Everything would be OK now, he told himself. Mary Ssanyu would be free, and her life could begin. And Cross would never have to see Azubuike again. He went to the shower and felt good under the hot water.

Back in the room, he stretched out on his back on the couch, his feet hanging over the couch's arm. He turned his head and looked at her. She was beautiful, tall and elegant. He could not see her face under the blanket, but her face was in his memory. Her skin was clear, her dark eyes bright, her cheek bones high, and her mouth was perfectly shaped, full and sensuous.

Finally sleep overcame the woman. Her tears and sobs stopped. Her breathing was steady and deep. Cross closed his eyes, but she filled his thoughts as he tried to sleep. He awoke suddenly and started for his pistol lying on a table under a lamp near the couch. He had put it there after Mary had gone to sleep. At first he thought it was a dream, but when his eyes focused in the dark of the room, a three quarter moon trying its best to light the room, she was standing at the side of the couch. Her hand was on his shoulder. She was naked.

"Come to bed with me," she whispered.

They made love until mid-day sunlight flooded the room through the window drapes. They lay in bed; he was holding her close, her head resting on his chest. She slept for another hour while his vision was locked on her face. There had been many women in Joseph Cross' life, but none like Mary Ssanyu. She was beautiful, a beauty Cross had not seen before. And their lovemaking had been gentle, slow, and wonderful. She had whispered, "I am so happy, Joseph my love."

Later they shared a shower and laughed together at little jokes. They dried each other and made love again on the wet floor of the bathroom. Mary watched as Cross shaved. She touched his bare back and shoulders. She gently touched the two scars of bullet wounds, one high on his shoulder and the other lower on his side. She pressed her breasts against him and they fell to the floor to make love again.

When they were both exhausted, they dressed, and Cross had some food sent to the room. Strong coffee, melon, and scrambled eggs. They ate their fill and laughed. Mary had not been this happy since Paris, so many years ago, when she looked forward to school every day.

After a breakfast that was filled with laughing, laughter that Mary Ssanyu had not done or heard since being sold to Azubuike, Cross took her shopping to the stores that catered to Europeans. At first the sales people in these stores did not want to sell to an African dressed in camo fatigues, but Cross' money bought their services.

He bought Mary six dresses, four pairs of expensive slacks and five blouses. Mary tried on dozens of pairs of shoes before she found four pairs she liked. Cross had to laugh as she had fun discarding shoe after shoe, enjoying the pleasure of new things. He hugged her and told her, "You are like every woman in the whole world when it comes to buying shoes."

He bought her underwear and bras, and she insisted

he come into the dressing room with her as she tried each one on. And finally, he bought her two handbags and a suitcase to carry everything in when she would leave Africa. As they started back to the hotel, she stopped in front of a shop that sold European cosmetics. He followed her inside, and she spent an hour selecting everything a woman would want and more.

At the hotel they brought the packages up to the room, and she quickly stripped out of the camo fatigues she had worn the day before when they escaped from Azubuike. She tossed the fatigues into a far corner, wishing never to see them again.

Cross sat on the couch and enjoyed watching the woman try on each piece of clothing, model what she was wearing, and then try on the next. They laughed, and they ordered food up to the room, roast chicken and a bottle of good Champaign. They ate, laughed some more at silly nothings, and they went to bed and made love until dusk.

The next morning Cross took Mary to see the old man, Ruben Dekker, who found and sold whatever anyone wanted to buy. His bent and old legs managed to carry him to Joseph Cross as Cross walked into the little shop. He at first took Cross' hand in his, thought better of it, and took him into his arms.

"It is so good to see you, mijn oude vriend," Ruben said falling into the Dutch language he had been raised in. En deze mooie vrouw?"

"English, Ruben, please," Cross said laughing.

"I am so sorry, Joseph. I mean, who is this beautiful woman?"

"Ruben Dekker," Cross said, introducing the two formally. "This is Miss Mary Ssanyu. She is a very good friend of mine, and she needs your help."

"She is then my friend, also," Ruben said as he shook her delicate hand and bowed slightly. She smiled, and Ruben fell in love with her immediately. "Tell me, Miss Ssanyu, how you came to know this very good man?"

Mary looked at Cross, wondering what she should say. Cross answered Ruben's question by saying, "It's a long story. Let's sit, and I'll tell you."

Ruben pulled three old bamboo rattan chairs from a dusty corner of his shop and placed them in the center of the room. They sat, surrounded by shelves of dusty cans of food, straw hats, used shoes and boots, a few shirts, and anything else Ruben thought someone would buy.

Cross told him in detail all that had transpired over the past few days. Ruben turned pale under his thick grey beard. Memories of his childhood, the beatings from his adoptive parents in Holland, long days working in the fields, and then the years on the road, looking for some peace and solace filled his head. Tears filled his old eyes.

Ruben apologized deeply when Cross told him about the skinny, ragged man whom he had once fed and was now a maniac and cannibal who worked slaves to death.

"I am so very sorry, Joseph," the old man said. "Why did I feed that boy? Why did I ever bring you to him?"

Cross touched the man's shoulder and told him not to worry. "Everything will be alright now, Ruben," Cross said. "You couldn't have known. You have no responsibility for any of this. You are simply too good a person, Ruben, old friend. You take too many vagrants into your home. You feed too many people who need a meal. Please don't stop doing that."

Ruben tried to smile to say thank you for the kind

words. But he knew that if he hadn't helped Stephen Okeke, if he had not sought out Joseph Cross, the ragged boy might have died on the streets, and people would not be suffering now.

"Look," Cross asked, trying to pull Ruben's thoughts away from the General. "I want this woman to get out of Africa. She needs a passport. Can you arrange that?"

"And what Nation shall this pretty woman be a citizen of?" Ruben asked as he stared at Mary.

Cross looked at her, questioning, and she smiled as she answered, "France, please. I loved it so there."

Ruben nodded silently, sighed deeply, stood and took Mary into his back room where he took a photograph of her. The two returned, and Ruben told Cross, "Her passport will be ready tomorrow afternoon. Come back at 3 PM . . . with $1000, please."

Mary smiled, knowing now she would be safe and free. She wanted to go to Paris where she had attended school. Cross agreed and said he would send her there. They spent that night in the bed in Cross' hotel room. They made love and ate food and drank wine. They laughed. Life was suddenly good for both of them.

The next afternoon, when they had Mary's passport, Cross gave her $5000.00 in cash and the bag of diamonds. "Take them to Amsterdam," he told her. "See Hienrich Van der Mullen. Any taxi there can take you to him. He will buy the diamonds at a fair price if you tell him I sent you. They aren't worth much, but it will be enough for you to leave and start a new life. Then go to Paris and disappear. Contact only me . . . No one else . . . If you ever need anything. Anything, understand? I will always be there to help you."

He drove Mary Ssanyu to the airport. He bought a

first class ticket for her to Amsterdam with a stop in Berlin and another from Amsterdam to Paris.

As she started to board the plane, she asked, "Why are you doing this for me? Is it because I brought you into bed?"

"That was wonderful, Mary. I'll never forget you. You are beautiful and very, very sexy. I loved our time together. But I'm doing this because I don't like Azubuike. I wish there was a way I could get everyone away from him. But for now I'll be happy getting you away from him. Be happy . . . Change your name . . . Get a job . . . Be someone he will never find. Start a new life. Don't tell anyone else where you will settle."

She kissed him lightly as a tear fell from her eye. She turned and almost ran for the gangway to the jet that would take her to freedom. She sat next to a window, and as the jet taxied down the runway and took to the air, she looked at her homeland below. She wished there had been some way to stay there, to do some good for her people, to rid the land of Azubuike and all the suffering he had brought to her people.

Cross waited inside the terminal and watched the jet load the passengers. He wanted to get one more look at the beautiful woman but only saw her walk up the stairs of the gangway without turning around. He watched the jet as it rolled slowly towards the runway and then took to the air. It flew her to a life he hoped would be good for her, a life that would eventually erase all the nightmares of her years with Azubuike.

That was one year before Margaret Fullsome came to beg Joseph Cross for help.

CHAPTER FIVE - The Beginning

Joseph Cross had kept the letter Margaret Fullsome had received demanding ransom for her son. The postmark was Geneva, Switzerland. Without a return address on the envelope, Cross could only speculate. There were three people in Geneva who would willingly deal in Azubuike's blood diamonds regardless of their source. Three people who believed money was more important than human lives.

Arnaud Deschamps was a jeweler who settled in Geneva after spending seven years in a French prison for jewel theft. He decided that making jewelry and selling it for more than it was worth to people with too much money was a better way of life than stealing jewelry from those same people. It had been suspected that he was a receiver of stolen jewelry, gold and silver that he melted down, gems removed and re-cut, if necessary, to fashion into new jewelry. He had once tried to sell blood diamonds to Cross.

Charlotte (Lotte) Koch was a swindler, a con artist who bilked wealthy people out of their money by first stealing their jewelry and then asking for a reward for its return. She used middlemen, her employees, to pose as the thieves. She was a vivacious socialite who threw extravagant parties throughout Switzerland and the South of France. It was at these parties that she picked the next very expensive necklace or bracelet or jewel encrusted pin to steal. Lotte would sink to any level if profit were to be made, even being the buyer and seller of blood diamonds, which it had been rumored she had done more than once.

Lars Ruscher was a Swiss National, a former Interpol Agent, who decided after a few years with Interpol that he could make a better living on the other side of the law.

Lars had a good education in the Arts. His job with Interpol was to investigate thefts of works of art and jewelry. He put his experience to good use by stealing works of art and jewelry rather than recovering them from other thieves. Cross had run across the man more than once trying to peddle blood diamonds in Geneva, where Lars had bought an expensive home.

One of them wrote the letter for Azubuike. Cross knew that. It could be no one else. All three were educated and were capable of good handwriting. He understood that if he were going to help Mrs. Fullsome, he would have to start there.

But there was still something burning in the back of his mind, something that was bothering him. Why did she come to him? He could not get past the fact that Mrs. Fullsome hated him. Her entire political career had been formed by vocally and publicly expressing her hatred of him. Of course, that had been good publicity for Cross. The world seemed to be attracted to 'bad guys.' Men wanted to brag about having met him and 'what good friends they were with Joseph Cross.' Women wanted to tame the 'bad boy.' On an almost daily basis women would offer themselves to Cross with the fanciful idea that he would fall in love with them. Most of these women, trying to get close to him, were turned away by the staff at the Rochester Club. A few . . . A very few . . . made it up to Cross' apartment for one night and then were escorted out the front door of the Club. All Mrs. Fullsome's protestations against Joseph Cross did was advance her political career and put more money in Cross' pocket and women in his bed. 'Why did she come to him,' he thought.

But his curiosity would not let him ignore her pleading. The day after she had come to The Rochester Club, Cross drove to the estate outside of Royal Tunbridge Wells that the Fullsomes called home. It was an ancient estate, hundreds of years old, long lost to overbearing British inheritance taxes by a family who had owned it for ten generations. It wasn't the grandest estate in the whole of England, nor was it the grandest Joseph Cross had seen, but it was big enough.

The grounds of the manor were miniscule compared to the thousands of acres once a part of the estate. All of the farmed acreage, the pastures where sheep and cows had grazed, the forests that had once held deer and foxes as game for the landed gentry, had been sold off, piece by piece over the years.

A few tall trees, unkempt and slowly dying of age and disease shaded a gravel drive that curved to the front doors. A large pond was to the right, banked in stone. Pond flowers bloomed in it, and two nasty tempered white swans had made a home there. The water had once been clear and stocked with trout. It, too, had been ignored by the Fullsomes, and the water was now dark and without fish.

Cross had not phoned ahead. He didn't want anything to be miss-assumed as placing him in a subservient position. Asking for an appointment would put Mr. Fullsome in charge. Cross had come to be used to being in charge after so many years as a powerful criminal underworld leader. He knew that Taylor Fullsome was at that position in his multi-continental businesses that he worked from 'home,' home being the four story, eleven bedroom house he had bought some years before.

Cross knew that Mrs. Fullsome would not be at home

when he called on her husband that day. Parliament would be in session; she would not be so upset about her son's kidnapping to not attend. Her career would always be centermost in her mind. Cross was sure he knew her well enough to be assured of that.

He parked his Jaguar at the front of the manor house, at the wide, grey granite steps and went up to the big, carved, British oak doors. There was some dispute with the butler, who came to the door when Cross pulled the ancient chain that rang a bell inside the house.

"If you do not have an appointment, I am afraid Mr. Fullsome cannot see you," the short, pale, and puffy butler said very officiously, his stubby red nose held high.

"Tell you what," Cross said as he pushed his way past the man into the hallway of the house. "You go tell him his wife was at my apartment the other night at half past six in the morning. She and I had drinks together. Go tell him that, and see if he wants to see me."

The butler walked away, very royally, in a snobbish huff, turning to look over his shoulder at Cross every now and then. He left Joe Cross standing in the long hallway, looking around at the suits of armor lined up like ancient soldiers on parade. Swords and flags were on the walls, and big paintings of someone else's ancestors were hanging in the Fullsomes' home. Less than two minutes later, Taylor Fullsome walked through one of the many doors that lined the shadowy hallway.

"Just who the hell are you?" he called out loudly, his voice echoing throughout the tall hallway as he walked towards Cross, his footsteps loud on the marble floor. He walked to the side of the carpets lining the hallway as was his habit, not wanting to wear down what he had spent money on. "I warn you, I have staff, and I will phone the police!"

Cross, seeing Mr. Fullsome for the first time, thought he would need his staff if he was going to throw Cross out. Mr. Fullsome was little more than middle age, perhaps not yet sixty years old, but overweight, and with a bulbous red face that foretold of high blood pressure. His stomach protruded grandly, and his jowls hung long and loose over his three chins. His hair was thin and had not been combed yet that day, nor had he shaved. He wore bright blue silk pajamas, the buttons of the top ready to be ripped away trying to keep the pajama buttoned over his fat stomach. His feet had been squeezed into heavy leather slippers that were lined with rabbit fur.

Cross walked to him, held out his hand, and said, "I'm Joseph Cross. Your wife came to see me the other day."

Fullsome had a vacant look of not understanding on his face. He didn't take Cross' hand. Cross said, "About your son . . . You know . . . Robert . . . Your son."

"What about my son?" he asked.

Cross was confused; had he been set up for some fall by the MP who had been hounding him?

"You are Taylor Fullsome, aren't you? You are married to Margaret Fullsome, the Member of Parliament? You have a son named Robert who has been kidnapped for ransom?"

"And what bloody business is it to you? Are you with the Police? You sound like an American."

"You're telling me you know nothing of your wife coming to me? Asking for my help?"

"Of course not!" the man shouted. He took two steps backward, putting what he hoped would be a safe space between himself and this man who stood taller than him.

"Mr. Fullsome, I think we need to talk. Is there a place we can sit and hash this out?"

"Hash this out?   What the bloody hell does that mean? You're a bloody American, aren't you?"

"May we go somewhere and sit?" Cross asked, trying as hard as he could not to laugh at the fat man whose bluster was making his puffy, chubby face even redder than normal.

"Very well," Fullsome said haughtily.   He turned suddenly and spoke to his butler who was standing nearby. "Have two of the gardeners come to the house. Have them wait should I need them."

He started to walk away and spoke to Cross without turning to look at him. "We can talk in my office. But I warn you that I will call my staff in should I need them."

Cross followed Fullsome into what Fullsome referred to as his office. It was a grand room of expensive, very contemporary furniture.   Every electronic device and computer available filled the room.   Six big television screens had news channels on from around the world, the volume on each turned off, the spoken words on each flashing in typed letters across the bottoms of the screens. Big computer monitors with the latest stock market reports from Europe, the Americas, Russia and China were lined up along the wall to the right.

Fullsome's desk was an eight by five foot, hand carved, mahogany monstrosity. Modernistic renderings of animals and people had been cut into every inch of the dark wood, obviously Cross thought, by someone who had had too much to drink. He stifled a laugh, not wanting to offend Fullsome until he had what he wanted. The top of the desk was crowded with more computer screens and keyboards. Lined up on the left of the desk were four telephones, each a different bright color.

Bookcases lined two of the four walls, all filled with books of law from around the world. A small silver and glass cart stood nearby, holding several crystal decanters of the very best liquors the world had to offer. Underneath, on the bottom shelf, were a half dozen bottles of wine lying on a rack on the sides, and big crystal glasses to go with them. Cross wondered if any of them were from one of his smuggling and black market operations. Taylor Fullsome was a multi-millionaire, but Cross imagined he was also cheap and would seek out expensive wines on the black-market if it meant buying them at an under market price.

Fullsome sat behind his desk, falling heavily into the big black leather chair. He did not invite Cross to sit. He leaned back in the tall chair and asked, "Did I understand, sir, that you allege my wife was in your apartment at half past five in the morning?"

"Is that what you care about, Mr. Fullsome?" Cross asked. He pulled a chair from the left corner of the desk and put it directly in front of it.   He sat in the chair, leaned back, crossed his legs casually, looked directly into Fullsome's eyes and asked, "What about your son?"

"What about him, sir? He has chosen his way of life. What more is to be said?"

"Do you have any idea where he is?"

"I do," Fullsome said.   "But why in heaven's name should I discuss this with you?"

"Because your wife discussed it with me . . . And asked for my help."

"I don't believe that, Mr. Cross."

"Phone your wife, Mr. Fullsome," Cross said. "Tell her to come home, and the three of us can talk."

Rather than go to the phone, Fullsome reached for a cherry wood, cedar lined cigar box at the edge of his desk. He took a fat cigar from the box and slowly snipped the end with a shiny brass cutter. He lit it with a gold lighter and blew the smoke towards the ceiling. He looked at Cross and said in a subdued voice, "My wife seldom does as I command. She is very independent. She stands in Parliament against my wishes."

Cross reached across the desk, pulled the cigar box towards him, and took a cigar from it. Fullsome made no effort to stop him. Not having a tool to snip the end, and not being offered one by Taylor, he bit the end and spit the fragment onto the floor. He lit the fat cigar with his own gold lighter, the one with the diamond on it which he let Fullsome see. He drew deeply and blew the smoke directly at the man.

He looked at Fullsome, smiled, and said, "Be a man. Phone her and *tell* her to come home. Tell her you don't care what the hell she's doing. Tell her this concerns your son and nothing is more important to you . . . And should not be more important to her."

Fullsome thought about that for a moment and then, with a shaking hand, he reached for one of the four phones on his desk. His finger had a hard time finding the right phone buttons as he slowly touched the numbers on the pad, dialing his wife's private phone in her office in Parliament. He waited.

A woman answered the phone and told Taylor that Mrs. Fullsome was on the floor of Parliament. "Tell her that her husband wants to speak with her," he said trying not to sound frightened.

"But . . . But Mrs. Fullsome . . ."

"Go right away," he said a bit more forcefully. "Tell

her it is a family emergency. Tell her I want to speak with her now."

He heard the phone being laid on the desk top. He waited . . . And he waited some more. He held the phone to his ear and smoked his cigar nervously, once or twice choking on the smoke. An inch of ash fell from the cigar onto his pajamas, ignored or perhaps not noticed by Taylor.

Minutes passed like hours. Joe Cross was smiling steadily, his eyes locked on Fullsome's, watching the man sweat and shiver. He drew on the big cigar and blew the smoke towards Taylor. Taylor laid his cigar in a crystal ashtray, coming close to missing the ashtray and almost letting the cigar fall onto his desk. He wiped sweat from his forehead with his free hand. After a minute or two of waiting, he reached for his cigar but found it had gone out. He tossed it angrily across the room. Finally, Margaret Fullsome came to the phone.

When she answered, he told her in a not very strong voice, almost apologetically, that she should come home. Cross listened as Taylor spoke. "Yes Margaret, I know you're busy . . . Yes Margaret. . . You see, Mr. Cross is here . . . Yes Margaret . . . Now stop that right now, Margaret . . . *MARGARET! SHUT UP!*" he yelled. He sat forward in his chair and spoke loudly, "I demand you come home this minute. Tell them you have more important business! . . . *SHUT UP!* You come home right now!"

Fullsome slammed the phone down, took another cigar from the box and lit it. He drew deeply on the cigar, smiled broadly and said, "Mr. Cross, believe it or not, that felt good. Is it too early for a brandy? Or would you prefer coffee?"

****

An hour and a half later Margaret Fullsome climbed from her chauffeur driven Bentley and stormed into the house. She brushed past the butler, pushing him aside, and threw open the door to her husband's office. "What do you mean talking to me like that!" she shouted as she stomped across the floor. "And what the hell is he doing here?" she asked, pointing a shaking finger at Joe Cross.

"Mr. Cross and I have been talking about Robert," Taylor said. "You asked for his help without consulting me. Now he and I have consulted, and we have come up with a plan."

"How dare you . . .!" she shouted. Her face was flushed red with anger.

"Sit down, Margaret!" Taylor shouted as loud as his wife had. He slapped his open hand down hard on the desk top. "And shut up for once in your life! Robert is in great danger. Mr. Cross has told me about this African who is holding him hostage."

Margaret Fullsome, MP, who was used to ordering people and having them do exactly as she told them to do, did sit finally, and she reluctantly listened. Cross related his experiences the year before with General Simba Azubuike. He told her of the slaves, the small but drugged army, the nightly entertainment of torture, the tall, steel I-beam where people were burned alive.

As he told her all of this, her face went gradually paler. "My God!" she said. "Can that be real?"

Her husband said, "I had no idea, Margaret . . . If Mr. Cross is telling the truth, we must do something. I am going to give Mr. Cross six million American dollars . . ."

"But the ransom is five million," she said interrupting her husband.

Cross smiled, spoke up and said, "I'm going to make arrangements to pay the ransom, maybe a little less than he wants. I'll bargain with him. The other million will be for my expenses and for a backup plan in case I fail to convince Azubuike to release Robert."

Margaret asked, "Do you mean he may take you captive as well as Robert?"

"Mrs. Fullsome," Cross said. "Azubuike is insane. He may do anything. I need a backup plan. I have no intention of being his slave or being that man's late night snack before bed."

Her husband stood and spoke up; maybe for the second time in his marriage to the MP, he spoke with authority and with strength. "I am giving Mr. Cross what he needs, Margaret. If you don't like that, then stay out of it."

She said nothing, again perhaps for the first time in her marriage to Taylor. Taylor sat again and drew on his third cigar since Cross walked into his office. He blew the smoke up to the ceiling once again, obviously thinking about something. He drank deeply from his fourth glass of cognac. Then he said, "Tell me about your backup plan, Mr. Cross."

Cross leaned back in the chair. He at first didn't want to tell them what his plan was; the more people who know a secret, the less likely it would remain a secret. He recalled an old adage he had heard somewhere, *'If three people know a secret, the only way for it to remain a secret is to kill two of them.'* But he had to justify the one million dollars he was asking for. So he said, "I'm going to Geneva first. I want to find out who wrote the ransom demand."

"Do you mean it may not be from this General fellow?" Taylor asked.

"Exactly. If I find the note was written *for* Azubuike

and not as some con game, I need to know who is buying Azubuike's diamonds. I will go to Amsterdam to find out.

Margaret asked, "Does that matter?"

"There are three major markets for blood diamonds, Mrs. Fullsome.   Moscow is the biggest market, but the Russian Mafia run that, and it's useless trying to deal with those people. If the Russian Mafia is behind this, I will step away, return your money to you, and you can deal with them directly. Please don't ask me to do anything involving those people.   The   other   two   are   Berlin   and   Amsterdam. Amsterdam is a bigger market than Berlin. I need to find the person buying from Azubuike . . . if it isn't the Russian Mafia. I need to know how his diamonds get to the buyer and how the money gets back to him."

Taylor Fullsome asked, questioningly, "Why? Why do you need to know that?"

"If I go to see Azubuike in person, I'm not going to walk into his hellhole with cash in a suitcase. He'd take the cash and kill me. If I go to speak with him, I will reach a bargain and have the money transferred to him. I need to know   how   his   money   is   transferred   and   where   it   is transferred to."

"And your backup plan?" Margaret asked.

"That I will keep to myself." Both Margaret and Taylor nodded, understanding that Joseph Cross was about to put his life at risk for them, for their son. They knew they had to defer to him, and they did not insist on knowing what he wasn't willing to tell them.

Cross was invited to stay for lunch, but he declined. He didn't like Margaret Fullsome, MP any better than he had every day for the last several years. And he found Taylor Fullsome to be too fat, too rich, and too unmanly to spend time with.   Taylor was a man without a conscience and without a soul. His businesses hurt many people in order to make him a very wealthy man. That was an anathema to Cross. He had no desire to spend time with him. Being near Taylor Fullsome made Cross feel like being somewhere else.

He would get Robert Fullsome away from Azubuike if he could, but not for Robert's parents. Cross had other ideas, and he would use Robert's kidnapping to do what he wanted to do.

Both Taylor and Margaret walked Cross to the door. She stopped him as he was about to leave and asked, "Why? Why are you doing this?"

"I have my reasons, Mrs. Fullsome," he answered. "One of them happens to be that it is the right thing to do. The other reasons I will keep to myself."

CHAPTER SIX – The Search

Lars Ruscher had settled into a two hundred year old house overlooking Lake Geneva. The house was a grand, late Edwardian mansion with a private boat dock where Lars' 65 foot yacht was tied. The five acres of land surrounding his home was fenced in an eight foot tall, grey-stone wall, and the property was maintained by a staff of six gardeners. Lars had a household staff of three maids, a chef, two kitchen assistants, and a butler. But Lars could afford it.

Lars was a master jewel and art thief, but Lars kept his house clean. What that means is he never stole anything in Switzerland. His frequent excursions outside of that Country, to every corner of the world, brought him the wealth that he lavished upon himself. Age was beginning to catch up to Lars. He realized that, and he seldom did what is commonly called 'cat burglaries,' that is climbing the outside of buildings to break and enter. His thefts were more discrete, well planned, and sophisticated. They required more research and a study of electronics to overcome alarm systems. But what this extra work brought were the very best of jewels and works of art the world had to offer Lars.

Cross called upon Lars at his home unannounced, surprising the man who hadn't seen Joseph Cross in several years. Cross had Billy Volgar accompany him to Geneva. He thought a little intimidation from the ugly giant might be necessary.

There was only one gated entrance into Lars'

property; the wrought iron gate was open the day Cross and Billy arrived. The long drive from the street to Lars' front door was over paver stones that had been laid sixty years before. Age and use had worn them down so that the car bounced along slowly as it approached the big home.

At the front door, solid oak that had been sheathed in bronze three years ago by Lars, Cross first knocked and then rang a doorbell and then knocked again. The butler, an elegant middle-aged man in a muted, pin-striped suit with a red carnation in the lapel, opened the door and stood wordlessly, questioning with an arrogant frown, just who would be calling on Lars Ruscher without an appointment. He looked over Cross' shoulder at the ugly giant standing behind Cross. His first instinct was to slam the door shut and run away, but Cross spoke before he could move.

"Tell Lars Joseph Cross is here to speak with him," Cross said. "He knows who I am, and he'll want to see me. We'll wait inside," he finished as he pushed his way past the man. Billy followed; the scowl on his face was enough to make the butler stand aside.

Lars was surprised to see Cross; even more surprising to Lars was the big man who followed Cross into Lars' home.

"Why! Joseph Cross!" he said as he walked to Cross, his arms held wide in greeting. Cross resisted hugging the man but shook his hand.

"And who is this?" Ruscher asked.

"He's with me," was all Cross would say. "We need to talk, Lars. Where?"

Lars hesitated at first, wondering what trouble he might be in with someone like Joseph Cross. Cross, he knew, could be good to do business with – everyone made a profit when doing business with Joseph Cross – but he was not the kind of man to have angry with you. The fact that he brought Billy Volgar, whom Lars knew of but had never seen before, at first frightened Lars. He had done nothing to anger Joseph Cross; at least he didn't think he had. But he smiled a thin smile and waved the two men to follow him.

Billy walked a few steps behind the two men down the entrance hallway to the far end of the house. His heavy footfalls echoed throughout the big house. Lars opened a door on the right and stood aside as Cross walked into the library. Billy followed Cross and Lars into the room, closed the door behind him and stood with his back to the door as Cross and Ruscher took seats in the room.

The library was small but lined on all walls with tall bookshelves that were crowded with rare, very valuable volumes, many stolen by Lars over the years. An overstuffed couch, an antique Lars had stolen in his younger years, and two armchairs sat in front of a fireplace that held logs but no fire. A small wheeled cart of bright brass and glass was nearby. It held two crystal decanters and a few glasses. The room's air was clear, but the age of the books lent a not unpleasant perfume to the room.

Lars, being Swiss, spoke both German and French since he was a child at home. He had learned English in school and could speak that language with only a minor trace of a sophisticated European accent at all.

"So, Joseph," he said as he stood at the cart and poured two glasses of twenty year old Scotch whiskey over ice. He handed one to Cross. He looked at the door where Billy stood. He at first wanted to offer a drink to him, but thought better of it. Getting too close to Billy Volgar might be dangerous.

He asked Cross, "Are you here to buy diamonds or

sell them?"

"What makes you think I'm interested in diamonds," Cross answered. He leaned back in the comfortable chair, crossed his legs, sipped at the excellent Scotch, and smiled in a friendly manner.

"Why else would you come to Geneva? Would you be here to buy a new wrist watch?" Lars laughed nervously. He fell backward into his chair and held his glass so tightly his knuckles were turning white. "I doubt you would bring cash to deposit into one of your numbered accounts. You have people to do that for you. And you have brought with you a very formidable body guard. What else can Switzerland offer you?"

"Information," Cross answered as he tasted the smoky whisky. He laid the glass on a small table next to him and said, "I want to know what General Azubuike is doing now."

"General who?"

"Come on, Lars. You know who I'm talking about. The blood diamond General."

Lars looked over Cross' shoulder at the giant of a man standing at the closed doorway. Billy had folded his bearlike arms across his chest and glared at Lars. Lying to Cross would not be a good idea, Lars thought. "So, I cannot fool the American master of the trade!" he said and smiled. He leaned back in his chair, trying to look at ease, and sipped at his glass of Scotch. He then said, "Alright, of course I know who the man is."

"Have you bought from him recently?" Cross asked.

"Joseph, I buy very little in the way of poor quality diamonds. His diamonds are almost all of poor quality, as you must know. Oh, now and then he has a good one . . .

But most are good for industrial use and little more. A few can be cut into small diamonds for jewelry . . . But only a few. He seems to produce quite a few diamonds I am told. Is that why you came to visit me, Joseph?"

"I need to know who is buying from him. If you know, it will be worth your while to tell me."

"And how will it be worth my while?" Lars asked. He sat forward, his innate greed for even more wealth taking control of him.

"I'll pay you, of course," Cross said and looked toward Billy Volgar, suggesting that there might be an option if Lars did not cooperate. Lars saw this, and the unspoken threat was understood.

"How much?"

"What it's worth," Cross answered. He was trying to keep his patience under control and not call Billy Volgar to pick the man up and shake the truth out of him. He didn't like Lars Ruscher. Lars was a thief, and although he preyed only on the wealthy of the world, he flooded the market with the things he stole. No matter what he stole and what he sold, he always made a profit for himself. But doing so lowered the price of everything by selling everything quickly, below market value. He didn't discriminate to whom he sold; he sold to fences of stolen merchandise, to insurance companies who paid to recover what Lars had stolen, and to corrupt government officials. Others in the criminal underworld suffered the reduced market value caused by Lars.

Lars leaned back in his chair and sipped at his whiskey. His hand was shaking visibly, beads of sweat formed on his forehead. He stared at Cross and then looked at Billy Volgar standing at the door, nearby. He thought he had better say something, and that something perhaps should be the truth. Seeming to withhold the truth, or tell a lie that Joseph Cross knew was a lie, may not be a very good idea.

"Arnaud Deschamps," Lars said finally. "I've heard he is buying poor quality diamonds. I don't know from whom. But much of what he buys is poor quality."

"What about Lotte?" Cross asked. "Is she still in that sideline business?"

"Ahhh, Charlotte Kamp," Lars said dreamily, memories of her naked body lying on his bed flashing through his mind. "She is still, after all these years, a beautiful little scamp, isn't she? I haven't seen Lotte in over a year. I understand she is spending an inordinate amount of time in Nice, living with an old Baron or something, in his summer villa. She is probably robbing him blind without him knowing it. And I wouldn't doubt that she has had a new Last Will made for him that leaves everything to her. I doubt that she has the time to be dealing with blood diamonds."

"Alright," Cross said. "If you're telling me the truth, it's worth five thousand. I'll wire transfer the money once I know you haven't lied to me."

"Five thousand what?" Lars asked, leaning forward greedily once again. "Euros? Pounds? Dollars?"

"Dollars. I don't have time to be trading currencies."

"Fine, and cash will do."

"I'll wire transfer it. I'll be leaving Geneva in a day or two. I don't like sending cash in the mail. Give me the account you want it sent to."

****

The Rive Gauche District of Geneva is an upscale shopping District with many expensive department stores and jewelry shops. The streets of the Rive Gauche are crowded with the young and wealthy of the world who spend their money freely. The restaurants and bistros are famous for their grand and often exotic cuisine prepared by chefs from around the world.

There is a thin, unnamed and dark alley off of the Rue du Rhône. It is an alley of one hundred year old paving bricks that are covered with mold and mildew and spilled trash almost everywhere. The tall buildings that encompass this alley keep the sun from ever penetrating into its dank gloom. And the un-numbered doorways of a rat infested series of cheap and small apartments line both sides of the alley. Arnaud Deschamps had claimed one of these for himself.

He slept on a thin mattress on a bed with rusted, squeaky springs. He ate, when he had money to buy food, sitting on a rusted metal chair, at a battered wooden table with a warped leg that caused the small table to wobble. He worked at another small table, his work bench, this one metal, covered in torn vinyl, where he had the reputation of cleaning blood diamonds of their dirt and crusted mud, and melting stolen gold and silver jewelry after removing the gemstones. He did this work mainly for other people, most often petty thieves who paid Arnaud little for the work he did.

Cross had a difficult time finding the alley and the doorway to the stairs that led down one flight to Arnaud's basement home and workshop. He knocked on the cracked and warped wooden door and knocked again. The door was locked, but Cross could hear music from inside, a cheap and static filled radio perhaps.

He stepped aside and told Billy Volgar to open the locked door. Billy took the knob of the door into one of his bearlike hands and twisted it, breaking the lock. He put his shoulder to the door, and it slammed open. Arnaud was standing against the wall opposite the door, holding a small, old revolver, shaking uncontrollably.

Billy reached under his suit jacket and started to pull out his big .45 semi-auto. Cross touched his arm and stepped in front of him.

Arnaud Deschamps spoke only French, an uneducated and often guttural French dialect of the streets of Paris. Cross spoke to him in French.

"Arnaud," he said, holding his arms out in front of him. "Please, it's me. Joseph Cross. You remember me, don't you?"

Arnaud Deschamps was a small man, thin, and that day he was unshaven. His rapidly greying hair, greasy and uncombed, hung long over his ears. He wore thick glasses rimmed in cheap black plastic, white tape repairing one broken stem. He wore a faded plaid shirt that was two sizes too big for him that he had found in a trash bin months ago. The breast pocket was torn and hung loose. His dirty blue jeans were two sizes too big for him. They hung loose and baggy. His jeans were belted with a length of rough cord.

His hand, holding the small revolver, was shaking; his finger was on the trigger, the hammer cocked, which made the gun very dangerous even if old and uncared for. Cross looked down as a brown mouse ran across the room, jumping over Arnaud's scuffed shoes. It retrieved a crumb of bread that had fallen to the floor the last time Arnaud had eaten. It quickly devoured it and returned to the hole in the wall it had come from, once again jumping over Arnaud's feet.

"I don't know," Arnaud said, not noticing the mouse, his voice weak and full of fear. "Did you come to hurt me?"

"No, of course not," Cross said gently, smiling, trying to reassure Arnaud. He took a few steps toward the little man. "Please Arnaud . . . I'm your friend . . . You remember me, don't you?"

"I think so," Arnaud said. He lowered his arm ever so slightly. "Joseph? Joseph Cross? I think I remember you."

"Put the gun down, Arnaud. I just want to talk to you. There's some money in it for you if you talk to me."

"Money?" Arnaud said, encouraged by the promise of cash. He let his arm fall to his side.

"Why not put the gun on the table?" Cross suggested. He pulled out his money clipped cash and took a one hundred Swiss Franc note from it. He held it out, offering it to Arnaud. Arnaud's eyes lit up as he saw what to him was an extravagant amount of money. He dropped the revolver on the little kitchen table and reached out for the bill. Cross walked to him and let the little man take it quickly.

"What do you want?" Arnaud asked.

"Blood diamonds," Cross answered simply.

"I don't have any . . . Haven't had any in a long time . . . I can get some . . . maybe . . . How much?"

"Do you do business with General Azubuike?"

"Who?" Arnaud asked. His face, honestly questioning the name, told Cross he was not trying to hide the truth. Arnaud would not be able to lie without his face revealing the lie. He was a small man, beaten down by life, with nothing close to heroism inside of him. If he lied, Cross would know it.

Cross looked at the beat up old metal work bench that crowded the small one room basement apartment. On it he saw a few pieces of not very expensive jewelry that Arnaud was in the process of removing small, inexpensive gem stones from. There was nothing in the room of any real value. And except for the radio with the tinny sound, there were no electronics at all in Arnaud's home.

The single room was filthy with months of cleaning undone. Cobwebs hung from the ceiling and corners. Cheap, cracked plates lay in the sink, unwashed. The small bed next to the wall held a pile of dirty sheets and dirtier clothes. The man had nothing. Cross pulled another one hundred Swiss Franc note from his money clip and laid it on the table with the bent leg.

"Thank you Arnaud," Cross said. He was not the man Cross was looking for. "Are you alright? Can I do anything for you?"

"No . . . It's the damn police . . . They won't leave me alone . . . I can't get the good stuff anymore . . . I won't go back to prison, you know. I'll kill myself first. No one brings the good stuff to me anymore because the damn police are always watching."

Cross thanked the man again and gave him a third one hundred Swiss Francs. Billy followed Cross out of the little room and up the stairs. "Where do we go now, boss?" Billy asked.

"I want you to go back to London. Take a commercial flight, and leave the Gulfstream with me. Leave your gun, the 9MM, in the Gulfstream. Make sure the Club is in good shape. Mike Finnegan is bringing in a shipment of wines next week. You'll have to meet him and make sure they get to the Club. In the basement. No one is to know about this, OK?"

"I don't like that. I don't like that at all," Billy said. "I don't like leaving you alone. Where are you going, boss?"

"I'm going to Nice to see Lotte Koch. I don't think she's going to give me any trouble. After that, if I need you, I'll get in touch with you. Stay handy, OK?"

****

Charlotte Koch, or Lotte as she was known, had found a man in his late 80s, a man with a title and a lot of money. The man, Baron Eric von Rustien, did have a lot of money, some inherited and more acquired by buying and selling industries and real estate over a sixty year working career. What he didn't have was a title, save for what he had taken on. He had assumed the title 'Baron' after ten years of building wealth so that he would be welcomed into European society.

His name was really Eric Rustien. He added the 'von' when he assumed the title. Lotte didn't care about that. She did care about the many millions of the Baron's money she could spend and move into one of her bank accounts.

The morning after leaving Geneva, Cross rented a Lexus at the Nice Côte d'Azur International Airport. He had made several phone calls inside the airport, to friends who would know Lotte, and found the estate that she had taken up residence in. He drove there, not having problems with the roads. He had spent many, many months in Nice, so he knew his way around. And he had an estate of his own in St. Tropez.

The Baron's estate was a grand building of carved grey stone, three stories tall, on a small piece of land, high enough in the hills to afford a good view of the Mediterranean and allow Mediterranean breezes to cool the summer heat. Lotte greeted him at the door. She had been told by the people Cross had contacted that he was in town, wanting to see her.

"Oh Joseph darling!" she said, smiling and holding her arms out to embrace him. "It's been too many years."

Lotte spoke English with an educated German accent, as flowery, refined and genteel as a German accent can get.

Cross took her into his arms and kissed her lightly on both cheeks. "Lotte, my love," he said. "You get prettier every time I see you. You must be using some kind of magic."

"Magic," Lotte said as she led Cross into the house. The inside was not as elaborately grand as Lars Ruscher's home, but it was elegant and warm thanks to the two foot thick stone walls. "Plus good Plastic Surgeons," she added with a laugh. "Come into the sitting room. It's too early for lunch, but I hope you will join me later. Perhaps some coffee?"

"Coffee would be great, Lotte."

They sat next to each other on a couch upholstered in Asian silk. Lotte edged very close to him, her hand firmly on his knee at first, then his thigh, as they waited for a man servant to bring a silver tray of coffee to them. A young man, tall and with the build of someone who spent a lot of time in the gymnasium, walked into the room with the coffee service. He stopped suddenly when he saw Lotte sitting so close to Cross. A look of displeasure, perhaps jealously, crossed his tanned face.

Lotte squeezed Cross' thigh even harder and looked up at the young man. She was enjoying herself, making her lover jealous. "Put the tray on the table, Peter" she said to him. "You can leave now . . . And close the door after you, please."

"I gather he shares your bed occasionally?" Cross asked.

"Occasionally," she answered. "When I need him."

Lotte poured the strong, steaming coffee into a delicate china cup and handed it to Cross. He took his, but Lotte held off pouring coffee for herself. She left her hands free to place her right hand on Cross' thigh once again as she edged even closer to him. Cross thought she might be in his lap pretty soon.

In the next half hour they reminisced about old times, good times, fun times they had shared. They laughed and tried to remember names of restaurants and the many police who had chased them around Europe. Lotte and Cross had shared many adventures throughout Europe, associating with the very best thieves Europe had to offer. They would buy the best, and, working together, they would send Police of every Nation out chasing red herrings as they smuggled what they had bought.

Lotte looked deeply into Cross' eyes and said, "And the sex was good, too, my love."

"The best," Cross lied. Lotte had been a demanding lover and a woman who leaned toward leathers and chains. Not to Cross' liking. But to keep her friendship and her business, he had relented and acted as if he were enjoying it. Several years had passed since they had slept together; Cross was determined to have still many more years intervene.

"Did you come to rekindle that flame, my love?" she asked.

"I wish I could," he lied. "But I have business to take care of."

"Oh that is a shame, Joseph," she grimaced, her

lower lip stuck out in an exaggerated, childlike pout.

"I hear you're living with a man, Lotte. What would he say if he found us in bed together? Or if he found you with that muscle bound child you're keeping around?"

She squeezed his thigh and slid her hand closer to his crotch. "The man . . . As you say . . . Is 89 years old and bedridden. He barely knows where he is anymore. His time on this earth is short."

"That's too bad," Cross said, trying to sound sincere. "My deepest condolences."

"That is not necessary, Joseph. You know me . . . Shhh! Don't tell anyone . . . I'm in it for the money," she laughed. "Does that surprise you?"

"You can do nothing that would surprise me, Lotte." And they both laughed.

Together, they finished the silver pot of coffee and sat back, quiet for a moment, and then Lotte took her hand from him, slid a few inches away, and asked, "What is the business you have come to see me about, Joseph?"

"Bad business, I'm afraid. Do you know General Simba Azubuike?"

"The General?" she asked. "Of course I know that loathsome man. I sometimes buy the few good diamonds he has for sale. I've seen better, but they are easy to dispose of."

"Have you bought any recently?"

"No . . . Not in the past six or seven months. Lars would know that better than I."

"Lars Ruscher?" Cross asked. He was surprised to hear the name.

"Yes," Lotte said. "When he has good raw stones from the General and needs quick cash, I buy them . . . At a steep discount, of course."

"Lars Ruscher?" Cross asked again.

"Yes, why? Is there something wrong?"

"Lars told me he doesn't deal in Azubuike's diamonds. He said you and Arnaud Deschamps buy from the General."

"Well then, Lars is lying. I, of course, know of Azubuike but I have no direct dealings with him." She was looking directly into Cross' eyes as she said this, and without diverting her eyes, she sipped at the last few drops of her coffee.

'She might be lying,' Cross thought. She was good at that. She made a very good living out of lying. And if she were lying, he would ensure she never lied to anyone again. If she were lying, Billy Volgar would be sent to see her.

"So how does Lars get his hands on Azubuike's diamonds?"

"Oh, Joseph, I thought everyone knew that," she said, smiling, as she would to a child who asked a childish question. She carefully placed the delicate cup and saucer on the tray next to the silver pot, sat back, crossed her legs, showing a good deal of her shapely calf, and said, "Lars is an aficionado of short wave radio. It is his hobby. Didn't you know that? He brags about speaking with people all over the world. When Azubuike has some stones to sell, he speaks with Lars on the radio."

"Do you mean that Azubuike has a short wave radio set up at his compound?"

"Why yes," Lotte said, surprised at the question, as if everyone was supposed to know that. She was amazed that Cross did not know. "You really must keep up to date on what is occurring in our world, Joseph."

Cross spent another hour with Lotte Koch, trying to determine if she was telling the truth. It seemed she was, because when Cross thought about it, dealing in a few thousand dollars' worth of poor quality diamonds would not support the royally elite lifestyle Lotte was used to.

Lotte was a con artist, a thief, and a receiver of stolen goods who made a grand living by bilking old men out of their money. She would not waste her time on a few thousand dollars of poor quality diamonds, unless she could make easy money at it. So, Cross came to the conclusion that Lotte was not lying.

****

When Joe Cross arrived back in Geneva, he drove his rented Lexus directly to Lars' lakeside estate. The tall, wrought iron front gate was closed this time and locked electronically. Cross could not find a manual lock, and there was no keyhole. Yet the gate would not open when he pushed on it.

There was a speaker under a grill at the side of the gate, built into a tall grey-stone column. Cross pressed the button and waited. He pressed the button again, and then he held the button down. Still no one answered.

It was late afternoon, and dark clouds were rolling in over Lake Geneva from the North, foretelling cold spring rain. He could come back, he thought, but would that do any good? Lars would know what Lotte had told Cross. So Cross looked up to the top of the eight foot tall stone wall and began to climb. The stones made climbing easy. The rough stones supplied good handholds and footholds.

He stopped at the top of the wall, sitting with his legs hanging over, and looked across the estate's grounds. No one was there; the gardeners were nowhere to be seen. He climbed halfway down and dropped the last few feet of the wall to the grass below. He stepped onto the paver stone drive on the inside as the first few drops of rain began to fall. He looked across the five acres of grounds once again and started towards the house. Across the lawn, from Cross' left and from behind the big house, two gardeners were walking towards him. One held a shovel, the other a rake.

They called out in German, "Wait! Stop! Who are you?"

They were not small men, and they didn't look very happy. Cross ignored them; he felt for the butt of his pistol, the pistol Billy had left in the Gulfstream, tucked into his belt at his side and quickened his pace.

He got to the front door of Lars' estate before the two gardeners could get to him. The sky quickly grew dark with black clouds, and rain started to fall heavily. A breeze coming off the lake was rapidly changing to an icy wind. Cross twisted the big brass doorknob and pushed the tall, bronze sheathed, oak doors open. He had half expected the hinges on the heavy door to squeak loudly, but they were silent as the doors swung open. He was surprised that the door was not locked. Had it been, he thought, Billy should be there to rip the damn doors off their hinges. Lars was standing inside, trying to smile, but obviously frightened.

He was wearing expensive looking, gray, casual slacks and a light blue silk shirt that hung loose outside the slacks that draped over his bare feet. Lars was fiddling nervously with the buttons on the shirt. His eyes revealed the shock and perhaps a little fear he was feeling at seeing Joseph Cross inside his home.

"Joseph! You're back once again! What a surprise!" he said. He started twisting his hands in front of him and forced a smile.

The two gardeners stood on the porch, behind Cross, in the open doorway. They were breathing heavily and still holding the shovel and rake, but they made no movement towards him. Without looking behind him, Cross pulled his jacket aside to show Lars the pistol at his waist. He said, "Tell your lawn guys to go back to work. You and I need to talk."

Lars waived an arm, and the two men turned and walked away, leaving the doors open. Lars' butler, a man of some forty or fifty years and not built to be a danger to anyone, side-stepped quickly around Cross, leaving a wide berth, and closed the doors. He disappeared hastily into a room off the hallway.

"Shall we talk in the library?" Lars asked.

"I'd rather go see your short wave radio setup, Lars. Don't lie to me. Billy Volgar isn't with me, but I can have him here in a matter of hours."

"Of course," Lars said. He was sweating now, his eyes shifting, his voice shaky. "It is a hobby of mine, you know. I speak with people everywhere, you know. Just a hobby, you know. Why, the other day I was speaking with a young boy in Greenland. Can you believe that? Come . . . I will show you."

Lars turned and walked with unsteady and nervous steps to the end of the hallway. He opened a door on the left and stood aside. Cross waived him in and walked behind him into a small room. The room was filled on three walls with tables and shelves of electronics. Small lights were flashing, and a faint buzzing came from a few of the dark gray and black boxes. A microphone sat on a small table with a laptop computer next to it.

Lars pompously waived his arm as if showing off his machines, and tried to smile, imitating pride in his electronics, but nerves were apparent in the crooked smile. Cross knew nothing about shortwave radios but assumed that Lars would have only the best, as he demanded in every facet of his life.

Cross looked around the room and then asked, "So this is what you use to talk with Azubuike?"

"Azubuike?" Lars said, feigning the question, but his eyes told Cross he was lying. "I don't talk with Azubuike."

"Please don't lie to me, Lars. We've known each other for too many years. Don't get me wrong here, but I know you'd do anything for money. You've been buying blood diamonds from Azubuike. You pay him pennies, and he thinks he's getting a good deal. You and he communicate by radio. He tells you when he has a supply to sell. I know that, so it's a waste of your time and mine to deny it. If you want to deal with someone like Azubuike . . . Well, that's between you and your conscience. Now, don't insult my intelligence. Tell me that I'm right."

"Alright, Joseph," Lars admitted. "I do buy what he has to sell. Judge me if you will. Once a month . . . On the first day of each month . . . He calls me, and we discuss what he has."

"Only on the first day of each month?"

"Yes . . . Once each month. Often he has only a few diamonds. Occasionally he has a good supply."

"And how does he get his diamonds to you? How do you get the money to him?"

Lars pulled a wheeled, low back office chair away from the desk on which the microphone and laptop rested, and he sat. He was breathing easier having told the truth, but his face remained pale with anxiety. He was frightened, and Cross knew that was good for getting at the truth.

He was afraid of Joseph Cross, as most people in the crime and smuggling business throughout Europe were. Cross had a reputation, a reputation for being smart but also for using violence when he had to. He preferred to not use violence, but he also knew that in his world, violence was sometimes very necessary. Lars said, "There's a middle man . . . In Amsterdam . . . Do you know Hienrich Van der Mullen?"

"Hienrich?" Cross asked, surprised that Van der Mullen was involved as a middle man or in any way at all with Simba Azubuike. He had done business with Hienrich for many years. He had trusted the man. Then a terrible thought entered his mind. Cross had sent Mary Ssanyu to Hienrich when she escaped from the General. Was that a mistake? He had to find out if he had put the woman in danger.

Cross took a deep breath. He started to pace around the room, touching the electronics aimlessly without really looking at the boxes. He had to think; he had to keep Lars talking. Overwhelming fear raced through his mind. He cared for Mary Ssanyu. He had wanted her to be safe and to live a good life. He had sent her to a man who might well have sent her back into that maniac's hands. If that had happened, he had to save her once again. He had to get as much information as he could. He stopped pacing, turned to look at Lars and asked, his voice quavering "So Hienrich receives the diamonds and sends the money on to the General. How does he do that?"

"I don't know, Joseph. I truly don't. I wire transfer the money to him via the Banco De Las Islas, and he buys the diamonds for me. I have no idea how the diamonds get to him. I truly don't. Hienrich then sells the diamonds for me. I never see the damn diamonds. Often he merely sells them for what I paid for them because of their poor quality. Sometimes he pays me a profit. He keeps a small percentage for himself. I have to trust Hienrich, don't I? I truly never see the diamonds. I pay for what Azubuike describes, and Hienrich returns a profit to me via the same bank if there is a profit. It is small business, but it is business. I often do not make a profit, but I never have a loss."

"Why doesn't Hienrich buy directly from Azubuike?"

"I'm not sure," Lars answered. "I've asked him that, but he won't tell me. I think he doesn't want to tell anyone he buys diamonds from that man. People in our business know Azubuike and often stay away from him. Those who deal with him acquire a very bad reputation. I think perhaps I am a middle man as you Americans say, rather than Hienrich being the middle man for me. I'm not sure."

"Has Hienrich ever mentioned a woman . . . A very attractive African woman . . . A woman who came to him some time ago to sell diamonds?" Cross asked.

Lars' forehead wrinkled. He was wondering what this had to do with Azubuike's diamonds. Joseph Cross had a reputation with women, Lars had heard all the stories, but why this one woman? Honesty once again, he thought. The truth might keep Billy Volgar from him.

"Once, a long time ago, Hienrich told me he had some diamonds . . . Blood diamonds, he said. He said they didn't come from Azubuike. He said some woman brought them to him. He asked if I wanted to buy them . . . In the usual way, you know. We made the deal, and I made a few hundred. That's all I know . . . I swear; that's all I know. Was that the woman you speak of?"

Cross slammed his fist down on the table top, hard enough to make the microphone jump.

It was the twentieth of May. In eleven days Lars and Azubuike would make radio contact. In eleven days another transfer of money through Hienrich to Azubuike would take place. Cross had ten days, before that transfer could take place, to find out if he had sent Mary Ssanyu into danger or to freedom. He knew he had to use the upcoming diamonds deal to his advantage if he were to free Robert Fullsome . . . and Mary Ssanyu if he had made a mistake sending her to Hienrich.

He took a step closer to the seated Lars and told him, "I'll be back here early on the morning of the thirty-first of May. If you tell anyone I was here . . . Including Hienrich and Azubuike . . . or that I'll be back here . . . I'll send Billy Volgar to take care of you. Do you know what that means? Do I make myself clear?"

"I understand, Joseph. I understand. But why? Why is this so important to you?"

"That Lars, is none of your business. Just be here when I come back, and keep your mouth shut."

CHAPTER SEVEN - I Had To Tell Azubuike

Hienrich Van der Mullen was a short, stooped over little man who wore old clothes that he had bought second hand years ago, and he struggled even to spend his money on these. His mouse-brown hair had gone uncut for months because he couldn't part with the few coins a haircut cost. He had long ago given up shaving because razors were too expensive for him. And the thought of paying someone else to shave him was anathema to him. He had an old pair of rusty and dull scissors that he used as best he could to cut his own hair back off his shoulders and trim his beard when it hung below his neck.

He was a man who had an obsession for counting money. When others enjoyed hobbies, sports, or family, Hienrich would spend his hours at a table counting coins and paper money of many Nations and denominations, stacking them neatly, tenderly. He would arrange them one way and then rearrange them as a child would when playing with tin soldiers.

His other obsession was acquiring money by any means. Buying and selling blood diamonds was not his only business. He was a receiver of stolen goods of all kinds. Petty thieves would bring their cache of whatever they could pilfer – radios, televisions, auto tires, cheap jewelry, anything that anyone could steal – and he would pay a pittance of the value and resell everything quickly for a profit. But the thieves knew he would buy anything, so they brought anything to him.

Hienrich liked to store his money in the five safes he kept in his home along the Jordaan District of Amsterdam. He had first one small wall safe installed in his bedroom, then a second larger one, then a still larger one cut into the concrete floor of the basement, and finally a big, thick, standing safe in his bedroom where he could be close to his money. Each was filled with cash: paper money of every denomination and from every Country in the world, and coins of gold and silver. He never kept gems or jewelry, or gold or silver that was not coins. Hienrich would spend a pleasant, warm, Sunday afternoon locked inside his dark, musty and dusty home counting his cash.

He didn't trust banks or anyone who would invest his money for him. In his twisted mind, every person he met wanted his money. He kept his home filled with pistols and rifles and shotguns in every room, for fear of someone breaking in to steal his money. His sleep was constantly broken by dreams of people stealing his money from him. It was not unusual for him to stuff his old, torn, dirty pillow case with paper money so he could sleep near it. Having his money lovingly close at hand was what he enjoyed.

Hienrich bought the small building where he lived when the Jordaan was a working class district, when property was cheap. It had been a vacant warehouse for several years when he acquired it. When he bought it, the ceiling of the third floor leaked in the rain, the floor in a room on the second floor was unsafe to walk on, and the plumbing ran rusty water when it would allow water to flow at all. But the building was cheap, and that suited Hienrich. He thought of having repairs done, but that meant spending some of his money. He could not bring himself to do that. He would live with the inconveniences.

He put a small bed with squeaky springs on the third floor; he thought the third floor would be harder for a thief to get to while Hienrich slept. On the ground floor he had a small wooden table on which an electric hot plate rested so he could cook whatever he found cheap, or could steal, at the markets. There was an old toilet at the rear of the ground floor. He suffered the rusty water but at least he didn't have to pay someone to change the pipes.

Cross had dealt with Hienrich many times over the years, buying good diamonds from him and then smuggling them to a buyer somewhere in the world or to London where they would be cut or re-cut. Cross had trusted the strange little man; as far as trust could extend in the business they were in. Cross knew he was a bizarre and maybe demented man. At least Hienrich had never tried to cheat him. Business honesty was important when two people conspired in some criminal activity.

That is why Cross had sent Mary Ssanyu to him with Azubuike's diamonds. He had trusted that Hienrich would buy the diamonds for a price perhaps a little lower than their value, but a few Dutch Guilders meant nothing if Mary's freedom came with them. Mary would be on her way to a new life with enough money to at least start that new life.

But Cross hadn't known back then that Hienrich did business with Azubuike. Yes, they were often blood diamonds that he bought from Hienrich, but he had not known that these often came from Azubuike. He should have asked, he thought. He should have known. His conscience was wracked with the guilt of maybe having made a mistake.

Now Cross had to find out if Mary had sold the diamonds they took from Azubuike and gotten away, or had Hienrich sent her back to Azubuike? Had Hienrich somehow gotten word to Azubuike? Or, had he innocently told Lars, and had Lars told Azubuike that Mary was there? Was Mary truly safe?

Hienrich greeted Cross warmly and welcomed him into his home. Hienrich brushed Cross' hand aside and took him into his arms, hugging him as one would hug a dear friend or close relative. Cross was put aback by the near stench of the man's unclean clothes and unwashed body. His breath was foul and his hair greasy. Inside the old warehouse was filthy, and rats and insects scampered freely across the dirty floor.

Hienrich was wearing heavy and threadbare brown corduroy pants that were filthy enough to be able to stand on their own. He had a green plaid sports jacket on, one that he had found in a trash barrel some months ago. His sockless feet were wearing torn Nike's that were two sizes too big for him.

Hienrich's home had not changed since the last time Cross had been there, one year ago. The few pieces of furniture were as old, dusty, and worn as Hienrich was and as Cross remembered. There was a smell of dampness and dirt permeating the place. He watched as families of cockroaches scampered across the floor and up the walls. But Hienrich was happy to see Cross. "Ahh, Joseph," he said speaking in Dutch-German, smiling behind a beard that needed the old scissors that he used on it. "It is so good to see you once again."

Hienrich could speak no English, and Cross could speak only a little German. Cross could understand most of what Hienrich said. Hienrich tried to understand what Cross said. They were barely able to communicate if each spoke slowly and repeated much of what was said. Hand gestures helped.

They sat at the small kitchen table with the hot plate

which Hienrich pushed aside. Hienrich pulled a bottle of inexpensive vodka from the back of a cupboard in what he called his kitchen. He filled two mismatched glasses, and they drank to each other's health.

"So why are you here, Joseph? To buy or to sell?"

"Unfortunately, neither, Hienrich. I need some information."

"And perhaps I have information to sell, Joseph," Hienrich said. He smiled a greedy little smile under his uncombed beard and moustache, anticipating more cash filing his boney, dirty hands.

"I have a thousand American for the right answers," Cross said. He knew Hienrich would bargain for more and one thousand dollars was merely a place to start.

"If what you need, Joseph, is important . . . It must be worth more than that," he said, rubbing his hands together. He leaned back in his chair, his face lighting up with anticipation. He smiled under his moustache and beard, showing off broken, yellow and black teeth.

"How much more, Hienrich?" Cross laughed. He had been through this so many times with the man over the years. It was all in good friendship in the past. A joke they shared. But this time Cross had to know if he had sent Mary Ssanyu into danger or freedom. So the laugh was forced.

"That depends on what you want to know. Ask, and I will tell you how much it is worth."

Cross paused and looked deeply into Hienrich's eyes. The smile fell suddenly from Cross' face. There was danger and warning in his glare. The smile disappeared slowly from Hienrich's unshaven face In return. The cheery red blush of his cheeks faded to white. This was different, he realized. This was not the usual business he and Joseph Cross had done in past years. This was not about diamonds. He knew of Cross' reputation as someone not to be on the bad side of.

Cross shifted in his chair, leaned forward resting his elbows on the table in front of him, and asked, peering into the old man's eyes, "Do you do business with Simba Azubuike?"

"Simba who? What a strange name."

"I've spoken with Lars Ruscher, Hienrich," Cross said simply, in a low tone.

"Ahh then," Hienrich said as he filled his glass with vodka. His hands were shaking, and some of the vodka missed the glass, spilling onto the dust covered, warped wood of the table top. "Since you know already . . . Of course I know the man. I've never met him, but I buy his diamonds, and I act as middleman between Simba and Lars. Lars tells me when diamonds are available. He wires money to me, and I buy what I want from him. Most of it I sell to others and keep a fee for myself. Since you know that, I will not expect to be paid. That is only fair." Hienrich was frightened; something was wrong here. He hoped that an offer of free information might save him from danger.

"Do you know Mary Ssanyu?"

"Who?" Hienrich asked, his forehead frowning in honest questioning. He was either a very good poker player, or he wasn't lying. Cross saw that on the man's pale, frightened face.

"Some time ago I sent a woman to you. She had some diamonds to sell. She is tall, African, beautiful."

"Oh yes," Hienrich said brightly. "I remember now. She had a leather bag. Most of her diamonds were of poor quality, but a few were very good. Why do you ask?"

"Did she tell you where the diamonds came from?" Cross asked.

Hienrich's forehead creased in thought again. Why was Cross so interested in this woman? A lover who spurned him and ran off? He doubted that. Cross usually became bored of women before they tired of him. The diamonds? Could she have stolen them from Cross? Not if he sent her to him. Was she to divide the profit of the sale with Cross and didn't? No, Cross would not have come to Amsterdam after all this time for a few thousand Gilders. Then why? He told himself he had to be careful. Cross was a dangerous man.

"I'm trying to remember," Hienrich lied. "No, I don't think so . . . But I assumed they came out of Africa. They were typical . . . And she was African after all."

"Where did she go after she left you?" Cross asked.

"Where? I have no idea."

"She said nothing, then?"

"No . . . wait," Hienrich said forcing a stiff smile. Maybe the truth was the best avenue. He decided he had to tell bits of the truth anyway, a little at a time until Joseph Cross was satisfied. "I think she said she had a plane to catch. I think she said she would do some shopping with what I gave her. Yes, that's what she said. She said she would buy things for a day or two. She seemed to like that idea. She seemed happy."

"And she just left . . . And you haven't seen her since?"

"She had a taxi waiting," Hienrich said; there was pleading in his weak voice. He was sweating now. He took a rumpled, filthy handkerchief from his threadbare jacket pocket and wiped his forehead. He twisted the handkerchief in his hands. He tried to pour vodka into his glass, but his hands were shaking uncontrollably. He spilled most of it and put the bottle down, nearly dropping it to the floor. He asked, "Why are you asking this? What has she done to you?"

Cross asked, "Did you tell anyone she came to see you?"

"No, I don't think so."

"How do you and Lars communicate?"

Hienrich wiped his forehead again, smiled nervously, and said, "By phone, of course. Sometimes by wire."

"Did Lars keep any of Mary's diamonds or did you sell them all?" Cross asked and sat forward, leaning his elbows on his knees.

"Come to think of it . . . I think Lars did keep one or two of the good stones. I sold them for him, of course."

"And did you tell Lars where you acquired them? From whom?"

So that was it, Hienrich thought. Something happened to this Mary Ssanyu, and Cross was involved somehow. Well, he had nothing to do with whatever happened. If it was Lars . . . Then let Lars take the punishment.

"Yes, of course," Hienrich said, feeling relief as a weight was slowly removed from his shoulders. "I told Lars of the woman. I had no idea where the diamonds came from, of course, but why? Did something happen to this woman?"

"How do the diamonds from Azubuike get here?" Cross asked.

"A man brings them," Hienrich answered. "A black

man . . . A tall man . . . A thin man but muscular . . . A well-dressed man . . . A man who has a military bearing. He wears good clothes and says very little. He has never said a word to me. He merely hands me a small bag with the stones and goes away."

Cross got to his feet abruptly. He knew he had made a mistake. Not knowing Hienrich and Lars were associated was a mistake. All his adult life, since leaving the United States Air Force so many years ago, he had done nothing without knowing everything about the deal he would be involved in. Yet he let this woman he cared about walk into danger. His head was filled with fear, guilt, and regret, as well as anger. Revenge was what he needed now. If Mary Ssanyu had been brought back to Azubuike, people would die.

If she was dead, if Azubuike had her murdered, there would be hell to pay, he promised himself.

****

Cross waited in a coffee shop three blocks away from Lars' home in Geneva. He drank coffee, one cup after another, not tasting the strong, bitter brew. He ignored the sticky and sweet pastry on the table in front of him, and he thought of what he had to do. Guilt was engulfing him. He was frightened of what had happened. He had no way of knowing for sure, but Mary Ssanyu may well have walked into a trap. And he had sent her there. He couldn't shake the terrible thoughts of what might have happened to her. She had not contacted him since he had sent her on her way. He had no way of contacting her. He didn't know where she had settled . . . If in fact she had gotten away safely.

He waited until the dark of night, until the streets of Lars' neighborhood would be empty. The coffee shop closed; he was the last customer to leave as the door was locked behind him. He walked aimlessly in the rain until it was time. He found an alley at the back of the five acre estate, behind Lars' home. A brick wall, covered in green vines ran the length of the rear of the property. Shards of broken glass were embedded along the top of the wall. Cross took off his jacket and slung it across the wall, covering the glass. He climbed over and dropped to the wet grass below. He pulled his jacket off the wall, ripping it on the glass. It was ruined and useless. He dropped it to the ground and walked on.

Lars' Edwardian mansion lay ahead. It was dark; no lights were on inside. Cross found a small window at the rear of the house on the ground level and forced open the locked window using the small thin bladed knife he carried.

He climbed into the dark home and found himself in the kitchen. Knives hung from a magnetic rack on the wall above a big, oak cutting board. 'No,' he thought. 'That would be too easy,' he said to himself in a whisper. If Lars had done what Cross felt he had done, he would kill him with his hands only. Close up, very personal. That would be the revenge he would seek.

He found the stairs leading up to the second floor and to Lars' bedroom. He took one slow step at a time, walking softly. The carpeted stairs were solid and did not signal his presence. There was a dim light coming from under a door at the top of the stairs. He went to that door and quietly opened it a few inches, enough to peer inside. Lars lay in bed, snoring loudly. A book lay open, the cover up, on Lars' chest where he had put it as sleep overtook him. A small bedside lamp with a thin shade over it threw off dim, pale, yellow light.

Cross stepped into the room and walked silently to Lars' bedside. He eased the book away from Lars, placing it on the nightstand. He touched Lars' shoulder softly. He touched his shoulder again and shook him gently. Lars moaned and turned, trying to focus. His eyes broadened when he realized Joseph Cross was standing there over him.

Lars jumped and tried to roll away but Cross grabbed him by his arm and pulled him out of bed, throwing him onto the floor on his back. He fell on top of Lars, one knee on the man's chest, his hands grabbing Lars' pajamas at the neck.

"What! What!" Lars managed to say in a scream.

"Quiet! Make any noise and you're dead! Now tell me you son of a bitch," Cross growled. "Mary Ssanyu. She brought diamonds to Hienrich in Amsterdam. You bought them. Tell me what you did after that."

"I don't understand . . . What? . . . Why? . . ." Lars was whispering as best he could. Abject fear filled his face and eyes. Color drained from his face. His lips were wet with spittle.

Cross pressed his knee down into Lars' chest. He pulled the man's head by his hair off the floor and backhanded him across his mouth.

"Once again Lars," Cross whispered in an angry growl. "Mary Ssanyu . . . What did you do after Hienrich phoned you?"

"I don't . . ."

Cross didn't give him a chance to lie. He pulled Lars to his feet and hit him across his jaw. Lars fell back onto the bed. Cross pulled him up once again. Lars' mouth was bleeding; he tried to scream for help, but another punch to the side of his head silenced him. Black unconsciousness fell around him.

Lars woke to find himself tied painfully at his chest and ankles to a chair. His arms were twisted behind him; his wrists had been tied so tightly he could not feel his fingers. The electric wire from two lamps Cross had tied him with was biting into his skin, blood seeping around it.

Lars looked around and realized he was in the room on the ground floor that held his radio equipment. He spit blood out of his mouth. His vision was clouded; he shook his head, but the pain was fierce. Slowly his sight returned. Cross was standing in front of him.

Cross said, "I'm going to ask you once more. Mary Ssanyu . . . Did you tell Azubuike she was in Amsterdam?"

"Please, Joseph . . . Please."

Cross backhanded the man across his face and said, "Tell me, Lars and I'll go away."

"You will? You will not hurt me?"

"Tell me, Lars," cross demanded.

"Alright," Lars said trying to smile. "I felt I had to tell Azubuike. I mean, if the woman was from Africa, he would want to know after all. She might be in competition with him. I had to tell Azubuike. I do business with him, don't you understand? I had to tell him. I do business with him. If I withheld anything from him, the business might end. I didn't know she belonged to him. I just told him because she was African, and I thought he might want to know."

"What did Azubuike say he was going to do?"

"He said nothing, Joseph . . . He said nothing."

"How long did you wait before contacting Azubuike?" Cross asked.

"I didn't wait," Lars said. "Hienrich phoned me and told me about the diamonds and the woman. When Hienrich told me about her, I knew Azubuike would want to know, so I spoke with him on the short wave."

Cross paced back and forth around the small room, in front of Lars Ruscher as Lars began to cry. Cross stopped and turned to look down at the man. He asked, "Do you know what you've done, Lars? That woman was a sex slave owned by Azubuike. Eventually he would have tired of her, and she would have been killed. Her life was not life, it was terror and misery. And you may have sent her back there."

Cross paced around the small room for a moment or two. He stopped, turned to Lars and said, "When Azubuike kidnapped Robert Fullsome, you wrote that note to Margaret Fullsome, didn't you? Azubuike told you to do that, didn't he? Don't lie to me, Lars."

"I'm sorry Joseph. I didn't know," he said through his tears. He was wailing loudly, enough to draw the attention of household staff. But Cross didn't care. He touched the pistol at his waist. There were things more important than life.

Cross walked behind the chair holding Lars. He slowly put his right arm around Lars' neck and his left arm behind Lars' head. He locked his right hand at his left elbow and slowly choked the life out of Lars Ruscher.

He left Lars tied to the chair. Carefully, he retraced his steps since entering the house and Lars' bedroom. He wiped everything he had touched clean, leaving no finger prints. He left the house quietly, through the window he had entered, picking up his torn jacket from the lawn as he climbed the wall, and disappeared into the dark of night. The house servants would find Lars the next morning. The police were called. The body was taken away. An investigation was pursued. No arrests were made.

Cross knew, in his nightmares, what had happened. Hienrich told Lars. Lars told Azubuike. The man who brought diamonds to Hienrich had found Mary, and she was back in the hands of Simba Azubuike. He knew that was what had happened. If Azubuike knew Mary had left him and stolen his diamonds, he would seek revenge. There was no doubt about that. He was furious, with himself as much as he was with Hienrich and Lars. That night, lying in bed, he fought back tears thinking of her.

CHAPTER EIGHT - Is Helen Around?

Tenerife is the largest of the Canary Islands. Those islands sit off the northwest coast of Africa. Spain owns the Islands, and Tenerife is a tourist destination, particularly during the celebration of the Carnival of Santa Cruz de Tenerife. It is a week filled with music, dancing, street parties, parades, drinking and young people seeking the sun and sex.

Tenerife is also the home of Manuel Hernandez Maria Rodriguez de Santa Anna. Manuel, or Manny as he is known to criminals across the world, is the very best there is at shifting money around the world in order to hide it from Governments everywhere. He had been a master at the art of money laundering before the days of computers. His skills at accounting and record keeping were unsurpassed. Today, with the help of his assortment of powerful computers, his mastery continues.

In spite of his corpulent weight, Manny looks younger than his sixty-six years. His smile is constant, his teeth white and perfect. He is very active, especially chasing the young women who vacation in Tenerife. His face, however, is constantly red, his cheeks are always puffed and red veined, and his fat lips are always wet with drool in anticipation of his next meal. Manny likes his food; that is to say as kindly as possible that Manny is enormously fat.

Joseph Cross has had a long term relationship with Manny. Cross has filtered millions of U.S. dollars, British Pounds, Euros, and practically every other currency of the world through Manny, making both of them a nice profit. And he and Manny are friends who enjoy each other's company, cognac, and cigars.

But Manny has a sideline business. Manny is a clearing house for companies that offer military mercenary services. When a specialized military or high security job is needed – be it a small operation or a large overthrow of a government – Manny is contacted, and he goes through his list of mercenary groups to find the group of specialists needed to do the job. Each group has earned its reputation for professionalism. Without that reputation they would not be on Manny's list.

Years in the past Joseph Cross was hired to smuggle a boatload of arms and ammunition into Southern Africa. Upon delivery he was paid an additional $10,000 to accompany a small mercenary group of German and French professional soldiers who would deliver the guns to their final destination.

On the way to delivering the weapons to a very private army of white settlers fighting rebels in the African bush, the group Cross was with attacked and wiped out a camp run and financed by Cubans, where native black African terrorists were being trained. Killing the Cubans and the men they were training was the easy part. He had manned a Belgian 7.76 mm light machine gun mounted on the top of the cab of one of the trucks.

Cross then stood by and watched as the Germans and French then went on to slaughter the inhabitants of the small village where the training camp was located. No one survived, not one woman or child. He did not take part in the murders. Manny had arranged that operation.

The day Cross' jet landed in Tenerife was a clear, sunny, hot day in May. He had only a few days before Azubuike would want to speak with Lars over the short wave radio. There was a lot to do and to plan.

He carried a gray leather attaché with him as he walked to the car rental stand at the airport. He rented a nice, red E-Class Mercedes Cabriolet convertible in deference to the sun and put the top down to take full advantage of the perfect weather. He weaved his way slowly and carefully through the throngs of tourists. Cross wished he could move faster; there was a lot to do in a short time.

The streets were crowded with vacationers. The beaches were crowded with young people who chased the sun; the men were muscular and tanned; the women were all in the smallest of bikinis and tanned. 'One day,' he thought. 'One day when this is all over I'm going to have to spend some time on the beach here.'

Cross drove the Mercedes along the winding roads, driving faster where he could. Manny's house was isolated on the south side of a hill overlooking the Atlantic amongst fields and forests. It was fenced, and the two acres were heavily wooded inside the fence and outside. The house had been built twenty years ago by the best construction companies and had been designed by the best modern architects money could buy. It was strikingly modern, all wood and stone with grand windows along the south and west walls of the house, so that the magnificent sunsets could be enjoyed. The expansive roof was covered with red, Spanish clay tiles. The lines of the house were intended to make anyone looking at it say, "WOW!"

There was a gate at the road through the forest leading to Manny's house. The gate was closed but not locked. Cross got out of the car and opened it. He drove through the gate, stopping to close it behind him, and drove on to Manny's house.

At the door he rang the doorbell. There was no answer, and Cross' knocking at the front door of the house brought no one to the door. He walked around the side of the house to the rear along a slate stone path lined on both edges with masses of colorful flowers. At the rear of the house he found Manny sitting in his garden, under a tall willow tree, on a double wide padded chaise, almost big enough to hold his bulk.

Manny was dozing, half asleep in the shade of the willow tree in the warm afternoon, a tall glass of something icy in one hand and a long cigar in the other. Manny opened his eyes and saw Cross walking towards him. He dropped the cigar onto the lawn as he reached for a pistol lying on a table next to him.

"Whoa Manny!" Cross called out. He stopped walking, dropped the attaché onto the ground, and held his hands high over his head, smiling and laughing. "It's me . . . Joe Cross."

Manny pushed his bulk from his chair and managed to stand, shading his eyes with the hand holding the pistol while his other hand still held his drink. He was fatter than Cross remembered and so fat that he had a hard time pushing himself out of the chaise and an even harder time standing. He gave up trying and sat back as he smiled and said in Spanish accented English, "Joseph? Is that really you, Joseph?"

"It's me, Manny. Now put that damn gun down."

Manny shook the sleep from his brain. He laid the gun on the table and tried to pick up his cigar from the lawn, but his enormous waist wouldn't allow him to bend over that far. He sat back and rubbed his eyes. Cross stepped lightly to Manny and picked up the cigar for him. Manny took it gratefully, still trying to bring Cross into focus.

Manny's native language was Spanish, but he could converse in heavily accented English, German and French. He spoke in English as he said, "It *is* you, isn't it, Joseph? Come sit near me. My eyes aren't so good as they once were. I have some nice sangria. You must have some. It is cooling in the heat."

Cross pulled a wicker chair close to the man and sat near him. Manny squinted and said, "You haven't changed, Joseph. You are as thin as always. We must spend some time together so I can put some meat on your bones. How long has it been?"

"It's been a couple of years, Manny. And you're even fatter than I remember," he said as he patted the fat man's stomach.

They both laughed, Manny shaking his 380 pounds as he laughed. "But I am not yet so fat that I cannot bring a young lady or two into my bed!"

"You better go on a diet, Manny," Cross said jovially. "If you don't, you're going to explode and send balls of fat everywhere. And besides, pretty soon you're going to need a bigger bed if you want someone in it next to you."

"Oh, Joseph! The ladies seem to love me . . . Perhaps for the money, no?" But I do love my food! And you're too skinny, my friend. You need to take a lesson from me!"

They laughed again, and Cross leaned back in the chair next to Manny. Manny grasped an icy glass pitcher of red sangria, many citrus fruits floating on top, and filled a tall glass for his friend. Cross took it and sipped at it, laying the glass on the table.

He had carried the thick attaché with him and had placed it on the grass between the two of them. They spoke for fifteen minutes, reliving old times and old deals that made money for both of them. They laughed some more, and Cross enjoyed the sweet, fruity sangria.

Manny put a silver torch lighter to his now unlit cigar and then asked, "So, Joseph. And why are you here? Did you just wish to talk of old times?"

"No, Manny. I have business. I have six million American dollars with me . . . In the attaché. I need you to keep it for me, and when I send word, I want you to wire transfer five million of it . . . Or whatever amount I tell you . . . to where I tell you."

"And the other million?"

"My expenses and your fee. And there's more than that if I need it. Plus . . . And I hope I don't shock you too much . . . Is Helen around? Do you know where she is? At least part of that is to pay her."

"Helen! Helen! Are you crazy, Joseph? Do you know what they call her?"

"Yes, of course. 'Helen-a-hand-basket.' But I think I may need her expertise."

"If you need *her* . . . You must be in real trouble, Joseph. Tell me."

It took Cross a full half hour to tell Manny everything, starting with the MP Margaret Fullsome's visit to the Rochester Club. He left out nothing except his murder of Lars Ruscher. He told Manny all the other details, including all he had seen at General Simba Azubuike's compound.

"So the five million is ransom. And this Mary Ssanyu . . . She is important to you? You think Azubuike has her?"

"I hope Azubuike doesn't have her, but I think Lars may have told him, and Azubuike sent people after her in Amsterdam. If so, I have to set her free. If she is there . . . I sent her into trouble, and I have to get her free of it."

Manny crushed out the stub of his cigar and reached for another. He offered one to Cross who declined. Cross enjoyed a quality cigar, but they were a thing of relaxation to him. He could not relax, not when the thought of the woman possibly being back in Azubuike's hands was filling his mind.

Manny blew a cloud of smoke into the air, looked Cross eye to eye and asked, "So that is why you killed Lars?"

Manny knew, of course. His connections were worldwide. Lars' body had been found, but the police had no leads to the killer, certainly not to Cross. But Manny knew, having heard Cross' story; who else would have killed Lars as he had been killed? It was a murder of revenge, not of theft or disputed love. Cross was likely the only person seeking revenge. At least that was Manny's opinion.

And his assumption was proved correct when Cross confessed, "I couldn't take the chance of him contacting Azubuike," admitting to the death. "If Azubuike has the woman, that maniac may not know I sent her to Hienrich Van der Mullen in Amsterdam. If he doesn't, then I'm safe, and I can ransom the Fullsome boy, and I can get her away from him. If he does know I sent her away . . . I'm in trouble. That's why I need Helen. If Azubuike knows, and he has Mary, I want to get her away safely, and I want to live long enough to do that."

"That, Joseph my friend, is a huge task," Many said. He sat forward and put his hand on Cross' knee as a father would when giving guidance to his son. "You have not asked for my advice, but I feel I must give it in any case . . .

Go home, Joseph. Go home. You are going to get yourself killed."

"Thank you, Manny, but I can't go home. I made a promise to that damn MP Fullsome and her husband. If I get her son back, she'll leave me alone. She won't hound me and my business anymore. That will be like cash in the bank. It will take a really big burden from my shoulders. If Mary Ssanyu is back with Azubuike, I must set her free. It's my fault if she is there. So, my choices are very limited, Manny. Will you handle the money for me?"

"Of course, Joseph," Manny said, placing his fat hand on Cross' arm. "But I will not take money from you for this. I will send it where you want . . . And I will return it to Mrs. Fullsome if you are killed. I will pay Helen, but I won't take blood money from you, my friend."

Cross smiled and shook Manny's hand. In his type of life one only makes a few friends who can be trusted. Cross knew that Manny was a friend who could be trusted. Billy Volgar was loyal as well as one who could be trusted. Trust and loyalty, to Joseph Cross, were equal on the scale of morality. And they were rare commodities in his chosen life or, for that matter, in any life.

Cross spent two days and two nights at Manny's home. Time was running short. Azubuike would try to contact Lars as scheduled. Cross spent the night in sleepless worry. Manny did everything he could think of to make Cross comfortable, but for Cross there was too much food, too much wine, and too much liquor and not enough time. Manny made a few phone calls, and mid-morning of the third day Helen d'Neuville arrived.

Helen d'Neuville was the CEO and sole shareholder of Solutions Militaires Internationaux, in English: International Military Solutions, a company that provides the very best soldiers the world has to offer whenever and wherever the very best are needed. Her company provides security services to international corporations, governments, and the very, very rich. And her company also provides small armies of professional soldiers to fight small wars that seldom reach the news media. The jobs she takes are very expensive, and in many cases cash is paid, and no record of the job is kept.

Helen d'Neuville was a tall, well-built woman whose father was French and whose mother was Swedish. She inherited her Viking good looks and blond hair from her mother and her love of military life from her father, who was an officer in the French Foreign Legion. Almost all officers in the Legion are French and are the very best and toughest officers France has. The soldiers of the Legion are from every corner of the world, many running from what awaits them at home, but few will ever be an officer. Helen was born in Paris while her father was away fighting in the many conflicts of post-colonial Africa and Southeast Asia.

When she was just 21 years old, Helen led a small group of former Legionnaires, who were working as paid mercenaries wherever they could, into Rwanda to rescue her father when he and seven of his men, providing transportation security, were ambushed. When the ammunition her father's squad had with them ran out, they were taken prisoner. Helen and her mercenaries attacked the small village in the dark of night, where they were being held, killed everyone there, and rescued her father and the four men who had not been killed before Helen arrived. From that day on Helen was known as the bloodiest mercenary killer money could buy.

The black Mercedes limousine came to a stop at the end of the gravel drive of Manny's home. The driver quickly got out of the stretched limo, and a second man jumped from the passenger side of the front seat. They both held MP5 machine pistols at the ready. They scanned the area on both sides of the car before opening the rear door for Helen. She got out of the limo slowly, dramatically.

She was wearing custom made desert camouflage jodhpurs and a hip length jacket that fit her seductively, open half way down, emphasizing her breasts that were covered with nothing but the jacket. On her feet were tall combat boots, polished to a mirror shine. Around her waist was a polished black leather belt from which hung a polished black leather holster that held a Sig Sauer P226. Her head was uncovered; her long blond hair was braided, hanging left and right to below her shoulders. Her broad shoulders and masculine stance were overshadowed by her large breasts.

Helen stood tall, looking around Manny's grounds, enhancing her arrival in theatrical fashion. She walked along the slate path, one guard in front of her and one behind her, as Manny had told her to do when she arrived. Then she stopped and smiled at Cross and Manny. They were sitting under an umbrella that shaded a table on Manny's stone patio. Manny was taking up almost all of a couch, while Cross sat on a cushioned armchair. She smiled and waved at them from the flowered path that led from the front of the house around the side and to the patio.

Both of her guards were looking left and right for any possible ambush, their machine pistols at the ready, as she walked to the two men. They walked up the broad granite steps to the patio, and Cross stood as she approached. Manny tried to stand from his couch, but his bulk made it too difficult, so he just gave up and remained seated, grinning an apology.

Cross pulled a chair from the table. Helen sat and thanked Cross saying, "Oh, Joseph, mon amour. I've wanted to meet you for so many years, oui? You know I've been in love with you forever, pauvre de moi." Helen was raised speaking French, but she had learned enough English and German to communicate with the men who worked for her. She spoke English with Cross and Manny.

"Helen," Cross said as he stared at her breasts, "your reputation in everything precedes you."

"You make me blush, Joseph, no? My . . . how do you say it . . . My sexual prowess . . . It is far larger than rumors would have it. I must show you one day, no?"

The three laughed; the two guards stood nearby, not laughing, keeping their gaze moving. Manny was smoking one of his big cigars. He had a leather cigar case near him, lying on the glass table. Helen reached for it, took a cigar from it, bit off the tip, spit it away, and put the cigar to her lips. One of her guards raced forward with a lighter. Helen drew deeply, inhaling the sweet smoke, and blew a cloud of pale gray smoke skyward.

Cross and Manny were drinking more of Manny's cooling and sweet sangria from tall glasses filled with ice. Manny offered one to Helen, who leaned back in her chair, throwing out her big breasts until the buttons on her jacket threatened to explode, and said, "I adore the champagne, Manny. You have some, no?"

It took only a few minutes for one of Manny's servants to bring a silver ice bucket holding a bottle of Dom Perignon to the table. When it was opened and her crystal flute filled, Helen drank greedily, finishing three tall glasses quickly. Then she went back to her cigar. She blew smoke directly at Cross and asked, "So, my darling Joseph. If it isn't sex you want . . . And I do hope you desire for me to take you to the bed right away . . . What is it you want?"

Cross finished his glass of the fruity red wine and said, "I'm going to see Simba Azubuike. I may need you to come get me out of his jaws."

Helen laughed loudly, thinking Cross was joking with her. But his face told her he was deadly serious. The humor washed away from her quickly. She said, "Joseph, you are fou . . . What is the word? . . . Crazy, no? . . . Why go to him?"

"He's holding a young man for ransom. I promised to pay the ransom and bring him home."

"Then you are the crazy one, and you aren't the man I thought you were. You have become the legend in our world, mon ami. You are doing the good thing? For what?" She paused and stared at Cross. Then she asked as she leaned forward towards him and smiled greedily, "You are being paid the great sum, no?"

"Expenses only, I'm afraid."

She sat back in the chair, and a questioning frown filled her Nordic face. "You know that man, Azubuike . . . He will eat you for dinner, no? He will take your money and kill you and also the man you want to . . . sauvetage . . . what is the word? Rescue, no?"

"That's possible, Helen," Cross said. "That's why I need you to come get us out if that's necessary."

Helen drank two more tall flutes of the champagne while she thought and did not take her eyes from Cross' eyes. The bottle was nearly empty, but without being asked, Manny's butler brought another to the table. She asked, "Why me?"

Cross answered, "Because you're the best . . . And you won't have any compulsion about killing everyone to get the job done. I don't need prisoners, in other words. But, I may want to kill Azubuike myself. There is a situation that may call for that."

Helen thought about that, drank some more champagne, smoked the cigar, stared at Cross and then said, "It is a woman, then? Why else would the famous Joseph Cross want to kill a man? What could he have done to Joseph Cross? Vengeance? No, not . . . Revenge . . . Is that the word, no? And you are not the hired killer. You have the big man . . . Billy Volgar . . . for that. It must be a woman. It can be nothing else, no?"

"It is a woman, and if Azubuike has her, I want to kill him myself. If she isn't there, you can kill him."

She laid the flute on the table and sat forward. A very serious expression came across her face. Her voice fell to a conspiratorial whisper. "We need to talk about the money," Helen said. "How many soldats . . . soldiers . . . does this Azubuike have?"

"A few dozen, but they are paid with drugs. I've seen them. Their weapons are not maintained, and they are disorganized. I think only a few of the AK's can be fired. Most will probably blow up if the trigger is pulled. They wear rags; they are dirty and skinny. But they are still dangerous, I think. Drugged out men with guns can be very dangerous. Each of them carries a really big bolo . . . A machete. And there are some boys . . . Children . . . Who have guns. They, too, all carry some kind of big knives or machetes. I didn't see any artillery, but there may be some.

"There is one outpost on the road, about a mile from the compound. There is only one road in to his compound, and there are a few men stationed there along the road. They may be drugged. When I saw them last, they were asleep, but I can't guarantee it now. They need to be disposed of. There may be radios for communication, but I didn't see any. The villages nearby are probably all afraid of him and may report anyone on the road to save their own skins. And he has people in Europe who work for him."

"And Lars Ruscher, he worked for him? That is why you killed him, no?" she asked.

"You know that?"

"Of course I know that. Only the police don't know."

"Will they ever know?" Cross asked.

"Certainement . . . I say certainly I think . . . but not from me."

"So will you be my Plan B?" Cross asked.

"There is the many things you don't know, and that is the dangerous thing, no? I assume time is such that to gather intelligence, this is not possible. You want this to happen soon, no?" She paused, finished another flute of the champagne, crushed out her cigar on Manny's stone patio under her boot, and asked, "How do I know when you need me to come . . . when you need to be rescued? Will you shout very loud?" she laughed.

"I will need one of your people to go to Lars' home in Geneva right away. There is a short wave radio there. If three days after I get to Azubuike's compound, you haven't heard from me via the short wave radio, come get me. Don't wait, for God's sake. If I'm dead, kill everyone except an English young man named Robert Fullsome and an African woman named Mary Ssanyu. Even though my liver will upset his damn stomach, it may not kill him. If I'm dead, make sure he is dead, too."

"And how should I know if you have the success? If you are free?" she asked.

"I will use the short wave radio. Your man will be Robin One, and I will be Robin Two. If I say anything else as my call sign I will be in jeopardy. If I say . . . To wire transfer only half of what Azubuike wants . . . Then you will know I am safe. If I say to wire transfer all of it, assume I will be dead soon after saying that. Have your man contact Manny. He has the cash and knows what to do with it. Have your man at the short wave radio make some comment about the weather where he is. Say it is raining hard but he will make the transfer anyway. If I say anything at all about the weather, stay prepared but don't attack until you hear from me again. If I say nothing about the weather, attack as soon as you can."

"That is good Joseph. But I will be paid if I attack or not."

"That is understood, Helen. If I'm dead, Manny has my money, and Billy Volgar will see to it that you are paid as promised."

Helen said, "I will need the two dozen men and officers, oui? I will need the airplane, also. I have access to this, of course. I will not go in on land, oui? And I will need money, oui? Will you pay in Euros?"

"American dollars," Cross answered.

"That is good. Seven hundred thousand will be enough, oui?"

"That's a lot of money, Helen," Cross said.

"And tell me, Joseph, mon amour. How much is your life worth?"

That, of course, was a good question. Cross knew that the odds were better than even that he would not be welcomed by Azubuike. Azubuike may be crazy, but he would insist that the money be delivered before Robert Fullsome would be released, if in fact Robert Fullsome was still alive. And Azubuike could not be trusted. Once the money was delivered, both Cross and Fullsome might well be murdered, sliced up and served for dinner. And if Mary Ssanyu had been brought back to Azubuike, it meant certain death for Cross.

Understanding that, he said, "Seven hundred thousand sounds about right. Two hundred fifty thousand up front and the balance upon completion?"

"Agreed, Joseph, mon amour. Now let us deal with the terrain."

"Terrain is tough, Helen. The area is swampy for the most part. To the north is drier. That is where the only road I know of in and out is. It's really just a dirt path. It runs North and South. The road is dirt, rocky, and rough. To the west is swampy forest. To the East is less forest but still wet. To the south are shallow streams and muddy swamps. That is where Azubuike's slaves dig for diamonds. There was a guard post of sorts on the road to the north the last time I was there. It may still be there. As I said, better to eliminate that quickly. If you will parachute in to the north, that is the safest place to do it. The surrounding ground is fairly dry and grassy plains. South, East and West of the compound is too wet, too swampy. It is about a mile from the outpost to Azubuike. He won't see you drop in there. That is the safest place."

"Safe, mon amour, is always a good idea. But sometimes it is necessary to take the chance and do what seems the impossible, oui? I will use the parachute, but I will use it to be most . . . effect . . . Is that the word?"

Cross nodded, knowing Helen's reputation for doing what others would not do. "Consider," he said, "that if you do drop to the north at night, the outpost there will be an easy target. However, if you could drop to the east, into the forests and swamps, you could enter the compound absolutely unseen. There may be a clearing there, enough to land in. I don't know but you may see it from the air. If not, you'll drop into trees, and we both know how dangerous that is. Or, you could wait until the dark of night and drop right into the middle of Azubuike's little kingdom. From what I've seen there, everyone is pretty much asleep or drugged out after dark. It could be some of them are afraid to venture out into the night. The choice is yours of course, but I will need you there if what can happen to me does happen."

"I will need the maps, bien sûr . . . Of course . . . is that right, oui? Do I say it right? We will study, oui? We will find a way in, and I will save you, Joseph, do not fear. And when we are done with the study, we shall talk of sex, oui?"

"Sure thing, Helen," Cross said. He leaned back in the chair and laughed. "But first, before anything, get one of your people to Lars' short wave radio. Azubuike will call any day now about diamonds for sale. Answer when Azubuike calls. We need him to be kept in the dark."

****

Before leaving for Africa, Cross took Manny aside. The two of them sat in the shade of the big willow tree, smoking cigars and drinking Spanish wine. Cross knew he was walking into hell to confront the devil. He knew he might never get out again. There were things he had to take care of, a last will and testament of sorts. Manny was his friend and could be trusted.

He sat close to Manny and told him, "Manny, my friend, if I don't come out of this alive, and if the Fullsome boy doesn't come out alive, I need you to do two favors for me."

"You need only to ask, Joseph," Manny said. He touched Cross' shoulder gently. "But please . . . Do not do what you are going to do."

"Sorry, I have to, Manny. Please, do not send any of the money you are holding for me back to Margaret Fullsome, regardless of what she asks. Try to locate Mary Ssanyu. If she is still alive and away from Azubuike, give her one million dollars and tell her to run away again. If I'm not successful, Azubuike may try to find her."

"Of course, Joseph, but . . ."

Cross stopped him and said, "Send one million dollars to Michael Finnegan. Billy Volgar can tell you where to find him. Have my lawyers sign over all my ships to Michael. Send the rest of the money . . . Whatever is left after Paying Helen and Michael . . . To Billy Volgar. Tell him to get the lawyers to transfer ownership of The Rochester Club to Billy and his son jointly. His son is in Australia. He's a Doctor there. Don't let Billy argue with you on that. They can keep the Casino or sell it, but tell them my advice is to keep it and have Billy's son run it. There is a warehouse of black market goods and guns in the Thames warehouse district. Billy knows where that is. That should go to Michael with the boats. In the safe in my apartment is a bag of diamonds. I want them to go to Jacob Rosen. Billy knows where to find him."

"Joseph," Manny said, almost in tears. "Do you really think you will not return?"

"If Helen does her job, and if I can stay alive for three days . . . I will survive. If Azubuike knows about Mary Ssanyu . . . Well, just do what I ask of you, old friend."

"It will be done, Joseph. It will be done."

CHAPTER NINE - The First Day

Cross' Gulfstream jet landed in Kampala. It was the 29th of the month, two days before Azubuike would try to contact Lars Ruscher via the short wave radio. He would have diamonds, dug by his slaves, to sell. There would be an answer by one of Helen's men who was monitoring the radio. But would the General hear what he wanted to hear?

Azubuike would be expecting to make a deal with Lars for some diamonds. When all he heard was intentional static that Helen's man caused, and twisted words Azubuike wouldn't understand, Cross hoped he would not suspect that Lars was dead and his own end was near. He hoped Azubuike would think perhaps bad weather was interfering with the signal. Those things happen after all. Cross hoped Azubuike would wait a day or maybe two and try again. Hope was all Joseph Cross had.

The note Lars had sent to Margaret Fullsome said she would be contacted in one month's time. It would be another week or perhaps more before instructions to deliver the money were sent to her. When Cross showed up with the ransom, Azubuike would be suspicious. Why hadn't they waited as they were told to do? Why Joseph Cross? That was not what he had told Mrs. Fullsome to do. Since the man was insane, Cross believed he might take some insane measures to ease whatever paranoid fear he felt, like killing young Robert Fullsome and Cross, too. Cross had to get Robert and Mary away before that happened. Time was not to Cross' advantage.

If he could talk to Azubuike and arrange for the release of the Fullsome boy quickly, he could be back in Kampala, alive and well in a day or two. Add to that, he would need to be assured that Mary Ssanyu was safe and not in the maniac's hands. If she had been returned to him, he would have to find a way to free her. If he could not do all that within three days, if he were dead or his mission had failed, Helen d'Neuville and her small army of mercenaries would drop out of the sky, and the killing would begin. When that happened, if he were still alive, he would have to protect not only himself but Robert and Mary, also.

When he stepped down from his Gulfstream, it was raining. He was wearing a light cotton bush jacket and light weight slacks. He wished he had taken his broad brimmed hat from the plane where it waited with his camping gear.

There were three uniformed men of the Ugandan Special Police Force waiting for him. They were waiting for him inside the terminal, keeping dry, watching behind big glass windows as he ran from the jet through the rain. All were dressed in crisp and clean uniforms, tan in color, with rows of badges and ribbons across their left chests. All wore dark sunglasses and black, hi-peaked, military hats with polished brims pulled low over their eyes. Their slim waists were belted in shining black leather, and on each belt a polished black holster hung, each holding a big semi-auto pistol. The stern and fearful expressions on their faces did not change as Cross walked into the building. He shook the rain from him and tried walking past them, but they stepped in front of him, two of them grabbing hold of his arms, to stop him.

Cross had seen their kind before. They were tough, ruthless thugs who beat people senseless whenever they thought it necessary. They were from a special branch of the local police, a left over throwback to the Idi Amin era of murders, fear, and violence. The 'Ugandan Maalum Polisi Nguvu' – the Ugandan Special Police Force – were a force that had little to stop them from doing whatever they wanted to control the population. He also knew that the higher echelons were readily open to bribes.

"Mr. Cross," the one seemingly in charge said, as the other two held tightly onto Cross. He wore silver badges on his shoulders, some sort of rank that made the others subservient, Cross assumed. "Will you please to accompany myself inside?"

"Why?"

The man smiled, revealing perfectly white teeth, each rimmed in gold, but there was menace behind the smile. Cross tried to see the man's eyes but the black glasses prevented that. "It is to make the examine to your passport . . . And to speak with my Colonel."

There was no place to run to, so Cross followed the three policemen into a side door of the Kampala Airport. The door was solid metal without glass. It was locked by an electronic keypad. A simple four digit code was punched in; Cross watched and memorized the numbers in case he needed them again.

They walked slowly down a thin hallway not accessible by passengers in the airport. It was all gray concrete, dark, hot, and humid. It smelled of stale, still air, and only a few dim lights along the ceiling lit their way. They stopped near a dead-end wall, and a door to his left was opened by one of the officers. Cross was roughly pushed through the doorway.

Inside the small room, a table and two gray, metal, folding chairs almost filled the space. The room smelled of dead, sour air, along with an odor of unwashed bodies that floated aimlessly in the room. And on a wall to the left, stains of dried blood streaked the wall down to and onto the floor.

Colonel Okello Owusu sat at the table, glaring up at Cross. He wore an olive green uniform, pressed to a crisp sheen, with red and yellow braiding encircling his right shoulder. Five medals, hanging from colorful ribbons, lined the top of his left breast pocket. He wore no hat, revealing short cropped hair flecked with premature gray. His eyes were covered by very dark, black, metal rimmed sunglasses. His dark eyes could not be seen through the sunglasses. From across the table Cross could smell the cheap cologne the Colonel was famous for. He had smelled the cologne a few times before, each time he had a run-in with the Colonel.

The Colonel was one of the officials at the very top of the Ugandan Special Police Force. Even his superiors and the Country's politicians were fearful of the Colonel. He had recruited the loyalty of a few dozen of the fiercest of the officers under him. They did his bidding, no matter what that was, in exchange for the money he paid them. He and his associates had become wealthy – by Ugandan standards – by demanding taxes that did not exist and taking bribes as often as they could. And he was not exactly a friend of Joseph Cross.

"Mr. Cross," Owusu began. He stood so that Cross could see him placing his hand on the big pistol holstered at his side. He made no effort to extend his hand towards Cross. "Sit, please," he said and pointed towards one of the metal chairs, the one that had the slightly bent leg.

Cross sat in the other chair, crossed his legs, leaned back, and tried to look casual and bored. But he knew there could be trouble. He had a history with Colonel Owusu, a history of the policeman trying to catch Cross smuggling diamonds out of Uganda without paying the Colonel for that privilege.

The Colonel, as with so many other policemen around the world, had been unsuccessful in catching Joseph Cross, but he kept trying. And he was the only Ugandan Special Police Officer Cross had never been able to bribe. Owusu would take money from anyone . . . But not from Cross. He hated Cross for making a fool of him so many times over the years, smuggling diamonds right under the Colonel's nose without ever being caught.

Cross had tried to bribe the Colonel to simply leave him alone. But Owusu would never take the bribes. Instead he wanted a cut of the profit of the diamonds he knew Cross was somehow smuggling, and Cross was unwilling to do that. It had become a matter of pride with the Colonel. Cross was insulting him. Cross had eluded him for so many years, he now wanted to jail Cross more than he wanted Joe Cross' money.

Cross said nothing. He looked around the barren room; he looked behind him at the three Officers who stood against the wall on either side of the closed door, the only door out and away from the Colonel. He waited. Finally, Colonel Owusu sat and leaned back in his chair. He broke the silence.

"Why are you in my Country, Mr. Joseph Cross?" Colonel Owusu spoke in very near perfect English. One would have to listen intently to hear the slight remnants of any accent of the African language the Colonel had been raised in. Being of wealthy and influential parents from the Idi Amin era, he had been educated at a private English school in South Africa, from the earliest grades through college.

"Vacation, Colonel," Cross answered casually, with a thin smile. "Only a vacation. I'm going to go into your back country and take photos of some wild life. Lions and giraffes and things like that. Work at my casino in London has been keeping me very busy. You know . . . The Rochester Club? . . . I've told you about that haven't I? You should come and spend some time there . . . As my guest of course."

Owusu ignored the invitation. He knew inside of himself that it wasn't the casino that kept Cross busy. It was smuggling diamonds. He said, "I didn't know you are a photographer. Where is your camera?"

"In my luggage, Colonel. I'll go get it for you if you wish." He started to stand but a hand on his shoulder from one the officers behind him stopped him. Owusu pulled the pistol from its holster and laid it prominently on the table. He snapped his fingers, and the two lower ranking officers standing behind Cross turned and ran from the room. They were back in a few minutes, time spent in silence inside the small room. The Colonel and Cross played a game of who would blink first as they stared at each other. Neither lost as the door to the room opened, breaking the spell each held on the other.

The two officers carried Cross' two brown leather suitcases. They laid each on the table and opened them. Owusu stood and began rifling through them. He tossed clothes on the table and onto the floor. Cross just sat and watched, not moving or saying anything. It didn't take long for the Colonel to find the case that held Cross' Nikon camera and its two lenses.

Owusu held the camera, turned it over in his hands, looked through the view finder, and tried to find a way to open it.

"It's a digital camera, Colonel," Cross volunteered. "It doesn't open . . . No film."

"Where would one hide diamonds in it, then?"

Cross smiled and answered, "What diamonds, Colonel? I have no idea what you're talking about. As I said, the camera is to take pictures of your wonderful Country's wildlife, that's all."

Owusu said nothing for a moment or two. He took the time to light a French cigarette, elaborately pulling one from a gold cigarette case that was studded with small diamonds. He lit it with a gold cigarette lighter, the gas flame shooting up two inches tall. The Colonel was famous for many things, one of them being his use of that lighter on people he wanted information from. Cross took notice of the ring on the man's right hand, a thick gold band with a beautifully cut diamond that Cross estimated to be at least four carats, maybe five.

The Colonel let the cigarette smoke curl slowly from his mouth. He smiled again and demanded, "Your passport, Mr. Cross."

"Why?" Cross asked. "Immigration is outside, not here."

"Oh, you will not need to go there, Mr. Cross," Owusu said and smiled dangerously. "May I call you Joe, as so many others do?"

"No," Cross answered. "I think Mr. Cross will do. Formalities . . . You know, Colonel. Now, may I leave for immigration?"

"That is for the common people, the ordinary people, not the special people . . . Like you and me. I will hold your passport until you have finished your . . . Vacation was it? Photography I believe you said. It will be returned to you when you leave my Country. And at that time, you and I can look over all the magnificent pictures you will take home with you. Of course, if you have no pictures . . . You will not be returning home, will you now?"

Cross relented and reached inside his bush jacket pocket. He pulled out his blue American passport and handed it to the Colonel. Cross didn't care; it was just one of a dozen passports he had from a dozen different Countries. He could have a new one made up in a matter of hours back in London or in Paris or in Rome or in Geneva, or in a handful of other places. None of them were real after all.

"Thank you, Mr. Cross. Now you may take your bags and leave. Please enjoy your . . . Photography vacation I think you said?"

"I need to rent a car," Cross said. "And then I need to get my camping gear out of my plane. Is all that going to be OK with you, Colonel Owusu?"

"Of course," he said jovially. "These officers will help you. Good bye for now, Mr. Cross. I will look forward to seeing you again before you leave my Country."

Owusu stood, crushed out his cigarette on the floor, put his pistol back in the holster, and left the room. Cross picked up his clothes and folded them as best he could as he put them back in the suitcases. But he didn't want to spend too much time there, so his packing wasn't very neat. Most of the clothes were just stuffed back into the suitcases. Two of the police officers closed Cross' bags and lifted them from the table. They carried the bags as Cross led them down the dark hallway and back to his Gulfstream.

While a tent and other camping gear were being unloaded by the jet's pilot and co-pilot, Cross went to the terminal, followed by the two officers. He rented a Land Rover that would take the rough road to Azubuike well enough. When it was loaded with his suitcases and all the gear from the jet, he waited until the police officers were not near and spoke quietly to his pilot, "Get out of here as fast as you can. Get back to London. Don't wait for anything. Don't file a flight plan. Just go. Let Billy Volgar know where I am."

The pilot nodded and discretely handed Cross a small bundle wrapped in black cloth. The two Police Officers were standing near the Land Rover, smoking and talking in the heat of midday. The rain had stopped, and the afternoon began to bring the air and humidity quickly into the 90's. Steam was rising off the concrete of the airport. They didn't notice Cross hiding the Beretta M9 with three extra clips of 9MM ammunition from the bundle under his bush jacket.

Cross waved an overly friendly good bye to the two officers as he drove away and watched his Gulfstream jet taxi to a runway and take off for home. He saw in the rearview mirror the two officers yelling and running after the Gulfstream. Cross laughed as he realized the police assumed the jet was supposed to wait there to take Cross home. The Colonel wouldn't like that, but it was too late to stop the Gulfstream as it rose into the clouds and disappeared from view.

****

The broad, four lane, well paved and divided highway from the airport south out of Kampala soon turned into a two lane, poorly paved road that ended at the beginning of the dirt road that would take Joe Cross back to Azubuike.

The narrow, dusty road south had not changed much since the last time Joe Cross had visited General Simba Azubuike a year before. There were more potholes, and there were fewer animals grazing along the side of the road. It seemed to be drier than he remembered, dustier, maybe with less vegetation.

Two hours into the slow drive he stopped to stretch

his legs and relieve himself. There was a dark mound a hundred yards away. He walked to it and found two elephants, dead, rotting in the sun, their skin split from the heat and oozing white fat. They were covered with thousands of flies. The stench was unbearable. The elephant's ivory tusks had been hacked off by poachers to be sold illegally around the world.

Vultures were circling overhead. They were not landing to feast on the dead carcasses. That told Cross that some bigger meat eating beast might be nearby. He looked around at the tall, brown grass that was everywhere. Some of it was moving; he hoped a breeze was there but worried it might be a big cat. He quickly returned to the Land Rover and locked himself inside before he became some big animal's dinner.

As he drove on, and the Land Rover bounced along the unpaved, rutted road, all he could think about was what he might expect when he got face to face with the maniac he would have to deal with. He had a pistol with 60 rounds of ammunition, and he had a hope that Azubuike didn't know anything about what had occurred since their last meeting.

If Mary Ssanyu had successfully escaped and was living a good life in Paris, as Cross hoped she had, then he might just be able to successfully pull off the ransom of the Fullsomes' son and bring him home.

Azubuike might know how to keep people frightened of him. He might know how to keep his small army drugged enough to do what he told them to do. He might know how to keep an income flowing in from the blood diamond trade. But Azubuike wasn't smart enough to out-talk Cross. He knew that's all he had to go on. Joe Cross' ability to talk his way out of trouble, and the fact that Azubuike's greed would work against him, were Cross' only advantages, all he had to keep himself alive.

He drove for hours, moving slower than he wanted to due to the rutted, rocky road. The Land Rover bounced along, and he was tiring. The afternoon wore on; the heat was oppressive. Leaving the car's windows rolled down did little but let the heavy air move around inside and around him. He made two more stops along the road, spending no more time in the heat and sun than was necessary, in order to stretch the soreness from his legs and back, and to relieve himself. He drank water freely from one of the four thermos jugs he had brought with him. He thought he might eat something, but worry kept him from having any appetite at all.

The Big African sun began to sink towards the horizon, and the air began to cool slightly. The night hours, he knew from experience, could be cold and dangerous. Animals hunted at night. He didn't want to be the one who was hunted. He put more pressure on the gas pedal and tried to ignore the rocks and potholes in order to get to Azubuike before total darkness.

After kicking up clouds of dust and bouncing along the unpaved road for what seemed to him to be forever, Cross came upon the outpost Azubuike had established a mile from his village. Cross knew it was about twenty minutes outside of the compound by foot and only a few minutes by car. He slowed the Land Rover as he got closer to the little, round, straw-thatch roofed hut with its thin walls of dry sticks and mud. The thatch was brown and old and only thinly covered the little hovel, most of the fronds having fallen off or blown off. Brown grass and dry, red dirt lay all around what was supposed to be a guard post.

Three of Azubuike's men were there; two were asleep at the side of the hut, stretched out prone in the dirt, avoiding the late afternoon sun in the little shade provided by the thatch covered hut. The third was sitting on his haunches smoking a long, fat . . . something . . . rolled in a piece of paper. 'Probably ganja,' Cross thought. There was a dusty and old AK-47 and an even older British Enfield rifle lying in the dirt in front of the hut. Standing against the wall of the hut were two long, fierce looking spears.

He slowed the Land Rover to as slow as it would go without stopping. Neither of the two sleeping men woke, and the man smoking had his eyes closed as he was wrapped in the smoke of the strong drug. He drove past them, sped up a little, and then drove as fast as the rutted dirt path would allow. None of the three 'guards' stood. They were useless, he thought, and would not cause Helen any trouble if she chose to parachute in north of the compound and approach down the dirt road.

He thought again, as he drove, that the area of the hut would be a good place to parachute into. The ground was dry and hard. Too far east or west, and certainly south, the ground soon turned marshy and swampy and often thickly treed. If Helen dropped from the sky there, the guards would be quickly and quietly dispatched. They would not be a problem for her and her men. Chances are that the guards, deep in drugged euphoria, would not even notice the parachutes landing all around them.

But then she would have a mile, twenty minutes by foot at the most, less at a 'double time' pace, to travel to get to the village. Cross didn't know if Helen would attack from there. They had spent days studying maps and discussing options, but Helen would not discuss her plans with Cross. She said if he were captured by Azubuike he might be forced to tell him how Helen would enter the compound. She was right of course. Not knowing was the best way he could ensure that Helen would come to his aid if he needed her. He would leave that up to her, knowing she was the best at her trade.

Shortly, on the horizon, Cross saw the tattered shacks of Azubuike's compound. Wisps of smoke from open fires twisted up to the darkening sky. The faint glow of the fires could be seen in the darkening night.

As he had remembered, the compound was surrounded by cut acacia thorn bushes that encircled the encampment. They were piled six to eight feet tall, and four to five feet thick. It was certainly enough to keep animals out. The thorn bushes would make a very good defense and would be difficult for people to breach. The wall of thorns was left open where the dirt road met it, an entrance passage into Azubuike's compound. If Helen came in, it would have to be through that breach, rather than through the acacia wall. Or, she might, he thought, just drop right into the compound in the dark of night. He laughed and thought, 'That would be just like her. Do what no one else would think of doing.'

As he got closer, there was an acrid stink filling the air. A low cloud of thick black, oily smoke hung heavily over the huts in the still air. Cross drove into the compound and came to an abrupt stop. In the middle of the compound, where he had seen the steel pole standing upright the last time he was there, were the burnt remains of a human being, chained to the steel pole. Whiffs of stinking smoke rose from what remained of the body.

Cross climbed slowly out of the Land Rover. He felt his stomach turn, and he retched at the side of the car. He had seen a lot of death in his lifetime, deaths from wars and murders, but nothing of the sort that passed for amusement for Azubuike. The man had to die when this was all over, Cross promised himself. Getting Robert Fullsome out and being assured of Mary Ssanyu's safety would not be enough. He could not walk away and leave that man to his disgusting pleasures.

A dozen of Azubuike's 'soldiers' came running towards him. They were dressed in what best could be called rags, the remains of shorts and pants. Some wore torn and dirty shirts, others were bare-chested. Most were bare footed; some wore sandals made of twisted palm fronds. They were all screaming at once, waving their old rifles and machetes in the air. One of them stumbled and fell to the ground; his old British Enfield rifle hit the ground and fired, and another of the men fell with a bullet in the back. The others seemed not to care or even notice that one of their compatriots was dead.

Cross was quickly surrounded by the ragged, skinny men. Fists and rifle butts pummeled him to the ground. Lying there, in the red dirt, Cross rolled into a ball trying as best he could to protect his head and balls. Unconsciousness engulfed him finally.

He awoke lying on the polished wood floor of Azubuike's big hut. His clothes had been stripped from him, leaving him naked. He was bleeding and bruised; he took a deep breath and choked on a nose and mouth full of blood. The room was spinning around inside his throbbing head. He was on his stomach and tried to push himself to his feet. Someone said something in guttural Swahili. Then Cross was kicked in the stomach. He cried out in pain and rolled away.

Someone spoke again, and a bucket of muddy water was emptied on Cross' head. He gagged and spit bitter water and blood. Two men then pulled him to his feet and dragged him across the floor, leaving a trail of blood behind them. They let go of him, and he fell to his hands and knees. He fought to keep from collapsing to the floor. The pain he felt was intense and coming from every part of his body. But he pushed it aside and straightened his back as he knelt.

When he could, he wiped the water and blood from his eyes and looked up. Azubuike was sitting in a tall backed chair on the raised platform. The chair had been painted a bright red. It was not the same chair Cross had seen him sit on during his last visit to Azubuike. It was bigger, taller, and wider to accommodate Azubuike's massive bulk. He had built himself a gigantic throne to hold his bulk and to rule his little fiefdom from.

It was more elaborately carved than his previous chair. Carved palm trees rose along the sides of the throne. Delicately carved animals filled the throne's back that rose three feet above Azubuike's head. The arms of the throne were carved snakes, covered in gold leaf. Every other part of the throne had been painted a bright red. It was beautiful, but it was a crazy dictator's chair.

The floor of the platform it stood on had been painted red to match the throne. The zebra skin of the last throne Cross had seen had been replaced by the skin of a male lion, its head resting on the floor and used as a foot stool by the General. Animal skins, zebras, antelope, leopards, and crocodiles, lay everywhere on the platform around Azubuike.

The General was wearing a bright yellow uniform of sorts, roughly tailored and ill-fitting, that was covered in medals and ribbons. He had a cape draped across his shoulders. It was so long that as he sat it fell to his ankles. It was bright blue, and the collar was fashioned from the mane of a lion.

Cross wiped his eyes again, and his vision slowly returned. Azubuike was fatter than Cross remembered. So fat that he barely fit in his new throne. His eyes were wide and gleaming, bulging from their sockets. He was leaning forward, smiling broadly, and obviously enjoying seeing Joe Cross on the floor, bleeding and in pain. His fat, red lips were covered with foamy spittle as he smiled down at Cross.

The man, Cross recognized, was even crazier than Cross remembered. The past year had done nothing good for the man.

He was laughing in a demented cackle, pounding his fist on the broad arm of his chair, and he was rocking back and forth. While Azubuike was laughing uncontrollably, Cross looked around the big room. There were five of Azubuike's soldiers in the room and two more standing on either side of Azubuike. And to Cross' right, kneeling on the floor below the platform, head bowed, and chained at the neck, waste, and ankles was Mary Ssanyu.

Mary, like Cross, was naked. Her head had been roughly shaved, leaving her bald and bleeding in spots. The chain around her neck was attached to the chain around her waist and was not long enough to allow her to hold her head upright. The chains at her ankles, likewise, were attached to the chains at her waist and not long enough to allow her to stand. Her hands were bound with leather straps behind her back, leather that was wet when her hands had been tied and now was shrinking, cutting into her wrists. She was bent, her eyes were swollen shut from beatings, and her body was bruised and bleeding.

Azubuike managed to stop his raucous laughter. He struggled to push himself from his throne, falling back into it twice before being able to stand. The guard on his left reached out a hand as Azubuike came close to falling. The General stopped laughing and glared at the man who backed away quickly. The General took hold of a stick that had been fashioned into a cane, except that this cane had mean looking thorns running down it to the floor. An ivory handle had been fastened to the cane; Azubuike's fat hands covered it, holding tightly to it.

Azubuike stepped gingerly off of the platform, down the three steps, and across the floor to stand in front of

Cross, who remained on his knees. The General's long cloaked dragged behind him.

"So, my friend Joseph," Azubuike said. "You have come to visit me . . . Perhaps for a cup of tea?" He laughed again, loudly, cackling like the maniac he was. Spittle dripped from his fat lips.

"No!" he shouted. "You Americans drink coffee, don't you?" He laughed uproariously again. Cross looked around the room at Azubuike's men. They were not laughing; in fact the two who had been at the sides of Azubuike's chair remained there staring down at Cross. They were the only guards in the big room who did not appear to be drowsing in a drug induced stupor. They seemed well fed and strong, well dressed in clean military fatigues, and they held tightly onto clean and well cared for AK-47s.

Azubuike walked, struggling with his cane and his extreme weight to get back up the steps onto his platform. It was apparent that no one dared help him or touch him. Azubuike had bought his power, with drugs, with money and with women. But Cross knew that purchased-loyalty lasted only so long as the price was paid. That was the weapon Cross knew he had to use. Take away Azubuike's purchase power, and he will not be a king who no one can touch.

Azubuike fell into his throne and with some effort raised his fat legs enough to rest his feet on the lion's head. He was breathing hard from the effort of returning to the big chair. He coughed and spit thick phlegm onto the floor in front of him.

"You are a strange man, my friend Joseph," he wheezed and spat again. "You must have no fear. But you must fear of god, Joseph. Do not you fear of god?"

"If there is a God in heaven . . . I respect him. I am aware of his laws, even though I don't always obey them.

But do I fear God? I don't believe God is to be feared."

Azubuike raised his hand, and one of his drugged out soldiers standing near Cross slammed the butt of his rifle onto Cross' back, between his shoulders. Cross yelled in pain and fell forward.

"You must learn to fear god, my friend, Joseph . . . *BECAUSE I AM GOD!*" he shouted in a maniacal, high pitched scream, pounding his fist on the arms of his throne.

Cross pushed himself up to his knees. He moved and twisted his shoulders feeling for broken bones. The pain was terrific but he could move, and that told him nothing had been broken. He looked up at Azubuike and said, "I knew you had been given the heart of your god, General . . ."

Another of the soldiers quickly hit Cross in his stomach with the butt of his rifle, buckling Cross over. Azubuike leaned forward and tried, unsuccessfully, to stand. He screamed in a booming and threatening voice, "I am not a General! *I AM GOD! I AM THE KING OF ALL GODS! YOU WILL ADDRESS ME AS GOD!*" He sat back and breathed deeply after the exertion of screaming in a high pitched voice that signaled insanity. He said in a calmer voice, "Or maybe you can address me as king since you are who you are, my friend Joseph. You have my permission to call me king."

"Alright . . . king . . . Why are you kicking the crap out of me?"

"Why are you here, my friend Joseph?"

"To arrange the ransom of Robert Fullsome."

Azubuike laughed again, slapping his hand on one of his fat knees. "You are joking, my friend Joseph! You are telling me a good joke!"

"I was asked to arrange for payment of the five million

dollars, king. It's not a joke."

Azubuike pushed himself from his throne once again. He stood on unsteady fat legs, holding tight to his cane. He said, "You do not have money with you, my friend Joseph. You brought a gun but nothing else."

"The money will be wire transferred to wherever you want it. I take the Fullsome boy, and you get the money. No tricks."

"Oh, my friend Joseph. No tricks you say? You are to be trusted, you say. You are honest, you say. That is so good, my friend Joseph," he laughed. "But I have a question. Do you know this woman?" Azubuike asked, pointing a fat finger at Mary Ssanyu, on her knees at the side of the room, kneeling below the platform, and chained painfully.

Cross looked across the room at Mary, chained and bent. She had been beaten badly; she was cut and bruised over her entire body. How long had she been there? Cross could only imagine. A year must have been a year in hell. But she was alive, and being alive meant Cross might still be able to save her and get her away from the mad Azubuike.

She turned her head to the left slightly. Her eyes, swollen almost shut, made an effort to open. She could barely focus, but she knew it must be Cross. No other white man would be there. In a barely visible motion she shook her head and then lowered her head once again.

He got the message. If he were to get Robert Fullsome and himself out of there alive . . . And somehow rescue Mary . . . He had to deny knowing her.

He said, "She looks familiar . . . But I don't think I know her."

Azubuike exploded in laughter again. He fell back

hard onto his throne, almost tipping it backwards. When he stopped he said, "Oh, my friend Joseph. This is the woman I sent with you when you were to buy my diamonds. This was my wife, Mary Ssanyu. Now do you remember?"

"I might recognize her if she weren't chained and if she hadn't been tortured."

Azubuike laughed again. He said, wiping a tear of laughter from his eye, "Do you remember telling her to run away? Do you remember telling her to sell my diamonds and run away?"

"Why would I do that?" Cross answered, hoping to outtalk this crazy person.

"Do you love her, my friend Joseph?"

"Of course not . . . I don't even know her."

Azubuike raised a fat arm and waived to one of his ragged, drugged soldiers, speaking in an African dialect Cross had never heard before. The man dropped his AK-47 heavily onto the floor and walked to Mary. He stood behind the kneeling woman, pulled his ragged shorts down to his knees, bent and entered the woman roughly. Mary screamed, but the chains kept her from escaping the man. She screamed in pain once again, and then the man stood, pulled up his torn shorts and walked away.

Azubuike looked directly at Cross while the rape was happening, grinning an insane grin, enjoying the torture that brought him so much pleasure. Cross watched the rape but in spite of what he wanted to do, he did nothing, he said nothing, and let no expression cross his face to betray the disgust and anger he was feeling.

"So, my friend Joseph," Azubuike said in a near whisper. "What do you think of that?"

Cross remained kneeling and turned his head slowly

away from Mary and glared at Azubuike. He took a deep breath to regain some small bit of calm. He said in a muted voice, "I think it's disgusting and savage . . . But she means nothing to me. Why would she?"

Azubuike laughed again and said, "So my friend Joseph. I will give you some time to think about this, and then perhaps you will tell me the truth."

Cross started to say something, to say anything that would keep Azubuike talking, because Cross was confident he could talk his way out of this. But before he could say a word, a rifle butt connected with the back of his head, and a sea of black unconsciousness washed over him.

CHAPTER TEN - The Second Day

It was the dark of night when Cross awoke. He was inside a hut of some kind. He was next to a wall of thin poles that let the cold night air in. He was lying on the wet, muddy, red-dirt floor of whatever hut he was in.

The smell inside the hut was that of urine, defecation, and death. It hung heavily in the stagnant air, and Cross found it difficult to breathe because of it. His stomach turned, but he fought back the urge to vomit.

He heard someone uttering a low moan, filled with pain. He tried to move, to push himself to his feet, but his hand slipped in the filthy slick mud, and he fell back. The slight movement caused pain on his right ankle. He could see nothing but shadows in the pitch black of the hut. His hand went to his ankle and felt the chain. A rough shackle was wrapped at his ankle. He pulled it and found, without being able to see, that the length of chain was fettered to someone lying next to him.

As his eyes became used to the dark, he started to see the shadows of the forms of other people lying as he was, in the mud. Someone was crying softly; someone was coughing; the moaning started again. There were a few whispered words in a language Cross again didn't understand. He lay back in the mud. Even thinking about sleep was useless. His mind was filled with thoughts of escape and the many ways he could kill Azubuike.

The sun rose slowly, and little by little some light found its way through the thin sticks of the wall of the hut. The bitter cold African night was beginning to warm. That morning warmth was causing the stench of the filthy hut to get worse.

Cross pushed himself up on his elbows and looked around; it was a long hut, thin but long. There were a number of people lying in the mud, all seemingly chained together. Cross sat up and put his hand to his ankle. A thick, rusty iron ring circled the ankle, a heavy chain attached to it, a keyed padlock fastening it closed. Then he heard a voice.

"You're white," the voice whispered.

"What?" Cross said loudly.

"Quiet! Don't talk loud! You're white. Who are you?"

Cross looked down the line of chained people. Halfway down, a young white man was sitting up. At least Cross thought the man was white. He was covered with dirt and mud, but under the filth, Cross could recognize another white man.

"I'm Joseph Cross," he answered in a whisper. "Are you Robert Fullsome?"

"How do you know me?"

"I came to pay your ransom."

"Well, you're not doing a very good job at that now, are you?" the young man said, snickering, and he lay back in the muddy filth.

"What's happening here?" Cross asked. He turned to lean on one elbow, trying as best as he could to not move the chain so as to not cause the slave lying next to him any pain.

Robert sat up again, leaning on one elbow also. He looked at Cross and said, "You don't know? We're their slaves. We dig for their diamonds."

The young man lay back in the mud once again. Cross tried to stand, but the chain was heavy, and the person at the other end of the chain cried out in pain as Cross pulled on the chain. It was a woman chained to him who had cried out. In the early morning light Cross recognized that he was naked, as was the woman and everyone else in the mud hut. They were covered in mud and filth. Most were mere skeletons, mud covered skin over bones.

Cross stood and moved closer to the woman so as not to move the chain. There was enough light to see that the woman's ankle was covered in blood and the filth of the hut's floor. Robert Fullsome called out in a whisper, "You better sit down. They don't like us to stand before they tell us to."

Cross lowered himself and sat in the muddy filth. He pulled his knees up as far as the chain would allow and hugged them against the still early morning cold.

He said in a soft, whispered voice, "You said these people dig diamonds?"

"Yes," Fullsome answered.

"Why hasn't anyone done anything about this? Why hasn't someone come here for you?"

"Shit, you're here, aren't you now? So bloody well do something."

And Cross knew he was going to do something. When Helen got there he would free these people . . . He would free Mary Ssanyu . . . And he would kill Azubuike. All he had to do was stay alive until Helen arrived. Two more days, he would have to wait two more days. He would keep his mouth shut and do as he was told, and hopefully he would be alive when Helen arrived and started the killing.

The sun was above the horizon and shown through the thin weave of the walls of the long hut. A door of roughly cut wooden plants that hung on leather hinges was opened, and a man, one of Azubuike's drugged soldiers, bent low in the opening, silhouetted in the open doorway. He said something, and the chained people groaned, pushing themselves to their feet. One by one, from Cross' left, the 'chain gang' walked out of the hut, bending low not for the doorway but from the endless days of pain and work in the African sun.

Cross, at the end of the line of chained slaves, was the last to leave the hut. He shaded his eyes from the bright light and called ahead of him to Robert Fullsome, "What's happening . . .?" One of Azubuike's men ran to him and hit him with a club hard across his shoulders and back. Cross started to fall to the ground but stopped himself. He arched his back once again to find if bones had been broken. It was painful, but he could move his arms. Nothing was broken. The hit he took, he realized, wasn't as hard as it could have been.

"No talk you!" the man who had hit him shouted in accented English. Cross turned as he walked and looked at the man. He was young, not more than a teenager. He was short, not fully grown, and he wasn't skinny as the other soldiers were. His clothes were dirty, but they weren't yet in rags. And he was forcing an angry, actor's stage-like scowl on his face. It was certainly a forced anger; the young man wasn't a very good actor. Cross sensed more fear than anger in the young man. He would keep his eyes on that boy. He might be of some help.

There were fourteen people chained at the ankles in

front of Cross, all naked and covered in mud and filth. Three of them were women including the woman chained in front of Cross. He looked ahead and found Robert Fullsome, chained five people in front of him. He was covered in red mud and filth from the hut, but his long, shaggy blond hair, as filthy as it was, told Cross he was not African.

The young guard had three others with him. Those three were from the ranks of Azubuike's soldiers paid with drugs. They stumbled as they walked, and they dragged their ill kept rifles along behind them in the dirt, leaving scraped trails in the mud.

The line of slaves walked slowly, dragging the long chain across the ground, for what Cross thought must have been half an hour. The line of Azubuike's slaves stopped at the edge of a ditch that was more than eight feet deep. Inside the ditch was a pool of water; a slowly moving stream of red, muddy water filtered through the shallow pool. There were woven baskets, wide and flat, lying on the side of the ditch. One by one each of the chained slaves crawled down into the ditch, each taking one of the baskets, and each began clawing at the red mud, some kneeling and some bending.

They scratched mud from the bottom of the ditch, putting handfuls of the stuff in a basket and washing it through the water they were standing in. Cross watched and found that they washed the dirt through the weaves leaving stones and pebbles behind in the baskets. They would then examine each stone to find diamonds. When none were there, they started the process all over again.

Cross followed the woman chained to him into the ditch. He held the chain so it would not do more damage to her ankle and tried to help the woman down the slick muddy walls of the ditch. He stood, looking at the others as they clawed with their fingers in the dirt. The soldier who had clubbed Cross stood at the edge of the ditch over Cross. He pointed to a basket and knelt down on the ground at the edge of the ditch. He said, "You dig now."

"Dig for what?"

"You dig now," the young soldier said. "Find diamond for god."

"That's what these people do?" Cross asked as he looked down the line of pitiful people. They were covered in red mud, and they splashed more of it over their heads and onto their shoulders.

The young soldier saw what he was looking at. In a low voice he said, "Sun," looking up to the sky. "Hot . . . Burn."

Cross understood. The red mud was all that was going to protect him from the burning African sun. He reached down and grabbed handfuls of the sticky mud and spread it over his shoulders and arms. He let it run down his back. The young soldier smiled and pointed at his head. He wore an old, sweat stained, grass-woven hat with a wide brim to keep the sun off of his head and shoulders. Cross had nothing on his head. He understood once again and spread a thick coating of mud on his head.

Another soldier, older and meaner looking, approached, staggering and dreamy eyed but looking angry all the same. The young soldier who had helped Cross jumped to his feet and began yelling at Cross in Swahili, waiving his club in the air. Cross knelt in the mud and began digging, filling the woven tray with mud and slowly washing it in the muddy water he stood in.

The heat of the morning increased as if the thermostat on an oven had been turned up. Down the chain line, to Cross's left, a man, chained next to Robert Fullsome, collapsed, face down, into the red mud. Two soldiers ran to the edge of the ditch above the person lying bent in the dirt. They screamed and kicked dirt and stones down on top of the man. Robert touched the man at his neck and at his wrist. He looked up at the two soldiers and said in Swahili, "Yeye ni wafu. He's dead."

The older of the soldiers took a key from his pocket and tossed it down to Robert. Robert caught it and unlocked the padlock at the dead man's ankle. The two soldiers raised their rifles and pointed them down at Robert, a message that he should not try to escape while the shackles were loose. Robert quickly removed the locked shackle from his own leg, the chain from it fastened to the shackle he had removed from the dead man, and fastened the chain from the dead man to himself, connecting him to the slave next to the dead man. The chain gang was once again locked together.

When the body was free of the chain, the younger of the two soldiers laid his rifle on the ground and jumped down into the ditch. He roughly grabbed the key from Robert and pushed him down into the mud. He picked up the loose chain, and then he took hold of the dead body by the ankles and dragged it up the side of the ditch, slipping and sliding as he crawled up. The older soldier bent and took the body at one ankle, helping to drag it up out of the ditch.

The two of them then dragged it a few feet from the ditch and left it there to bake in the sun. The chain gang returned to its work. Cross wondered if the body would be left there for scavengers to dine on.

He watched and noticed that the young man who had told him to cover himself with mud was standing by, watching, separate from the three drugged men. His face told Cross the boy was disgusted with what he saw.

Time had no meaning for Cross that day as he bloodied his fingers digging for Azubuike's diamonds. The heat was unbearable and beat down on Cross. His head throbbed, and he knew he was in trouble when he realized he wasn't sweating anymore. Heat stroke was close. From above someone was shouting. The chain gang stopped digging and fell to the dirt, sitting.

The young soldier who had tried to help Cross lowered a wooden bucket on a frayed rope. The slaves grabbed for it and fought over the dirty water. They pulled at the chains as all eleven raced for the single bucket. Robert Fullsome stood aside, and Cross stood watching in disgust.

Cross let the chains pull him with the others, but rather than fight for the water he sat down in the mud and watched. One wooden bucket for thirteen slaves. He looked across the line of slaves and saw Robert Fullsome. He was standing and looking down at the poor people struggling for a mouthful of water. Cross got to his feet and managed to stand close to Fullsome. He took the chance and spoke in a low voice, "Why aren't you drinking?"

Fullsome raised his arm and put a finger to his lips telling Cross to be quiet. The young soldier, standing at the edge of the ditch, looked at his fellow soldiers who were having a good time watching the chained slaves fight over the water. He turned to Cross and he, too, put a finger to his lips to tell Cross to be quiet.

The line of chained slaves was huddled together, fighting over the water in the wooden bucket. Robert and Cross were able to stand near to each other as they watched the poor creatures in the mud hoping to get a mouthful of water. The other soldiers grew tired of laughing at the slaves. They slowly walked away and sat in a circle, smoking whatever drug they had wrapped in scraps of paper.

The young soldier edged his way to the side of the ditch. He motioned toward Cross and Fullsome. Fullsome smiled and managed to move closer to Cross. He elbowed him. While the others were busy with their drugs, the young soldier tossed a small flask down at Fullsome. He caught it and turned his back to the other slaves.

He drank half the water in the flask and handed it to Cross who drained all the water from it. Fullsome quickly tossed the flask back to the young man, unseen by the other soldiers. He and Cross edged away from each other again. When the wooden bucket was dry, it was pulled from the ditch by the young man. He called to the other guards who reluctantly stood and walked back to the ditch. The line of slaves returned to their knees to dig into the red mud.

Time drifted by in the heat of the African afternoon. Then the man chained next to Robert yelled and stood. He waived a hand above his head and almost danced with joy. One of the soldiers knelt down, and the man threw the raw diamond up to the soldier. As the soldiers looked at it and talked all at the same time, Cross took the chance of whispering to Robert, "What's happening?"

Robert held a muddy hand to his mouth and whispered back, "If you find a diamond . . . You get food."

"And if you don't?" Cross asked.

"Then you don't eat."

The hot African sun was setting on the horizon at Cross' right. He took note of the direction . . . West . . . Knowing that would be important. In any battle, if you didn't know where you were, you would certainly die.

In the endless hours of the hot afternoon, several other slaves found diamonds, and they knew they would be given food that day. The bone thin woman chained next to

Cross began to cry, softly at first then in heavy sobs. Cross knew. She had not found a diamond again that day, and again she would not eat gain that day. She was clawing desperately in the mud with bloody hands. Cross figured she might not make it through the night.

He continued to dig slowly through the red mud, not really caring because he knew that rescue would be there shortly. He could do without food for a few days. And if he could get water from the young man, he would be able to survive. Then his hands loosened what anyone else would have tossed aside as a worthless stone encasing some crystal. But Cross knew it was a diamond.

He touched the crying woman's shoulder gently, softly. She turned her tear drenched face to him, her eyes blank with pain and suffering. He held the small diamond out to her. She looked at it in his hand, looked up at him, and then back at the stone. She was questioning without words. Cross gestured for her to take the diamond. She spoke in a language Cross could not recognize.

The young soldier who had given Cross and Robert the water said, "She say she too weak for sex." He forced a laugh.

Cross, kneeling in the mud, looked up at the man. He had a rusting AK-47 rifle slung across his shoulder and the mean looking club strapped to a piece of rope that passed for a belt. He was smiling.

Cross said, "You speak English very well."

The soldier said nothing.

"Tell her she can have the diamond . . . So she can have food today . . . I want nothing from her."

He spoke to the woman, and she looked at Cross, wondering if this were just some trick, some punishment for some unknown crime. Slowly she raised her hand that was merely bones covered with rough, bleeding skin, and held it out.   Cross dropped the diamond into her palm, and she closed her fingers around it. She smiled at Cross. And then she pushed herself to her feet and called out, holding the stone out, above her head proudly.

CHAPTER ELEVEN - The Last Afternoon

The afternoon wore on, sliding slowly into dusk, with the African heat beating down on the backs of the slaves, as they dug in the red mud. Cross knelt in the mud, making a show of digging but not with the effort of the others chained alongside of him. He glanced to his left and saw Robert Fullsome digging with still some strength left after his weeks of captivity. It was obvious the young man was beginning to waste away; his skin was beginning to hang loose on his arms. His ribs were showing, and his legs were getting near to bone thin. But he dug slowly, without stopping. He had not found a diamond yet that day. He knew the day was coming to an end, and he had resigned himself to another night of painful hunger.

A man at the middle of the chain stood and yelled, weakly, but he yelled, holding a raw diamond above his head. He, too, would eat that night. Then another man did the same. Robert, on his knees in the mud, had stopped digging. He was holding something in his hand. Then he stood, holding his diamond above his head. The others were crying, desperately digging in the mud, but they knew the day's work was almost done, and they had found nothing. That meant that a few of them would probably not be alive when the sun rose.

They were working south of the compound, in muddy swamps. Mosquitos and flies flew in thick clouds throughout the ditch they dug in, but as Cross quickly learned, the red mud the slaves covered themselves with was a means of keeping the biting insects off their bodies.

The sun had finally begun to set, and the air was beginning to cool off, thanks to a breeze coming out of the east. Cross took note once again of the direction of the setting sun, remembering the direction of the rising sun, and now knowing what was north and what was south. Important information when fighting the war to come.

The horizon to the east darkened with black clouds that were forming miles away over the flat, swampy landscape, foretelling a storm in the night. It would be cold in the slaves' hut, colder still when they had to lie in the wet and filthy mud.

The guards at the top of the trench started yelling and waiving. The slaves pushed themselves to their feet. The work day was over. They dropped their woven baskets onto the side of the ditch and began to struggle up the slick mud walls, clawing to pull themselves to the top eight or nine feet above. Several who slid back down the hill from weakness dragged others with them along with cries of pain. Cross grabbed the thin arm of the woman chained next to him and stopped her from sliding back into the deep ditch. He held the chain at her ankle to keep it from ripping at her inflamed skin. She looked up at him and tried to smile in thanks. He helped her and the next two slaves, up the hill. The guards at the top of the ditch were laughing at the good sport below.

When the chained slaves were all up, out of the ditch, they lined up, heads hung in despair. The line was one less than had come to the ditch that morning, the dead man's body lay where it had been dumped. The slaves were facing the compound so far away from them. Before they were marched back to the stinking hut where they would sleep and perhaps die, two of the soldiers unlocked Cross' ankle chain and pushed him away from the line of slaves.

Cross was led away, punched and pummeled by the two guards who took him from the slaves. He was clubbed and shoved all the long way back to the center of the compound, as the line of chained slaves struggled to walk to their miserable hut.

He said nothing when he was hit and made little defense. They seemed to take pleasure in punching him from behind, hitting him with the butts of their rifles and with the clubs they carried, but the hits weren't as heavy as they had been the day before. He stumbled once, tripping over some stones, but managed to keep himself from falling to the ground. He was clubbed across his shoulders for it but not hard enough to do damage, only to hurt.

His head was spinning from the day in the blazing sun and from lack of food and water. But he would manage, he would push the pain aside, until, at least, Helen arrived.

Revenge would come, he thought, as he patiently endured what they found so much fun in. In a day or two, all these men would be dead. He pulled himself upright, stretched, and continued towards the big thatched roofed building that was Azubuike's self-proclaimed palace.

The young man who had given him water was not with these guards. He had been with the two who had walked the slaves back to their hut. Cross wondered as he walked, just who that boy was. Why was he being kind to Robert? What was his motive?

Inside, he found Azubuike's great bulk filling the tall red throne on the bright red, raised platform. He wore the same, bright yellow uniform he had the day before but without the cloak. There were stains of dried blood down the front of his shirt. His fat feet, without shoes, rested on the lion's head on the floor. He was asleep, slouched down on his throne, his huge belly puffed out as he snored and farted loudly. The man was disgusting, Cross thought, but he certainly knew what it took to keep his demented little kingdom going. Drugs, slaves, women, and money from blood diamonds.

Two guards, not the same two as the day before, stood sentry on either side of Azubuike, each holding old, but clean looking, British Enfield rifles. And each had a shiny machete hanging in a scabbard from the military web belt each had around his waist. Again, these did not appear to be the drugged out 'soldiers' Cross saw everywhere outside. They were not thin, not bone thin as everyone else was. They were fed better than the other 'soldiers' Cross had seen. And their clothing was not rags. They wore tan fatigues that were clean and not ragged. Their tall combat boots were clean and polished.

Cross had been taking note of Azubuike's "army." There were perhaps three dozen of the drugged soldiers; none were well-armed save for the clubs and machetes each carried. The newest and best of their guns were the old, well used AK-47s, and there was a variety of other rifles, from old Enfield's to bolt operated hunting rifles. None were being well maintained.

There were perhaps eight or ten boys, children really, who wandered around aimlessly, carrying weapons that might explode if they ever tried to fire them. These boy soldiers would not be a problem for Helen and her men. But Cross didn't want them killed unless they put up a dangerous fight. He had plans for the people living under Azubuike's thumb. And he hoped that somehow these boy soldiers could be rehabilitated.

And then there were Azubuike's personal guards. Azubuike had a cadre of men who seemed to be his guards. These could be dangerous men, not drugged out, wasted men with useless weapons. He wished there were a way to warn Helen of these men.

Their weapons were newer, cleaner. And if they were drugged, they didn't show it. They may have some professional background; at least they looked as if they did. Cross thought they were being paid with something other than drugs. Money certainly, maybe women, and certainly better food than everyone else was getting. How many of them were there? How many more did Azubuike have? He had seen two the day before and now another two. Cross had to find out. And he had to know where they were housed.

The few drugged out criminal amateurs whom Azubuike referred to as 'his army' would not be a match for Helen's professional soldiers. But numbers count in battle, Cross knew. A couple dozen armed men, regardless of how well they were armed, might be able to kill a few of Helen's men, but not all of them.

These people could easily spread fear in remote areas for Azubuike. They might not use guns; they might hack people to death with their machetes or beat them to death with clubs. People from small, remote villages would have little chance of defending themselves against a surprise attack by these drugged men who probably didn't know what they were doing.

But Cross was certain they would be no competition for Helen d'Neuville and her mercenaries. Azubuike's personal guards might be another thing. If they could fight, they would fight. If there were just a handful, Helen could handle that. More might be a problem. Somehow he had to find out how many of them were protecting Azubuike.

Azubuike had to be bribing various government officials to leave him alone. Money and a handful of diamonds would be enough to allow Azubuike to rain terror down on the locals in such a remote area where government seldom showed itself anyway.   Those people would have to be dealt with also, after he killed Azubuike. They could not be allowed to appoint some other petty thug to keep the blood diamonds coming in to them.

Cross thought about all of this as he stood in the middle of the big hut, the three guards behind him. They were quiet and still as they watched Azubuike snore in deep sleep, slouched on his throne, his huge stomach bulging out of his yellow shirt.   Minutes passed as Cross shifted from foot to foot, waiting silently but still impatient.   He had nothing but contempt for this petty brute and warlord.   In his mind he kept going over that day when he had bought the diamonds from Steven and started him on his way to becoming the disgusting tyrant he was. But he had to wait . . . Wait until the dark of night the third day when rescue and killing would come.

Azubuike snored, and snorted and farted loudly. But it did manage to wake him. He pushed himself upright on his throne, rubbed the sleep from his eyes, farted again and finally focused his sleep hooded eyes on Cross. He tried to push himself up from his sprawl on his throne. He had a hard time doing it. The two guards at his side dared not touch him, even to help him.

"Ahhh! Is that you, my good friend Joseph? I think it is you. But you are covered with the red mud of my diamond mine!   Hah Hah Hah!" he laughed loudly shaking the building. He pushed himself up on one elbow and farted once again.

"Yes, king . . ." Cross started but was interrupted by the warlord's screaming rant as he tried, but was unable to raise himself out of the throne. He pounded his fist on the arm of his throne.

"*YOU DO NOT CALL ME BY THAT NAME! I AM NOW GOD! I AM NOW GOD! I HAVE THE POWER OF GOD INSIDE ME! I HAVE THE POWER OVER LIFE AND DEATH! I AM GOD!*"

"OK . . . god," Cross said, stifling laughter. "Yes, I am Joseph."

Azubuike settled back on his throne, and a cruel smile returned to his fat face. He pushed himself up on his right side and farted again, loudly and malodorous. "Please excuse that, my good friend Joseph. I had the heart of a dead slave for dinner last night, and it has been disagreeable with me."

"I can only imagine . . . god. What do we do now?"

"I have a bag, my good friend Joseph. A bag of diamonds to sell. But I am having trouble, my friend, Joseph. Do you know why I am having trouble?"

"Let me guess," Cross began. He looked around the room and saw two benches against the hut's wall to his right. He started to walk to one of them. One of the guards behind him reached out to stop him, but Azubuike raised a fat arm and smiled. The guard let Cross go. He sat on the bench, groaning against his stiff and bruised back and shoulders. Looking across the big room, he said, "Lars Ruscher won't answer his short wave radio."

"HAH! That is so right, my friend Joseph! And do you know why?"

"Because it isn't the first of the month?" Cross answered. He knew that Helen's man would ignore radio calls from Azubuike until the scheduled call on the first of the month.

"Ha Ha Ha Ha!" he roared. "You know that, my good friend, Joseph! You know my arrangement! You are so special, my good friend, Joseph! You know so much! You are so smart! That is why I like you so much, my good friend, Joseph!"

"I know a lot . . . god. Now what do we do?"

"Why will not this Ruscher answer my calls to him?"

There was no sense lying to Azubuike. Too many people already knew that Lars was dead. It was at least likely that Azubuike's contacts in Kampala had heard and had told Azubuike. A lie might get Cross killed. Keeping Azubuike talking by telling the truth was his only chance to stay alive.

"Probably because he's dead . . . god," he said.

"HAH! And, my good friend, Joseph, you know he is dead . . . How did you know this? Because perhaps you killed him?"

"You haven't lost any of your ability to delve into the enigmatic mysteries of life. The theory of Ockham's Razor certainly applies to your hypothesis."

"What does that mean?" Azubuike asked angrily, his smile dropping from his fat face, and with a hint of a threat behind the few words. Anything he did not understand had to be an insult to his paranoia filled brain. "Are those words an insult to god?"

"Forgive me. I mean . . . What I mean is you're smart . . . god."

"Yes," he smiled once again, at the false compliment, and relaxed back in his throne. "I am not only god; I am smart as you say, my good friend, Joseph. But you are smart also, aren't you? So you tell me . . . How do I sell these damn diamonds now that you have killed the man who buys them?"

Azubuike sat forward on his throne, his fat fingers grasping at the carved, gold covered snakes in the armrests of the chair. He glared menacingly at Cross. The guards at his side lowered their rifles and pointed them at Cross. The three guards who brought Cross to Azubuike started for him.

Cross leaned back and crossed his muddy legs. He smiled at Azubuike and said before the ragged guards could reach him, "I guess you have only one choice here . . . god."

Azubuike raised his hand once again, and the guards stopped in their tracks. He glared angrily at Cross for a moment and then asked, "And what is that choice, my good friend, Joseph? And if it is not a good choice, you will die here, and I will eat your liver tonight."

Cross took a deep breath because he now knew he would be able to get away alive. Azubuike's greed, insanity, and stupidity were working in Cross' favor. But he had to get away immediately because Helen and her mercenaries would arrive the next day, and when they arrived, the killings would start, and that killing, what Cross anticipated would be a short but violent fire-fight, might take out Robert Fullsome and Mary Ssanyu . . . And Cross himself.

He took the chance that the insane brain inside of Azubuike's head would not reason that he could send his diamonds directly to Hienrich in Amsterdam. He took the risk and said, "I am the only person you have right now who can buy your diamonds, regardless of their quality. Even your best stones are valueless unless you can get them out of Africa. You can spend months seeking out someone else, but what do you do until you find someone? Where do you get the money you need to keep your army going? I will give you fair value for them and maybe a bonus to seal a long term arrangement."

"HAH! And you have such cash in your back pocket,

my good friend, Joseph? HA HA HA HA!" He pointed a fat, bent finger at Cross as he laughed.

"Thanks to you . . . god . . . I don't have any back pockets. In fact I don't have any clothes at all. No, I will use your radio, and my people will have half of your money wire transferred anywhere you like."

"Half?" Azubuike asked suspiciously. Hey pushed himself forward on the throne and yelled, "Half! You would steal half of god's money! I should have you ripped apart and cooked!"

"Not steal . . . god," Cross said. "Look, you need money to keep your kingdom going and maybe even grow. Your source for cash is dead. I am alive. You know me. I'm always in the market for good diamonds. I can be your new source. I will pay half their value now and half when I'm safely back in London. I will buy what you produce from now on, no questions asked, and a fair price will always be paid. I will be your new source, your new bank so to speak. I will take the risk of smuggling them out of Africa. All you will have to do is let me know when you have diamonds, and that can be done when I take Lars' radio to London with me. It's easy . . . There won't be any interruption in your flow of cash . . . god."

Cross paused a moment to allow Azubuike to understand what he had said.   Then he added, hoping to seal the deal that would keep him alive and free Robert and Mary, "Plus, I can get you the five million for the Fullsome boy. All I need is to get out of here . . . With Fullsome. I will have half his ransom wire transferred with half the price of the diamonds. When Robert is back home, and I am in London, the balance will be wire transferred, and your money will be flowing in."

Azubuike had a strained look on his face as he

considered what Cross had said. He had a hard time understanding what Cross had told him. His fog clouded brain twisted with the words as he tried to figure out if what Cross said was good or not. His insanity was getting in the way.

It was all spinning around inside his warped brain like a tornado of jumbled words. Five million dollars was what he had wanted for Robert Fullsome. He tried to understand what Cross had said about the five million. He could use that to recruit more good soldiers for his personal guard and buy more drugs for the others. Cross said he could give that to him, at least he thought that is what Cross had said. Plus, he had to have some source to buy his diamonds. Maybe Cross could deliver all of that, maybe. Maybe Cross could be trusted and maybe he couldn't.

His head was throbbing trying to work out what to do. Finally, he told himself he had to accept what Cross said; there was no other solution to the problem he faced now that Lars was dead. And Cross was right in risking that Azubuike never considered sending the diamonds to Hienrich for him to sell. And when someone else became available to buy his diamonds, he would have Cross killed. That was it. He felt good that he had come up with the right thing to do. Get the money and then kill Cross when he could.

A slow smile crawled across his fat face. He sat back once again and said, "Oh, my good friend, Joseph. We have a deal."

"Not so fast . . . god," Cross said. "I want something in return for our deal."

"And what is that, my good friend, Joseph?"

"Robert Fullsome has to come with me, or I can't get the five million from his parents."

"Done," Azubuike answered quickly. "But if you have lied to me, you both will die."

"And one other thing . . . god. I want Mary Ssanyu."

"HAH! And what use do you have for that ugly pig?"

Cross could have told Azubuike the truth; that his guilt for having sent the woman into danger was weighing heavily on him. But Azubuike was an animal and insane. He wouldn't be able to understand the truth. He wouldn't understand compassion and guilt. It had been a long time since he had felt compassion, and Cross doubted Azubuike had ever felt guilt at anything he had ever done.

So Cross had to tell a lie that the fat man would believe. He said, "I need to profit from this to cover all my expenses. I intend to sell her to some Arabs I know who can make good use of her."

Azubuike erupted in a burst of laughter. His whole body was shaking as he rocked back and forth. A dark stain erupted across his pants as he emptied his bladder without realizing it. "That is so good! That is so good! Take the pig . . . She is yours."

"One other thing . . . god," Cross said as he stood from the bench against the wall.

"Be careful, my good friend, Joseph," Azubuike said seriously and ominously. The laughing had ended as his eyes glared red down at Cross. "You may ask too much."

"What I want . . . What I want is a bath and my clothes and my Land Rover and my pistol. It would be difficult to go north looking like this and on foot."

Again Azubuike broke out in sudden, loud laughter, reverberating through the big hut. "Oh, my good friend, Joseph!" he said too loudly as he laughed, pounding his fists on the chair's arms. "You are such funny! Is that how it is said?"   He laughed again, doubling over his enormous stomach and slapping his fat knees. Then, suddenly, he stopped laughing and he looked menacingly across the room to Cross. "First you have my money sent. Then you have the bath."

"Look . . . god . . . We are entering into a business contract. The whole world must know how smart you are. How could anyone not recognize that you are now god? How could the whole world not know that you are more intelligent than anyone else in the entire world? So . . . god . . . You must show the world that you know a contract must benefit both parties. How could you not make it clear to the whole world that you know that? You want your money, and I want what I want. Without me you have nothing. Send me back to the pit, and you have nothing. Kill me, and you have nothing. Eat my liver . . . And you'll get heartburn and an upset stomach. I am the only person who will buy your diamonds and who will get your five million for Fullsome."

Cross sat back down on the bench, silent for a moment, his legs crossed casually, leaning back against the wall behind him as he stared into Azubuike's eyes. He was taking a risk, but he hoped that Azubuike's greed and insanity would work positively for him.

After what Cross thought was a full minute of silence between the two of them, he said, "First a bath . . . Then my clothes . . . Then Robert Fullsome and Mary Ssanyu at my side . . . Clean and clothed . . . Then my Land Rover and my pistol. Once I have these things, I will agree to help you. I will use your radio then to initiate the wire transfer. You can have someone go to Kampala and draw the money from the bank there. Take it or leave it."

Azubuike was silent for a time, trying to think, trying to weigh his options. He struggled to reach down into a wooden box at the side of his throne and pulled from it a long cigar. He bit a big part of the tip off and spit it across the floor. A guard quickly held a gold lighter out, and Azubuike drew deeply. He blew gray smoke out and said threateningly, "Why must I trust my good friend, Joseph?"

"Because I gave you my word . . . god. You know me. In business I never lie. I helped you once, remember? . . . And I will help you again."

"I do remember. You were kind to me in my previous life. Without you, I might have died and not raised myself up to be god. And does my good friend, Joseph trust me? Do you trust me not to kill you after you use my radio?"

"Hell no," Cross answered and smiled. "But I'm your last hope to sell your diamonds. And without me you'll never get the ransom for the Fullsome boy. Without me all you'll get is a meal or two of the boy and me."

Azubuike broke out in loud, raucous laughter again and threw the newly lit cigar to the floor to the right of him. It lay burning a hole in the leopard skin rug there. He stopped laughing finally and sat forward, breathing heavily. A cloud of madness suddenly swamped across his face. His eyes flamed and bulged. He stopped breathing, and his fists clenched tightly the armrests of the chair. Anger had replaced the laughter, and the insane anger was now controlling him.

But Cross was right in believing that Azubuike's need and greed for money would give Cross what he wanted. Azubuike waived a fat arm, and one of the guards standing at his side bent to listen to him whisper. The guard stood upright and spoke to the soldier standing nearest to Cross in an African language Cross couldn't understand. The two soldiers who took Cross from the diamond trench pulled him roughly to his feet. They pushed at him and pointed at a door at the side of Azubuike's throne platform, telling him with pointed rifles to walk in front of them to it.

One of them opened the door, and Cross stepped up three carpet covered stairs into a grandly furnished room, Azubuike's private home. The walls of this big room were not the mud and thatch of the other buildings in the compound. They were made of finely honed and finished dark African woods, put together by craftsmen who knew what they were doing. The roof of the room was raised by thick, highly polished beams to a central peak. No rough palm thatch finished Azubuike's roof as all the other huts were made. His apartment had a solid roof, painted white, with two big and gaudy brass chandeliers hanging from it.

Chairs and couches lined the walls; all were covered in the skins of zebra, lion, leopard, antelope, and giraffe. A huge bed lay in the center of them room, covered in pillows and animal skins. There were electric lamps that were lit, lighting the windowless room. There was a mélange of prints of paintings, old master and modern, hanging everywhere with no order to them, some in cheap frames, and others just roughly pinned to the walls.

Thick Asian carpets covered the polished, wood plank floor. A well-constructed oak and marble topped bar, six feet long, was filled with bottles of every kind of liquor one could ask for. And protruding from a wall nearby was an air conditioner that buzzed quietly, cooling the room. Cross smiled, now understanding where a lot of the General's money went.

The guards closed the door, leaving Cross alone in the grand and expansive room that was behind the wall, separating it from Azubuike's throne platform. He left muddy footprints on the carpets as he walked around the room, enjoying the cool air. He went to the bar and found several bottles of cognac. From behind the bar he pulled out a large, crystal glass, filled it halfway, and drank deeply. The cognac burned as it went down and made his head spin pleasantly, but it also gave him some strength. He shook off the affects and poured a small amount more into the glass. He raised the glass and whispered a toast, "Here's to you, Azubuike, you son of a bitch." He drained the glass and laid it on the marble top of the bar.

Behind a door, in a white painted wall that held a dozen framed prints, he found an overly large bathroom with a white marble walled shower prominent. It was big enough for three people or, as Cross laughed at the thought, one fat bastard. He turned the faucet and held his hand under the running water. He was amazed that there was actually hot water. This had to be a very private chamber, kept by Azubuike for himself alone. He couldn't imagine the egomaniac sharing this with anyone.

He stood under the needles of steaming water for a long time. Mud and filth washed from him and filled the tiled floor of the shower. He was in no hurry to get out of the shower, so he let the mud filter down the drain slowly. His back ached from the beatings he had received from the clubs, his shoulders were stiff, and he smelled like an overused outhouse.

On a shelf inside the shower there were several bars of sweet scented soaps, all wrapped and unused. Cross assumed that Azubuike didn't use the shower very often. The few times he had gotten close to him, Azubuike smelled like a pile of elephant shit that had been rotting in the African sun. A stiff brush was hanging near the soap. He scrubbed himself hard, ignoring the cuts and bruises that stung under the brush. Being clean was more important than the stings of washing.

When he was clean, he stepped from the shower and toweled himself with a thick, soft, white cotton towel that was hanging from a gold towel bar near the shower. He found a gold and ivory handled straight razor, the kind barbers once used, at a deep copper sink. There was a still unwrapped bar of some soap with French words on the wrapper. He lathered with that, shaved and decided not to use any of the selection of highly perfumed colognes lined up on a glass shelf, under a tall gold-flecked mirror, above the sink.

When he stepped out of the bathroom he found his clothes, freshly laundered and pressed, laid out on a zebra skin covered couch. Next to them were his wrist watch and his wallet. He checked inside the wallet and found all the cash gone but all his credit cards still there. Cash the soldiers could use. They had no use for credit cards in their remote compound. But he wasn't about to complain about that. His holster was on his belt. His pistol was not there.

Dressing quickly, he returned to Azubuike's "throne room through the door on the platform." No one was there; the cigar Azubuike had tossed away lay on the leopard skin on the floor, burning a brand into the skin. The big door that led outside was open, letting early evening light and a cool breeze into the building.

Cross stepped outside into the cool, early evening air that soon would be cold. The black storm clouds were racing from the east towards the compound. Both Robert Fullsome and Mary Ssanyu were there, both still naked, filthy, chained together at the ankles, hands tied behind their backs with leather straps, and kneeling in the dirt. At least, Cross thought, Mary's chains keeping her bent low had been removed.

Six of Azubuike's drugged-out soldiers were surrounding them, struggling to keep their eyes open from the drugs they lived on, pointed their assorted dirty and rusted weapons at the two while they Cross stepped down onto the dirt and said as strongly as he could, "I want them unchained and cleaned up. And I want them dressed."

None of the guards made any move, nor did they reply. Robert, keeping his head bent and while not looking at the guards, spoke softly in Swahili, translating what Cross had said. The guards seemed to understand most of what he said. They looked at each other, wondering what to do. Azubuike was nowhere to be seen. Cross repeated his demands, this time louder, and Robert softly translated, in a voice muted with fear, once again. He spoke to Cross without raising his head, "Please be careful. If you anger them they will kill you."

Cross replied by shouting and demanding even louder. This time Robert did not translate. One of the guards finally went to the two chained people, unlocked the shackles, and cut the leather straps, and the two stood, keeping their heads bent. Cross spoke, "Inside, both of you. There's a shower inside in the back room, and I'll find some clothes for you. Hurry . . . Quickly before somebody changes their mind."

Robert held Mary by her arm, his hand around her waist, and helped the weakened woman up the stairs. The two almost ran into the big hut, followed by Cross. Mary knew where Azubuike's apartment was, but she hesitated, feeling the fear that had been beaten into her. Cross pointed them to the door of Azubuike's private quarters and gave Mary a gentle push to make her move.

When the three stepped inside, they found the fat General was in there, sitting on a couch, smiling, drooling spittle from the corners of his fat lips, and clapping his hands like a child at Christmas. Two of his personal guards stood at his side. These were the few men Azubuike had who were well dressed, well fed, and well-armed. They locked their eyes on Cross, their faces twisted in angry, dangerous scowls.

"Oh! Oh, my good friend Joseph!" he said laughing

loudly; clapping his hands together, the sound echoing throughout the room. "I heard you yelling at my men. I just love the way you demand when you are frightened!"

"I'm not frightened," Cross said, trying to sound like he wasn't frightened. He didn't want to die, but he knew there was a time and place for him to die. He had accepted that fact. So he swallowed hard and took a step forward, towards Azubuike, to signal that he wasn't frightened. "I know you can kill me any time you want. I can accept that. I've been on borrowed time for many years. If I die today . . . That's just fate. But I also know that when you kill me, you will lose millions of American dollars for Fullsome, and you will lose your only source for selling your diamonds. So I guess I'll stay alive for the time being anyway."

The smile fell suddenly from Azubuike's fat face. He sat forward, struggling not to fall back onto the couch. "And I want that money, my good friend, Joseph. I need that money."

"You'll have it . . . god. As soon as Mary and the Fullsome boy are ready, I'll leave with the diamonds, and in a few short days you will be rich . . . with the balance of the money. But first, I need to use your radio . . . And I need my pistol."

Azubuike laughed again, this time a forced, more dangerous laugh. He wasn't clapping his hands together; his eyes were piercing and fiery as he scowled angrily at Cross.

The General pushed himself to his feet, falling back onto the couch once, and finally standing with the aid of his thorn encrusted cane. He walked, waddling like a very fat duck, past Cross who did not step aside for him, leaving his private quarters, into the big room that held his throne. The guards followed the fat man as he shuffled heavily across the polished wooden floor, leaving the door open behind them. Cross went to it and closed it softly. Azubuike struggled to walk to his throne and fell into it. He was breathing hard after the exertion.

Cross, Robert and Mary were alone in the apartment. He quickly led them to the bathroom and told them to shower and clean themselves up. Mary asked in a weak, hoarse voice, "Why?"

"Because I'm getting you out of here," Cross said. "Now hurry. We don't have much time. That fat bastard may change his mind."

Cross left them and walked quickly out onto the throne platform. He walked past Azubuike, and down the three steps to the floor of the throne room. He stopped in the middle of the floor, turned slowly to face the dictator, and said, "First, I want clean clothes for Mary and Robert. And I'm waiting to hear my Land Rover delivered outside. I want water for the three of us. And I want my pistol back . . . Loaded."

Azubuike once again raised an arm and spoke loudly to one of the soldiers standing across the room, at the open doors. The soldier ran outside, and within a minute Cross heard the engine of his car. He waited in silence with Azubuike glaring at him. What Cross didn't know was that the fat maniac was trying to figure out how to kill Cross and still get the money he needed so badly. But his warped mind could not grasp any option other than to do what Cross demanded. Killing Joseph Cross would be easy. But then what? He kept his rage inside of him, even though he wanted to see Cross torn apart and burned.

His supply of drugs was dwindling, and he needed those drugs to keep his small army from leaving him. His personal guards, who were not kept on drugs, were there for the money and the female slaves. The slaves he had, and he could get more when needed, assuming he could keep his 'army' together. It was the money he needed. There were people in Kampala to pay off, as well as his guards. They wouldn't hear of delays in their payments. And he knew no other way of getting it than to do what Cross wanted.

After Azubuike had finished giving whispered orders to the guard at his side, the guard quickly and without warning, turned and ran to the back room where Mary Ssanyu and young Robert Fullsome were. It took what seemed like an eternity to Cross, with Azubuike not moving his angry glare from him, for the guard to return with Mary and Robert. They had showered, and Robert had shaved off his weeks old beard. They were dressed in new khaki pants and shirts, Mary's hanging limply on her bone thin body. They wore new brown leather boots; Mary's were too big for her, but she didn't seem to mind.

Mary's cut and bruised face, one eye being closed and badly bruised, would take time to heal, but she smiled, showing her spirit was healing already. Both were anxious to get away from Azubuike. They tried not to run, but they wanted to get to Joe Cross' side as quickly as possible.

The guard then walked to Cross and handed him his Berretta pistol. Cross checked the magazine, found it full, and he pulled the slide back finding a round in the chamber. He slid it into its holster. He was handed two spare magazines, found them fully loaded, and slid them into their holders on his belt. He turned around to check once again on the Land Rover. It was still there, the engine running. He said to Azubuike, "OK, now to the radio."

Azubuike nodded his fat head and finally leaned back on his throne, still breathing hard. He reached down into the box at his side and pulled a cigar from it. He bit the end off, spit it onto the floor, and held the cigar to his lips as the guard at his side quickly lit it. Azubuike would not take his red eyes from Cross as he drew deeply and blew a cloud of smoke in Cross' direction. Insane hatred filled his face; his fat body was stiff as he fought to restrain his desire to cut the three people apart.

The guard who had brought Cross his pistol walked to Cross and handed him a slip of paper. It was Azubuike's Kampala bank's wire transfer instructions. He led Cross out the double doors of the big thatched roof building, followed meekly by Mary and Robert, holding tightly to each other. They did not know exactly what had transpired, but somehow Joseph Cross seemed to have freed them. What would come next was still unknown to the two of them. They would be quiet, do what they were told, follow Cross, try to stay close to him, and hope for the best.

The three of them were led around the big building to its rear, past a dozen stinking barrels of trash that Cross hoped did not hold the uneaten remains of one of Azubuike's cannibalistic dinners. The odor was foul and choking. They covered their mouths and noses as they walked past the barrels; the guard seemed not to care. Perhaps even the soldiers who were not drugged had become so used to Azubuike's excesses that foul stenches did not bother them anymore.

Behind the big building was a small mud and thatch hut, in poor condition, leaning to one side but still standing. The palm thatched roof was covered in a bright blue plastic tarp to keep the weather out. An electric wire hung from the edge of the thatched roof and connected with a generator a few yards away. The generator was inside a tall, lean-to shack, better built with better wood and roofed in tin. More wires ran from the generator to Azubuike's private living quarters. More than a dozen five gallon cans of gasoline, needed to run the generator, were stacked nearby.

The generator was humming, explaining to Cross how there were hot water and electric lights in Azubuike's home. Two of Azubuike's ragged soldiers were sitting on the ground in front of the little hut, in the red mud, old rifles lying in the dirt next to them.

Cross was trying to keep track of how many soldiers Azubuike had. They were all terribly thin, all dressed in little more than rags, all armed with old and dirty weapons that may or may not fire when needed. There were children no better off than the drugged out soldiers. But he knew there was a contingent of guards, the men who were always very near Azubuike, one of whom had taken Cross to the small hut. They seemed better fed, better clothed, and better armed with AK-47s that were clean and seemed to be well cared for. He needed to keep count of them. He had seen four of these men so far, but he knew there might be more. That would be the biggest trouble for Helen.

The two soldiers lying in the dust were obviously on some drugs, as were most of the others Cross had seen. And he remembered the young soldier at the diamond pit who had given him water. He was not drugged. This would be important to be remembered because Cross had decided that he had to destroy Azubuike's little hell-hole of a kingdom, whether he managed to get out alive or not. He had to know how many of Azubuike's people would . . . Or could . . . Fight.

Inside the tattered little hut, Cross found, sitting on a wooden table, a big, and ancient by modern technological standards, short wave radio. Studying it, he found a switch that looked like it might turn the radio on, so he flipped it. Lights flashed, and a dented speaker buzzed.

Robert and Mary stood outside, looking in, wondering

just what was happening. Cross pulled a battered metal chair away from the table and sat, hoping the chair would not collapse under him. He found the bandwidth that would connect him with Helen's man, waiting for the call at Lar's radio in Geneva. The man Helen had sent there would listen to the code words Cross would speak.

He spoke slowly, hoping the static would not wipe out his words. "Robin One, this is Robin Two." Any other opening words would mean Cross was in very grave danger. He repeated the call signs and then repeated them again. At first there was no answer. But the man had to be there, he had to be waiting.

"Robin Two," came the answer finally, crackled and filled with static, but understandable. "This is Robin One, go ahead."

"I want half of the ransom money and an additional fifty thousand dollars wire transferred to Azubuike right away," he began. He gave the man the transfer instructions.

"Understood, Robin Two. Half the ransom money plus fifty thousand. The weather here is very rainy, but I will make the transfer in any case."

"That's good, Robin One. The weather here is hot. I will be home soon."

Helen's man would contact Helen who waited with Manny Rodriguez. No money would be transferred as they had planned. Cross had managed to get away. Helen d'Neuville would get the message, and she would not come to his rescue. He was safe. She would wait for Cross and for whatever he had in mind.

CHAPTER TWELVE – The Deal

Azubuike was still sitting on his throne when Cross was led back to him, Robert and Mary at his heels. He spoke to the guard standing next to Cross in an African language. Cross could pick up only a few bastardized Swahili words, that he understood to be very demeaning insults. Robert, understanding what was said, whispered in Cross' ear, "He doesn't like you."

"I sort of got that," Cross said.

When the short conversation ended, Azubuike smiled broadly and waived his fat arm in the air. One of Azubuike's personal guards ran down from the platform and roughly pulled Mary and Robert away from Cross. They didn't speak, and Cross said nothing, each knowing that it would be useless to argue with a crazy person. They were led up the three steps onto the throne's stage and stood next to Azubuike. He continued to smile a vicious and frightening smile, the smile of a crazed lunatic who held people captive. He looked at Cross and said in a whisper, "You have called for the money to be transferred. I received the knowledge of this. Now, the money will be transferred, and I will have a lot of money. Why should I not kill you all?"

Cross sighed a deep breath. Azubuike did not know that the wire transfer would not take place. If Cross could get away before Azubuike became aware of this, then he was safe. All he had to do was convince Azubuike that he had to let the three of them go.

Cross took a step forward and said, "Because when you kill us, you lose two and a half million dollars, the price of your diamonds, and a source to sell your diamonds in the future. Does that make sense to you . . . god?"

"And why shall I trust you, my good friend, Joseph?"

"I've explained that already . . . god. In business I always keep my word. As long as you and I are alive, I will buy your diamonds. That is a promise."

"And if I keep the bitch with me for another year . . . Just as what you call the insurance?"

"Then our deal is off. Kill me now, and when your cash runs out, try to find someone else to buy your diamonds. My organization is very large . . . And very dangerous. You know about Billy Volgar . . . He will kill anyone who does business with you, if you kill me and Robert and Mary."

Azubuike glared down at Cross, crazed anger engulfing him. His hands were balled in fists as they hit the carved arms of his tall throne. He was sweating, and foamy drool covered his chin. He was trying to think through his options, but his insanity would not allow clear thinking. All he could consider was getting the cash he needed and his desire to murder this Joseph Cross who seemed to Azubuike to be in command. No one, he told himself, could dare command him since he became god. He would not allow it. He was certain that with a mere wave of his hand he could bring an end to the entire world. That was the awful power he knew he had since he became god.

Finally, he came to the conclusion that he really had no choice but to get his hands on the cash, all of it. He had promised money from the ransom to people in Kampala who would protect him. Those payments had to be made. Cross would have to leave with Mary Ssanyu and Robert Fullsome and the bag of diamonds. But he would then insist that Cross come back to him to receive more of his diamonds. No more transfers. Cross would have to come to him to get more diamonds. On one of those return trips, after Azubuike had found another buyer, he would kill him. He would rip him apart very slowly. He would make this Joseph Cross suffer before dying.

"If you go now, when will my money be received? When will the transfer be made?" Azubuike asked, his voice low, almost a whisper, more of an animal's growl.

"As soon as we are on my plane, in the air, back to London, you can expect what is due you," his double entendre' not understood by Azubuike.

"Alright," Azubuike grumbled. He tossed the small leather sack of diamonds to Cross who caught them and smiled, knowing he had won. Azubuike waived his arm once again, and one of the guards at his side pushed Mary and Robert towards the stairs and down to Cross.

He led them out to the waiting Land Rover. All the camping gear Cross had arrived with was in the rear of the big auto. His suitcases were there, but they had been opened and rifled through, and then roughly closed. He didn't care what was missing; the important thing was to get away . . . Alive. Cross started the engine and looked at the gas gauge. The tank was full. Azubuike had his supply of gasoline. Cross had seen the cans next to the generator.

There was a great deal of grumbling and yelling of threats and braggadocio amongst the ragged, drugged guards as Cross drove away with Mary and Robert, both of them in the back seat, huddled together and slouched down in the fear that had been instilled in them over the time of their capture.

He didn't stop as the drugged guards chased the

Land Rover out of the compound, beating the car with their clubs and machetes. He didn't want to give them the opportunity to pull the three of them out of the vehicle. They kicked at the Land Rover and hit the big car with rifle butts and clubs and clumps of red mud as it inched its way past them. Cross had his pistol lying in his lap, ready if he needed it.

Some of Azubuike's boy soldiers stood in the dirt road outside the compound, chanting, waiving machetes and rifles in the air, and screaming profanities that only Mary and Robert could understand. They moved aside as Cross moved the Land Rover slowly through the crowd. He didn't want to hit or hurt any of them; they were children after all, he told himself.

But Cross knew that Azubuike now needed him alive if he were to have a market for his diamonds. There was no one else. That false hope of Azubuike's gave Cross some protection. It would take time for the fat man to find another market, and Azubuike didn't have time. He needed to keep his "army" drugged or they might turn on him.

When they were well out of the compound, leaving the soldiers behind them, Cross floored the accelerator, and the Land Rover raced away, leaving a cloud of red dust, stones and pebbles behind them that engulfed Azubuike's men.

Cross didn't slow when they reached the outpost guard shack. Two skinny guards were asleep in the shade but awoke suddenly as the Land Rover sped past them. They jumped to their feet and started screaming, waving their rifles in the air. One of them shouldered the old Enfield and pulled the trigger but the gun wouldn't fire. He tried again but the gun was so old and dirty, it was useless.

For an hour they bounced north along the rutted, dirt

road in silence, Cross driving faster than the road really allowed. There was a dented and dirty, American G.I. aluminum canteen of water lying on the floor of the back seat. Robert took it, opened it, and handed it to Mary. She drank deeply, nervously. Robert asked, "Mr. Cross, do you want some water?" hinting that Mary shouldn't drink all of the only water they had. She handed the canteen to Robert and smiled apologetically.

Mary reached forward and touched Cross on his shoulder. She said, "Why do you rescue me?"

Without taking his eyes off the dusty road in the darkening night, Cross said simply, "Because you needed to be rescued." She squeezed his shoulder gently. He glanced down and saw her hand of bones, knowing that had he not come to Azubuike when he did, she would be dead in a few days or weeks. She had suffered for almost a year; she would not be able to suffer much longer.

They drove on in silence along the bumpy and rocky road for another hour. They passed a herd of giraffes and saw a few elephants encircle a calf, protecting it, as the car passed by. A leopard chased after them on the driver's side of the car for a few hundred yards, pacing the fast moving Land Rover, and then shot off to the side and away from them.

Robert was slumped against the door of the Land Rover, asleep and snoring softly. Mary looked at the young man and smiled. She felt safe, for the time being at least, and for the first time since being captured and returned to Azubuike. But she had no idea what the future held for her. She easily and deftly climbed over the front seat and sat, twisting her now boney hands together nervously. Finally, she found the courage to ask, "What will happen to me now?"

Cross finally slowed the Land Rover and began trying to avoid the bigger potholes and rocks. It was very dark now, and the Land Rover's headlights did little to light the road ahead.

He took his eyes from the road and, for the first time since she had been washed and dressed, took a close look at Mary Ssanyu. She was thinner than he remembered her, much thinner; her face was badly swollen and bruised and cut; her cheeks were sunken; her eyes were circled in dark rings; one eye was swollen and closed; her head had been roughly shaved, leaving cuts that had not yet healed. But she was still beautiful. With freedom and some good food, Cross knew, her dark skin would one day be smooth and seductive once again. Life would return to her, but she would never forget the hell she had suffered under Azubuike. He asked, "What do you think will happen to you?"

"I don't know . . . If I am to be sold, please kill me instead . . . I will kill myself if you will not. That beast told me you would sell me."

Cross laughed and then apologized. "I'm sorry," he said. "I don't mean to make light of your situation. You are safe, please believe me. You will not be sold to anyone. I lied to Azubuike to get you away from him. I feel terrible about what happened to you."

"But are you not responsible for what happened?" Mary asked. "You sent me to that Van der Mullen man. You must have known what he would do to me. You must have known that the soldiers would take me and send me back to . . . Back to . . . Back to the devil."

"Soldiers?" Cross asked. "What soldiers? What do you mean?"

"I was shopping for clothes . . . Preparing to leave . . . When two men . . . African men in uniforms . . . They dragged me from the shop. They injected me with something . . . I was quickly unconscious. I awoke on an airplane. I was soon back with . . . With that man and was soon being beaten by him. You knew this would happen?"

"I promise you, I didn't know. I had trusted Hienrich to help you, but I did not know that he was doing business with a man in Switzerland named Lars Ruscher. Hienrich stupidly told Ruscher that he had purchased diamonds from an African woman, and Ruscher told Azubuike that you were in Amsterdam. I didn't know any of this until I confronted them both a few days ago. Then I knew you were in trouble, and I had to come," Cross said, his eyes on the road once again, trying to avoid the larger rocks. "I didn't know . . . and Ruscher is dead now."

"Dead? How? Did you kill him?"

"Yes. He needed to die for what he did."

"Then you did not know that I would be sent back to . . . Azubuike?" She said the name in a fearful whisper.

"No, I didn't," Cross said softly. "I am so very sorry. I thought . . . I honestly thought you would be safe. But you said soldiers came for you. What soldiers? Who? And how did they get you back to Azubuike?"

"They were soldiers, as I said. Africans. Police I think. They did not speak except to order me. I screamed, but no one would help. They threw me into the back of a car, and I felt the needle in my arm. I awoke on an airplane, as I said . . . A big one I think. And I was quickly taken to Azubuike."

"Soldiers, you said. Maybe police?" Cross asked. "Their uniforms . . . What were they like?"

She had to think for a moment; her eyes, still swollen and one shut completely, closed in thought. She answered,

"Tan . . . Clean . . . Well pressed."

"They black . . . Africans?" he asked.

"They were Africans," she answered. "That is what I cannot understand. In Holland . . . In Amsterdam . . . African soldiers?"

"Did you see any insignia? Badges . . . Anything?"

"Yes!" she said. "I remember now. I had forgotten. On their shoulders was the flag of Uganda."

"That explains it, then," Cross said. "I know what happened, and I think I can fix it. Once you are safe that is."

"What will you do?" she asked.

"That is not for you to know," Cross answered and smiled, knowing what he would do.

They were quiet for a while, bouncing slowly along the dirt road. Cross began humming a tune. Mary interrupted to say, "Then what will happen to me now?"

"The three of us will stop in a hotel in Kampala for a day or two. Longer would not be safe. We will rest and eat and regain some strength. My plane will come there, and we will leave Uganda and Africa. You will never return. I will take you out this time and insure your safety forever."

She spoke again, saying, "But I have no passport."

"You don't need one, Mary. I'll take care of that. We will fly to London and land at a little RAF runway left over from the war. No one uses it but me, and it is very isolated. The British authorities won't know you've arrived."

"But how do I leave Kampala? Without a passport they will not let me leave, and they will send me back."

Cross looked at her again and said, "Mary, you will not go back. I promise you that. Money can buy anything, even the blind eyes of the airport officials. The people at the airport will get a lot of money from me to look the other way as we leave."

Mary smiled and asked, "In your London, what will happen, then?"

"We will be met by a man I trust . . . Billy Volgar. He is big and ugly. You must not be frightened of him. He's my good friend, and I trust him with my life. He will take you to my home where you will stay for a few days. You can recuperate there. My doctor will visit you there. Billy will protect you . . . Nothing will happen to you. You can rest and eat some excellent food. He will take you shopping for clothes and anything else you want. Nothing will happen to you while Billy Volgar is next to you."

"And what will you do?" she asked.

"I'm going to take Robert home to his parents. I have a lot of money I got from them for saving him. It was supposed to go to Azubuike, but I intend to keep it and use it for other purposes."

Both were quiet for a minute or two; Cross swerved the Land Rover suddenly to miss a pot hole in the road. It woke Robert momentarily, but he quickly laid his head back against the window and went to sleep.

Mary gazed out the side window that was now covered in dust and dirt. The grassland they drove through was dark in the night, but the sky was full of millions of stars. She smiled. She spoke quietly, almost in a whisper, still looking up at the night sky. "You will go back there, won't you? You will kill Azubuike, won't you?"

"Something like that," Cross answered and smiled, because he knew what was going to happen, and he felt very, very good knowing it.

"That is good," she said as she nodded her approval and wiped a tear from her eye. She turned to him and tried valiantly not to cry as she asked, "And what will happen then?"

"By the time I get back, after you have been in London for a week or two, Billy Volgar will have a passport made for you, and you will have several suitcases of very good clothes. You will pick a place where you would like to live . . . Anywhere in the world but far from Africa . . . And I will send you there. You will be safe, and you will start a new life. You will have money for the rest of your life. Is that OK with you?"

Mary stared at him, frowning, deep in thought, trying to understand what she was hearing. She asked, "Why?"

"Because . . . It's the right thing to do," Cross answered and they drove on to Kampala in silence.

CHAPTER THIRTEEN – I'm Going To Kill Azubuike

Cross, Mary and Robert found a small hotel in a back street, a drab part of town where a small room could be had for one of the better diamonds that had been dug by Azubuike's slaves. Cross did not want to use his credit cards, and all his cash had been stolen back at the compound. The diamond would certainly draw attention but not the direct attention foreign money or credit cards would attract. If someone was looking for them, they would look at the better hotels, the more expensive places, in the better parts of town.

They arrived at the hotel as the sun was rising. Dim early morning light flooded the streets. In that part of town people were beginning to stir, and small shops were just opening. Cross and Robert and Mary went to the room, where they slept behind a locked door until the sun was setting once again. Mary took the only small bed, Robert and Cross lay on the floor, which was more comfortable than the muddy slave hut. Cross' pistol lay very close to him.

Cross was the first to wake up. The three had slept the day away. The big African sun was settling for the night behind Kampala's tall buildings and would soon be below the horizon. He quietly left the room and went out onto the streets. Another small diamond bought some cooked chicken and several bottles of good beer. Mary was awake when he got back to the room; Robert was still asleep. Mary was crying as she sat on the edge of the bed.

"What is it, Mary?" Cross asked. "What's wrong?" He went to her, dropping his cloth bag of food and beer on the bed. He put his hands on her shoulders and felt her body quaking with the tears.

"I thought you had left me," she said through her tears.

"That's not going to happen, Mary. I told you I was going to take care of you."

"Then do not leave me alone again, Joseph. Do not leave me alone."

He gently lifted her from the bed and took her into his arms. She was fragile; he felt that, and he was careful as he held her. Her head rested on his shoulder as he let her cry. When her tears were exhausted, she lay back on the bed and curled herself under the thin blanket.

Robert had awakened and was watching as he lay on the floor. Cross looked down at him, and Robert nodded, understanding.

"I have to go out for a few minutes," Cross said. "There's food in the bundle. Try to get her to eat something. And stay with her until I get back."

Cross was able to make a collect phone call from the lobby of the hotel to his London casino, and the next day his Gulfstream jet landed at the Kampala Airport. The pilot left the jet carrying a briefcase. A few handfuls of American dollars bought his way past the police and immigration. By taxi he found the hotel where his employer was waiting.

The briefcase was filled with cash, both dollars and British Pounds. Cross took the case, thanked the pilot and gave him instructions. The pilot returned immediately to the jet to prepare it for a return to London. The fuel tanks were filled, and he filed a flight plan indicating a flight to Rome with no passengers aboard. The lie was standard procedure for the pilot who had been in Joseph Cross' employ for several years.

Later that evening, after the three had showered and Robert and Cross had shaved, Cross took Mary and Robert to a restaurant and watched them fill their empty stomachs with food. Cross ate very little. His thoughts were filled with the coming days and what he had to do. With the money in the attaché, Cross led his party through Ugandan Customs and Immigration, handing out money as needed to easily bribed police and various officials who, as they stuffed money into their pockets, did not ask for passports or anything else before letting them through the airport.

Cross kept looking behind him and in the crowds all around them for Colonel Owusu and any of his Special Police. But with enough cash handed out, they were able to speed through the airport and get onto the Gulfstream without trouble. As the jet started to taxi out to the runway, Cross finally could breathe easily.

His jet took off without problems from the control tower, the operations people there having received cash from Cross, and headed up, above the clouds, for London. Cross was buckled into a seat at the front of the plane. He looked behind him, at Mary Ssanyu and Robert Fullsome, sitting together, buckled into a leather couch at the rear of the plane. They were holding each other, hugging each other tightly, and both were crying, letting out all the pain and anguish they had felt while captives of Azubuike. Cross knew they would be alright. Time would heal the physical wounds but perhaps not the memories. He saw both as strong people who could overcome whatever was placed in front of them. He hoped the nightmares would eventually fade into the past.

When the jet leveled off, Cross got up, stretched his stiff and aching muscles, and went to the bar. He pulled a crystal snifter from a cabinet and poured a very large cognac. He drank half of it, savoring the burning of the liquor as he swallowed it. It would take weeks to recover from the beatings he suffered at the hands of Azubuike, but the thought of what he would do soon was a good medicine that pushed the pain away. He smiled at the thought of putting a bullet in Azubuike's head.

He held the glass and looked back at the two people he had rescued. They were smiling and laughing now, wiping the tears away. Cross tried to imagine what the two had suffered, but it was too much of a terrifying thought to dwell on. He felt terribly responsible for Mary Ssanyu's year of suffering. Robert had months of pain, but it was money that saved them both.

Both were bone thin and bruised. Their cuts had been washed clean and would heal. A week or two of good food and rest would take care of them.

Both got to their feet and went to Cross. Mary hugged him tightly, her head on his broad shoulder. Robert took Cross' hand in his and said, "Thank you Mr. Cross. But to merely say 'thank you' isn't enough. How do I thank you?"

"Come with me to see your parents," Cross answered.

"That goes without saying," Robert answered. "But there must be something I can do to thank you."

Mary pulled herself from Cross and turned to Robert, "Mr. Cross must be trusted," she began. "He did not have to help me, but he has helped me twice. I owe him my life, and you owe him your life. Do as he asks of you. There is a reason he wants you to accompany him to your parents. It is not for you to know why at this time. You will learn that reason soon enough. Never question him. That will be a way of thanking him."

Robert nodded and looked hungrily at the bar of liquors. Cross grinned and said, "Help yourself. I'm going to make some sandwiches for us. I'm suddenly really hungry."

****

The Gulfstream jet slowed as it reached the Mediterranean Sea and European continent. The pilot began flying a zig-zag pattern, flying very low to the ground. Landing at the small airfield outside of London had to take place at a certain time of day, when people would not be out walking, and cars would not be driving by. Those aboard had to be patient and wait for the dark of night.

Cross watched his two passengers as the sky darkened. Mary had stretched out on the leather couch, and Robert was slumped in the overstuffed chair next to Mary. Both were asleep, exhaustion, food and liquor finally catching up with them. Cross tried to sleep, but he found that impossible. Thoughts of the coming days filled his mind. Pictures of fat Azubuike lying in the mud with a big hole in his forehead, his brains and blood spilling onto the ground he had defiled for so many years, filled his mind.

They had been asleep for over two hours when the jet's sudden dive from altitude woke them. Mary jumped to her feet, and Robert sat up, holding onto the chair's arms. "Don't be afraid," Cross said, smiling to comfort them and ease their worry of the plane crashing. "It's important to land quickly. We will be less noticed that way. Better buckle up, though. The landing will be rough."

The three sat and fastened seatbelts around them. Both Robert and Mary squeezed the arms of their chairs tightly, worrying in spite of Cross' assurances. The plane's steep dive ended quickly as the pilot pulled back suddenly on the controls, and the Gulfstream met the ground. The old runway was short and rutted and filled with weeds, but Cross' crew had landed there many times before and knew how to handle the quick stop.

Robert and Mary stood, anxious and nervous. Cross remained seated. The cabin door was opened, and the three climbed down, Mary and Robert very cautiously, not knowing what to expect. They looked around guardedly, the fright of having been in Azubuike's hands still fresh in their minds. The night air was cold, but it wasn't raining. A wind was blowing out of the east which foretold rain coming soon.

In the darkness, not too far from where the Gulfstream sat, its engines still running, was a long black limousine, its rear door open, waiting for Cross and his two guests. Standing at the side of the limo, holding the door open, was Billy Volgar. As Mary and Robert passed him to climb into the limo, they looked up at the giant, who was head and shoulders taller than either of them, not sure what to make of him. Billy was smiling, but even his smile was fierce and foreboding.

Cross sat in the back with the two, while Billy climbed into the front seat, next to the liveried chauffeur. The drive was long and tiring, but by four AM they were pulling into the underground garage of The Rochester Club.

The elevator ride up to Cross' home was like a dream to Mary Ssanyu, who hadn't seen such luxury in so many years that much of what she saw was hard to believe, something out of a child's imagination. She smiled and touched and wondered at everything, the polished wood and brass, the framed paintings, everything, as they stepped from the elevator and walked through the doors and into Cross' apartment.

They stopped at the top of the three steps leading down to the big fireplace. Cross said to them, "Mary, Billy will show you to the guest room. Get some sleep. Robert, you'll have to make do with a couch out here, I'm afraid."

"Anything, Mr. Cross. Anything," he said, exhaustion and sleep filling his tired eyes. He was relieved at being free once again. He had months of torture to put behind him. Sleep was the best medicine.

"In the morning, say goodbye to Mary. You and I will be driving to your parent's home, and you won't ever see Mary again."

Robert looked at the tall woman and then at Cross and asked, "Where will she go?"

"She hasn't decided yet . . . But when she does, no one will know, not even you. She must be protected."

Robert nodded, understanding a little, but fatigue was overtaking him rapidly. He took the steps down and collapsed onto the circular couch that lined the fireplace area. He curled himself onto the couch, pulling his knees up and resting his head on his arms. He was asleep almost immediately.

Cross turned to Billy and said, "Show Mary to the bedroom. I'll get a blanket for Robert. Then you and I need to talk."

****

The two men sat in the kitchen, Cross drinking coffee and Billy drinking tea laced heavily with cream and sugar. Billy said, as softly as his gravel filled voice would allow, "I'm glad you made it back, ain't I. I was bloody afraid."

"Thanks for that, Billy. But the worry is over now. I'm back, and everything will be OK."

They sat in silence for a minute or two. Cross knew what he had to do, and nothing, not even Billy Volgar, would change his mind. And Billy knew what his boss was going to do. The thought frightened the big man who had never been frightened of anything before.

Billy drank some of his hot tea, put the big, cracked mug down on the table and asked, "You're goin' back there, ain't you?"

"I have to, Billy. Don't worry. Everything has been arranged, and everything will be OK."

"Then I'm going with you, ain't I."

"No, Billy," Cross said and patted the big man's arm. "I've made some plans that don't involve you. But there are things you need to do." Cross explained, "For two weeks I want you to take care of the woman. Never leave her side. See to it that my Doctor comes here and examines her thoroughly. No reports to anyone but me on that. Get her the best food, anything she wants. Take her shopping and buy her clothes and whatever else she wants, plus suitcases to carry everything. Get her a passport and some IDs. Off the black market, of course. She needs to decide where she wants to go, but not under any circumstance back to Africa. Have the attorneys set up funding for her, enough to keep her for a few years and allow her to start a new life somewhere. When I get back, we'll see her off."

Cross paused for a moment or two, holding the steaming mug of coffee tightly, and then said, "If I don't get back . . . Well, Manny in Tenerife knows what to do. Check with him and do whatever he tells you. I've left very specific instructions with him. Don't argue with him, just do what he says."

Billy put his cup of tea down and stared roughly at Cross. He said in his bearlike growl, "What the bloody hell you mean, *if you don't get bleedin' back?*"

Cross drained the mug of coffee, laid it down on the table, smiled and explained, "I'm going to kill Azubuike." He went on to tell Billy everything that had happened since Margaret Fullsome came to him, asking for his help. He told him all the details; he told him of his beatings and of his time as a slave. He told Billy about how the people were suffering, how the slaves were being starved and worked to death. He told him of the boy soldiers and the drugged men who carried dirty guns. He told him about Azubuike's penchant for cannibalism and torturing people for his pleasure. He ended by saying, "The man has to be stopped, Billy. He's hurting too many people."

Billy said, "That's a bloody damn job for me, boss. Bloody hell! You ain't gonna' do that and get out alive, now, are you?"

"No, I have to do it. Whether I live or die, it's personal now. I started that maniac, and I have to bring him to an end, too. Don't worry, everything will be alright."

Billy did not tear his eyes from Cross as he sipped at the tea. Then he asked, "Why?"

Cross laughed nervously and said what he had said so many times in his life, "Because it's the right thing to do."

CHAPTER FOURTEEN - Follow My Lead

Cross needed an extra day to set things up, so Mary and Robert spent that day relaxing in Cross' apartment, eating the food they needed to regain their strength, and talking quietly to each other. Neither of them wanted to talk of their months of hell at Azubuike's hands. As much as they tried to avoid speaking of their trials in Africa, however, they soon found it almost medicinal, a true catharsis, to finally be able to talk about what happened to them, to let loose the memories of all the horrors that had built up over the months and years. They often cried, holding onto each other for comfort, and they sometimes laughed, but not often.

Cross and Billy Volgar left them alone that day. They were busy doing other things. Cross had set a task for his lawyers, writing contracts and delving into the past of Margaret and Taylor Fullsome. He had stayed on the phone for most of the day, talking to contacts he had all over the world. All of them were criminals or businessmen who worked closely with criminals of one sort or another. All of them had worked with Joseph Cross before. Some owed him for making them wealthy, some for having saved their lives.

The result was that no one would ever do business with Simba Azubuike again if Cross did not survive what he had to do. Some of them did it because they liked Joseph Cross and owed him something. Others did as he told them for fear of Billy Volgar.

Dinner was brought to the apartment that evening from The Hunter's Room restaurant downstairs. Mary ate lightly, obviously deep in thought of what her future would be. The memories of the years she had been trapped with Azubuike were not easy to lose. Fear and worry weighed heavily on her. But Robert gorged himself on food he hadn't tasted in many months. He was free, he was home in England, he was young, and being young he felt invincible, as all young people feel. Each passing year wears away at that feeling that nothing bad can happen to the young until, with age and experience, caution rules their lives, as it would eventually rule Robert's life. Both Cross and Billy sat at the table with the two, Cross eating lightly and Billy eating everything he could get his huge hands on. Four bottles of good red wine were opened and finished, Billy drinking most of the four.

The talk was light and not about Africa. Billy had to bring Robert up to date on the missed months of football matches of course, and The World Cup Robert had missed. Mary laughed at the two as they got excited in their sports back and forth. Cross only shook his head, being used to the British fascination with their sports but not understanding it. Soccer and cricket were complete mysteries to Joseph Cross. Oh, he went to the games now and then, often at the excited insistence of Billy Volgar. But watching American football and baseball on his satellite TV system, and going to a horse track for a day in the rare British sun, were the sports he took pleasure in.

The next morning Robert said goodbye to Mary Ssanyu. Robert would accompany Cross that day, not questioning what they would do. He and Mary hugged and whispered a few words and kissed. She held his hand as he and Cross stepped into the elevator, reluctant to see him go.

The elevator doors shut, leaving her standing in the hallway, Billy Volgar at her side. A few tears, of both joy and sadness, sprung from her dark eyes.

Cross drove his Jaguar out of the underground garage into the grey of the morning rain. Robert Fullsome sat in the passenger seat, nervously twitching and rubbing his hands together. They were on their way to see his parents, whom he hadn't seen or spoken with in over a year. He didn't know what to expect from his parents, who hadn't made any attempt to contact him in that time.

His father would be the hardest on him, he thought. There would be recriminations about the life he had chosen. But life worshipping money as his father did was not what Robert Fullsome wanted. In Robert's mind, life was more than garnering personal wealth. His mother would be emotional, and he expected her to overwhelm him with guilt at first, and then berate him for putting her to so much trouble.

They drove in the steady rain to the Fullsome's estate outside of Royal Tunbridge Wells. It was only a forty mile drive, but the heavy rain and slick roads made the drive almost two hours long.

As they got closer, Robert's anticipation of what he would face at home grew. He gazed out the rain soaked window as the countryside passed by. They slowed to drive through quaint country villages of small, moss covered, slate roofed houses and shops. A few stone cottages with thick thatched roofs stood lonely in fields of wheat at the edges of the villages. Cross sped up as they passed cattle in stone walled, green fields. Thick leafed trees offered some shelter from the rain to wagon horses, massive in size, whose ancestors had carried armor clad knights into battle. "It hasn't changed much," he said, almost speaking to himself.

"How long has it been?" Cross asked him.

"I don't know . . . A year . . . Maybe a little more. And of course there is the time with . . . In the diamond ditches. You lose a sense of time . . . Down there." He couldn't say Azubuike's name; it caught in his throat as if he had tried to swallow a clump of thick mud, and it came close to making him gag. "I guess I haven't spent much time at home since I started at Eton. I was glad to move there . . . To start school, I mean. I didn't like Eton. It's too snobbish, you know? I had nothing in common with the students there. But I was very happy to leave home."

He turned away from the window and looked toward Cross. He said, "Can you imagine what it must be like to grow up all alone? Mother was too busy with her politics, and father was never home. He had to make money, you know. Or so he explained to me every time he missed one of my birthdays . . . Every Christmas . . . Everything that is important to a child. I had a Nanny, of course. An angry old witch who had forgotten how to laugh a hundred years ago."

Cross hadn't thought of his own childhood in many, many years. It was best, he knew, to put those years away in some distant closet, lock the door, throw the key away, and not bring them out again. Memories held too many beatings by a drunken father and too many laughs from schoolmates as he went to class in hand-me-down clothes, often torn and always disheveled. But he pushed those memories away and concentrated on what he had to do that day.

They entered a miniscule village, consisting of two colorfully ancient Pubs with thick, thatch roofs and eight little shops, three of which were abandoned and boarded up. It called itself Wilshire Market. Unkempt rose bushes and tall weeds that had been ignored for years lined the cobblestone walkway in front of the buildings. Cross thought that perhaps a hundred years ago there may actually have been a market there for the farmers to sell what they grew. Modern times and too many years had watched the young people move to the cities and leave the farms, leaving Wilshire Market to lie rotting in a slow death.

The two Pubs seemed to still be active, however. Inside them, old men with gray hair and gray breads, wearing heavy work clothes and coats, were smoking pipes and cigarettes while drinking their dark beer. They stared out the dirty windows at the strange sight of an expensive motor car driving slowly by. Old trucks and older tractors were the norm. There was no money left in Wilshire Market for new, expensive autos.

Driving on for another thirty minutes, they found the entrance to the Fullsomes' home and turned down the thin, graveled road. The Fullsomes' big house lay before them. As Cross remembered from his last visit, it was dark and unwelcoming. He saw out of the corner of his eye a sad grin race across Robert's face at the sight of the home he had left. He pulled the sleek, black Jaguar to a stop at the front door and turned to Robert. He said, "You owe me, boy. I saved your damn life. Follow my lead and do what I tell you. If you don't, I'll collect the debt you owe me. Do you understand?"

"Anything you say, Mr. Cross. Anything you say."

It was mid-afternoon that Saturday as they got out of the car. The rain had slowed to a misty, grey drizzle, but the air was cold from the rain. Cross held an attaché case. Robert wondered what was in it, but he knew he shouldn't ask.

The Fullsomes' butler opened the door as they approached, before they could knock. He looked past Cross and said, without feeling, as if Robert had just gone down the road to the pub for lunch, "Good afternoon, Mr. Robert." Robert was standing behind and to the right of Joe Cross, knowing he had to follow Cross in all the things that would happen that day.

They walked inside and found Margaret Fullsome in the hallway. "Oh my God!" she cried out in a choked whisper. "Robert, you're home."

She ran to him and threw her arms around him. He hugged her and whispered in her ear, "It's good to be home," telling the lie through some semblance of kindness, even though he didn't mean what he said.

She stood back and held him at his shoulders, looking her son up and down. "You're so thin. My God! What happened?"

"Not now, mother," Robert said. "Is father at home? Mr. Cross wants to speak with both you and him."

The MP nodded, looked at Cross and saw the dangerous expression his face held. She led them to Taylor Fullsome's office, holding tightly to her son's arm. The man was at his desk, a telephone to his ear. Without stopping his conversation, he waived the three in and pointed to a couch and chairs. He went on talking into the phone, speaking about some business that would bring in yet more money, until Cross walked to the desk and ripped the telephone cord from the socket on the floor.

"What the bloody hell do you think you're doing!" the man yelled.

"I've brought your son home to you," Cross said. "Don't you have anything to say to him? Aren't you glad to see him?"

Taylor looked at his son, sitting next to Margaret on the brocade covered couch. She had her arms around him, hugging him close to her. Robert's arms were at his side, not touching his mother at all.

He said, "Of course I'm happy that he is home . . . And alive in spite of what he put himself through. Everything that has happened is your fault for not listening to me, Robert. And I hope you will not be stupid enough to run off on another adventure. I've had your place at Eton held for you, Robert. And you will return there on Monday next," he said with finality.

Robert started to say something, but Cross stopped him with an upheld hand. He said to Taylor, "You know, you're a real son of a bitch."

"How dare you! How . . ."

"*Shut up!*" Cross shouted. "You're going to listen and do exactly what I tell you to do."

Taylor stood and glared at Cross. He was fat from years of sitting at his desk making money, and he was shorter than Cross. He wanted to look angry, but inside all he felt was fear. Cross turned to Margret Fullsome and asked, "Mrs. Fullsome, do you remember Billy Volgar? You met him at my casino."

"Of course I do," she answered. "The man was frightening. How could I ever forget?"

Cross turned back to Taylor and said, "If you don't put your fat ass back in your damn chair and listen to me, Billy Volgar will come here tomorrow. Ask your wife if you want that to happen."

Margaret Fullsome looked at her husband and said, "Sit down Taylor, for God's sake. The man is dangerous."

Taylor sat but could not hide his pent up anger. His face was flame red, and his breathing was short and heavy. "Alright, you bloody bastard," he said. "I'm sitting. Now before I phone for the police, tell me what you want."

Four phones sat on the desk, each had been connected into a socket on the floor at the side of Taylor's desk. Cross pulled the three remaining wires out and tossed them across the desk. He said, "You're not phoning anyone. You're going to sit there and listen to what I have to say. And then you're going to shut up and listen to your son instead of talking to him. Got it?"

Taylor Fullsome said nothing. The color had drained from his face, and a nervous twitch fluttered at his left eye. Beads of sweat formed across his forehead.

Cross pulled a handsomely carved chair with a Chinese silk upholstered seat and back away from a wall and put it next to Taylor's desk. Taylor looked shocked and said, "That is a very expensive and rare piece of furniture. It is not used for seating." Cross smiled and sat, crossed his legs, and began, "I did what you asked. Your son is home and safe."

"And you paid the five million American dollars ransom?" Taylor asked.

"I paid none of it. The man holding Robert thought I did, but in fact I still have all the money you gave me."

"Then none of the ransom was paid?" Margaret asked.

"Correct," Cross answered.

"Fine," Taylor said as he sat forward. "I will take your check to return the money then."

Cross smiled again and told him, "Sorry, but you're not getting any of it back. I have expenses, and in a few days I'll have more expenses. Anything not used to cover my expenses will stay with me. My fee, so to speak. And I have an idea what I will do with some of it."

He turned in his chair and looked directly at Robert Fullsome. Robert sat next to his mother on the couch, but he had edged away from her. She had let him go, and her arms were now folded in her lap. Robert had been sitting forward, elbows on his knees, his hands folded as if he were praying, listening intently to what Cross was saying. He had no idea what Joseph Cross was up to, but he was interested. There had to be a reason why Cross insisted he accompany him to his parents. He didn't ask, and he had promised to do what Cross told him to do.

His forehead frowned in wonder at what he was hearing. No one had ever talked to his father as Joseph Cross was speaking to him. He looked back and forth from his father to Cross. Cross had said nothing to him about what he would do. He wondered what would come next.

Cross, before saying anything else, looked around Taylor's big office. The room was walled in mahogany; the ceiling was fifteen feet tall above them, coffered dramatically with a large crystal chandelier hanging in the middle, casting weird dancing lights across the walls. Bookcases were on every wall, all filled with law books of every Nation, accounting ledgers, and a few small pieces of sculpture. In one corner a very large globe stood in a cherry wood stand. There were paintings on the walls, all framed elegantly and expensively. There were TV's and computer screens everywhere, but there was nothing personal in the room; no photos of family, no trinkets or souvenirs of any kind. It was a cold room, designed for making money and nothing else.

He turned back to Robert and asked, "What will you do now? I mean, will you go back to Eton, or if it were possible would you do anything else?"

The young man lowered his eyes in deep thought, but it took only a moment or two for him to raise his head, smile and look back and forth from his mother to his father. He said proudly, "If I can, I want to do something to help people. I'd like to help those poor people in Africa . . . Where I was, I mean." That, he now knew, was why Cross insisted that Robert go with him. That was what Cross had planned and hoped to hear.

"That's what I was hoping you would say," Cross said and smiled, satisfied that his intuition was right. He stood and paced around the room and then stopped, turning to Robert, and said, "I'm going to give you one million American dollars of the five I took from your parents. What will you do with it?"

Robert sat up very straight and proud and said, "I will go back to Africa and open a hospital . . . And maybe a school."

"Good, you have your million."

He then turned to Robert's father and said, "And you are going to help your son. Your lawyers will work with mine to set up a charitable trust for your son. You will fund it with five hundred thousand British pounds a year, enough to support his hospital and school. Enough to hire doctors and outfit an operating room and anything else he wants. And if he needs more, you will give it to him."

"That's bloody ridiculous!" Taylor barked. He was frightened, his face was red and he was sweating. "I won't do it! I will report you to the authorities. You can't threaten me! I will see you in court!"

Cross sat once again in the chair no one was supposed to sit on and pulled up the attaché case he had brought with him. He laid it heavily on Taylor's prized desk. He had made dozens of phone calls in his apartment as Robert and Mary rested. He had criminal contacts all over the world, and he had police and government officials from many Countries willing to help him for the cash he would pay.   The results of his time on the phone were in the attaché.

He paused . . . 'For the affect,' he thought, as he grinned straight at Taylor Fullsome.   Then he opened the case and took a thick manila folder from it.   He opened the folder and peered one by one at the pages of paper it held.   He then took the first and laid it on Taylor's desk.   Taylor looked down at it but could not bring himself to touch it.

Cross, still grinning and very satisfied that everything was going as he had planned, said, "This is proof that five years ago you illegally transported and sold to Syria's dictator-president Bashar Al-Assad, chemicals that had been banned by The United Nations.   He used those chemicals to produce poison gas.   I have the shipping records and sworn statements from five people involved in the shipment."

He took a second sheet of paper from the folder and laid it on top of the first.   Taylor looked as if he would faint.   His eyes were wide and his breathing short and fast.   Cross said, "Four years ago you sold materials to Iran that they needed to expand their nuclear production facilities.   Those materials were banned by the United Nations.   I have again the shipping records and sworn statements."

Cross closed the folder and tossed it on top of the papers on Taylor's desk.   He said, "I have records of very nearly every illegal thing you've done over the past ten years.   I'm sure there are other little business deals you've done, but I'm equally sure these will do to put you out of business and into jail for a very long time."   Cross paused once again.   Taylor was sweating; he was scared, knowing he had been exposed.   Margaret Fullsome was about to get up to go to him.   Robert took her arm and stopped her.

"All this will remain between you and me . . . If you agree to fund your son's hospital and school.   If you don't agree . . . I will turn all this over to the police and the United Nations. But Billy Volgar may get to you before the authorities do. You may be able to hide from the police. I doubt you will be able to hide from him."

Cross turned to look at Robert. He was sitting back and laughing. His mother was crying. Her only thought being that if any of what Cross had ever went public, her political career would end very suddenly.

Taylor Fullsome's face was reddening, and his breathing was very short and forced. He was overweight and not in any semblance of good condition. Robert saw this and went to him for fear he was going to have a heart attack or stroke. He touched his father's shoulder and wanted to say or do something to calm his father, but there was nothing he could do and nothing he really wanted to do.

Margaret rose and stood with her son. She could not bring herself to touch her husband as Robert was doing. In her mind, twisted with politics and ramifications of the truth, she was forcing the wish that her husband would die then and there. That seemed the easy way out for her. Taylor's death would be the assurance that what this man, this Joseph Cross, this criminal, had on Taylor would not be made public.

Racing around in her mind was the terrible thought of her political career coming to a crashing end. The publicity would sound a death knell to her wish to one day be Prime Minister.

Taylor looked from his son to his wife. He saw some worry, perhaps compassion, in his son's face. He saw only contempt in the tear filled eyes of his wife; he did not see any love or compassion from her. He scowled at Cross, squinting to peer through a thick fog of terror. He stammered, "How . . . How . . ."

"I am in a similar business to your own, Mr. Fullsome," Cross said as he stood and closed the file of Taylor's crimes in the attaché. "The difference between you and me is that I have a conscience. There are things I will not do to make money. It appears there is little you won't do to make a buck. You sicken me, Mr. Fullsome. I've killed people like you because they sickened me. But I won't kill you . . . Because you will support your son's enterprises for as long as he wants and needs that support. I have contacts all over the world who seem to like me more than they like you. On any particular day of any particular week, I will know what you are doing. I will know every illegal thing you do. I will know every time you send your son money, and I will know when you don't. Now, what is your decision? Help your son . . . Or take your chances?"

CHAPTER FIFTEEN - The Kill Plan

Tenerife was warm and sunny the day Cross arrived, a change he appreciated after several days of rain in the England that was his adopted home. He drove south across the hills of the Island, slowly, the top down on the rented BMW. He needed time to think, away from the pushing and shoving of business in London. He stopped at an attractive inn and slowly drank two bottles of good Spanish beer as he pondered the soon to come future.

Before leaving for Tenerife, Joe Cross had busy days of work to do. It had taken five days and more threats thrown at Taylor Fullsome, and the appearance of Billy Volgar at the Lincoln's Inn offices of the Solicitors for both Joe Cross and Taylor Fullsome. Fullsome and his Solicitors were, of course, reluctant to set up the charitable trust that would fund Robert Fullsome's hospital and school. Cross was ready to grab Taylor Fullsome and throw him through a wall, or perhaps just hand him over to Billy Volgar. But in the end, the papers were signed with much grumbling, swearing, and empty threats from Taylor. Robert at last walked away happy with a cashier's check for one million American dollars in hand.

As everyone walked out of the Solicitor's offices Cross took Robert aside. The young man was ready to run off and get started, somewhere in Africa, anywhere in Africa if one were to ask him. When Cross asked, Robert could not tell him where he would establish his hospital or for that matter how he would go about it. He was a young man with grand ambitions but with little thought of how he would see those ambitions into reality. Cross would see to it that he got the help and advice he needed. Cross told him to wait a week or so, and he would be able to help Robert find a place. Robert trusted Joseph Cross; after all, were it not for Cross, Robert would have died, chained to Azubuike's slaves. He would wait and follow Cross' lead.

They were alone the following afternoon in one of the small Pubs in Wilshire Market, near Robert's home. The pub, named 'The Ploughman' one hundred and twenty years ago, was dark and cool inside. A weather beaten wooden sign hung over the door, a farmer walking behind a plough painted on it, the paint peeling away with the years. The heavy wooden beams of the rafters and posts were black with age but still strong, having been crafted from some of the last of thick native British oak. The table Robert and Joe Cross sat at was not nearly as old but it was brown wood and beaten and scratched after years of use. The place smelled of age and beer and pipe smoke, not an unpleasant smell, but one of history that was fading fast in the modern Britain.

They were talking of small things, meaningless things, each trying to avoid the truth of what would happen soon. But Robert could not wait any longer. On the second pint of beer, Robert asked Cross, "You're going to kill General Azubuike, aren't you?"

"What I do . . . Or don't do, is none of your business, boy. At least for the next couple of weeks," Cross answered. "You will hear from me, and you will have a chance to build your hospital. Just wait with you mother and father until you hear from me. Don't do anything, and don't talk to anybody. You need to trust me . . . And I need to trust you. If I can't trust you . . . Well, you won't like what happens to you. I'm not a man to be fooled with or lied to."

"Alright, Mr. Cross. You saved my life. I owe you so much. I doubt I will ever find a way to repay what I owe you. I will, of course, do as you ask. But is it because of me . . . or Mary Ssanyu? You like her, don't you? You're very angry at what happened to her, aren't you?"

"It's because of neither of you," Cross answered. "Don't over estimate your own importance, boy. I have no intention of discussing Mary Ssanyu with you. I have reasons for everything I do, and right now none of those reasons include you."

"Alright . . . I can accept that. But why did you insist that father finance my endeavors?"

"Why do you think?"

Robert lowered his eyes and twirled his mug of black beer across the table top, causing a mini tide pool inside the mug. He was thinking. He looked up and suggested, "Because you don't like my father?"

"That's part of it," Cross answered.

"And you don't like my mother," Robert said.

"She's been a royal pain in my ass for years, Robert."

The young man was thinking again. He asked, "But there's another reason, isn't there?"

Cross sat back in the hard wooden chair he was sitting in. He crossed his arms, looked Robert square in the eyes, and said, "OK, if you insist . . . I started Azubuike in his life. Without me and what I did years ago, he would not be the fat bastard he is today. I have a lot of payback owing for that. I want to put an end to his little hellhole. I want to make up for some of the bad I'm responsible for."

"So, I'm guessing you want me to build the hospital

there?"

"Yes I do," Cross answered. "Now listen to me because I'm going to tell you what to do, and if you don't do exactly what I tell you to do . . . You can go home and be a good son to your parents. I will tear up all the contracts and send Billy Volgar to collect that million dollars from you."

****

That was Cross' last day in the U.K. before opening hades' gates and letting loose the dogs of hell. The following morning he was on his Gulfstream and headed to Manuel Hernandez Maria Rodriguez de Santa Anna's home in Tenerife.

Cross left the little Inn and drove on to Manny's home. He looked up at the blue sky above as he drove. Soft, billowy, white clouds drifted across the Island. The air was scented with the ocean's salt and masses of flowers that grew along the side of the mountain's thin road.

Manny was waiting for him. He had phoned Helen d'Neuville the day before, when Cross told him he would be there. Manny and Helen were on the patio, drinking cold white wine, waiting for Cross to arrive. Her two guards, with machine pistols in hand, stood nearby, keeping watch.

Manny had brought his cedar humidor of big Cuban cigars onto the patio. He offered one to Helen. She took one hungrily, bit the end off and spit, and then lit it with Manny's gold lighter before one of her guards could get to her with his own lighter. She drew the sweet smoke into her lungs and smiled gratefully. The white wine was good, but she preferred champagne or something stronger. She would not complain because the wine was sweet and refreshing in the mid-day's heat. She finished the first bottle with little help from Manny and watched as a second was opened by one of Manny's servants. As she watched the cork being pulled, Manny's eyes were locked on Helen's exposed cleavage under the military camo shirt she had left half unbuttoned.

They heard the BMW pull to a stop at the front. Manny put his glass down on the table and said to Helen, "I hope you're ready for this. Joseph Cross is a dangerous man, and he won't stop until someone dies. He will have certain specifics he wants done. It will be dangerous work I think."

Helen placed her burning cigar on the edge of the crystal ashtray on the table. She looked up at the blue, cloud dotted sky. She thought for a minute, trying to find the right words. Then she looked at Manny and said, "Danger is of nothing, oui? The plan, that is the thing. When the plan, it is good, the battle, it is also good, oui? The danger, it is removed when le plan est bon, oui?"

They looked up as Cross approached. He wasn't smiling; that told them that he was ready and The Angel of Death was nearby, following him closely, in his shadow. He sat in a chair between the two without greeting either of them. He asked Helen, "Are you ready?"

"Oui, I have the men I need. I have the dollars you sent. I have the weapons, and I have the avion . . . How you say? . . . The airplane? Is that the correct? What I do not have is the plan, n'est-ce pas vrai?"

Cross reached into his jacket pocket and retrieved a slip of paper. He unfolded it and laid it on the table. "I drew this on the flight down here. I didn't have full freedom to explore Azubuike's compound. This is what I saw and what I know. There may be more, but I doubt what I didn't see will be dangerous."

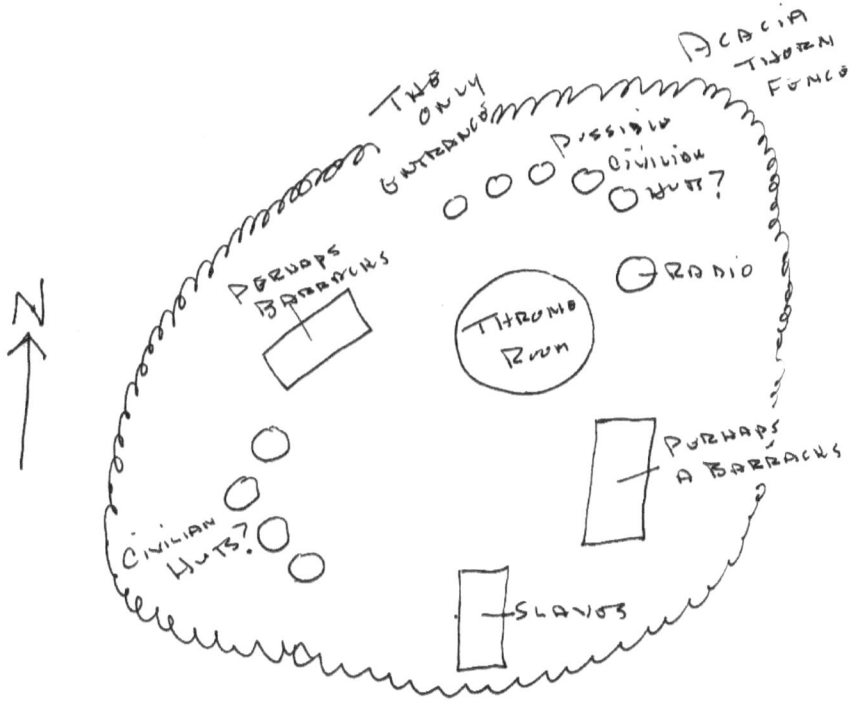

Helen picked up the paper and examined it closely. She asked, "And Joseph, mon amour, how big is this . . . I do not know the word . . . This place, oui?"

"I call it Azubuike's compound for lack of anything better. It's perhaps two hundred yards at the widest point. It's a ramshackle place, not really built to any plan," Cross answered. He knew what Helen had to do, and it would be difficult, but he had to be truthful with her. "Look, I didn't have the opportunity to explore the entire compound. I was too busy digging God damned diamonds with the slaves. But I know enough."

"You were working with the slaves?" Manny asked, astonished to hear this.

"Azubuike was making his point the hard way . . . For me at least. I was beat up, knocked unconscious, and when I woke up, I was chained to a line of slaves in a filthy hut. I spent the day digging diamonds chained to the slaves. Azubuike wanted me to know he was powerful, at least in his own mind. But I was able to look, and I saw some of what he had there.

"I can only guess what a few of the mud huts are used for," he continued. "I saw a few women, and I saw children, so some of the huts must be for them. I'm guessing the women I saw were for the guards. I doubt there are families there as we know families. I saw Azubuike's soldiers coming and going from a couple of the bigger buildings. They have to be barracks or something like that. I know where the radio shack is and where the slaves are kept. I've been inside Azubuike's throne room and his private quarters at the rear of his throne room. The rest is only conjecture."

"There is a lot to be the assumption, Joseph," Helen said. "Tell me of the soldiers."

"Most are not really soldiers," Cross answered. "They are drugged, ragged, thin, and they carry old weapons. I'm guessing they get more drugs than food. And their weapons are old and dirty. But everyone carries a machete and a club. There are four men that I saw who are not drugged, but there might be more of them. They carry good, clean weapons. Their clothes are not rags and they look well fed. They look professional. They may be experienced. They are the most dangerous. There are also a handful of children who carry old, dirty guns. Outside the compound, about a mile north, there is a roadside check point. I saw three men there, and all were in drugged-out sleep. They will need to be taken care of, but they should not be a problem. If they are approached quietly, they'll probably be asleep and easily disposed of."

Helen looked deeply at the paper again. She understood that Cross had been held captive and did not have the freedom to gather perfect intelligence. She had been in a few battles with less intelligence at hand. "And the fence?" she asked. "It is as you say thorn? And how big it is?"

"How tall?" Cross asked. "Perhaps four to six feet, but it is irregular. It is maybe three or four feet wide. Again irregular. It looks like it may have been assembled quickly, without much plan. It's all acacia that had been cut and piled up. The thorns are very big and very sharp. It is meant to keep animals and people out . . . And maybe to keep people in. It would do a good job at that. But the entire thing is dry. It will burn easily."

"And who is to do the burning?"

"I will," Cross answered.

"You will then go in before I go in?" Helen asked. "You will not use the parachute?"

"I am going in early. I will take out the little outpost on the road. I need five of your men to come with me. I will leave three there to protect our rear. If anyone comes to help Azubuike it will have to be from the north. I will burn the thorn fence. That will be your signal to parachute in. It will be dark, the middle of the night. There will be a new moon when you drop in. It will be very dark, so the fire will be easily seen. Circle above, high enough so the engines won't be heard below, until you see the fire. The fence is dry and will burn quickly, as I said. I want to wait until the dark of night when most in the compound are asleep. I need you to drop in quickly and quietly. If anyone is awake before you are there, the two men with me and I will take them out. But we can't hold out for long, so make it a HALO drop."

"Oui," Helen said. "We do the 'high altitude, low

opening' drop . . . How you say? . . . bien? . . . Good? I am to drop into the compound? Not outside?"

"The terrain inside the compound and to the North is fairly dry," Cross explained. "To the West and East is marshy forest. Too wet and wooded to drop into, especially at night. To the South is swamp and very wet. Your best bet is to drop directly to the North, outside the compound where it is nothing but dry grassland. Use directional chutes. If some of your men land inside the acacia wall that won't be a problem, just stay close.

"That is good," Helen said. "And how do we . . . How do you say? . . . Get out, is that the word?"

"I have a plan," Cross said. "There will be another plane, a small cargo carrier. It will land on the dirt road as it can . . . After you've done your job. There will be cargo onboard that will have to be unloaded quickly. Once it's unloaded, you and your men will get on board and be flown out. It will be big enough to take you all out. It might be a tight fit, but it can carry everyone."

"And you, Joseph? You will not come also?"

"No," Cross answered as he leaned back in the chair. "I have some things that need to be done. I'm going to stay for a few days."

"You will stay, mon ami?" Helen asked. "I do not understand."

"You will understand once your job is done, Helen. Until then, what I do is my business alone. Just be there and kill everyone who needs to be killed. One other thing," Cross added. "The children with guns. I want them disarmed and not killed if possible. If they fight . . . Kill them. If they can be disarmed, then do so. And unless the women fight, I want them alive. Most of those people are slaves of one sort or another. If the women don't dig diamonds, then they are probably sex slaves. They deserve a chance at life. The drugged soldiers and Azubuike's personal guard should all die."

"What of this Azubuike?" Helen asked. "You do not make mention of him?"

"Don't kill him," Cross answered. "I want him alive."

"But . . ." Helen started.

"No buts," Cross answered. His eyes were locked on Helen's. She had never met Joseph Cross before, but she knew of his reputation. He was strong, she knew. He was dangerous, and she knew that also. It would be unwise to disagree with him too strongly. 'Perhaps,' she thought silently, 'One day I will have to kill him. But not now.'

CHAPTER SIXTEEN – James Hoffman

Robert Fullsome was in his bedroom at his parents' estate. He was packing three small suitcases with everything of his that could fit in them. Clothing was the most important thing, but so much of these things were too heavy weight for the heat of Africa. He left most of his clothes in the closet and bureau.

Books, of course; he couldn't do without them. Poetry, those were important, so he carefully placed three anthologies in the largest of the suitcases. He ran his hand across the books on the small shelf at the back of the room, deciding which were important enough to take with him. Faulkner was always a good read; he packed two of his books. And Steinbeck, of course.

He pulled his old, dog-eared copy of his childhood Bible and flipped through the pages. He had to laugh as he saw all the underlined passages and side-bar notes he had written, questioning things that a young man wasn't supposed to question. He tossed that in the suitcase. Four more books on the social sciences were squeezed in. There was no more room for books. But he could always get more, he thought.

And he packed the big .38 revolver Joseph Cross had given him. He held it in his hands before putting it under some shirts. It was heavy, very heavy. Robert had never touched a gun before. As a child he played sports and chased little girls, but he never played 'cowboys and Indians' or war as so many of his school mates did. His father hunted and killed small animals proudly. He had insisted Robert accompany him on these hunts, until Robert was old enough to say 'no'. Could he ever use the pistol? He wondered if he could actually kill another human being. He put it in the smallest of the three suitcases, wrapped in several pieces of his underwear.

On top of the bureau, were three silver framed photographs: one of his mother, one of his father, and one of his sister, Elizabeth. She was the lucky one, he thought as he held her picture and smiled at the memory of her. At nineteen, she had escaped their family and had married a Spanish businessman, Jose Maria Santiago. She lived in Madrid. She had a family, three children and a good husband who provided well for her. She was happy. She had never come back, and Robert hoped she would stay away forever.

Robert had seen her several times in the past five years. She was glowing with happiness and in love with her husband; she was raising a son and two daughters and would, she assured him, never return to their unhappy home in England. He carefully packed her photograph in one of the suitcases and left the other two sitting face down on the bureau. They were not important; they would only be hard memories of an unhappy past, a past that would be best forgotten.

The door to his bedroom opened suddenly, hitting the wall hard. He turned and saw his father standing in the doorway. His bulk filled the open doorway. He hadn't shaved that day, and he was still wearing the wool pajamas he had slept in. "What the bloody hell are you up to, Robert?" the man growled.

Robert sighed a deep breath and answered, "I'm packing, father. That should seem obvious."

"You are really going to do this, aren't you, Robert?"

"Yes, father. I'm really going to do this."

"Why?" Taylor asked. "You have a future here, Son. Your place at Eton . . ."

Robert slammed one of the suitcases closed, locked the two latches, and said, interrupting his father, "You made an agreement, Father. The contracts have been signed."

Taylor took three steps into the room and smiled proudly, throwing out his chest as if he had just made the goal that won the game, as he said, "Any contract can be done away with. Don't be an ass. Stay here, and when you have finished school you will join my company. Everything will be yours in a few years. I have worked my whole life for your future, Robert."

"Please Father. It's done. I have a few things to do, and then I'll be off to Africa. It's what I want to do. That is *my* future, Father. Can't you understand that? Can't you understand that I don't want a future like yours? Can't you understand that I have my own mind? Why must you always hate and disapprove of everything I want? I'm not like you, Father. I'm nothing like you."

Taylor Fullsome shook his head, unable to understand that his only son would not be part of the empire Taylor had built. He had lost a daughter to some trivial Spanish banker or some such thing. Good riddance, he would always tell himself when he thought of her. To Taylor, a daughter was only something to produce grandsons who might work with him someday, making money. But his daughter's children, his grandchildren, were not to be part of his life. They were far away, and he had never so much as seen them or talked to them. But Robert, his son, was a disappointment; the only son he would ever have, and now he would lose him, also.

There was little he could do, he knew that. He had been forced to go to London to sign the contracts. He had met with his attorneys and with Joseph Cross' attorneys. And he had seen Billy Volgar standing there, in a corner, huge hands folded in front of him, and a bulge under his left arm that Taylor knew had to be a very big gun.

Billy was silent; he stood watching and waiting. The threat that was Billy Volgar was obvious but silent. No, Taylor would do nothing to spur the ire of that ugly and frightening man. Taylor would walk away from his son. He had no options left. He would go on with his life because business and money were really the only important things to Taylor. Everything else was on the periphery of his life and his dreams.

Robert watched his father turn and leave the room. There would be no goodbyes, no hugs, no loving wishes. There would be contacts in the years to come, when Robert needed money for his hospital and school. And somewhere in the recesses of his mind was the hope that some good would come of that arrangement. Maybe, like Scrooge's ghosts, using his money for something good might change Taylor.

He went back to his packing. In his mind was the decision that he would never return to the Fullsome Estate. His life was just beginning. The past was not his life; it was all just unpleasant memories. No more doing what he was told, hoping for a 'thank you' or a 'good job' that never came. No more would the only words spoken by his parents be criticisms. And spinning around in the back areas of his mind was the hope that he would never see either of them again.

Margaret Fullsome walked into his room and went to her son slowly, hesitating, because she was afraid. She took him into her arms and hugged him to her as she cried softly. He was taller than she, a fact he had never realized before. He looked over her head, out the window with the old, yellowed, lace curtain that he had always hated. Her presence had always been dominant, like the proverbial gorilla in the room, until that day. He put his arms around her to try to comfort her, but he knew that the only comfort she would take would be him telling her he wasn't leaving.

"Please stay, Robert," she whispered. "You don't have to work with your father. You can enter politics." She moved away from him slightly, looked up at him, and smiled as if it were a new thought, not a hope she had held inside of her for years. "I know all the right people. I can help you. You can be a success there, you can stand for Parliament, and you can do good for people right here at home."

"No, Mother. I'm sorry, but I am leaving." He pulled himself away from his mother's arms and took two steps back, away from her. He looked at her; her face was aging and puffy under her thick make-up, showing years of politics and tensions and pressures. He wondered if there was any love left behind the wrinkles and grey strands only partially hidden by the false color of her hair. Could she love anything but power? Could there be any small ember of love left in her heart for her only son?

"I have to do this, Mother. Inside of me there is this driving need . . . This passion almost, to help people. I have been given the opportunity by Mr. Cross, and I will not let him down. I wish you could understand, Mother. I wish you could listen to me and understand."

"Tell me, then," she asked as she wiped the tears from her eyes, spreading the black mascara and blue eye shadow across her cheeks. "Where will you be? What will you do?"

"I've been told what to do by Mr. Cross. I intend to do exactly what he has told me to do. I cannot discuss it with you or anyone else. Perhaps I'll write when I get settled; we'll see how I feel. And perhaps someday you might visit. I think you'd like some of the things I'm going to do. And it might enhance your political career. But for now, I cannot tell you anything more."

"But Robert . . ."

"Mother," Robert said, trying to be compassionate, but too many years of being ignored by his mother as she climbed the political ladder left little room for love or compassion. "I'm going. It's something I have to do. Can't you imagine the good that will occur when there is a hospital and school in some wilderness area, serving people who have been ignored by the world for too long? Can't you see?"

"The Government has spent millions over the years in aid to African nations. I have sponsored several bills to do this. Why you? Why is it so important that you do what others might do?"

"Because I have to," Robert said. He smiled as the thought raced into his thoughts. "And as Mr. Cross would say, 'It's the right thing to do'."

★★★★★★★★★★★★★★★

Robert drove his old Vauxhall sedan to the small, isolated and little-used airfield where he and Joseph Cross and Mary Ssanyu had landed. He parked at the side of a rusted Quonset hut, out of view of motorists who might pass by, as he had been told to do. Evening was fast approaching; the air was cooling, but there was no rain. The small WWII airfield was deserted. Grass and weeds were growing in the cracks of the concrete runway. Birds had nested on top of the old control tower with the broken windows. Rabbits ran free, feasting on the wild vegetation.

Robert got out of his car and pulled his suitcases from the trunk. He stood, holding them, one in each hand and one on the concrete at his feet, and looked around at the lonely place. No wonder, he thought, that Joseph Cross used this old airfield. What better place for his kind of business. There was nothing there but trees thick with undergrowth, and the nearby country road that was little used by anyone. He laughed and turned to enter the decaying, old building. He had received a phone call from Cross the day before with instructions to go there and wait. "Don't ask questions, boy," he had said. "Just do what I tell you to do. Wait there."

Inside, he lit a new Coleman lamp that was on top of a new folding camp table. He looked around the room. There was a cot with a thin mattress, and a new, neatly folded blanket and a fresh, white pillow were lying neatly on it. A small, round table that held a propane camp stove was across the room. On the table were a stack of magazines next to a single metal plate, a tin cup, and a knife, a fork and a spoon. There was an AM / FM radio on the table. And at the back of the small room was an old toilet that Robert hoped actually worked. Next to it was a sink, as old as the toilet. It was dripping water from the faucet, so he was confident he would not go thirsty.

Hanging from the steel wall was a long steel shelf. Cans of food were lined up on it, and a can opener lay in the middle of the cans. It was basic food, beans, canned meats, and canned pastas, but it would do.

He would spend the next several days there, waiting. He would wait for a man to arrive with word from Joseph Cross. He had been told by Cross that if, after a week, no word came, then Joseph Cross would be dead, and Robert would be on his own to do whatever he wanted. The million dollars would still be his, but Joseph Cross would not be there to help and guide him.

****

Cross left Tenerife that afternoon. He left his Gulfstream on the Island and flew a commercial jet to Kampala, Uganda. He sped through customs using one of many passports he owned, this one a British passport in the name of James Hoffman. He wore a dark blue business suit, one bought off the rack, the kind of suit so many mid-level businessmen wear. He wore black plastic rimmed eye glasses with plain, nonprescription glass. It wasn't much of a disguise, but he hoped it would be enough.

He did not stop looking for Colonel Owusu and any of his police. But he and his men were not there. The Colonel had been checking the passenger manifests for people arriving on a daily basis. The name James Hoffman meant nothing to them.

His first stop was by taxi to the Kampala branch of Barclays Bank, where he withdrew $50,000 in cash, American dollars, that he had wire transferred there the day before.

With the cash in a briefcase, he took another taxi to the offices of the Ugandan State Government. His business there was completed in less than an hour. He left the building without the briefcase and without the money, but with a manila envelope filled with papers.

A third taxi took him back to the airport, where he bought a first class ticket to London. He would rest there, in his private apartment on the fourth floor of his casino, for a day or two, review his plan to be sure he had thought of everything, and then begin the little war and the killing.

At the airport he walked to the gate and passed two of Colonel Okello Owusu's Special Police Officers. They were dressed in the crisp and clean uniforms Cross was very familiar with. They wore thick black sunglasses to hide their suspicious eyes, and their peaked caps were at a swaggering angle. They smelled of strong and very cheap cologne.

As Cross walked toward the departure gate, the two Officers glared at him. They spoke to each other, back and forth, and then they ran to catch up with him. They thought they recognized the man, but they weren't sure. They called out loudly for him to stop, calling out 'Joseph Cross!' over and over again, but Cross walked on, slowly, through the crowds, as if the two officers were calling to someone else. The taller of the two stopped in front of Cross and spoke in broken English.

"I see passport," he said. He stood very close to Cross, close enough for Cross to smell the fish, peppers and spices the Officer had for lunch; the smell almost overwhelmed the strong cologne.

Cross pulled the passport in the name of James Hoffman from his pocket and handed it to the officer, innocently and questioningly. The officer opened it slowly and turned the pages, one by one, very deliberately. Cross waited, saying nothing, smiling slightly. The Officer held the passport up with the photo page open, next to Cross.

"This is you?" he asked.

"Certainly," Cross answered in his best feigned British accent. "Who would it be?"

He looked at the stamped page showing this James Hoffman had arrived in Uganda that morning.

"You come here today?" the man asked. "You leave here today?"

"Yes, that's right."

"Why?" he asked, closing the passport but not handing it back to Cross.

"Business," Cross said. "Look, my plane is going to leave in a few minutes. May I please have my passport back?"

The two Officers looked at each other, and the shorter of the two said in better English than the first, "There is a small exit fee. You will pay that now."

Cross understood. He took his old, cracked leather wallet from his pocket and pulled two ten Pound notes from it. He handed one to each of the officers. Their eyes lit up at such a fortune.

The taller of the two said, "You pay more."

It was not a question but a demand. Cross had twenty-five Pounds left in the wallet. He pulled two more ten Pound notes from it and handed them to the man, holding the wallet open in front of them. They saw him give them everything he had, except for one single five Pound Note. They did not know that Cross had three thousand American dollars on his gold money clip. They stepped aside, and Cross went to his plane.

CHAPTER SEVENTEEN - Diplomatic Pouches

It was unusually cold the night of the raid. A steady breeze from the northeast had been carrying unseasonably low temperatures, for Africa, with it. It foretold of rain soon to come with it. That would not be good if Helen were to drop in while it was raining. But she and her small army had overcome such obstacles before, and Cross knew she could do it again.

It was ten minutes past two AM. The three guards at the roadside outpost, on the dirt road a mile from Azubuike's compound, weren't aware of the cold air coming out of the northeast. They had been chewing khat leaves and smoking ganja all day. They were euphorically half asleep at their posts. Before being driven to the outpost they had each been given three hand rolled cigarettes of rough tobacco laced with cocaine. They had smoked one each in the back of the old truck and had finished the others quickly, all the while chewing mouthfuls of khat. Oblivion engulfed them; a herd of elephants could have marched over them, and they would not have realized it.

They lay in the dirt, outside the old mud hut that was supposed to be their shelter, dozing in half sleep. They did not hear the small plane land on the bumpy road a few hundred yards from them.

Cross climbed from the single engine plane first,

followed by five of Helen's mercenaries. They pulled rucksacks and five HK MP5 SD silenced submachine guns from the plane. Cross wore a web belt that held a Beretta M9A1 pistol. All were dressed in black camos, their faces blackened with dark of night camo paint.

As the six men walked toward the mud hut outpost, the small prop airplane turned and took off into the cold wind. When it was gone, the silence of the night was broken only by the sounds of big hunting animals in the distance, calling out their threats and warning others of their territory.

A small fire had been laid in the road in front of the hut, the dying embers and final wisps of smoke curling into the night, unnoticed by the drugged guards. One hundred feet from the outpost, Joe Cross and his five followers stopped. Cross motioned to three of the mercenaries and waived them on.

Quickly and silently they went to the hut, and without a sound, they killed the three guards with knives. The sounds of gunshots, even silenced shots, would carry for miles in the cold night air. Silence was vital. They pulled the bodies into the hut, and the three mercenaries remained there to cover Cross' rear as he and the two remaining mercenaries walked the mile to Azubuike's compound.

The thorn walled compound was dark and quiet as the three men approached. A strong smell of burnt flesh wafted towards them. Helen's two men looked at Cross, silently asking what the smell was. "It's bad," Cross whispered. "Try to ignore it . . . If you can. It's what we're here to put an end to."

They circled around the outside of the acacia wall, stepping carefully until they found a somewhat isolated place in absolute dark. Using machetes, they cut through the thorns at the rear of the compound rather than use the open gate at the dirt road. Entering from the road would have been too obvious and could have been seen by anyone still awake. They walked slowly into the compound, stepping quietly so as to not wake or alarm anyone.

The few buildings blocked most of the cold wind blowing in from the northeast; acrid smoke filled the air and was being blown towards the three men. A few fires in front of a couple of the small huts burned the last of their scraps of wood as Cross and his men walked without a sound across the compound. A man, dressed in dirty rags of a flowered shirt and brown shorts, bent to crawl out of a small hut nearby. A quick burst from a silenced MP5 laid him dead in the dirt. They stopped in their tracks and looked around. What small sound there was from the shooting seemed not to wake anyone.

Cross stopped in front of the big round building that was Azubuike's throne room. He told the two men to wait outside. They turned their backs to the big building, standing guard at the foot of the stairs. Cross took the three steps up slowly, not wanting to make any sounds. He opened one of the double doors, a rusted hinge squeaking too loudly. He spat on it and spat again. The squeaking subsided.

Inside was pitch black and very still. Cross pulled a flashlight from his belt and lit it. He waived the beam slowly from right to left, across the big room. He stopped suddenly when the light rested on Azubuike sitting on his throne, smiling broadly. Standing next to him, his hand on the tall back of the throne was Colonel Okello Owusu, grinning as broadly as Azubuike.

Azubuike was dressed in wrinkled green fatigues and his long cloak of lion skin. He struggled to stand and stood without thinking to pull the cloak around him. He took a couple of steps forward, almost tripping over the lion's head rug. He stood at the edge of the red platform that held his red throne, his face looking maniacal in the light of the flashlight. He said, "Why, Mr. Cross. You are later than I expected. But you are here in any case. It is so very good to see you again."

Cross did not turn when the electric lights were switched on, flooding the room with bright light. There were six of Owusu's Police standing around at the walls, each armed with an M16 rifle. They began to laugh, first one and then another, until all six had been joined by Colonel Owusu and Azubuike.

The doors behind Cross opened. Helen's two men were pushed roughly into the room by three more of Owusu's Special Police Officers and four of Azubuike's personal guards, the few of his men who were well armed and not drugged. Helen's men were clubbed with rifle butts and fell to the floor. They had been disarmed outside, and their rucksacks and weapons belts had been taken from them.

Colonel Owusu had stopped laughing; a deadly serious cloud had come across his face. Azubuike fell back onto his throne. The Colonel was looking down at Azubuike who was laughing insanely, uncontrollably, slapping his hands on his fat knees. Spittle was flowing from his lips, mucus ran in long streams from his nose, and his eyes were wide and bulging. Sweat was streaming down his forehead and across his face.

Owusu had no love for this fat maniac, but for years Azubuike had funneled money to him, to buy his ignorance of all the horrors Azubuike was responsible for. The Colonel looked up, pulling his gaze from Azubuike. He looked around the room. Azubuike's guards stood stoically, not laughing. He looked across the room at his men who were still laughing. He raised his hand, and all of them stopped laughing immediately and came to a stiff attention, clicking boot heals together.

It took Azubuike a few seconds to realize he was the only one still laughing. He slowly looked around in wonderment, unsure of why no one else found it humorous that Joseph Cross had walked into his trap.

He pushed his bulk from his throne once again and stood on unsure, fat legs, holding tightly to his thorn encrusted cane. The room was filled with silence as he took two uneasy steps forward and then said, "Take this man, my good friend Joseph, take him out and burn him. I wish to smell his burnt body."

Azubuike's four men stepped to Cross but were stopped when Owusu said in a soft but commanding voice, "No."

His nine Officers rushed to Cross and the mercenaries. They stood between them and Azubuike's men, their backs to Cross.

Azubuike looked up at Owusu who stood a full foot taller than he and a hundred and fifty pounds lighter. He silently questioned Owusu's insult. 'How dare this man say 'no' to me,' he thought. He didn't have the words to speak; his anger was flaming.

Owusu looked down at the corpulent little dictator, standing there and looking up with burning eyes. He said, "I want to speak with him."

He spoke in Swahili, telling six of his officers to take Azubuike's guards outside and keep them there. They left and closed the big doors after them. Three of the Colonel's officers remained to stand guard over Cross and his two men.

He again waived his arm, and his three officers took Cross and the mercenaries by their arms. Owusu pointed to the door at the side of the throne's platform that led to Azubuike's private quarters. They walked through the doorway; Owusu stepped down off the platform, following them, leaving Azubuike gaping open mouthed, shaking uncontrollably, his twisted mind unable to comprehend what was happening. He slouched back on his throne and lost control of his bladder, spreading a dark stain on his pants.

Owusu stationed the three Officers outside the room, their backs to the closed door. Inside he was alone with Cross and the two mercenaries. Owusu stood in the center of the room and spat onto the floor. He said, "That man is disgusting."

"But he's your friend, apparently," Cross said.

"He buys what you may call friendship, Mr. Cross."

"So like everyone else, you have a price?" Cross asked.

"That is a roundabout way of getting to what I want to speak with you about," Owusu said. He paced back and forth in front of Cross, the two mercenaries standing to the side, near the closed door, waiting for the opportunity to attack. Stopping, Owusu pulled his gold, diamond encrusted cigarette case from his pocket and took a cigarette from it. He held the case out, offering one to Cross, who declined.

Owusu stood very close, in front of Cross, smoking his cigarette in quick, deep breaths. He glanced at the two men who had come with Cross. Their faces, painted with nighttime camo, were blank, but Owusu sensed the danger they carried with them. They had the unmistakable look of professional soldiers about them. He said nothing, and his face did not reveal the worry he had that these men had not come alone with Joseph Cross. There had to be others like them out there somewhere.

Cross finally broke the silence by asking, "So what the hell do you want to talk about? Are you just delaying my burning at Azubuike's stake?"

"You will not burn . . . Nor will you die today, Mr. Cross. I have other plans."

"OK," Cross said. "So what are those plans? What the hell do you hope I'll do for you?"

Owusu laughed and said, "It is what I will do for you, Mr. Cross. I am sickened by that man out there. I can no longer tolerate his excesses. He is not worth caring about anymore."

"So what?" Cross asked. "Go put a bullet in his damn head if you want to. Just get to the point."

"The bullet in his head . . . that will come later. For now I must plan for after his death."

"And you have some plan for me?"

"That also will come later, Mr. Cross," Owusu said. "I like the money that I have been receiving from this . . . Operation, shall we say. I want that money to continue."

Owusu said nothing more but stared into Cross' eyes for a moment or two, waiting for Cross to come to the realization of what Colonel Owusu wanted. He inhaled the last bit of smoke he could from the cigarette, crushed it under the toe of his boot, on an antelope skin rug, and lit another. But Cross said nothing. He thought he might know what the Colonel wanted, but he would wait to hear it from the man himself. If Owusu was going to kill Azubuike, then Cross thought he should just go do it. What did that have to do with him?

"Again," Cross said. "So what?"

Owusu turned and walked to a couch that had been

upholstered in giraffe skin. He sat and waived toward a chair, inviting Cross to sit. As he sat in the soft armchair not too close to the Colonel, Cross said, "Cut to the chase, Colonel. You want something from me. Money? That can be arranged. Anything else? . . . We can talk about that. But let's stop wasting time."

"Tell me how you intended to kill Azubuike," Owusu said and grinned a satisfied grin.

"How did you come to the conclusion that I was planning on killing Azubuike?"

"Please, Mr. Cross. I am not a stupid man. I was educated in English schools in South Africa, you know," he said very proudly. "I've told you this. You came here with these soldiers," he pointed to the two men standing at the door. "You would have no other motive."

"So just tell me what you think I was going to do," Cross said, getting frustrated at the game Owusu was playing.

Owusu dropped his half smoked cigarette onto the floor and crushed it under his boot on a leopard skin rug. He lit yet another cigarette and blew a cloud of smoke towards the wood beamed ceiling.

He smiled again and began, "You came to my Country with cash and bought permission to build a hospital. Oh yes, I know everything that happens in my Government. You used a strange passport and bribed two of my officers with a great sum of money. Secrets do not exist, no matter how much you paid people to keep a secret. Very strange, I thought at first. Then I realized that a short time ago you had come to this place to rescue Robert Fullsome, which you did very successfully. And what did this young man want? Again I thought about that. Robert Fullsome foolishly wants to do some good in this world. He is young and unwise and has not yet learned what the world really is. In a few years he may learn the harsh realities of life, the evils that exist in men's hearts. He will learn . . . If he is to survive . . . That money is what the world's engines need for fuel. He will learn of the corruption that is everywhere, and he may learn to live within that corruption. But for the time being you will help him build that hospital, correct?"

Cross did not answer.

"Where would this Robert Fullsome build that hospital, I wondered? He could do that anywhere in the world with the financial backing of his parents . . . And your backing, of course. It was not difficult for me to come to that assumption. I am not a stupid man, you see. You and Robert's parents . . . The three of you . . . Have wealth beyond dreams . . . Beyond my dreams in any case. But if you and he had plans to build it here . . . Then you would have to kill Azubuike first. That fat fool would not allow a hospital to be built here, of course.

"I knew you were coming," Owusu continued as he blew smoke towards the ceiling. "I was told that your small plane had left The Republic of Congo. So, I came here and waited. I thought if you did not come here, then I would kill that fat man myself. If you did come here, I would let you do that. And you did as I thought you might. But you surprised me, Joseph Cross. You did not come alone to kill the fat man. You arrived with two very professional looking soldiers. What was that all about? And further, if there are two, there are more. With more there will be a lot of killing. So further, once again, I assume you intended to do more than killing, you are here to wipe out everything Azubuike had here." Owusu laughed, satisfied that he had been right.

Cross thought, relieved that Owusu did not know about the three men he had left at the outpost. But what good would that do if he could not contact them? And

Owusu had only guessed that a small force of men would be arriving very soon. All he saw were two men with Cross. He was only guessing. If Cross could keep him guessing, keep him unsure of what was happening, that would work in Cross' favor. He sat back in the chair, grinned, and said nothing.

"But, of course, two men and you would not be able to do the job if you intend to kill everyone here," Owusu went on. "So, as I assume, you have others coming here, correct? You need not answer. I know I am correct. But the question remains, when will the others arrive? And how many more?"

He didn't know what was happening, and he was scared. He didn't have enough men to hold off a large scale assault. He knew that, and he was trying to get at the truth. The fear hadn't materialized on his face as yet, but he was worried. And he could not get Joseph Cross to say anything. His temper was rising.

Cross was beginning to get exasperated with Owusu's droning on. He decided that he would use Owusu's fear and worry. It was time to take the lead, to get aggressive. He sat forward and said, "Get to the point, Colonel. Kill me, or get to the point."

Owusu crushed out his cigarette, again on the leopard carpet. He also sat forward and said, "I want you to kill Azubuike, and I will take over this operation. You need not bring the help I know has to be coming. I will kill whoever else needs to be killed here . . . At your direction of course. After that is done, you will handle the sale of the diamonds, and we will split the profit evenly between us."

So, Cross found, Owusu was scared. He was stabbing in the dark at more soldiers coming to help. He had no way of knowing, but he was scared that he would be overwhelmed and killed along with Azubuike. Cross had to keep it going as long as he could. But if he couldn't set the acacia on fire, Helen might not arrive at all. Time, that's what he needed. Time was in short supply. He had to reach for any opportunity to do what he needed to do.

"Why should I kill Azubuike? Why don't you kill him?"

"My reputation is at stake, Mr. Cross. Eventually it would be common knowledge that I killed him. I can't have that."

"But you can kill everyone else? All of Azubuike's soldiers, his personal guards, the slaves and boy soldiers and anyone else you think should be killed?" Cross asked. Owusu was beginning to get uncomfortable with the direction the talk was taking. It showed on his face.

He took the time to light yet another cigarette, trying to calm himself and take control of his temper that was rising to the surface. Then he said, "Those people are nothing. They are insignificant in the greater scheme of what I want. No one will miss them. No one will care if they die."

"And so, after I kill Azubuike and you kill a couple dozen others, you will take over the diamond operation here? And you will free the slaves and make this an honest and legal diamond mining operation? Is that right? Am I correct?"

"Those people, Azubuike's slaves, they are also not important," Owusu said, waving his arm as if brushing aside the thought of the human beings being held in chains. "They are nothing, and they will continue to dig our diamonds. I will supply the slaves; you need not worry about that. I am not a cannibal as Azubuike is. I do not torture people for entertainment. These people will receive food and water and care enough to keep them alive . . . But they *will* dig diamonds for us. I assure you of that. You can certainly see the sense to that, can't you?"

Cross knew he had to be careful. If he said something Owusu didn't like, the result would be the same as if he had said something Azubuike didn't like. Owusu would kill him. So he asked, "Can I think about that? I mean . . . I like the idea of the money, and diamonds are easy to dispose of. I just need time to think about the process . . . I mean, I need to think about how we will make the trades and all that."

He needed time to get to the acacia and set it ablaze. He had to stall, and he had to keep Owusu thinking he was close to a deal.

"Tell me one thing, Mr. Cross. I asked you before, how did you plan to kill Azubuike? Why come here with only two soldiers?"

"As I said, Colonel . . . I need time to think about this," Cross answered evading the question.

"And suppose I turn over your two comrades to that maniac out there?" Owusu asked. "Will that speed up the process?"

"If you do," Cross answered, "Then you have lost my cooperation. Find someone else to buy your diamonds."

"And then I will kill you?"

"No one lives forever, Colonel. I've been on borrowed time for years. Today may be the day I die. I can accept that. Fate may be calling my name. But if you need me, you will cooperate with me as you want me to cooperate with you. And my friends here will remain safe and well fed while I think about it."

Owusu crushed out the third cigarette on the leopard skin carpet at his feet. He leaned back and stared at Cross as he thought.

Cross waited and then said, "I have something I need to know, Colonel."

"And just what is that, Mr. Cross?"

Cross leaned back in the chair and smiled. He said, "A couple of years ago I left here with a small bag of diamonds and a woman, Mary Ssanyu. I sent her to a man in Amsterdam who I thought would see her to safety, away from Azubuike. But that man told the wrong person she was there, and that man told Azubuike. She was picked up by Africans in good uniforms. She was returned to Azubuike and suffered a year of torture and suffering. Those were your men, weren't they?"

"Mr. Cross," the Colonel answered with pride in what he said. "I am a powerful man in my Country. Not only do I have my own police force, but I have control of security in each of my Country's Embassies and Consulates around the world. Those were people at my Consulate who report to me."

"Why did you send her back to Azubuike?" Cross asked.

"That woman was the property of the fat man," he said shrugging his shoulders to say it should have been obvious to Cross. "She is not important. Any property stolen from anyone should be returned to the rightful owner, don't you agree?"

"And you believe that people can be property?" Cross asked, smiling to hide his anger.

"Of course," Owusu said. "I know that Americans do not think like that. But the rest of the world does not think as you do. In Europe, in Asia, in Russia, in South America, and all through Africa, the lesser peoples, the unimportant people, the surplus peoples, they are and should be the property of the better people . . . For their own good, don't you see? We can take care of them, feed them, house them, and clothe them as they cannot do for themselves. They are much better off as being the property of their betters. How many children starve because they cannot be cared for by their parents? Others, their betters, can feed them and care for them, and they have work to do. Oh, I don't like what that fat man out there does. Property, any property, should be treated well, as an investment, don't you see? I will not treat my workers who will dig the diamonds for me the way Azubuike treats them."

Cross told himself that there was no sense in arguing with this man. This man had revealed himself to be not unlike Azubuike. He would call his slaves 'workers,' but they would be his slaves, his property. And knowing it was Colonel Owusu who had sent Mary Ssanyu back to many months of torture, sealed Owusu's fate. He would die along with Azubuike. But Cross would be patient and wait for the surprise Helen d'Neuville would be bringing with her when the gates of hell would be opened.

Cross asked, changing the subject so that the Colonel would not realize how much Cross hated what he had said, "So your embassy people do all of your bidding?"

"Of course."

"And that is how the diamonds get out of Uganda? In diplomatic pouches?" Cross asked.

"Of course," Owusu answered. "It is a good way to smuggle, Mr. Cross. The pouches and those who carry them walk past immigration freely. No one may examine a diplomatic pouch. Anything may be carried in a diplomatic pouch, even diamonds. Don't you wish you had such access to make your smuggling operations easier?"

Cross smiled but did not tell the Colonel that he had

access to diplomatic pouches from a half dozen Countries, a privilege he paid handsomely for but a privilege that made smuggling much easier.

CHAPTER EIGHTEEN – The Gates Of Hell

Colonel Owusu and Joe Cross returned to Azubuike's 'throne room,' followed by the two mercenary soldiers. Azubuike was slouched on his tall throne, asleep and snoring loudly. In his sleep he farted noisily. Owusu's Officers were laughing but stopped when their boss entered the room. They came to a quick and stiff attention, clicking their boot heals together loudly. As Cross and his two men walked into the room, they followed.

Owusu walked across the room to the steps up to Azubuike. He took the steps slowly, a look of disgust on his face. The Colonel carefully touched Azubuike's shoulder like he was touching some foul and dirty animal, and shook the fat man awake. His look of revulsion as he looked down at Azubuike was plain to see by everyone.

Cross and the two mercenaries had retreated to a far corner of the big room. They stood in a tight circle, debating silently what could be done to keep themselves alive. They shared a thought that they could take Owusu's three Officers and Owusu himself. But there were others outside, and any noise of a fight would bring them into the room, and they had guns.

Azubuike and Owusu remained on the little red stage, Azubuike on his throne, Owusu standing to the side, both looking down at Cross talking in whispers to the two men.

The three officers Owusu had with him were standing in front of the stage, looking up at their Colonel, their backs to Cross, waiting for his orders. Owusu moved to them and bent low. They whispered back and forth.

Azubuike was not happy at what he was seeing, both from Cross and the Colonel, and what he was not hearing. He pounded his fist on the arm of the chair and yelled some obscenity; Owusu just smirked at the fat man's demands and ignored him.

Everyone in the room turned at the shouting from outside. Even Azubuike managed to rise from his chair. "MOTO! MOTO!" were the cries. Cross knew the Swahili word for fire. There was a fire outside . . . Somewhere. There was confusion outside. People were running in all directions, shouting and screaming.

Cross started for the door, but Owusu's men ran and stopped him. The door of the building was flung open by someone outside, and Cross could see the flames surrounding the compound, lighting the night. The acacia thorn wall was on fire. Someone had set the entire acacia thorn barricade on fire. Someone had set the signal for Helen d'Neuville and her fighters.

The lights in the room went dark suddenly; the only light coming in was from the flames outside. A muffled shot from a silenced pistol rang out. The bright flash of the near noiseless gunshot was like a bolt of lightning from the side of the throne stage. Owusu fell dead onto the stage. He lay in an expanding pool of his own blood, a bullet hole in the back of his head.

Owusu's three Officers were dark silhouettes against the light of the fire outside. They froze for a moment, long enough for three more muffled shots, and the three Officers fell backwards to the floor, each with a third eye in the middle of his forehead. A voice, little more than a whisper, could just be heard. "Close the friggin' door, will you now. Before one a'them bloody bastards comes in."

Cross knew the voice. The Irish accent was unmistakable. He motioned to one of the mercenaries who ran to the door and closed it. The man pulled a bench from the wall and wedged it against the double doors, the best lock manageable at the time.

The two soldiers ran to pick up the M16 rifles of Owusu's dead Officers. Joe Cross ran to the stage, jumped onto it and took Owusu's pistol. The two mercenaries looked at Cross through the dark, waiting to be told what to do. Then the lights came on, and the little Irishman, Michael Finnegan, walked out of Azubuike's private quarters through the hidden door behind the throne. He walked quickly, and soon he was standing next to Azubuike, holding his Makarov pistol with a silencer protruding from the barrel in his right hand, pointed at the fat man's head. A bottle of Irish whiskey was in his left hand.

"What the hell . . ." was all Cross could manage to say.

"Aye, and didn't I know you'd be surprised," Finnegan said, smiling. He stopped long enough to take a deep drink from his bottle.

"How did you get here?" Cross asked.

"Didn't that bloody giant bastard Billy Volgar want to come, now? He and me, we don't trust any of these foreign bastards you been dealin' with, don't we now? But how could that bloody beast Volgar hide from anyone? There ain't nothin' here big enough for him to hide behind now, is there? The only bloody thing bigger than him is a bloody elephant, now ain't it? He'd be seen by all the bloody bastards from here to bloody Kampala. So here I am

Joseph, and didn't I save your bloody life once again? Now you have to bloody admit that, don't you?"

"And how the hell did you get here?" Cross asked.

"Didn't I steal a bloody truck in Kampala and drive here down that bumpy bloody road, now? Me and Billy Volgar talked Manny into tellin' us what the bloody hell you was up to. And didn't I know you'd need me help once again. So I set fire to the hedge bushes like *you* was supposed to do, now didn't I? It was too bloody easy. There was cans of bloody gasoline out back near the bloody generator, wasn't there? These blokes don't know nothin', now do they? I was walking bloody well right past 'em and they paid me no mind, didn't they now?"

Finnegan took another long drink from his bottle of whiskey and then said, "Now, shall I put a bullet in this fat bastard's head?"

Cross said, "No," and walked to Azubuike. He stood next to Michael and looked down at the fat cannibal he hated so much. Yes, he wanted to see Azubuike die, he wanted to see him suffer as much as he had made so many others suffer. But that had to wait. There was more to do first.

As Cross glared down at the fat man, gunshots started outside. Helen had arrived, and the dogs of war had been let loose. He wanted to run for the door, but Michael stopped him.

"No, Joseph," he said softly. "Aye and wouldn't I love to be out there, too. Me Irish blood is boiling for the killin'. But let them do what they have to do. Wait here until the bloody murders are over. Keep your hands clean, now, won't you?"

Cross nodded. Finnegan was right of course. Helen's mercenaries knew what they had to do. They were the professionals. But there were people out there who Cross wanted to survive. There were women and children. There were boys who deserved a chance at life. And there was the young man who had given Cross water that afternoon as Cross, chained to Azubuike's slaves, dug for diamonds in the muddy ditch. That simple act caused Cross to want that young man to live. He had to know why that one young man, among all the others, had shown some kindness.

He looked at his watch and then sat on the steps at the edge of Azubuike's throne. He looked at his watch again. He waited, listening to the violence outside, and then he looked at his watch again. Twenty-five minutes dragged by, and the gun shots slowed, and then they stopped. Silence.

The door to Azubuike's throne room slammed open, pushing the bench away, and tearing one of the doors off its hinges. Silhouetted against the flames of the little village burning outside was Helen d'Neuville. She was dressed in black camo fatigues that were covered in blood. She held a Heckler & Koch MP7 machine pistol in her right hand and a blood soaked machete in her left. A wisp of smoke drifted from the barrel of the gun. She dropped the machete to the floor, and in one quick motion she took the empty magazine from the gun and put a full one in its place. She stood in the doorway and looked around the room. Her two men smiled at seeing her. She nodded her approval, all the recognition and thanks they would get from her.

"Mon amour," she said looking across the big room at Cross, standing at the edge of the platform. "It is done . . . What you paid for, it is done."

Cross looked at Helen's bloody fatigues. He said, "You're hurt."

She looked down at her clothes and then smiled. "No, mon cheri, Joseph. This, it is the blood of the dead, no? Do not worry for me. But I do love you for the worry. I must take you to the bed for to say thank you."

"Did you kill everyone?" Cross asked. He was frightened that he had opened the gates of hell outside and too many people had fallen through. Not everyone under Azubuike's control needed to die. What did she do?

Helen took a few steps closer to Cross. She had camo paint streaked across her face that made her smile look very dangerous. She spoke softly, a whisper filled with dire warning, "You asked for me to do the job. You paid for the deaths. You, mon amour, said you want a few of these . . . these people . . . to not be dead. You must have the reasons for that . . . I do not know these reasons. But I did what you paid for."

She took two more steps closer to Cross and raised her machine pistol, holding it in both her hands. Finnegan turned his pistol from Azubuike's head and held it toward Helen.

Helen ignored Finnegan and took two more steps closer to the platform and Cross. The smile dropped from her face. She said, "These people who would fight are dead. These who did not are not dead." She paused for a moment, thinking, and said, "I do not have the words in English. Pour ne pas me faire confiance est dangereux."

"I think I understand," Cross answered. "I should trust you, I know that. You are the professional here . . . I'm not. You have the reputation of doing the job you are paid to do. I'm sorry if I offended you."

Helen lowered her machine pistol back to her right hand, allowing it to hang by the strap at her shoulder, and she smiled again. Finnegan moved his pistol back and laid the barrel against Azubuike's temple. He asked, "And just how bloody long do I keep the pistol on this big black fella? Are you gonna' kill him or not?"

Cross turned to him and said, "Not yet. I have something that needs to be done first. Find some rope. Tie the bastard up on the floor, Michael . . . feet and hands. Stay with him. No one gets near him, understand?"

"Sure, and I understand, Joseph. But can I sit in his bloody chair once he is on the bloody floor?"

Cross laughed and turned away. He stepped down off the platform and walked toward the door, Helen following him outside. He stood atop the three steps and looked around. Bodies lay everywhere in the dark night. Only the dying flames of the acacia provided any light. Smoke from the fires filled the air, dampening the odor of death.

Helen's men stood amongst the dead, some smoking, others resting against the sides of the few mud huts that had not been torched. They were all dressed in black fatigues; their faces were painted black, and each had blood splattered on them from the killing. On the covered porch of what once was Azubuike's throne room were the bodies of Owusu's police officers. All were dead.

As they looked at the carnage, Cross said, almost as an afterthought, "You've got three men a mile up the road. At the outpost. There are bodies there, too."

"I shall send people to them," Helen answered. "Shall I have the bodies brought here or leave them, Joseph?"

"Bring them here," he answered. "I can't leave that kind of evidence around."

Helen called loudly to a few of her men, ordering in French. They ran off to the truck Michael had driven from Kampala and sped up the dirt road to the north.

Cross looked to the left and saw the line of slaves who had dug diamonds for Azubuike and had been starved and beaten for their labor. They were standing naked and shivering in the cold dark night as a couple of Helen's men broke the padlocks holding them chained together.

A group of women were standing together to his right, hugging each other tightly. A few children were standing amongst them, hugging closely to the legs of the women, fear and tears streaked across their dirty faces. They were shivering in fear; their eyes were wide with terror.

In the center of the compound's field, sitting in the dirt, were seven men, all ragged and thin. Four of them were in a drugged, dreamlike state, their eyes clouded and staring off into some world only they could see. They didn't know what was happening all around them. Two of the others were not drugged. They were the remnants of Azubuike's personal guard. The last was a young man, barely out of boyhood. He was frightened, trembling in the night's cold and damp air. It was the young man, a boy really, who had given Cross and Robert water while they dug in the ditch.

Helen had walked to Cross and was standing next to him. He was unaware of her standing there. When he realized she was next to him, he said, "That young one. Did he fight?"

"No, mon amour. He dropped his rifle very fast, and he fell to his knees. He had his arms over his head, no? This I do not understand."

"I want to talk to him."

Helen called out to two of her men in French and pointed at the prisoner. She curled a finger, calling him to her. He was grabbed roughly by the arms, and pulled to his bare feet. They pushed him forward roughly. He stumbled and fell to his knees. Helen's soldier was about to hit him with the butt of his rifle. Helen called out, "Ne pas lui faire de mal!"

He was lifted to his feet once again, and he walked slowly to Helen and Cross. He stood in the dirt at the bottom of the stairs and looked up at the two. He asked, in a soft and quavering voice, "Are you going to kill me?"

Cross asked, "Do you recognize me?"

The prisoner looked up at him with squinting eyes in deep thought. It was dark, and the only light came from inside the throne room, behind Cross. The acacia fence had burned to embers, leaving only smoke in the night air. He was trying to see someone he knew. To him, Cross looked something like the muddy prisoner from weeks ago. He said, "Were you once digging for diamonds?"

"Yes," Cross answered. "That was me. Why did you give me water?"

"I felt sorry for you," he answered.

"Come inside," Cross said. He turned and walked into Azubuike's throne room, the young man following but stepping cautiously in fear around the dangerous looking Helen d'Neuville. She told her two soldiers to follow him inside.

CHAPTER NINETEEN – Out Of The Ashes

Inside the big throne room, Azubuike lay on the floor below his throne platform, face down, his hands and feet tied with a rough hemp rope. Michael Finnegan was slouched on the fat man's red throne, one leg across the gold painted arm of the chair, his bottle of Irish whiskey in his left hand, his Makarov pistol in his right. Colonel Okello Owusu lay dead on the floor at Michael's side.

Cross and Helen followed the young man into the room. Cross closed the door behind them to leave the scene of slaughter hidden outside. He leaned the broken side of the door against the opening. The bodies of Owusu's three officers lay where they had been killed, in an expanding pool of dark blood. The young man looked at the death, froze in his tracks and turned to Cross. "Are you going to kill me?" he asked.

"Not if I get the right answers," Cross answered.

"Ask me," he answered quickly, pleading, hoping there was a chance he might live.

"OK. Why?" Cross asked. He started to walk in a circle around the young man who was sweating and trembling in fear.

"Why what? I do not understand," he answered.

"Why did you give me water when I was in the pit?

And I want the truth. Don't give me any shit about feeling sorry for me. There were others there, too. You didn't give them water."

"I remember you," he said, staring directly up into Cross' eyes, his head tilted slightly in thought. "You were not like the others. I am Christian . . . But Azubuike could not know that. I do not want to die. If I do die I want my soul to go to heaven. I wish I could have saved all of them . . . But I couldn't. I felt sorry for you . . . Because I knew you were from outside . . . I felt you might be Christian . . . Like me. And I felt you had some good to do here. So I gave you water."

"And Robert Fullsome?" Cross asked. "You tried to help him, too. Why?"

"He, too, was here to do some good. I could feel that . . . Inside of me."

"Who are you? What's your name?" Cross asked.

"My Christian name . . . My Baptized name . . . The name I prefer . . . Is Bartholomew Thomas."

"OK, Bartholomew Thomas," Cross asked, smiling. "So you say you're a good hearted Christian. Tell me who the twelve Apostles were."

He smiled, threw his shoulders back, and stood up straight and proudly. There was a possibility . . . a chance . . . that he would live through the horror all around him. He began, "Simon who is called Peter. Andrew who was Simon's brother. James and John, his brother. Philip and Bartholomew, whom I am named after. He is sometimes called Nathanael. Thomas and Matthew. James and Thaddaeus. Simon the Cananean . . . And of course Judas. You see . . . I am Christian, and I am educated."

Cross looked at Helen, questioning without words,

silently asking if the boy was right. Helen shrugged her shoulders. Neither he nor she knew if the young man was correct, but he sounded assured naming the twelve. He turned to Michael Finnegan and asked, "So, is he right?"

"And how the bloody hell am I supposed to know that, Joseph? I ain't seen the inside of a church since I was thirteen bloody years old. The Church ain't never done me any good, and I ain't never done any good for the Church," Michael answered and drank the last few drops of whiskey from the bottle. He looked at the empty bottle and tossed it across the room where it smashed against the wall.

Cross turned back to the young man and asked him, "OK, so what should we do with Azubuike? A bullet in the head? . . . Or should we tie him to his stake and burn him like he has done with so many others?"

Bartholomew Thomas turned and looked at the fat man lying on the floor. His pants were wet with urine, and his bowel had opened, stinking the entire room. His eyes were bulging, and he was breathing fast, his mouth full of foaming spittle. Azubuike understood the words being spoken and feared what would happen to him.

The young man turned back to Cross and Helen and said, "No, that would not be right. There has been enough killing. He has done enough killing. It must end."

"Then what the hell do I do with him?" Cross asked.

"He must face justice."

"You mean hand him over to the Government?" Cross asked. "After killing Colonel Owusu? I'm afraid that would cause more problems than I'm ready to handle."

"No," Bartholomew said. "The tribes. He has terrorized them for many years. They will judge him, and justice will be done."

Cross looked again to Helen who again shrugged her shoulders. He told Bartholomew, "OK, you got it."

He spoke to Helen, "Have your men take Azubuike to that rat hole where he kept the slaves. See if you can put some of those chains on the bastard. Drop him in the mud and shit. Have two men guard him. Then have your men drag these bodies outside with the others. I'm going to have Bartholomew Thomas here do something, but I want you to watch him closely. If he does anything stupid . . . Kill him."

Helen nodded, turned and left the room. Bartholomew smiled and nodded quickly.

Cross walked to Michael, leaving Bartholomew standing alone near the bodies on the floor. He walked up the steps to the throne Michael was sitting on. He leaned down and whispered in Michael's ear. The little Irishman jumped from the tall chair and walked down the steps, off the stage, past Bartholomew, and out the door, slamming it closed behind him.

Walking back to Bartholomew, Cross said, "I'm going to have you do something for me, Bartholomew. If you do what I tell you to do, you won't be hurt. Understand?"

"Yes, sir," he answered quickly. "I understand . . . But I can't kill anyone."

"You won't be killing anyone," Cross said and smiled. "I want you to gather all the people out there together. The women and children, and the slaves. Not the soldiers. Bring them . . . In here I guess . . . After these bodies have been removed. Let them see Azubuike tied up and dragged from here out to the slave hut. Keep the people in here. Go back to his quarters and find food. There might be food in the buildings behind this one. Azubuike had to have stocks of some food somewhere. If his soldiers have any food, get it, too . . . All you can. Give it to the people. . . They probably need it. And water, too. See if there are any medical supplies anywhere. If not, get whatever Helen's men have. Clean and bandage their wounds, particularly the slaves. And get them some clothes, too. Do what you can for these people."

"I will do that," Bartholomew answered quickly. He smiled and asked, "You trust me, then?"

"No," Cross answered simply. "But there's no place to run, is there? If you do run or do something stupid, I will have you killed, understand?"

****

The African sun rose slowly; perhaps it was afraid of seeing what the slaughter had wrought. Azubuike lay in the filth of his slave hut, screaming profanities in every language he knew. He rolled around as far as the chains and rope would allow, covering himself in the filth he had kept his slaves in. He kicked at the thin walls, shaking the hut, almost bringing it down. The two men guarding him stepped into the hut, and as one kicked him in his stomach the other hit him across his head with a rifle butt. Azubuike yelled and howled like the insane man he was. Blood oozed from his bruised forehead across his glaring eyes. The two guards left him in the filth and stood outside, smoking strong Gauloises cigarettes, pleased with the operation and the fact that none of their comrades were killed or injured.

The rest of Helen's men stood in the middle of the compound in groups, smoking and talking, some just walking around aimlessly, waiting for the next orders from their commander. The dead had been carried to the rear of the compound and would be buried later that day, before the heat could get to the bodies.

Bartholomew had gathered the freed slaves and the women and children to Azubuike's throne room. They had stood in the cold mud and watched as the man who had once terrorized them was dragged by his ankles out of the throne room, across the wet red mud, and thrown into the long hut that had been the prison for the slaves. As they walked in, they stared down at the dead and the pools of blood.

Bartholomew had indeed found food for them and some shirts and pants for the slaves. Cross watched closely from the open door of the throne room. As Bartholomew raced back and forth to find food and water, one of Helen's men was close behind him.

The freed slaves ate voraciously, at first ignoring the clothes in favor of eating food and drinking clean water they had not seen in too many weeks to count. The women of the compound ate cautiously, unsure of what was happening but grateful that there was food without beatings and rapes. The children were in such a state of shock that they ate little, but they did drink the water given to them. The water seemed to outwardly calm them, but they would not leave the skirts of the women. They stood, dazed and shivering in the middle of the nightmare.

A few of the boys, former child soldiers of Azubuike, stood against the walls, trembling in fright, with eyes clouded by the drugs they had been given. It would be a long time before they could be returned to normal lives. Cross had no idea what to do with them. He would leave them for others to worry about. Perhaps Robert Fullsome could take care of them. At least they were alive, and maybe they had some normal life ahead of them.

An hour later Cross and Helen d'Neuville sat on the

steps outside the throne room, listening to the clatter of talk and dishes and pots and pans behind them, inside the big round building. Helen smoked a big cigar, and they passed back and forth between them a bottle of cognac they had found in Azubuike's private quarters. The African sun had fully risen and was heating what had been a cold and bloody night.

The air was clear, the last embers of the acacia had died and the smoke had drifted away; the sky was blue and brightening. A flock of marabou storks flew by overhead, noisy perhaps in joyous celebration of the end of Azubuike's terrible little empire. Encircling the compound were the gray ashes of the Acacia fence, the last remembrance of Azubuike's terror.

Helen looked sideways at Joe Cross, sitting next to her. He had a worried look on his face. Most of the camo paint that had covered his face that night had been streaked away by sweat. She asked softly, "So, mon amour Joseph, what is it that we do now?"

"I have work to do here," Cross answered. He sighed deeply and turned to look at her. "I have someone coming here soon who is going to open a clinic and later a school and full blown hospital." He paused, his forehead wrinkling in deep thought. He went on, saying, "This will be a good place soon, I'm sure of that. I hope so anyway. But what the hell do I do with Azubuike's people . . . Those soldiers and guards who are still alive?"

Helen drew deeply on her cigar, drank from the bottle of cognac, and then said, "My English, it is not the perfect, mon amour Joseph. But I think maybe it is the best thing that they should not walk free, if you understand what I say."

Cross turned to her and asked, "You mean I should kill them?"

"No, no, not you, mon amour. That is not for you to do that . . . I know. You are the good man who does what is good."

"But I've killed people," Cross said. "And I've ordered the deaths of people. You must know that."

"Oui, bien sûr, this I know. But when you kill, it is for the purpose that you see as good. No, this should be left to me, no? I do not have . . . What is the word? . . . Conscience? Am I right? Is that the word?"

"You mean you don't care who dies?" Cross asked. He was immediately sorry for having said that. He was tired, exhausted really. It was an insult of course, but he didn't mean it as an insult.

"No, I do care, bien sûr," Helen answered understanding a little of what Cross was feeling. "But I want to be sure they are the people who need the killing. And of course I must be paid, no? Even bad people I do not kill unless I am paid. Comprenez vous? I choose not to kill the good people."

Cross paused, hesitating to say what he wanted to say. He looked down, into his glass of cognac, twirled the brown liquid into a whirlpool, and then said, "But you do get paid to kill." It was more than just a statement; it was questioning why this woman could fight wars for whoever could pay her.

"Oui, and you paid me here," Helen said, waving her arm across the remnants of the slaughter. She inched closer to Cross and put her hand on his knee. "I kill these people so you would not die. For you . . . Do you understand? Are my words, they are correct? I, too, do what is right   . . . What I see as right. There are many things I do not do. As you do not do. Je suis désolé. Do I say it correct? Do you understand?"

Cross understood, and he knew it had to be done. Too many people had been suffering under Azubuike's maniacal rule. The governments weren't going to stop him. Society turned a blind eye to his insanity. Money was the justification for what the maniac did. Azubuike had been able to buy whoever he wanted. And if someone were to take his place, as Owusu had wanted to do, they, too, could buy a blind eye from governments. These people, Azubuike's soldiers, if allowed to live, might come back to set themselves up as petty warlords and start the cruelty all over again. No, it had to be done, but if he ordered these men to be killed, to be killed without a chance to fight, he would live with the killing forever.

He stood, took the bottle from Helen and filled his glass. He drank some more of the cognac. Helen said, "It is time for me to go, no? My work it is done. When will your plane be here?" She didn't like the idea of leaving Joseph Cross unprotected with Azubuike alive and a few of his better guards alive, also. But she had other work, other clients who would pay her for the work she did.

"It's on its way," Cross said. "It may be a day or two."

"That is not good, mon amour," she said. "I must leave. I have the plane on the way now. It will be here soon. I am sorry."

"You have a plane waiting?"

"Oui, of course. If you were to be dead, how am I to leave? It is as you say, the backup plan, oui? Is that the words?"

"That's alright, Helen," Cross said. "I understand. But first have your people collect all the weapons . . . Leave two of the best AK-47s and two of the best pistols and ammunition here for me and take the rest with you. Any that are not worth taking, damage them beyond repair and burn them. Make sure the prisoners bury all the dead. Have them dig a mass grave out behind the throne room, but make sure it's deep. I don't want animals digging them up in the night. Have your men go through every building to make sure nothing is hidden anywhere. Dig up the floors and search in the walls and thatched roofs. Open every box and barrel. I don't want any guns or drugs available after you leave. Secure the prisoners somewhere . . . Chain them somewhere if you can . . . Keep them all in one place where I can keep an eye on them, but make sure they are secured. I don't want trouble with them after you are gone. Then call your airplane in. And Helen . . . Thank you."

As she started to walk away, he called to her. "One more thing, please. Have your men tear down that . . . That thing," he said pointing to the steel beam where so many poor people had been burnt to death. "Get rid of it somewhere. I don't want to see it anymore."

CHAPTER TWENTY - You're Going To Let Them Go?

Helen stood on the bare ground in front of the steps and faced Cross. She took the few steps slowly, to be very near him. She was staring at him, thinking, considering. When she was very close, her hands went to his shirt collar. She pulled him to her and kissed him hard on the lips. She smiled at him and whispered, "You are the good man, Joseph. Someday, mon amour . . . Someday I will take you to the bed, no?"

Cross smiled and said, "Sure, Helen . . . Someday."

She walked away quickly and gathered her men around her. She gave them her commands, and they ran to do what they had been told. One man, carrying an American military AN/PRC-150(C) high frequency field radio, set it down on the ground and began calling for the airplane that would take Helen and her men away. It had been waiting across the border in Kenya since the sun had risen, waiting for the command to come to Helen and take her away.

Michael Finnegan walked to Cross' side and said, "It's done." Cross nodded and drained his glass of cognac.

****

Two hours passed as Cross watched the mercenaries do what needed to be done. A deep ditch was dug at the rear of Azubuike's throne room by the remainder of Azubuike's ragged army. The bodies of the dead were thrown in. Colonel Owusu and his police officers were dropped in last. They were covered with red dirt, three feet thick, and Cross felt that was a fit ending to Azubuike's terrible rule.

Two of Azubuike's personal guards remained alive. They stood to the side, arms crossed in front of them, contempt on their faces as they watched, while the digging and burying was being done by the ragged and thin drugged soldiers. Cross looked at the two; they were muscular, well clothed, and had been well fed. These were professionals, not the drugged out quasi soldiers Azubuike had kept to do the dirty work. The two felt that common labor was below them. Cross saw this and called to one of Helen's men to give them two shovels and make them dig. "Tell them their choice is to dig or die," he said. They spat on the ground, but they began to dig.

After searching all the huts and buildings, Helen's men found under the floor boards of Azubuike's private quarters a stash of drugs, a bag of raw diamonds, and bundles of cash of several different nations, all wrapped in plastic. Helen walked out of the big building and across the compound to Cross who was walking alone, looking at what once been a little hell on earth.

"You must come to the inside and see what it has been found," she said, a broad smile across her face. Cross followed her, slowly, still in deep thought about the coming days.

Inside Cross looked down at the pile of secrets Helen had found. He asked, "How much cash is there?"

"I do not know . . . It has not to be counted yet. But maybe when all is counted it might be a hundred thousand of your American dollars, perhaps?"

"OK," Cross said. "Count it, and you keep half as a bonus. Keep whatever currencies you want. The other half will go to the people who will be here soon to turn this nightmare place into something good. I'll keep the diamonds. Burn the drugs."

The morning slowly turned to a blazing hot afternoon. The work had been done. The former slaves had been fed all they could eat and were resting, most asleep on the floor inside Azubuike's big throne room where it was at least a little cooler than in the sun outside. Azubuike's soldiers were herded to the center of the compound and were sitting close together on the red dirt, under the burning sun. The boy soldiers had been gathered together and were sitting along the inside wall of one of the huts, under guard.

Helen and her men were relaxing in whatever shade was to be had, surrounding the defeated soldiers, waiting for the airplane that would take them away after a successful and very profitable fight.

Cross was seated on the steps of Azubuike's former palace, in the sun, perhaps hoping the heat would bake away the sin of having taken so many lives. Michael Finnegan walked quickly across the compound towards him, kicking up a cloud of red dust as he almost ran to his boss. His ever present bottle of Irish whiskey was not with him; a sour and worrying look crossed his freckled face.

He stopped in front of Cross and said nothing. "What is it, Michael?" Cross asked and smiled up at the little man. "Are you all out of whiskey?"

"He's gone," Finnegan said in a whisper. "He's bloody well gone."

"Who's gone?"

"That bloody bastard, Azubuike. That's the bloody hell who."

Cross stood quickly and looked left, to the long hut where Azubuike had been chained.

"That's not all, Joseph," Finnegan said. "Look at your bloody prisoners. That bloody kid, Bartholomew, he ain't bloody well there, either."

Cross jumped from the steps and ran across the compound to the slave hut. Finnegan followed, running hard to keep up. Helen saw this, and she, too, started to run, following the two. A few of her mercenaries followed her.

When they had reached the hut, they found the two guards who Helen had posted there, unconscious on the ground, inside the hut. Cross bent to look inside the slave hut. The stench of human waste was overpowering, but Azubuike was not there.

Helen asked, "Do I search for him, mon ami?"

Cross looked off, across the grass land and swamp surrounding the compound, thought for a minute, and then said, "No . . . He has nowhere to run. If the villagers find him, they'll tear him apart. It's that kid, Bartholomew, who pisses me off. I trusted that kid."

Helen asked, "You think the boy, he freed that Azubuike?"

"He either cut him loose and is running with him . . . Or he's dead somewhere. Either way, he can't go far."

As they stood talking, they heard the sound of an airplane in the sky. They looked east, under the high noon sun, and saw a plane slowly approach and begin to land along the dirt road outside the compound. At first it had the sun at its back and only the soft sound of the engines told Cross it was there. Then, as it came lower in the bright sky, he could see it.

The plane turned north and then south and touched down along the dirt road that led to the compound. The Beechcraft King Air bounced along the rutted and rocky path and came to a stop near the ashes of the burned thorn encrusted acacia wall of what was Azubuike's little kingdom.

Michael stood next to Cross and watched as Helen's men tore down the steel beam that had held so many unfortunate people as they suffered a cruel death at Azubuike's nightly entertainment. Four of them lifted the tall beam onto their shoulders and walked away with it. They walked a distance away, to the west, and dropped it in the muddy grass.

That was the last of the tasks Cross had ordered. Soon, there would be only memories of the pain, the suffering, the torture, the slavery. Soon, where Azubuike had once ruled, there would be only good. Soon, there would be a school for the children instead of drugs and guns. Soon, there would be a hospital instead of cannibalism.

Helen walked to the two men, carrying the two AK-47s Cross had asked for. She handed one to Cross and one to Michael, and asked, "Are you certain, mon amour, that you will stay? Come with us, s'il vous plait, or you may die here, no?"

"Thank you, Helen," Cross said. "You did a good job here . . . But I have more work to do here. Manny will send the balance of what I owe you to you."

"There is the ammunition, two pistols with many clips of the bullets, and several hand grenades on the porch," Helen said. "The money and the diamonds they are inside." She reached up and gently touched Cross' cheek. "Bonne chance, mon amour."

Cross looked around the compound. Much of it could be used by Robert Fullsome, but one thing had to go. He spoke to Helen, "One more thing. Set fire to that slave hut before you go. Get some gasoline from behind Azubuike's big house. Burn it to the ground and cleanse the land of it. I want only ash remaining, and let the wind dispose of that.

Helen called to her men, standing ready to leave, and gave the order. They ran to get the fuel, and in a few minutes flame and acrid smoke rose and filled the air. They watched it burn, throwing buckets of gasoline into the fire to make it burn hotter, and then without another word, Helen turned, waived to her mercenaries, and they boarded the plane.

Michael stood next to Cross as they watched the plane taxi and then take off. When it was airborne, Michael said, "I hope you've bloody well done the right thing, Joseph lad. It's just you and me now . . . And two bloody rifles." He laughed and then said, "Reminds me of the old days, now, doesn't it?"

"You think I screwed up?" Cross asked as the two of them walked to the porch of the big hut and its shade from the burning sun.

Michael answered, "You've got a couple of Azubuike's best back there, now haven't you? And all them bloody children that were raised to kill. You should kill them before they kill you, Joseph."

"Michael," Cross said as he sat on the covered porch next to a dozen boxes of ammunition, "You'd better sit down, because I'm going to tell you something that's gonna' knock your socks off."

Michael laughed and sat on the top step of the porch,

in the shade. He said, "You don't haft'a tell me, Joseph lad. You're going to let the bloody bastards go, now, ain't you?"

CHAPTER TWENTY-ONE - Dealing With The Devil

The women, the children, and the few boy soldiers had wandered off in small groups of three and four, seemingly aimless in their wanderings; some to the east, some west, all probably hoping to find what they had lost, their homes, their families, and their villages, or perhaps some family somewhere that might receive them well.

The children seemed the most confused and the most frightened at the prospect of what a new life might bring. Many of them had been born in Azubuike's kingdom and in their few years, knew nothing else.

Cross had sent them on their way, giving bottles of water to the women and their children and sending the boy soldiers off to follow the women. These dazed child soldiers wandered behind the women at a close distance, unsure of what to do, but afraid to be left alone.

Azubuike's remaining guards, dazed by withdrawal from the drugs they had lived for, wandered slowly away, still in delirium, following the women. They would not be well received by the villagers once word spread that Azubuike had fallen.

"What will happen to them?" Michael asked as the two watched.

"The women and children will go back to their tribes, their villages, and their families. They'll try to regain some life. They'll spread the news that Azubuike is no more. That can only be good. Maybe some semblance of a normal life and humanity can return here." Cross spoke knowing full well that what he said was merely a hope of his. He had no idea what would happen to those people, but he knew, at least, that they were finally free.

"And what of those two?" Michael asked, pointing to the two soldiers who walked faster than the others, north, up the dirt road, alone, away from the compound, pushing the drugged guards to the side as they left the compound, perhaps on their way to Kampala to seek out new employment. They were the professionals who had been paid in money and women.

"They don't have an employer," Cross said. "They'll search for one. War is all they know. Azubuike is no more, but there are enough revolutions, insurgencies, petty dictators and thieves in Africa that they'll find someone who will pay them."

"But the bloody bastard Azubuike, he really ain't no more, now is he? He's out there somewhere, ain't he now?"

"I have a feeling," Cross said, "That when some villagers find him wandering around they're going to rip him apart."

For two days Cross and Finnegan waited in the compound. They ate canned meats and drank a few bottles of Azubuike's liquors. And they walked about aimlessly, gazing off into the hot and blue African sky for the airplane they waited for.

Before Helen had left, as they gathered the women, children and prisoners together, Cross had sent Michael to the shortwave radio that had been used by Azubuike. Michael had sent the message that would be received by Helen's man stationed at Lars' home. The message would be sent on to Robert Fullsome. Robert would know it was safe for him to travel to Uganda and to the compound that would soon become his hospital and school. Michael had returned after sending the message and had told Cross, "It's done." And they waited for Robert to arrive.

****

The morning of the third day they awoke from a restless night's sleep in Azubuike's grand living quarters as the sun broke above the horizon and chased the cold dark of night away. They finished the last of the coffee and a few crusts of bread that would be their only breakfast. There was little food left; most of it had been consumed by the slaves, the women and the children before they left. Cross and Finnegan had tried to ration out the last of the food to make it last as long as they could. But there was little left.

"Bloody hell," Finnegan said as he drank the coffee. "They better get here soon, and they bloody hell had better have coffee with them."

"And I suppose a few bottles of Irish whiskey would be good, too," Cross laughed as he shaved in front of Azubuike's gold framed mirror. He used a straight razor he found in a drawer, ivory handled with elaborate gold inlay. It was very sharp, and Cross hoped it had only been used for shaving. The shower had stopped providing hot water when the gasoline needed to run the generator ran out. But cold showers seemed refreshing to the men considering the African heat.

They finished their coffee and started to walk outside to once again look into the sky for Robert Fullsome's airplane. They were shocked and surprised as they walked through the broken doors and stood on the covered porch. They were greeted by three small Toyota pickup trucks, painted in green camouflage, parked in the red dirt in front of them.   Each had a uniformed driver behind the wheel, leaning on the steering wheel, their side windows rolled down, and smiling at the good joke they had just pulled off. The second and third in the line had big machine guns, Belgian 7.76 mm guns, a type that Cross had seen before. They were mounted in the beds of the trucks, uniformed men standing behind them. Both guns were pointed at Cross and Finnegan. The first pickup truck had a man standing at its side, leaning casually against the fender.

He was an African, tall, slim and muscular, and very handsome. He was smoking a cigarette that was held in a fat ivory cigarette holder, yellowed with age, and clenched tightly in his teeth. He wore the clean, starched and pressed uniform of Colonel Okello Owusu's Ugandan Special Police Force, with the gold insignia of an officer on his shoulders. His tall peaked hat was pulled down low over his forehead and cocked at an arrogant angle.

He pushed himself away from the truck, slowly removed his dark sunglasses, and smiled, still biting onto the cigarette holder, showing off big, bright white teeth. Cross immediately thought of pictures he had seen of FDR, smiling with his cigarette holder clenched in his teeth, held high.

He said, "Good morning, Mr. Cross. And you also, Mr. Finnegan. I will ask some questions, Mr. Cross. If you answer truthfully . . . You may go. If you lie . . . You will die here. Do you understand?"

The man spoke in perfectly accented, British Public School English. His English was much better than Colonel Owusu's. Cross answered, "I understand. But who are you?"

"I am Captain Byron Nickels, Mr. Cross. I am so glad to meet you. I have heard a lot about you. It is an honor."

"In the hierarchy of The Ugandan Special Police, where do you stand?" Cross asked.

"A very good question, Mr. Cross. For the time being, I am in charge," Captain Nickels answered. "And I will remain in that esteemed position until Colonel Owusu is found. You see, the Colonel is missing. Isn't that very strange indeed? It has been several days since anyone has heard from him. But now I must ask a few questions, if you please. As I said, the truth will let you live. I presume Colonel Owusu is dead? Am I correct?"

Cross decided to take a chance. He could tell the truth, and the odds were that he would be killed or taken into custody and charged with murder. If he lied, he could be killed because he had the feeling that this Captain Nickels knew the truth. Either way, chances are, he would be dead very soon. So he lied. He said, "I don't know. The Colonel was here, but he left some days ago."

Captain Nickels turned and walked back to the truck he had been leaning against. He took the ivory cigarette holder from his teeth and spoke in Swahili to the man behind the machine gun on the truck in the rear of the small convoy. The man asked a question. The Captain nodded, and the man standing at the back of the machine gun raised it and pointed it at Cross and Finnegan. He paused for a second or two, smiled and pulled the cocking slide back, and began to fire.

Cross and Finnegan threw themselves onto the wood plank floor of the porch. Fifty rounds were fired just inches over their heads, but none hit either man. The bullets ripped through the thin wood and bamboo wall of the throne room, tearing the wall of the building apart.

When the firing ended, Captain Nickels said, "You may stand now, gentlemen, if you please."

Cross pushed himself to his feet; Michael stayed flat on the porch floor, looking sideways at the deadly machine gun. Captain Nickels laughed. He pulled his cigarette from the ivory holder, dropped it to the ground and crushed it out with the toe of his polished boot.

He took a pack of Players cigarettes from his shirt pocket. He dramatically put one in the end of the holder, took it to his mouth and lit it with a silver lighter. Almost as an afterthought, he held the pack out towards Cross. He said, "I am so sorry, Mr. Cross. Would you like a cigarette?"

"I don't smoke," Cross answered.

Michael, still flat on the porch floor, said, "I need one of them bloody things."

The Captain smiled and ignored Michael. He removed his peaked cap, wiped sweat from his forehead with a crisp, clean, white linen handkerchief, and said, "It is quite warm out here, don't you think? I would so like a nice cup of tea. May we retire to inside? It may be a bit cooler there. In the shade don't you know? My men will prepare some good English tea for us. I'm afraid I have no milk, however, worst of luck. I don't suppose you would have a spot of milk somewhere?"

Cross stood aside, and Michael pushed himself to his feet. He wanted to run, but he stayed at Cross's side. His hand went to the Makarov pistol tucked into his belt at his waist. Nickels saw that, laughed a little, shook his head, but said nothing.

The Captain walked up the steps and into Azubuike's former throne room, Cross and Finnegan following a few steps behind him. Inside, Nickels stopped and took in the big thatched roof building. Azubuike's big, bright red throne remained on its little stage. Dried blood stained the middle of the polished wood floor where Owusu's two policemen had been killed by Michael. Captain Nickels looked down at the big stain, turned to look at Cross, and smiled. The two AK-47s, the pistols, clips of ammunition, and the hand grenades were stacked against a wall nearby. Nickels looked at them and smiled again, walking past them as if they were insignificant.

The five officers who had come to the compound with Captain Nickels stepped quickly into the room. They went to the low stage across the room and there, using the stage as a table of sorts, with a small camp stove, began to boil water for tea. Captain Nickels sat on the edge of the low stage near the three steps and finished his cigarette in silence as Cross and Finnegan stood in the middle of the big room and watched.

Nickels looked again, past the two, at the two AK-47s leaning against the hut's wall near the still open door. Cross turned to look at them.

"Please don't even think about it, Mr. Cross," Captain Nickels said. "I assure you that I and my men are very good shots. And Mr. Finnegan, you may keep your diminutive pistol. Makarovs are rare these days, and that one you have may be old, but I dare say it is worth quite a few Pounds. I would not take it from you. But I assure you, you will not be able to fire even one shot if you remove it from your belt. Now, I will ask you once again, Mr. Cross. Where is Colonel Owusu?"

"You know he's dead," Cross answered. "You've no doubt seen the grave out back. Why do you ask if you know the answer already?"

"That's very good. The truth at last," Nickels said and

smiled falsely. He pulled the stub of his cigarette from the holder and crushed it out on the floor, again with the toe of his boot.

"Do you care that he's dead?" Cross asked. He had a suspicion, and he risked asking the question to see if he was right.

"And yet another very good question. I, of course, care as the Colonel is . . . Or should I say, was . . . My commanding officer. I respect the chain of command, as any good officer does. I was taught well at Sandhurst, you see."

"You know, Captain," Cross began. "I'm going to take a chance here. After all, I suspect that you will kill both my friend and me very soon, so what difference does it make, right?"

"Please be so kind as to ask your next question, Mr. Cross. I know I said I would ask the questions, but I am curious. Your reputation precedes you. You are said to be a thief but also a gallant gentleman. The tea is almost ready, so I do have a moment or two."

"OK, Captain," Cross said and started to walk a few steps toward the Captain. "Colonel Owusu made a lot of money taking bribes. My guess is not much of that money was filtered down to you.   Maybe some, but not a lot. Owusu being out of the picture now, probably puts you in charge . . . And probably promotes you to Colonel. All that cash . . . And Owusu's power . . . Now comes to you, right? So you're not exactly sad at Owusu's passing."

"Oh, Mr. Cross! You are as perceptive as I have been told," he said with a laugh as he slapped his thigh.

One of his officers brought a fine china cup and saucer of steaming tea to Nickels as Cross asked, "So what happens to us? How much do you want?"

The Captain sipped at the tea pleasurably, smiled gratefully at his officer, thanking him, laid the cup on the stage next to him, lit another cigarette, and said, "You paid two hundred eighty thousand Ugandan Shillings . . . A mere pittance . . . Pocket change, as you say. And what is that in American dollars . . . What? A hundred dollars? . . . For the permit to build a hospital and school here. You brought a great deal of money with you that day. A small case of cash in fact. I assume you bought more than a few permits. Bribes are always necessary, now aren't they?   But the bribes you paid do not purchase the protection of the law in such a remote place as this. Do you wish the protection of the law?"

"Protection from what . . . Or should I say who?" Cross asked.

"Ha! Oh, Mr. Cross, you are a man to fence with. Seldom do I have the chance to play this game with someone of your intellect."

Michel Finnegan took a step forward and said, "Bloody hell. You two can dance around all you bloody hell want. There ain't no Irish whiskey here, so can I have a cuppa' that tea and one of your bloody British fags while the two of you play your silly games?"

Captain Nickels bent backwards laughing at that. He said as he patted the stage, "Oh. Mr. Finnegan. Please, do come sit next to me here. A cup of tea shall be yours. I do love the Irish. When I was at St. Lawrence College at Gatwick there was this lovely little lass from Ireland . . . Well, we'll save that story for another day."

Finnegan walked quickly to the stage and sat as a police officer brought him a tin cup of hot tea. Nickels took the pack of Players cigarettes from his pocket and offered one to Michael. "A 'fag' as you say, Mr. Finnegan. I do love and dearly miss the British common language." Michael took the cigarette and lit it with a wooden match from the small box he carried.

"It would be lovely with milk and a little sugar, and a drop or two of the devil's own drink," Finnegan said as he sipped at the steaming tea. "But we all hafta' suffer at times, now don't we?"

Nickels laughed again, and as he did, Michael looked at Cross over the rim of the cup with a knowing gaze, asking without words if he should draw the pistol and kill all of them. Cross shook his head imperceptibly, enough for Finnegan to concentrate on his tea.

"Let's cut to the chase," Cross said, looking at the Captain. He took a few steps closer to Nickels. No one objected, so he walked to the low stage and sat a few feet away from the Captain, with Finnegan on the other side of Nickels. "How much do you want?"

Nickels laughed once again, rocking back and forth as he sat. He said, "How much of what do I want for what? You certainly are an American, aren't you now? Oh yes, they call you The Yank, don't they? Always the deal maker are we? Is everything about money, my dear Mr. Cross?"

"OK," Cross said. "If you don't want money, what do you want? I don't get it. You implied I didn't buy the protection you can supply. How do I buy it?"

The Captain stood. He crushed out the cigarette this time on the stage they were sitting on. He lit yet another cigarette from his package of Players and began to walk slowly back and forth in front of Cross and Michael. He didn't look at them; he peered down at the floor as he walked, while he smoked the cigarette down to a stub. He pulled it roughly from the holder and crushed it out on the wood floor this time with the heel of his boot. He turned suddenly and spoke in Swahili to his officers, "Kwenda nje."

The five uniformed officers stood at a sudden attention, clicking the heels of their polished boots together loudly. In unison they answered, "Ndiyo Kapteniyo!" They quick stepped in fine British military fashion out of the throne room, pulling the broken doors closed behind them, leaving their Captain alone with Cross and Michael.

Michael put his hand on the butt of his Makarov, thinking it would be a good time to kill the Captain and run, but Cross stopped him. He said, "Let's hear what he has to say, Michael. If the deal is worthwhile, maybe we all can profit."

Cross remained seated and turned to Nickels. He asked, "So what the hell *do* you want? Something your men can't know about?"

The Captain laughed once again and said, "Oh, I do love you Americans. Right to the point every time. No polite discussion, just get the business done."

He walked to the small camp stove that held the pot of tea his men had made. He filled his fine tea cup and sipped at it.

Cross was getting impatient. He wanted to know if he could make a deal or if he was going to die. He would fight, before dying, of course. Finnegan had his pistol, and the AK-47s weren't too far away. They had a good chance of living through a fire fight, even against the two machine guns outside. But what then? Nickels came looking for Owusu. Would someone come looking for Captain Nickels? He wondered how long the killing could go on. Would there always be someone else coming?

It surprised Cross when Nickels spoke after taking a

long time over his tea. "The money, old chap, will not do. One or even two payments will not be enough. You see, I wish to leave this horrid and hot Country. And yes, old chap, I was born here. But I was educated in Britain. I lived there for many happy years before being called back to serve my native land. And I do love that Country. You see, I wish to make a very early retirement and buy a small cottage, perhaps with a few acres, south of London. A few books, a good dog at my side, perhaps some grouse hunting, don't you know. A trip into London during the season. And if I am invited, I might spend some time at your wonderful Rochester Club."

"OK," Cross asked. "So what the hell are you getting at?"

"The diamonds, Mr. Cross. I want the diamonds and the income they will provide."

"So you want to be Azubuike the 2nd? You want to inherit his godforsaken little empire? You want to keep slaves digging and dying for you? And who the hell will run this place if you're living the quiet life of a country gentleman a couple thousand miles away? Not me . . . I hope you're not expecting me to provide you with diamonds because you don't have a snowball's chance in hell of getting me to do that."

"Ha! You are quite a wit, old man! I think you and I could be good friends when this is all over." Nickels laughed. "No, I would not expect you to run this for me. But your hospital will need money, I think more than Taylor Fullsome will provide willingly. Oh, yes. I know all about the deal you made with Taylor Fullsome. And I predict it will be a lifelong task for you to keep Mr. Fullsome's money flowing to his son. I think perhaps the diamonds will provide the funding Mr. Fullsome will be reluctant to provide. All I want is a small portion, perhaps only fifty percent."

"There is private funding, Captain, regardless of what you believe." Cross said. "We have no plans for the diamonds. And I, too, can make threats, Captain. If you know me, you must know that I don't make empty threats. I make promises that are always kept."

"Oh yes," the Captain said, nodding seriously. "I've heard of your Mr. Billy Volgar. I am sure he will convince Mr. Fullsome, over and over again, to pay what you want paid. But why risk his retribution? Taylor Fullsome is also a dangerous man, although he buys revenge rather than wreaking revenge with his own hands."

"I'll take that risk," Cross answered. "I have no plans to use the damn diamonds."

"Well then," Nickels said, in a more serious tone. "I suggest you make plans for the diamonds because I want them, and if I do not get them . . . Well, you and the Fullsome boy will not be very happy with the results."

"Oh for God's sake!" Finnegan screamed. "Do I haft'a bash your bloody heads together! You're acting like bloody little kids! Joseph," Finnegan said to Cross. "The man wants to retire. Use your damn Yank head! Either let me kill the bloody bastard or make an agreement to let him retire. *Hire* the damn people to dig the bloody diamonds! Pay them a living wage, for God's sake! But I ain't gonna' stand around here and watch you two be stupid for much bloody longer! I need a drink, damn it!"

CHAPTER TWENTY-TWO – The Long Days

And so the deal was made. Once the school and hospital were established and working, Robert Fullsome would offer employment to local villagers to dig for diamonds. They would be paid for their work rather than be forced into slavery. The diamonds would be sold, legally if possible, but sold in any case. Unspoken, Joseph Cross had it in mind to buy the best of the diamonds himself, quietly, off the books. Half of the profits would stay with Robert Fullsome to do with as he saw fit, and half would be sent to Captain Nickels, the soon-to-be retired country gentleman.

There was no paper contract, there was only a hand shake between Cross and Nickels and an understanding that if the payments were not made, the Ugandan Special Police Force would pay a very unwelcomed visit to Robert Fullsome. But Cross knew that once Nickels stopped paying his people in Kampala, they would not be willing to do what he told them to do. It would be up to Robert Fullsome to keep the payments going or to take the risk of stopping them.

That evening was spent enjoying a meal, the food as best as could be prepared from the stock of rations Captain Nickels had brought with him. And they enjoyed some good Scotch whiskey that Nickels always kept near. Nickels managed to find a half empty box of Cuban cigars that

Azubuike had stashed in the back of a closet. He handed one to Cross and one to Michael; each of his officers took one, and Nickels kept one for himself. The few cigars remaining in the box were stashed safely in Nickels' pickup truck.

The night was spent outdoors, where the cool air fanned by a breeze out of the east felt good. The eight men sat in chairs and benches as could be found around the compound and on the floor and steps of the covered porch; stories and jokes told by all were translated back and forth by Captain Nickels. There was laughter and camaraderie but Cross knew that much of it was forced.

The moon was not yet full that night but bright enough to cast eerie shadows throughout the once killing zone of Azubuike's compound. Sometime past midnight, a few shadows moved, and a small herd of horned antelope strolled casually through the compound, finding their way in where the acacia thorn fence had once stood.

Perhaps it was the meal or maybe the liquor, or even the good conversation, but it took Cross some time to realize that the antelope must have crossed the ashes of the burnt thorny acacia wall that had surrounded the compound. They would have left a trail in the ash. And when Azubuike ran away, he would have left a trail, also. That would tell him the direction Azubuike had taken and if Bartholomew had gone with him.

He stood, cigar in one hand and a clay cup of brandy in the other. The conversation stopped, and the men looked up at him. He asked, without looking at Captain Nickels, "Do you have a flashlight?"

Nickels said something in Swahili, and one of his officers ran to the pickup trucks. He returned with a long, black metal flashlight. "We call them torches, Mr. Cross.

But please take that one. What do you see?"

"Do you trust me enough to let Michael and me have a couple of pistols?"

Nickels hesitated but then told one of his men to retrieve the two Beretta pistols from inside the big hut. Cross took one and gave one to Finnegan, who drained his cup of whiskey, stood, and followed Cross into the night.

They walked slowly in the direction from which the antelope came, the flashlight exposing the tracks of the antelope. They skirted around a small hut, then the burnt remnants of another. Finnegan whispered as they walked, "You want to know how the bloody beasts got in, right? And if they left tracks, Azubuike would have left tracks, too. You want to know what bloody direction the bloody bastard went."

"Yes," Cross answered. "Knowing what direction he went might help us to find him . . . If he's still alive."

"You want him dead," Finnegan said. "I know that, Joseph. But do you want him dead enough to follow him across the bloody beast infested jungles of Africa?"

"It's mostly flat plains and swamp, Michael," Cross answered. "In spite of what you see in movies, there aren't many jungles in Africa. I think he'd avoid the swamps. Too many snakes and crocks. And I will follow him into hell if I have to so I can kill him. I was wrong not to do that when you wanted to put a bullet in his fat head. If the villagers find him, he's dead. But if he manages to avoid them, I want the pleasure of killing him."

They circled two more small huts, following the tracks of the antelope as they wandered through the night. Then they came to the rear of the ashes of a hut and found antelope tracks in the black ash of the acacia wall. But there was more than antelope tracks. The tracks were faint and walked over by the antelope, but it was obvious, even in the dark of night, that a person had walked through the ash before the beasts had. "Bloody hell," Michael whispered.

Cross used the flashlight to examine the ash. He said as he looked at it, "This is where Azubuike got out. He went north."

"And that bloody kid, Bartholomew," Michael added. "Not to forget that those bloody soldiers of his walked away north. Do you think they'll meet up with the bloody fat bastard?"

"The footprints are like they were running," Cross said, shining the light on the black ash of acacia lying on the ground. "And Azubuike was chained. He couldn't run with the ankle chains on. He couldn't have removed the chains alone. You're right; Bartholomew helped him for some reason."

"You're too bloody good, Joseph lad. I told you t'kill'em all."

"You're often more right than wrong, Michael. I should have listened to you."

Finnegan spat onto the ground and said, "He'll be comin' back, you know that, don't you, Joseph lad?"

Walking back to the big hut without speaking a word, they sat on the steps where Captain Nickels waited; worry was easy to see on their faces.

Nickels asked, "What is wrong, Mr. Cross? Did you find something?"

Cross told Nickels the whole story of the attack on the compound, without mentioning that it was Michael Finnegan who had killed Owusu. "I had Azubuike chained and tossed into a filthy hut where he had kept his slaves. Over there," he said pointing the flashlight to the pile of ash that had been the slave hut. "I made the mistake of trusting one of his guards, a young man who spoke well and professed to be a Christian. It appears that young man lied to me, freed Azubuike, and helped him to escape."

"That is quite unfortunate for you, Mr. Cross," Nickels said. "But it does not affect our agreement. When the sun is up, I will leave, and in one month's time I will expect the first of the money from the diamonds or the diamonds themselves. Send it by personal messenger to my office in Kampala. I will be Colonel Nickels by that time. From that point on, I will have an address in England to which you will send the money."

Finnegan thought for a minute and then said, "Excuse me. I don't mean to be an impertinent common Irishman in front of your lordship . . . But how the bloody hell can you control these good gunmen of yours from far and away in England?"

Nickels laughed again and patted Finnegan good naturedly on his shoulder. He said, "Oh I do love you Irish. And have no worry, my good fellow. Although I love England, I have no animosity to the Irish. Had I my way, I would let he whole of Ireland go their own way, don't you know. But as to your question. These men . . . And they don't speak English, no fear of that . . . They make little money at their employment. I will send sufficient funds to a few of them, officers of course, and they will respond as I wish. As long as our arrangement continues, there will be no trouble, and an element of protection will be granted."

"And what if that bloody cannibal shows up again?" Michael asked. "Will your people be here to help with that little problem?"

"Oh, I'm afraid not. That is your problem. My

protection will be from the greedier aspects of my homeland. The government and such, don't you know."

Cross spoke up, "But if Azubuike comes back with more killers and wipes out the hospital and school. Won't that end the deal you and I have? Won't that stop your retirement income?"

"Mr. Cross, I didn't expect you to be so naive. Azubuike was sending payments to Colonel Owusu. Owusu protected that man's operation here. How else do you think he could continue his abhorrent lifestyle? If needed, those payments will continue to me. You see, either way, I cannot lose. I will leave it up to you to decide who pays me. Do what you must to protect this place you seem to want so much. Or lose it to Azubuike. It is no concern of mine."

The remainder of the night was spent in the cool air, watching the stars light the sky, and talking of meaningless things. Only Nickels and Cross remained awake when the sun rose above the horizon to the east. The others had stretched out on the porch and were soon asleep. The Captain and Cross watched the ball of fire rise, and when it was fully in the clear sky, Nickels poked and kicked at his men. Michael stirred and sat up. There was much talk in Swahili, and things were packed into the pickup trucks.

Cross stood in the red dirt in front of the big building, watching. He stopped Nickels and said, "I want the guns and ammo."

"Of course, Mr. Cross. I almost forgot. Please do forgive me."

He gave an order, and his men removed the weapons and clips of ammunition from one of the trucks. They were placed, alongside the few hand grenades Helen had left, on the covered porch. The two AK-47s were laid next to them. Cross and Michael had kept the pistols they had been given during the night.

Captain Nickels said, "I'm afraid I have no food to leave for you, Mr. Cross. But I can spare some water." His men took a cardboard box filled with bottled water from one of the trucks and laid it next to the guns. "That should see you through, Mr. Cross."

Cross and Finnegan stood to the side to avoid the cloud of dust left by the three pickup trucks as they drove away very fast. When they were a mile down the dirt road and almost out of sight, Michael asked, "Are you going to keep that bargain you made with him, Joseph lad?"

"That's not up to me, Michael. All I want is to get the hell out of here. If the Fullsome boy wants to hire people to dig diamonds and send them to that bastard, that'll be his decision."

****

They sat in the shade of the covered porch that morning and into the heat of the African afternoon. They said little; there was little to say. Waiting was the hard part. Waiting for the airplane; waiting for Azubuike to return.

Finnegan napped, curled against the wood wall of the big hut, seeking the little shade available. Cross leaned against one of the rough wood posts that held the porch roof. He cleaned his rifle twice, making sure it would fire when and if he needed it. He took it across the compound and fired three rounds into the brush outside the compound. He fired three shots from the Beretta pistol. Then he returned to the porch.

Michael lay in the shade, his eyes barely open. He said, "Why waste the damn bullets, Joseph? You might well need them, now won't you?"

It was a quarter past four according to Cross' wristwatch when he heard the sound of the small airplane. He stood, woke Finnegan with the toe of his shoe, and grabbed up the AK-47 that he had laid on the porch floor next to him.

Finnegan jumped to his feet and picked up the other AK rifle, jacking a round into the chamber. "Who do you think it is?" he asked.

"I hope it's Robert Fullsome," Cross answered.

They stepped out into the blazing sun, shielding their eyes, and watched the small, single engine Beechcraft as it touched down and bounced along the dirt road from the north. It taxied slowly and came to a stop very near the entrance to the compound, almost the same spot Helen's airplane had stopped. The doors on both sides of the airplane opened, Robert Fullsome stepped out from behind the controls of the aircraft, and Mary Ssanyu stepped out from the other side.

They walked side by side into the compound. Robert was wearing blue jeans and a plaid shirt, which Cross knew were too hot and heavy for the climate. Mary was dressed more sensibly in tan shorts, a white shirt and sandals. Her hair, which had been roughly shaved off by Azubuike, was beginning to grow back over the scars left by the shaving. She had put on a few pounds and was no longer the bone thin skeleton Cross had rescued a few weeks ago. But the scars of being a tortured slave of Azubuike were apparent. Her wrists bore the marks made by the chains; her legs were scarred, and she walked with a slight limp. She tried to stand straight, but too many months of being chained and bent had crippled her.

They approached Cross and Finnegan, both smiling

broadly, expecting a grand welcome. As they got closer Cross growled, looking angrily at Mary, "What the hell are you doing here?" He turned to Robert and snarled, "You piloted the plane yourself, Robert?"

"Yes," he said. "I have a license. We made a few stops, and I flew it from The Republic of Congo."

"And what about her?"

Fullsome answered, smiling proudly, "Mary is going to work with me. She is going to run the school. We've made a bargain. Isn't that wonderful?"

"That's one hell of a stupid idea, Robert," Cross said. "How the hell did you get past Billy Volgar?"

Mary smiled and said, "Robert took me shopping. Billy seemed happy to have an afternoon off. We left England instead. Please don't blame Mr. Volgar. It isn't his fault."

Cross looked at Robert who was standing uneasily, a little nervous at what he had done. He spoke to Robert, "This is a dangerous damn place to be bringing a woman to. Especially one who has suffered so much right here."

Mary spoke up, saying, "But I want to help, Joseph. I need to help. Azubuike is no more. The danger is gone. I want my home to be safe. I want my home to flower. I want the children to have a good future here."

"I'm afraid Azubuike is not gone," Cross answered. "We had him in chains, but he managed to escape with the help of one of his soldiers. I don't know if he's dead or alive right now. If some villagers find him, they'll probably kill him. I don't know where the hell he is."

A look of profound fear clouded Mary's face. She grabbed Robert's arm for fear of fainting.

"But I thought . . ." Robert began. "I got your radio message."

"I know," Cross said. "Come inside, out of the heat. Did you bring any food with you? We should discuss the possibilities."

"I have a few boxes of food and water," Fullsome answered. "There are trucks on the way with building supplies and enough food and bottled water to last a month."

As they took three boxes from the airplane, Cross introduced Michael Finnegan to them. "I know what Michael looks like," Cross said, making an excuse for Michael's leprechaun appearance. "But he's the best I can think of when I need someone who can shoot and fight."

As they walked to the big throne room, Robert and Mary looked around at the burnt buildings and piles of ash left from the short war. They didn't ask any questions, but they both could imagine the blood bath that had taken place just days before.

"I don't suppose those trucks you have coming here have a couple dozen soldiers on them?" Cross asked as he led the way into Azubuike's throne room. Robert looked down shyly, not answering. Cross knew they were alone.

Inside they carefully avoided and stepped around the dark blood stains on the floor. Both Mary and Robert gazed down at the stains. Their stomachs twisted at the thought of the killing that had to be done if Robert was to build his hospital.

Nightmare memories of that place rushed through their minds. The past had to be washed away, but could the blood stains wash away? Robert thought he would have to do a lot of rebuilding if the big, circular hut were to be used.

They placed the few cardboard boxes from the

airplane on the raised throne platform. Cross and Michael dug through one of them and pulled a couple cans of beans and two cans of fruit from it. They passed a single can of meat between them, hungry enough to eat just about anything by that time. They ate ravenously while Robert Fullsome and Mary Ssanyu stood by and watched.

When they had eaten, Cross wiped his mouth with the sleeve of his camo fatigue shirt, looked back and forth between Robert and the woman, and said, "Until Azubuike is found and killed . . . You two need to get out of here. Get back on your plane and go."

"So you think he will return?" Mary asked.

"It's likely," Cross answered. "He had a good thing going here, and he's crazy enough to want it back. He has two of his personal guards out there somewhere. He may find them. If he's still alive, he'll be back. I don't think he'll know any other way of life."

Robert stood and walked around the walls of the big hut, his hands clenched behind his back. He stopped near Cross and looked at him. He said, "I won't go. There's too much to be gained here. Can we get the help of the police or maybe the Army from Kampala?"

Cross said, answering Robert's question, "I doubt Captain Nickels will risk his own life or that of his men. The way he sees it, he will profit whether you're here or Azubuike is here."

Robert looked up at Cross; his forehead frowned. He said, "I don't understand. Who is Captain Nickels?"

Cross explained the deal he had agreed to with Captain Nickels. Whether Robert or Azubuike paid him made no difference to the man. He cared for nothing, Cross explained, except for the money and a retirement life in

England. Robert was excited about being able to offer well paid jobs to local people, digging diamonds in what he called 'my diamond mine.' He didn't mention Nickels. All he could see was his future and his hospital. He seemed not to understand that if Azubuike came back, he would not come alone. He would kill everyone: Robert, Mary, and anyone else who would take his kingdom from him.

"You had some soldiers here," Robert said. "I have the cash. Can you get them back?"

"Those people do very specialized work, Robert. They fight battles. They are not cops. They would not sit here indefinitely waiting for Azubuike to come back. If they were hired to provide security, your cash would run out very quickly. They are very expensive."

"So I should just put this all behind me," Robert said, anger in his voice. "I should go home and tell my father he was right, that all this is just a waste of time and a childish fantasy?"

"I guess that's for you to decide, Robert. You have a decision to make. I've always felt that life is good and life is sometimes bad. It's how you face it that matters. I seldom run from anything, but I also weigh the risks and options. Sometimes I choose to turn my back and avoid trouble. That's what you need to do. If you stay, and Azubuike does come back . . . He will kill you and eat your liver; you know that, right? I can show you how to use the rifles and the pistols. But you'll have to fight alone. Are you up to that?"

"He's right, Robert," Mary Ssanyu said. "You should leave here . . . At least until that terrible man is dead."

"But what about you?" Robert asked. "You'll come back to England, also?"

"No," she answered too firmly. "I will stay here and

return to my village. I must help them; I must make them strong enough to keep Azubuike from terrorizing them again. I will teach them. Perhaps they will fight him before he regains strength."

"That's bloody crazy, woman," Finnegan said, the first words he had spoken since Mary got off the plane. How do you expect a bunch of farmers and cattle herders to fight like soldiers?"

"Perhaps I am crazy," she said. "But I must stay, anyway."

"And I will stay, too," Robert said. "If it means making the locals stronger before the hospital is built, we will do that together. I think if we organize businesses . . . Pay people to dig for diamonds . . . Improve their lives . . . Maybe they will want to fight off Azubuike. Maybe we could start a police force of our own. Maybe some of the young men will be willing to fight. I have money, Mr. Cross. Will you use it to buy guns and whatever else we will need?"

"Certainly," he answered. "I can do that. But I think guns cannot get here fast enough. That man is out there right now. He ran north. His few soldiers, the two professionals and a handful of his drugged men, went north. Sooner or later they are going to meet. He could be back any day now. There simply isn't enough time."

He looked at Finnegan with an unspoken question that Michael understood. Michael spat onto the floor and said, "Bloody hell, Joseph lad. It's never an end to fightin' the bloody devil himself with you, is it now. Well, I guess if I can beat the worst the bloody oceans can throw at me, I can manage to stay here with you."

"You mean, you two will stay here?" Robert asked.

"For a while," Cross answered. He pulled the Berretta

pistol from his belt and handed it to Robert. Finnegan did the same with his and handed it to Mary. They showed each how to fire them.

"Keep those with you at all times, and don't be afraid to use them if you have to. When your trucks arrive, do whatever you had planned. Michael and I will try to take care of Azubuike . . . If he comes back. If he's not here in a month, he won't be coming back. I'll assume some locals got him. Then we'll leave you two here and not worry about you. You'll be on your own."

"And what if he decides to wait until you leave?" Mary asked.

"That could happen . . . But I'm not going to stay here forever. One month, that's all, and then Michael and I are going home. The two of you are going to have to make plans to take care of yourselves."

CHAPTER TWENTY-THREE – The Nightmare

Cross and Michael walked the perimeter of the compound, along the ashes of the burnt acacia thorn fence. They first walked inside the perimeter, then outside. They walked through what had been the entrance of the compound and circled the compound once again. They carried their rifles slung over their shoulders and the spare clips of ammunition stuffed into their back pants pockets. Now and then they would stop and examine prints in the ash. All were some kind of animal tracks. They were looking for human tracks, evidence that maybe Azubuike would be back.

Nickels had given Michael a full pack of Player's cigarettes. He was careful about how many he smoked each day. They had to last. He lit one and let the smoke curl slowly from his red lips. He looked at the pack of English cigarettes and found he had only two left. He said, almost to himself, "Christ, I wish I had a bloody drink."

"And I wish I had one, too, old friend," Cross said. "But I'm better without it even though I know you're good with or without it. A clear head might be useful."

"Do you really think he's coming back?" Michael asked.

"I don't know. If the tribes out there don't get him, he may well want to regain what once was his. I just don't know . . . But we have to assume we'll see him again."

They circled the enclosed compound once again, in silence, and then Michael said, "This bloody place is too big for the two of us to defend."

"I had the same thought. We need to figure out a way to make a small, compact area defensible until we know Azubuike won't be back."

While waiting for Robert's trucks to arrive, the three men and Mary tore a few of the smaller huts apart, the few that had not been burnt. They took all the wood of any kind and the few pieces of furniture inside the huts, and anything else that they might be able to use to build a wall. They took everything to the center of the compound and formed a small wall around the porch of what once had been Azubuike's throne room. As an afterthought, they took the dried palm thatch from the huts they had torn down and laid it on the ground in front of the steps, a few feet away from their makeshift wall. In answer to Robert's question, Cross explained, "It'll burn."

After two days' work in the hot African sun, Cross was satisfied that they had a somewhat defensible position. The four stood on the porch and took in what they had built. Robert asked, "Do you really think we need all this against one crazy, fat old man?"

"Don't underestimate that crazy, fat old man," Cross responded. "He built a small empire out of nothing all by himself. It wouldn't surprise me to see him, right now, using machetes and knives to recruit people, promising them wealth if they will follow him."

"And don't forget the two soldiers you bloody well let go, Joseph," Michael added. "It's likely Azubuike went looking for them. I imagine they were well paid in money and women, and they just might want their jobs back."

"I haven't forgotten about them," Cross said, regretting that he didn't let Finnegan kill them. "I just hope they head north faster than Azubuike can catch up to them. And I hope Azubuike doesn't talk them into coming back if he does find them."

Robert seemed satisfied with that. But he asked, "What if they come back and not to the front door? I mean, the defense here seems pretty good, but the back is completely unprotected."

"You're right of course," Cross said. He grinned and patted the young man on his shoulder. "You're so right in fact, that you are going to go to the back of this big damn building and pile every damn piece of furniture in Azubuike's quarters in front of the door back there and any other place anyone could get in. Keep it so nobody can get in that way."

****

The sun finally set late that afternoon, but the darkness that enveloped the compound did little to cool the air. Cross sat with the three people who, with him, were to protect what Robert Fullsome hoped would change the area of remote Southern Uganda into a peaceful and humanitarian community. They had tried to sit inside the former throne room, but the heat and humidity of the still air soon drove them outside, onto the thatch covered porch. Not very often a slight breeze would waft past them. Animal sounds filled the night, predators hunting for a meal. Cross hoped they would find something to eat to keep them from making a meal of the four of them.

The black sky was filled with millions of stars, and the moon was still bright and night by night becoming full overhead. The four agreed that building even a small fire was not a good idea; the light from it would carry for a couple of miles and signal that they were there. So, dinner was cold beans, canned corned beef, and warm cans of Coca Cola.

When each had eaten what they could, Mary Ssanyu stood and said, "I am very tired. If you don't object, I will sleep on the floor in Azubuike's bedroom."

She turned before the three men could say anything and disappeared inside the big throne room. Cross watched her walk away into the darkness of the big hut. He wondered, without speaking the words, why she would come back to Uganda after so many terrible years of torture and pain. She was, he knew, a strong and very intelligent woman, but why would she put herself at risk once again?

The three men agreed that one would stand guard while the other two tried to sleep in the throne room, on the floor. Robert agreed to stand first watch, and Cross told him to wake him at midnight. Finnegan and Cross retreated into the big hut and finally found sleep, lying on the hard would floor, Cross using a big antelope skin rug for a blanket and Michael curling himself against the wall.

A nightmare of digging through the mud for Azubuike's diamonds filled Cross' sleeping mind. The acrid odor of burning human flesh wafted through the dream's air. A scream for help woke Cross suddenly and caused him to jump to his feet, but the scream was not in his dream. Finnegan was sitting up, his AK-47 in his hands. He pushed himself to his feet, and he followed Cross to the open doorway.

On the porch outside, Robert Fullsome stood, holding the Beretta pistol in both hands, out at arms' length. Five men, Africans who had painted their faces and chests in fierce streaks of white and red, were on the far side of the low wall they had built, waiving machetes, jumping, and yelling threats. Their eyes showed bright in the dark night. They were the remnants of Azubuike's drugged soldiers, returning to find what they had left behind.

Cross stood next to Robert and said calmly, "Shoot them."

Robert was holding the pistol so tightly in his hands that his knuckles had turned white. He was shaking, and his face had lost all color. He could not bring himself to put his finger on the trigger. Sweat poured from his forehead, his mouth hung open and spittle ran from its corners.

"Robert," Cross said calmly and softly again, "Shoot them."

"I . . . I . . . I can't," he said.

A burst of gunfire flashed from behind Robert. Finnegan had opened fire with his AK-47, and the five Africans were cut down.

Cross grabbed the pistol from Robert's trembling hand and pushed the young man back, toward the open door of the big hut. "Get in there and stay there," he said.

Robert slunk away, into the blackness of the hut. Finnegan pulled the empty clip from the AK-47 and put a full clip in its place. "You should never have trusted that boy," he said.

"You're right once again, Michael. But this whole damn thing is for that boy. I wouldn't be here if the kid didn't have this dream of making this a good place to live. I won't trust him again."

They walked side by side into the throne room. Robert was sitting on the floor, his knees pulled up to his

chin. He was rocking back and forth and crying openly.
Cross walked to the young man, bent and patted him on his
shoulder. There was nothing Cross could do for Robert; the
young man had learned a lesson the hard way. He had
learned that often times in life, doing something very bad
was necessary to finally accomplish something very good.

Finnegan walked to Cross' side and said, "Where's
the woman? The damn commotion should have her awake,
now, shouldn't it?"

Cross ran up onto the low platform and past the
empty throne. He ran into Azubuike's private apartment.
There was a candle burning there, throwing off very little light
but enough for Cross to see she was gone. All the furniture
that Robert had piled against the rear door had been moved
away. The door hung open, the stars and moon throwing
light into the room.

He closed the door and piled some of the furniture
back against it. He stepped out of the back room and
stopped. Michael Finnegan was on the floor, blood flowing
from his head. Robert Fullsome was standing, his arms
raised over his head. Azubuike, the two soldiers Cross had
let go, and Bartholomew Thomas stood facing Cross.

Azubuike was smiling an insane smile, his eyes big
and almost bulging from their sockets. The two soldiers held
old British Enfield rifles, pointing one at Robert and one at
Cross. Bartholomew was holding the club that he had used
on Finnegan's head and on the heads of Helen's two men at
the slave hut when he freed Azubuike.

Cross walked slowly towards them, eyeing his AK-47
that lay propped up against a far wall. He hoped Azubuike
had not yet seen it in the darkness. He had the pistol he had
taken from Robert. It was tucked in his belt, his camo shirt
hanging loosely outside his pants, hiding the gun.

"You're back," he said to Azubuike.

"You should have known, my good friend Joseph. You should have killed me. I would have killed you. You are not perhaps as smart as I thought you were."

Cross turned and looked at the boy Bartholomew. He asked, "Why?"

"He is my father," the boy answered, shrugging his shoulders to explain. There was neither joy nor any pride in the words, maybe some embarrassment. Just a shrug of his shoulders as if there was nothing else for him to do but help Azubuike.

★★★★★★★★★★★★★★★

When Finnegan awoke, he wanted to use his hands to wipe the blood from his eyes, but they had been tied tightly behind his back. He was lying in the dirt outside at the foot of the steps, outside what had been the small wall of wood he had helped build. It had been torn apart and was spread across the red dirt. It had been meant to be a defense against Azubuike. It turned out to be useless work in the blazing sun.

The sun was above the horizon, and daytime heat was building. He rolled onto his right side, and his vision began to clear. Nearby, a few yards away, he saw his employer, Joseph Cross, chained to the steel post that Azubuike's men had found a distance away.

They had carried it back and replaced it into the ground where it had been before. Bartholomew and the two soldiers were piling the wood that had been a defense in front of the porch of the throne room around Cross' feet.

Azubuike's great bulk was sitting on a low stool, watching and laughing insanely. White, foamy spittle filled his mouth and was dripping from his lips.

They had stripped Cross' shirt from him and found the pistol. Azubuike now had it tucked under his belt at his enormous waist. Cross hadn't tried to stop them. Something, he kept telling himself, something will happen. He had hoped there would be an opportunity, a chance. But he still had Robert Fullsome to protect. If he had tried to overtake Azubuike's two soldiers, not only might he die, but Robert Fullsome would surely die. He was determined to kill Azubuike. If he had to return from the fires of hell, he would return and kill the man. But he had to also protect Robert . . . If he could.

Finnegan rolled over onto his left side. He saw Robert Fullsome lying on the dirt a few feet away, his hands tied behind him. His eyes were closed and he was shaking as he sobbed.

Finnegan spoke to Robert, "Stop your bloody cryin', boy-o. What the bloody hell did you expect? You're in hell, kid. Life is bloody well like that. You win some, and you bloody well lose some, now don't you."

"But . . . But Mr. Cross . . . Jesus Christ!"

"Christ ain't got nothin' to do with this, kid. It's the bloody devil himself got us by the balls now. That man knows what waits for him. He's been on the edge his whole bloody damn life. He knew what his future was from the bloody day he started in this bloody business. Don't cry for him, son. Don't let that fat bastard see you crying. Spit in his God damned face if you get the bloody chance, boy."

Michael lifted his head from the red dirt and watched. The look on Azubuike's dark face was that of a madman. Spittle was dripping from his chin, covering his torn shirt, and sweat covered his fat face. He rocked back and forth on the small bench that struggled to hold his great weight, his arms wrapped around his knees. He would laugh uproariously and then suddenly stop, his eyes ready to leap from their sockets, and then he would laugh again.

The scrap wood and sticks that had been gathered were piled knee high around Cross. They covered the pile with the brown thatch that Cross had intended to light as a final defense. Cross seemed relaxed and only smiled down at the fat man. Bartholomew stacked the last of the wood at Cross' feet and looked up at him. Cross looked down and only shook his head. Bartholomew, a few tears filing the corners of his bloodshot eyes, mouthed the words, "I'm sorry . . . But he is my father."

Cross smiled and said, "I guess this kind of kills your chances at getting into heaven, doesn't it?"

Azubuike struggled to push himself to his feet. One of his soldiers ran to him and grabbed him by his arms, pulling him to his feet. This time, in his insane delirium, he let the man touch him. He stumbled and tripped over a few stones, walking in a daze-like trance to Cross. He bent as much as his bulk would allow and picked up a thin branch from the wood that would consume Cross. He jabbed the chained man across his stomach and chest with it, cutting Cross' bare flesh, and laughed at each jab. But Cross did not react. He didn't flinch or show any sign of pain. He was determined not to give this hated man the satisfaction of seeing him in pain. And he would not plead for his life, either. No, Azubuike would murder him no matter what, but Azubuike would not see him suffering.

The fat man looked up at Cross and spoke in a dreamlike sing-song, "I have bested you, my good friend Joseph. I have bested you, my good friend Joseph." He kept repeating the same eight words over and over. He tried to dance a little jig, but his enormous weight would not allow it.

Bartholomew could not look at the man, his father, as he rattled on. He lowered his eyes to the dirt at his feet. The two soldiers merely stood by and watched, seemingly not caring what was happening. They had left their old rifles and taken the two AK-47s, holding them casually as they watched.

Finnegan yelled, "You fucking bloody bastard! I'll rip you apart for this you bloody bastard!"

One of the soldiers walked slowly to him and kicked him hard in the stomach. Azubuike screamed and laughed wildly, "You are next! You are next! You are next!"

The second soldier lit a makeshift torch of grass and rags twisted at the end of a thin scrap of wood and handed it to Azubuike. As he did, yelling and shouting surrounded them. From between the huts, from three directions, dozens of men, dozens of women, and dozens of children came running. They carried clubs and wooden rakes and hammers and a few big machetes. Before Azubuike or the soldiers or Bartholomew could react, they were run over by the mobs. Whatever weapons the people carried were used to kill the soldiers quickly. Bartholomew was beaten to the ground and engulfed in a sea of Africans swinging whatever they carried. He was soon dead, cut to pieces by shovels and machetes.

Azubuike was knocked to the ground and beaten. The Berretta was pulled from his belt before he could reach for it. The voice, the voice of a woman who was standing behind Cross, called out above the fighting, "STOP! KUACHA! KUACHA!"

Cross twisted in his chains to see what had happened. Mary Ssanyu walked into the crowd of villagers.

They stepped aside almost reverently to allow her to walk past them.   She stopped at the steel beam Cross was chained to and called to a few men to break the padlock and handcuffs that were holding him.   It was done quickly, and Cross stepped down onto the red dirt of the compound.

"What the hell!" he started.   "What the . . ."

"Joseph," she began.   She pulled him down to her and kissed him on his cheek.   She said, "When I heard the screaming of those five men and the gun shots I had to be sure.   I had to be sure this man would not return.   The people didn't want him to return.   They had suffered enough. They came and put an end to it.   But you are hurt, Joseph," she said, touching the cuts on his chest and stomach.

"It's nothing," he said.   "What's happening here?"

She turned to look at Azubuike, on his knees in the dirt, his arms out to his sides, held there by two big men. Blood streamed from his nose and left eye, and from the cut on his forehead.   His clothes were ripped, and he was covered in the red mud he had once ruled.   He smiled a pleading smile at Mary and whispered in a quavering voice, "Mary Ssanyu . . . You are my wife . . . You must do as I say . . . Let me go, and we can live together as we once did . . . I will make you a queen . . ."

Before he could say more, she pulled the Beretta Cross had given her from the belt at her waist, raised it slowly, pulled the hammer back, and shot Azubuike once in the head.   He bent backwards at first and then slumped forward.   The men holding his arms let go, and the fat man fell face down into the red dirt that had been his petty kingdom.

CHAPTER TWENTY-FOUR – People Died For You

Michael and Robert were untied. Robert was shaking and ashamed. He could not go near to Cross and Finnegan. Mary found some water and a fairly clean rag. She washed Cross's wounds as he sat on the porch in the shade under the thatched roof. His shirt had been ripped off of him, but it was the only clothing available. He put the rag on and tied it at his waist.

He stood, and Mary watched as he walked to Robert Fullsome. The young man was trying to stop his tears. As Cross approached, Robert said in a quavering voice, "I'm sorry, Mr. Cross . . . I'm so sorry."

"All of this was for you, boy," Cross said. "People died for you. You better make something good from all of this, because if you don't, I will come back, and I will kill you myself. Understand?"

"I'm so damn sorry, Mr. Cross. I promise . . . I will build the hospital . . . I will build the school . . . I will make this a better place . . . I promise."

Cross took Robert's hand in his, and they sealed the promise. Michael and Cross walked away, side by side, leaving Robert behind, alone. They stood and watched as the villagers quickly dug trenches near the big grave where the others had been buried. The dead, including Azubuike, were buried. Mary fashioned a rough cross from some wood and pushed it into the red dirt. Instead of a prayer, she spat onto the grave and walked away.

The steel beam was once again ripped down and would never again stand to burn anyone. Mary was busy giving directions to the men and women to clean up the compound and tear apart all of the huts, except for the big throne room. The wood and thatch were stacked high and lit afire. Mary whispered to Cross as they watched the flames, "That putrid throne room will become a clinic until a hospital can be built. Perhaps the good that will be done there will cleanse the sins that were committed here.

She walked off to give more instructions. The compound would be unrecognizable soon. Even the red dirt was swept clean.

When the work was almost done, she walked back to Cross and Finnegan who sat in the shade of the porch of the only remaining building. She said without being asked, "These are the Bellawaa and the Ng'uluu people. They are Christians and have suffered severely at the hands of Azubuike. It did not take much for me to convince them to rid this land of him. They want a better life for their children. I hope to give it to them."

"I guess I owe you my life, Mary," Cross said. "How do I repay you?"

"It is I who owe you, Joseph," she said and smiled at him. "Without you, I would still be a slave to . . . him." She could not bring herself to say the fat man's name.

That afternoon and into the evening saw a celebration in the compound. Fires were built and food was cooked. People were dancing and singing and drinking some kind of local concoction that Finnegan drank too much of, arguing that without Irish whiskey anything would do. And in the middle of all that an old man, bent with the weight of age, with thick grey hair and a long beard, stood to bring a sudden silence to the festivities. He held a long staff of age-polished rough wood. He stepped to the center of the festivities and spoke in a deep voice graveled with age.

He spoke, and Mary translated for the three men. "He says it is by the grace of God that they are free. He says it is good to sing and dance, but they must also be thankful to God for their deliverance."

Michael whispered, "And maybe a small thank you sir to me and Joseph might be in order?"

"He says that he prays that the Englishman . . . That is you Robert . . . That the Englishman will allow a church to be built here next to his hospital and school."

Robert nodded and said, "Certainly."

Mary said, "He is saying a prayer now. It is best that I leave that to these people."

When the prayer was done, the flutes and drums and singing started again and went on into the early morning hours.

****

The following morning, six big Mercedes trucks, their beds covered in brown tarps that did little to hide the heavy load each carried, pulled into the compound. The loud engines woke the many people who had fallen asleep on the red dirt of the compound. Children began to scamper around, women started small fires to cook food, and the men gathered in groups, all talking at once. But all were happy and smiling and laughing, knowing that the evil of Azubuike was over.

Mary sat next to Cross on the steps of what was once the throne room as both watched all the activity, glad to finally see some happiness and to see all the children running and playing and laughing, some for the first time in their lives.

Robert and Finnegan went to the trucks and oversaw the unloading, directing what boxes should go where, where to set up big tents, where to put together a kitchen, where to stack all the building materials, and where to store all the food, medicines and hospital supplies.

Michael rushed from truck to truck, looking into boxes and crates as they were unloaded. When the trucks were empty, he stomped loudly to Robert and asked in an angry voice, "You ain't got no whiskey, lad? You ain't got no bloody whiskey?"

"I didn't think I'd need any, Mr. Finnegan. I'm sorry."

"Sorry don't feed the damn bulldog, boy-o," Michael said and walked away, mumbling under his breath.

Mary slid closer to Cross, handed him the two Beretta pistols and said, "I do not think I will need these any longer."

He took them and laid them side by side on the porch, next to him. She thought for a moment and then asked, "What makes people like Azubuike? What brought him to this place and what made him do what he has done? What was inside of him to make him so cruel?"

Cross put his arm around her shoulder, hugged her to him, and answered, "Satan often offers expedient ways to reach success. And all too often people's idea of success is power. I've met so many people who have tossed aside everything you think of as humanity in return for power . . . And wealth . . . And self-aggrandizement. The devil sits on everyone's left shoulder, Mary. The devil whispers in your ear. Some people listen and want quick, easy rewards. The devil . . . Satan from the pits of hell . . . who whispered in Azubuike's ear . . . Found a weak man, a man who was full of hate, who wanted revenge on the world who had treated him so badly . . . At least in his own mind. He sold his soul and got a bastardized little kingdom based on drugs and terror. He's dead now and probably burning in hell for all he's done.

She rested her head on his shoulder. She whispered, "I love you, Joseph."

He said without looking at the woman, "Come with me, Mary. You can have a good life in England. I'll see to that."

"No Joseph, my love," she said sadly. "I will stay here and run the school as Robert wishes. He speaks a little Swahili, but he needs someone to translate the dialects here. I will help him as best I can . . . And that's the least I can do. I will stay here because my people need some good in their future."

"I have to ask," Cross said. "What of the diamonds?"

She moved away from him, only an inch or two, and said, "Soon I will start a legal company. I will retain lawyers and file all the necessary papers in Kampala. I will register with the Kimberly Diamond Trust. I will hire people from the villages to dig for diamonds as well as work here in the hospital and school. And I will pay them well . . . And the diamonds will be legal and sold legally."

"What about Captain Nickels? You know he wants a cut."

"I will keep the bargain you made with Captain Nickels. I will do that at least for a time. Once we are established, and we have the people responding to us, once we have established a police force of our own, I think I will stop sending him money." She smiled and looked at Cross. She said with a laugh, "Then Captain Nickels can . . . Well, he can go perform a sexual act upon himself."

They both laughed, and Cross put his arm around her shoulders, hugging her to him.

There was food, and a kitchen was set up under a big tent. Soon a wood structured building would stand nearby, and the kitchen would be moved indoors. Joe Cross and Michael Finnegan ate well inside the big tent, and they agreed that maybe it had all been worth it.

Michael said as he cut into a piece of chicken, "Aye, and ain't the life with you Joseph lad bringing me nearer and nearer to the devil's own door. How much longer do you think we can go on with the adventures?"

"As far as I'm concerned, Michael me old friend of mine, as long as I can walk. Now wouldn't life be that boring without what we do?" He spoke in a put on Irish accent and laughed as he spoke.

The trucks were all finally unloaded, and two days later they prepared to leave. Robert came to Cross and Michael. He shook their hands and said, "I don't know the proper words to thank you. How do you . . . How do people like you do it? How can you risk everything like that? You almost died, and you seemed not to care."

Finnegan spoke before Cross could. He said, poking a finger into Cross' side, "This bloody terrible Yank bastard will tell you, 'Because it's the right thing to do.' I've heard him say that so many bloody times. But I think he likes the excitement, now doesn't he?"

Joe Cross added, "Robert, as you get older, I hope you will learn that occasionally you will find something worth dying for. All of us . . . Every man and woman on this Earth . . . Have a time to live and a time to die. You can't run from it . . . You must stand up to it and . . . As this drunken Irishman says . . . Do what is the right thing to do."

Finnegan said, "There's this here big truck out back that I bloody well stole up in Kampala. It'll stay here for your use, but I'd rip the bloody license plates off if I were you."

Robert Fullsome and Mary Ssanyu stood side by side and watched the trucks leave, taking Joseph Cross and Michael Finnegan away from them. They waived, and Mary cried. Robert whispered, "Don't let them see you cry. That's something Mr. Finnegan once said to me. They know they'll be missed."

THE END

www.ingramcontent.com/pod-product-compliance
Lightning Source LLC
Chambersburg PA
CBHW031426240626
47154CB00001B/219